Son of the Serpent

Also by Shauna Lawless

The Gael Song Series

Novels

Era I

The Children of Gods and Fighting Men

The Words of Kings and Prophets

The Land of the Living and the Dead

Era II

Daughter of the Otherworld

Son of the Serpent

Novellas

Dreams of Fire

Dreams of Sorrow

Dreams of Chaos

Son of the Serpent

SHAUNA LAWLESS

GAEL SONG: ERA II, BOOK II

HEAD of ZEUS

An Ad Astra Book

First published in the UK in 2026 by Head of Zeus,
part of Bloomsbury Publishing Plc

9 7 5 3 1 2 4 6 8

A catalogue record for this book is available from the British Library.

ISBN (HB): 9781035911325; ISBN (BROKEN BINDING HB): 9781035930364;
ISBN (XTPB): 9781035911349; ISBN (EBOOK): 9781035911363

Cover design by Susan Burghart
Typeset by Lumina Datamatics Ltd
Map design by Jamie Whyte

Printed and bound in Great Britain by Clays Ltd, Elcograf S.p.A.

MIX
Paper | Supporting
responsible forestry
FSC® C018072

Bloomsbury Publishing Plc
50 Bedford Square, London, WC1B 3DP, UK
Bloomsbury Publishing Ireland Limited,
29 Earlsfort Terrace, Dublin 2, D02 AY28, Ireland

HEAD OF ZEUS LTD
5–8 Hardwick Street
London EC1R 4RG

To find out more about our authors and books
visit www.headofzeus.com

For product safety related questions contact productsafety@bloomsbury.com

For my family

IRELAND
1169 AD
N
TORAIGH ISLAND
RATHLIN ISLAND
Rónnat's crannog
NORTHERN UÍ NÉILL
ULAID
AIRGÍALLA
BREIFNE
CONNACHT
River Shannon
To the ISLE OF MAN
Dúnmór
Kells
Hill of Tara
MEATH
DUBLIN TERRITORIES
Cluain Mhic Nóis
Clontarf
DUBLIN
DALKEY ISLAND
LEINSTER
Seir Kieran Monastery
Tree of Mag Adair
OSRÁIGE
Killaloe
SCATTERY ISLAND
LIMERICK
Disputed border between North and South Munster
Ferns
Hill of Carrig
FENNIT ISLAND
WEXFORD
WATERFORD
MUNSTER
Dun Domhnall
BANNOW ISLAND
CORK
Rathlin Island
Dublin
Seir Kieran
Wexford
Waterford
ENGLAND
WALES
Pembroke
Chepstow
London
Bristol
FRANCE
Rouen
Falaise
Paris

Characters

The Descendants of the Tuatha Dé Danann

Isolde (Is-old-a) – Daughter of Fódla and Murchad, sister to Aoife.

Broccan (Brock-an) – A warrior, son of Rónnat, cousin to Isolde.

Colmon (Cole-mun) – A warrior, cousin of Fódla and Rónnat.

Affraic (Af-frik) – A healer, mother of Báine, grandmother of Neasa, now deceased.

Báine (Bawn-yeh) – A witch, daughter of Affraic.

Étaín (Ay-teen) – A witch, daughter of Affraic, mother to Neasa, now deceased.

Shae (Shay) – A harpist, uncle to Gisela, now deceased.

Méabh (Mayve) – A cupbearer.

Gisela (Giz-ella) – A harpist, niece of Shae.

Senna (Senn-a) – A witch.

Siobhan (Shiv-awn) – A healer.

Fódla (Foe-la) – A healer, mother of Aoife and Isolde, now deceased.

Aoife (Ee-fa) – Daughter of Tomas and Fódla. Born giftless, now deceased.

Rónnat (Roe-nat) – A prophetess, sister of Fódla and mother of Broccan, now deceased.

Tomas (To-mass) – Former leader of the Descendants of the Tuatha Dé Danann, father of Aoife. A druid, now deceased.

Echna (Eek-na) – A druid, now deceased.

Neasa (Nee-sa) – A healer, niece of Affraic. Taken by the Fomorians, now deceased.

The Fomorians

Gormflaith (Gorm-la), known as Alys (Al-iss) – Sister to Máelmórda, mother to Sitric (deceased), Donnchad and Godfrey (deceased).

Máelmórda (Mal-mor-da) – Brother to Gormflaith, father to Cecile, now deceased.

Donnchad (Dunn-a-kha), known as Donn (Don) – Son of Gormflaith and Brian Boru, father to Angelo, half-brother to Murchad.

Angus (Eng-yus), known as Angelo (An-je-lo) – Son of Donnchad.

Cecile (Sess-eel) – Daughter of Máelmórda and Neasa the Descendant.

Olaf Tryggvasson (O-lav Trig-vass-on) – A former king of Norway. Not a Fomorian, but kept captive in bird form by Gormflaith.

Seir Keiran Monastery

Leofwynn (Leof-vinn) – Mortal, layperson at the monastery.

Aznar (Az-nhar) – Mortal, layperson at the monastery.

Ethel (Eth-ell) – Mortal, layperson at the monastery.

Dolag (Doll-agh) – Mortal, layperson at the monastery.

Banu (Bawn-oo) – Mortal, layperson at the monastery.

Cinnia (Sinni-yah) – Mortal who lives close to the monastery with her family.

Teafa (Tyef-a) – Mortal who lives close to the monastery with her family.

The Kingdom of Dublin

Asculv (Ask-ulv) – King of Dublin.
Eric (Err-ick) – Wealthy trader.
Hálfdan (Helf-den) – A trader.
Håkon (Hoe-kon) – An orphaned boy.
Sitric (Sit-rik), known as Sitric Silkbeard – Former King of Dublin, son of Gormflaith and Amlav of Dublin, now deceased.
Godfrey (God-free) – Son of Gormflaith and Olaf Tryggvasson, brought up by Sitric as his own son, now deceased.
Edysis (Ed-yah-sis) – Daughter of Sitric and his first wife Onguen, now deceased.
Brodar (Brow-dar) – A former king of Dublin, uncle to Asculv, now deceased.

The Kingdom of Connacht

King Ruaidrí Ó Conchúir (Rou-a-ree O'Connor) – King of Connacht, married to Gráinne, father to Róisín and Conchobar.
Queen Gráinne (Graw-ne-yeh) – Wife of King Ruaidrí.
Róisín (Ro-sheen) – Daughter of King Ruaidrí and Queen Gráinne.
Conchobar (Kru-hur) – Son of King Ruaidrí and Queen Gráinne.
Cathal (Ka-hul) – Younger brother of King Ruaidrí.
Cuan (Koo-an) – Son of Bardán and Tora, nephew of King Ruaidrí, nephew of King Godred of the Isles.
Bardán (Bar-dawn) – Brother of King Ruaidrí, father of Cuan.
Tora (Torr-ah) – Wife of Bardán, half-sister to King Godred of the Isles, now deceased.
Osán (Oss-awn) – Friend of Bardán.

King Tairdelbach (Tur-lough) – Former King of Connacht, father of Ruaidrí, Bardán and Cathal. Grandfather to Cuan, Conchobar and Róisín, now deceased.
Úna (Oo-na-gh) – Wife of King Tairdelbach, mother of Cathal, now deceased.
Fearghus (Fer-a-gus) – A warrior of Connacht.
Scolaí (Scull-lee) – A warrior of Connacht.
Blinne (Blin-yeh) – A woman of Connacht, a distant relative of King Ruaidrí.
Tóla (Toe-la) – King Ruaídrí's brehon.
Meallán (Myal-awn) – An orphan boy.
Eoghan (Owh-en) – Chief warrior of Connacht.
Ailill (Al-yil) – A warrior.
Brigid (Bridge-id) – A serving woman.
Eisten (Es-ten) – A serving woman.
Luchóg (Look-oo-g) – A clanless man/criminal/fuidir.

The Kingdom of Leinster

King Diarmait Mac Murchadha (Deer-mit Mac Murrough) – King of Leinster.
Domhnall (Doe-nall) – Son of King Diarmait, mother unknown.
Énna (Ay-nah) – Son of King Diarmait.
Eva (Eve-a) – Daughter of King Diarmait.
Connor (Conn-er) – Son of King Diarmait, currently a hostage of King Ruaidrí.
Riagáin (Ree-awn) – Translator for King Diarmait.
Caomhán (Keev-awn) – Son of Domhnall, currently a hostage of King Ruaidrí.
Olcán (Ul-cawn) – Son of King Diarmait's foster brother, currently a hostage of King Ruaidrí.
Brother Pádraig (Paw-drig) – A monk.
Brother Mark – A monk.

The Kingdom of Ulaid

King Maghnus Mac Duinn Sléibe (Mag-nus Mac Donlevy) – King of Ulaid.
Nuala (Noo-la) – Granddaughter of King Maghnus.
Dáirinn (Dawr-inn) – Granddaughter of King Maghnus.
Moncha (Muncha) – Granddaughter of King Maghnus.
Naoise (Nee-sha) – Stablemaster.

The Kingdom of Bréifne

Tigernán Ua Ruairc (Tier-nawn O'Rourke) – King of Bréifne.
Derbhfhorgaill (Derv-al) – Former wife of King Tigernán.

The Kingdom of Munster

Odhrán Ua Brian (Ur-awn) – King of North Munster, son-in-law of King Diarmait Mac Murchadha.
Cormac Mac Carthaig (Kurr-mick) – King of South Munster.
Finnén (Finn-yen) – Cousin of King Cormac.
Abbán (Ob-awn) – Cousin of King Odhrán, currently a hostage of King Ruaidrí.

The Kingdom of Waterford

King Ragnall (Rag-nall) – King of Waterford, father of Sichfrith.
Bjorn (Be-orn) – Friend of Cuan.
Brenna (Bren-na) – Wife of Bjorn.
Sichfrith (Sik-frith) – King Ragnall's son.
Ingvar (Een-var) – A trader and sailor.
Hvitserk (Vit-serk) – A warrior of Waterford.
Hara (Har-ra) – A warrior of Waterford.
Thorfinn (Tor-finn) – A warrior of Waterford.

Abbess Darlughdach (Dar-luch-ta) – The abbess of Kilculliheen, a nunnery just outside Waterford.
Sister Ruth – A nun at Kilculliheen.

Rathlin Island

Móirne (Morn-yeh) – A friend of Isolde, sister to Síoda.
Síoda (Shee-da) – Younger sister of Móirne.

The Anglo-Normans

Richard de Clare/Strongbow – Contested Earl of Pembroke, Lord of Striguil, an Anglo-Norman knight.
Alina – Natural daughter of Richard de Clare.
Robert FitzStephen – An Anglo-Norman knight.
Maurice de Prendergast – A Flemish knight.
Meilyr FitzHenry (My-lear) – An Anglo-Norman knight.
Hervey de Montmorency – An Anglo-Norman knight.
Miles FitzDavid – An Anglo-Norman knight.
Gerald FitzStephen – An Anglo-Norman knight.
Raymond FitzGerald, known as Le Gros – An Anglo-Norman knight, uncle of David FitzGerald.
David FitzGerald – An Anglo-Norman knight, nephew of Raymond FitzGerald.
Ranulf – An Anglo-Norman falconer.
William Ferrand – An Anglo-Norman knight, also a leper.
FitzHubert – An Anglo-Norman knight.
Walter – An Anglo-Norman archer.
Baldwinn – An Anglo-Norman archer.
Mildritha – A maid at Chepstow.

The Kingdom of the Isles

King Godred (God-red) – King of the Isles, uncle to Cuan.
Ragnall Godredsson (Rag-nall) – Son of King Godred.

Olaf Godredsson (O-lav) – Son of King Godred.
Viggo (Vee-go) – A warrior.

The Angevin Court

King Henry II of England – King of England.
Eleanor of Aquitaine – Queen of England.
Henry the Younger – Son of Henry II and Eleanor of Aquitaine.
Richard – Son of Henry II and Eleanor of Aquitaine.
John – Son of Henry II and Eleanor of Aquitaine.
Thomas Becket – Archbishop of Canterbury.
Theobold of Blois – Count of Blois.

Animals

Sleipnir – Cuan's horse.
Delaney – Eva's dog.

I shall not see a world that will be dear to me,
Summer without flowers,
Kine without milk,
Men without valour, captures without a king,
Woods without mast, seas without produce,
Wrong judgements of old men,
Every man a betrayer, every boy a reaver,
And the queen of the cowslip and clover will be
the only one to save us,
Two daughters she will have,
One to pass through death,
The other to destroy fire.

PART I

PROLOGUE

Cuan

Dúnmór, 1156

(Thirteen years ago)

"Faster!" Osán shouted.

I lunged forward as commanded, but the speed my father's master swordsman wanted was missing. I knew that before I turned to look at him.

When I finally lifted my eyes to meet his, Osán, who was standing at the edge of the training ring, grunted with disappointment. I tried not to scowl. He didn't like it when I did that. His disapproval was supposed to rouse me to greater heights. Make me move faster, strike deeper, jump higher. To show any signs of petulance or frustration would only make him push me all the harder. A punishment both for failing to move as he wished and for being unable to control my emotions.

"That's enough for today," he said, voice full of quiet exasperation. "I'll see you here at the same time tomorrow."

This early dismissal was unusual, but I didn't wait for him to change his mind. Quickly, I put the training sword away, and I was about to go home when my grandfather, who had been watching me train, called me over. I hurried to where he sat outside the feasting hall. He was old, so old he could no longer stand unaided, but he could still administer a painful clip to the ear when annoyed.

"Yes, Grandfather?"

"You're improving," he rasped as he sat forward in his wooden chair, his thin white hair fluttering in the breeze.

"Thank you, Grandfather."

"You need to work on your timing. You're quick, but you can't control it yet. You're all knees and elbows." As if to prove the point, he tapped his stick against the back of my knee, which made a soft clinking sound. "Tell your body to grow faster."

My cheeks burned, though I wasn't sure if it was joy from his earlier praise or embarrassment over how he had just described me. *All knees and elbows.* As if I could help it. My grandfather laughed at my reaction, at first dry and sparse, then building until he disintegrated into a coughing fit. "You are angry," he eventually got out once he had wiped his mouth. "Anger is good. I'm sure it hasn't passed your notice that the festival of Lughnasadh is tomorrow. And I'm also sure you've heard that your cousin Conchobar is coming to Dúnmór with his father to celebrate it with us. You'll need to use this anger to beat him in the training square. Last time was disappointing, was it not?"

"I'm ten now. He'll find it harder to beat me this time."

"We'll see." My grandfather smiled at my confidence. "You've grown, yes, but he will have grown too. He's eleven now. Twelve, maybe. I cannot remember." The pale-green cloth he had used to wipe his mouth fell on his lap, and speckles of red on the fabric caught my eye. My grandfather saw it too and tucked the cloth under his cloak, out of sight. "Now go," he snapped. "Tell your father I need him."

I scampered off to search for my father, but as I left my grandfather, I turned for a second to look at him. There was a yellow tinge to the old man's face today, and his skin sagged strangely under his left eye. It hadn't been like that yesterday. Perhaps I should tell my mother this, and about the blood when he coughed? She was the one who cared for him and sent for healers whenever a fever came.

My heart thudded against my chest at the thought of him falling ill again. I'd heard it said many times over the last year that my grandfather was dying. It shouldn't have been much of a surprise to hear these words. *He was old.* The oldest man I'd ever met. Father said God had blessed Grandfather with a long life and soon he would be with the angels, but I'd also overheard one of the slaves say that the devil didn't want him yet. *Kin-slayer*, he had called him. *Eye-taker*.

I had not repeated these words to anyone, but had wondered in the long, dark evenings what the slave had meant. *How could a man be so evil that the devil was afraid of him?*

As I made my way toward my house, I saw my father walking out of the stables, which were located behind the feasting hall. "Father!" I dashed toward him. "Grandfather wants you."

My father lunged toward me as I reached him, fast in the way Osán had described, and swept me up by the legs. Seconds later he was holding me upside down. "Does he now?"

Laughing, I threw punches at my father's stomach, which remained just out of reach, then wriggled my legs until my father started to laugh too. Carefully, he dropped me onto the ground.

"You're getting big," he said as I lay sprawled on the hay. "Soon I won't be able to do that."

"Good."

My father, a beast of a man, pulled me into a hug and ruffled my hair. "How did training go?"

"Fine."

"I was hoping for better than *fine*. I want you to put on a good show tomorrow."

"Against Conchobar?"

"Yes. Against Conchobar."

Frowning, I pulled out of his embrace. "I was only seven when he beat me last time. He was almost nine… and I was half his size."

"This time you're ten, and Osán has trained you."

"Why does it matter so much?"

In a way, this was a stupid question. This fight mattered to me more than to anyone. When Conchobar beat me last time, he'd hit me after the match ended and broken my nose. The shame of having to be led away by my mother, all covered in blood, had haunted my dreams ever since. This time, it would be different, and I couldn't wait to pummel Conchobar into submission. I'd dreamed of nothing else since I found out they were coming, but I didn't understand why it was so important to my father. *Or my grandfather.*

My father mulled over the question, then shrugged, a small smile building. "Because Conchobar is a little shit and needs to be put in his place. Just like his father."

"Why? What did Uncle Ruaidrí do?"

"Nothing to concern you." My father shook his head, his voice turning unusually stern and his smile disappearing. "You must be polite to your uncle when he comes. Do you hear me? You must be polite to Conchobar too. It's only in the fighting square that you can hit him. You know that, don't you?"

"Yes, Father."

"I can trust you, can't I, Cuan?"

"Of course!" I said this with such enthusiasm that my father hugged me again.

"You're a good boy. God has blessed me with only one son, but he has given me the very best. I'm proud of you."

My cheeks flushed hot, and this time it was I who hugged my father, holding him so tight that my arms ached.

"Well now," my father said. "Off you go. I believe young Dáire is looking for you." Giving my hair a last ruffle, he walked toward the feasting hall and Grandfather, while I went to my friend's house.

Dáire was waiting for me there. He had two nets in his hand, his face already smudged with dirt from the riverbank. Dáire was Osán's son, a year older than me, and as mischievous as it was possible to be. It made me wonder on occasion that Osán was so hard on me and not on his son, but not this day. Today I welcomed my friend's playful spirit and longed to leave the confines of the dun with him.

"Come on," he said, shoving a net into my hand. "Let's see if we can catch anything. I've been trying all morning and got nothing. Race you!"

Together we sprinted to the river. The dun was already in chaos as the people of Dúnmór readied it for our guests. If I stayed, my mother would put me to work. Fishing by the river with Dáire was heaven in comparison. We stayed there all day, leaving the shouts of my father and Grandfather and his men behind us, and only returned once it was dark and the smell of venison stew filled the air.

When I woke the following morning, I opened my eyes and found that my father was already dressed in his finest clothes and furs, ready to welcome his younger brother, Ruaidrí, to our dun. As the *tánaiste* and named heir of my grandfather, my father took his duties seriously, even more so since my grandfather had sickened. *If you are to be the next King of Connacht, better that your brother swears oaths to you now*, I'd heard my mother say to my father only two days ago. Father had nodded, but my mother had tutted when he said nothing.

Will Ruaidrí swear this? she had prodded.

He'll have no choice, my father had replied.

This morning there was no sign of worry upon my father's face. He winked at me as I stumbled over to the fire and warmed my hands, gave me a hug and kiss, but quickly left to be about his business.

"What's for breakfast?" I asked my mother, yawning as I sat down beside her.

My mother silently poured a ladle of barley oats flavoured with milk, honey and berries into a bowl and handed it over to me, her sharp eyes running over my face. "How are you always so dirty?" She leaned over to scrub my face with a cloth. She was distracted, though, and kept looking outside the house and toward the gates.

Wincing as she rubbed too hard over my cheek, I pulled back. "What's wrong, Mother?"

Mother shook her head, her light blue eyes paling to almost white as the morning sun streamed into our house. "Nothing,

Cuan. Your uncle and cousin will be here soon. I was just looking out to see if there were any signs of them. They did not say how many men they were bringing with them, nor whether they were coming early. I wonder if I should have the women prepare more stew?"

"Everything will be fine," I said. "I'm sure there is enough food to feed everyone five times over. You've been preparing for this visit for weeks now."

"That's true." She looked me over again, a soft smile growing this time. "Seeing as they aren't here yet, you're getting a good wash."

Knowing better than to argue, I did as she asked and scrubbed myself with the water she'd already poured into the washing tub, until not a speck of dirt lay upon me. Then I put on my best clothes and cloak that she had laid out on the bed.

Once I was ready, my father came in. While my mother had turned quiet this morning, my father was the opposite. He was louder than usual, for I'd heard him shouting several times at the warriors while I washed, and he moved about the house with the energy of a stallion that had been locked up all winter. It didn't take long for him to bang against the table and send one of the plates crashing to the ground.

"Bardán! You are part troll, I swear it!" my mother exclaimed.

Laughing at the face my mother gave him, my father came over to her, grabbing her by the waist to pull her close. She ducked down before he could kiss her, pushing him away and hitting him on the arm. "I don't kiss trolls."

This only made him laugh. "Ah, Cuan," he said to me. "Never marry a Viking girl. Their hearts are as cold as the countries they hail from." Mother hit him again, but this time she laughed, her anxiety falling away, and Father got a willing kiss.

"My mother was from the Isles, but my father was a Dubliner, as you well know," my mother said. "I'm Irish, too. Almost as Irish as you."

"Ha. Not quite, Tora. But it doesn't matter. I love you all the same."

My father pulled my mother closer to him again and whispered in her ear. "They are close now, my love."

My mother's face fell at these words. My father took a deep breath, then kissed her hand. "All will be well. I swear it."

"Be careful, Bardán," she whispered. "I've had strange dreams. Dreams of blood and fire."

"I'll be careful," he answered. "I've survived my two older brothers. I'll survive Ruaidrí too. While he's here, he'll swear his oaths before the clan and the priests, and before our father. All will be as it should be."

My father left then, leaving my mother to watch after him.

"Will you tell me what's wrong, Mother?" I asked, giving her a hug. "Don't pretend it's nothing. I'm not a little child anymore."

She forced a smile. "I'm just worried we don't have enough wine for the feast tonight."

"That's not true! Father bought in more from Dublin, so you know there's plenty. You… you and Father spoke of oaths and dreams of blood. What does that mean?"

She looked down at me and brushed her thumb over my chin. "I'm sorry, Cuan. Sorry for lying to you just now."

"Then what is it? Why is everyone so nervous about Uncle Ruaidrí coming?"

"Your grandfather is dying, little one. I don't think he has long left. The healer came to see him this morning, and he agrees with me. His heart is failing."

My breath stuck in my throat. I knew Grandfather was ailing, but to hear my mother say these words still hurt.

"I'm sorry, Cuan. You love him, and he loves you. That is a rare thing, you know. He loves almost no one. Your father, he loves a little. Ruaidrí, yes, there is something there for him too. His other sons, he loves not a bit. Everyone else is his enemy."

I knew this well enough. Two of my uncles had stood against my grandfather and tried to take the kingship of Connacht from him before I was born. He rewarded their treachery by removing their eyes himself, but my father, Bardán, had never betrayed him, and I had always thought Grandfather loved him in return.

"Why only *a little* for Father?"

My mother kneeled and rubbed my arms. "Your father is a safe pair of hands. Courageous. Strong. But to be a king in this world, you need to have ambition. Cunning. There can be no mercy in your heart."

"Father has too much mercy?"

"Perhaps."

"What about Uncle Ruaidrí?"

"The story you were told. That two of your uncles stood against your grandfather? The truth is… there were three. Ruaidrí only has his eyes because he found sanctuary in a church. His friend Tigernán of Bréifne helped conceal him, and Ruaidrí stayed hidden there until your grandfather had calmed down and swore not to take his eyes. Ruaidrí has no mercy. None at all, and he is clever and cunning. In the end, that is why your grandfather spared Ruaidrí, even though he had betrayed him. Kingdoms need clever men as well as strong ones to survive."

This made little sense to me, but my mother spoke with such certainty that I knew it was the truth. "It is my greatest wish your father will prove your grandfather wrong and that his mercy will make him the greatest king Connacht has ever known." She smiled then and hugged me tight. "Don't repeat what I said. I'm just worried, that's all. Once the clan names your father as the next king and everyone swears their oaths to him, I will rest easier. Even Ruaidrí will not break a vow made before the entire clan and before the priests. Now, get ready. Your good belt is by the table. Your training sword, too. You must impress our guests as well. For if your father is king, you will be king after him."

I nodded.

"Come, I will give you my father's sword to hold a moment. It will give you strength, and Odin's eye will watch over you."

My mother took a sword out from the wooden chest at the bottom of the bed. This was the sword that had belonged to her father, and she laid it on the mattress. It was long and heavy. Too heavy for me to handle, but oh, it was beautiful. Odin's eye was engraved into the hilt, and I rubbed my finger over it. The eye represented wisdom. *A dark wisdom*, my father had said. *A wisdom that the priests no longer liked to talk of.*

The horns sounded out long before I was ready to put the sword away, but no sooner did they blast than she placed it back in the wooden chest. "Now it is time to go."

My mother took my hand, her face now completely calm, and she smiled as she walked. Inside the gloom of our house, I had not noticed how much effort she had put into her appearance, but in the sunlight, she appeared to be an angel. She wore the silver orbs in her hair that her half-brother, King Godred of Dublin, had gifted her on her wedding day, and once she stepped outside, they glistened in the sun. So pale was my mother's hair that the silver seemed almost part of it. So different to the black, brown and copper hues contained within the hair of my father's kin. The men of my grandfather's dun couldn't help but stare at her.

Father held out his arm to her, then his other to me. "Ready?" he whispered into my ear.

"Ready," I whispered back.

We took our places at the front of the feasting hall. My grandfather was sitting in his chair with his wife, Una, at his side. She held their only son together, Cathal, on her hip. He was nearly two now, and he wrapped his arm around her neck and stared curiously at the newcomers to the dun. Cathal was a sweet boy, more fun now that he was running about the dun, and I stuck out my tongue to make him laugh, which he promptly did.

My father placed his hand on my shoulder as Cathal's laughter rose into the air, which focused my attention away from the boy and back toward the gate.

Uncle Ruaidrí, who had now moved past the guards, hailed some of them by name as he walked toward Grandfather. Conchobar followed. Uncle Ruaidrí greeted Grandfather and Una first, then held out his hand to touch his youngest brother's cheek. "Hello, Cathal," he said. "You are not so little anymore, little brother."

"Yes," Conchobar agreed. "He's bigger than Róisín, and she's a whole year older."

"Brother!" Ruaidrí said, leaving young Cathal to pat at Conchobar's cheeks, and opened his arms as he walked toward my father. "How are you, Bardán?"

"I am well, Ruaidrí. And yourself?"

My father and uncle embraced, both smiling as they took each other in. My uncle complimented my father on the dun. "When did you repair the walls?" he asked. "And you've rebuilt the feasting hall. With stone? When did you do this? Copying the English, are you?"

My father answered these questions and then complimented Ruaidrí on his growing family. "How many little ones are there at your dun now? Three? That's a lucky number." Conchobar, Ruaidrí's eldest son, said nothing as he came over to stand beside his father. He was still taller than me, but there was not such a difference as last time. He was skinnier than me too, especially around the legs and chest. With less weight behind him, he would be easier to force backward. Easier to push to the ground.

"You've gotten tall, Cuan," Uncle Ruaidrí said, placing his hand on my shoulder.

"Yes," my father said proudly, "as has your boy. Osán was about to take Cuan for his morning training. Perhaps Conchobar would like to join him?"

"What do you think, Conchobar?" Uncle Ruaidrí asked. "You fancy it?"

Conchobar smiled, and the two of us were led to the training square. Everyone continued to talk and laugh, as if this training session hadn't been prepared for and meant nothing, and perhaps it did mean nothing to some of them, but I could see from Conchobar's expression that he was eager for the fight to start. He'd been practising. I could tell this from the muscles in his arms, which were almost as thick as mine.

Osán gave us both leather armour for our chests, and he checked over both our training swords to make sure they were a similar length and style. "No strikes to the head," he said. "And do not move outside the square. If you do, you forfeit the match."

The two of us nodded, then Osán clapped his hands. "First one to get the other to the ground wins. Begin!"

Conchobar and I circled each other. He scrunched his nose as he looked down on me and swung his sword with his hand. I continued to circle. To watch. He was taller than me, but his movements were slow. Perhaps it was a trick to lure me in, but I didn't think so.

I sped up a little. Moved my feet the way Osán had taught me. *Balance is everything*, he had said. *You cannot be quick unless your body is in the right position, and your body cannot be in the right position unless your feet are.* I moved and moved, watching to see if Conchobar knew this lesson as well as I. I faked a lunge forward. He moved backward quickly, but his right foot moved too far back, and for a moment his body swayed.

I lunged again, swiping my leg behind his left. He fell to the ground in a heap and stared at me in shock. The match had lasted less than a minute, and already I had won.

Pushing himself up, he ignored Osán, who was announcing the match was over, but in his rage to get up quickly he had put all his weight onto one arm, and I swung my sword at this wrist. Into the dirt he went again. This time I pressed the blade of my wooden sword against his neck. A swell of pride rose up inside me, and though I knew I was not supposed to crow when I won, I couldn't help but smile.

"Don't worry," I said quietly. "I won't break your nose."

Conchobar glared and looked about to say something but then thought the better of it.

I had little time to bathe in my glory, for Osán clapped his hands, rushed toward us, and then lifted my hand as the victor. I gave the crowd a small smile, knowing that I couldn't acknowledge my victory too much. This was a practice match, even though

Father and I knew it wasn't. To behave as if I'd prepared or placed any importance on my winning would undo all the good work.

Knowing this, once Osán let go of my hand, I offered it to Conchobar. He gave me another sour look, but perhaps like me, knowing the significance of the fight, didn't want to pour any more import onto it by reacting, and took it.

"Balance," Osán said to Conchobar. "You must learn this. A warrior fights with their feet just as much as their arms. I will teach you this while you are here."

The polite clapping of the crowd suddenly stopped, and another sound replaced it. My grandfather, for all it was said he was dying and losing his wits, began to laugh. Low and rasping, the noise rose with the wind. If Conchobar and I had done our best to pretend this was just a bit of fun, Grandfather had undone it all without uttering a single word. My father couldn't help but grin. Ruaidrí made a point of congratulating me but said nothing to his son as he set his hand on his shoulder, leaving an awkward silence between the two.

Grandfather coughed then. A strange guttural sound that trailed away.

"Is it time to eat yet?" Ruaidrí asked. "We're tired after a long journey. Come, Father, where is all the good wine you've imported from Rome? Or was it Florence?"

"In the feasting hall," Grandfather replied, his breathing still not quite recovered. "Come, let us feast... and talk of many things. I'm not getting any younger... sitting out... in the cold."

My grandfather stood, and with the aid of two slaves walked a couple of steps between them, then without warning, he slumped forward. The two slave women held his arms tight but could not keep him standing. Grandfather groaned, slipped out of their grasp and thudded against the ground like a stone. He didn't even cry out, and once on the ground he didn't move. My father and uncle ran to him, asking him to speak, but Grandfather was silent. Pushing Ruaidrí away, my father lifted Grandfather into his arms.

"Tora," my father shouted as he made his way toward Grandfather's house. "Fetch the healer."

My mother rushed to the feasting hall, while I followed Father to my grandfather's house, which was situated at the back of the dun.

Perhaps I should not have entered the king's house, for children were not usually permitted to do so, but nobody seemed to notice me in all the confusion. My grandfather was already on his bed, a thick, black fur underneath his body. Still, he did not move. Not his arms, not his legs. Not even his head. At first my father shook my grandfather, using his hand to rub his chest, but soon he stopped and picked up my grandfather's hand. Gently, he kissed it.

Uncle Ruaidrí leaned forward and closed Grandfather's eyes. "God be with you, Father," he whispered.

These words shocked me, for I had not imagined that my grandfather was dead, only that he was sick once again and that the healer would make him better. The manner of this death, it had been too quick. He had been laughing one moment, falling the next. I stared at my grandfather, almost expecting him to laugh or shout or tell everyone to stop making a fuss, but I could see, even from the back of the room, that his face had turned pale. His lips, blue.

Father leaned over and kissed him on the forehead. Without a pause, five of the men in the room took out their swords and held them at my uncle's throat. Osán's sword was so close to Ruaidrí's skin that a small trickle of blood crawled down his neck.

"There is no need for this, Bardán," Ruaidrí said.

"Our father named me as his *tánaiste*, which means he wanted me to be the next king," my father replied, his voice unusually harsh. "Do you accept this?"

Ruaidrí nodded. "You are the next king. I will not stand against you."

My father pressed his lips tight together. "I want you to know that many have told me to take your eyes tonight."

"I'm sure they have, but do not listen to them. I knew Father was sick and you would be thinking of the kingship, and I still came here. I want to help you, Bardán. Meath presses us. So does Munster. Once they know our father is dead, they will move against Connacht. We need to be united, to fight as one, or they will destroy us."

"You speak the truth." My father took a deep breath. "But there can only be one king. You are my brother, and I don't want to hurt you. You are clever and I would have you help me make Connacht the first of all the kingdoms in Ireland, but to accept your help, I must be convinced of your loyalty. Once you turned against our father. Do you plan to turn against me?"

My uncle held out his arm, his fingers stretching toward my father. "I will help you, brother. I know what's at stake here, and you are the best man to lead our clan and kingdom. I will swear any vow you wish of me. I will swear on any Bible and in front of any bishop or priest."

My father took his brother's arm and held it tight. "Then I will name you as my war chief. Tonight, let us feast in honour of our father. Tomorrow we will call the men of the clan to vote on the kingship."

"As you wish, brother. With my vote for you, there is no one who would dare stand against you. You will be king. I swear it on our father's soul."

My father stared at my uncle. The swords didn't lower. In fact, Osán's moved ever so slightly upward, creeping onto my uncle's chin.

"Swear your oath to me now, Ruaidrí. Brother to brother. In front of our father's body and with God above watching us. Swear you will obey me. Swear that I am your king."

"I swear it." My uncle didn't pause, didn't falter. Didn't stutter. "I swear to all those things. You are the next King of Connacht."

My father gave a curt nod and gestured for the men in the room to lower their weapons and make their way into the feasting hall. Osán was the last to do so, but he did as my father instructed him. It was then, after everyone else had left, that my father noticed me. I half-expected him to scold me, but he winked instead and gestured for me to follow Osán.

Part of me didn't want to leave my grandfather, but the other part was eager to be away. He was dead now, and I did not want to meet his ghost, nor did I want to find out if it was an angel who came to greet him, or a devil.

The feast that night began in a subdued manner, but soon laughter was heard alongside the tears. Many stood up to speak about my grandfather. Stories of how he had won his kingship and of the battles he fought against the famous kings of Munster and Meath.

I listened, sitting between my father and mother, eyes wide as my grandfather's *ollamh* described one of these battles. His words were poetry, the battle he drew was so vivid I felt as if I had been there myself. It was only when my head had drooped twice in as many minutes that my mother took me back to our house.

"It's time for sleep," she hushed as she linked her arm with mine. "I've had enough stories for one night too."

"But I want to hear more."

Mother shook her head. "Your grandfather's funeral and the games that follow will go on for weeks. You'll hear every story at least ten times before it's over. Now it's time for bed."

Yawning, I lay down and dreamed of the glory that awaited me on the battlefield. I was a man in this dream. A man standing beside my father. *My father, the king.*

"Get up," Dáire hissed in my ear. Shoving a finger into my side, he jolted me awake. "Come on. Everyone's drunk. They won't notice if we take some of the new wine!"

I opened my eyes and stood, coughing as I breathed in the smoke that had built up in the house, and staggered outside beside my friend. My mother lay asleep on her bed, breathing softly, and didn't stir as we made our way out. She would not like that I had left at this time of night. *Perhaps I should not…*

"Hurry," Dáire whispered, his voice more full of mischief than normal as he dragged me toward the feasting hall. "They've finally brought the expensive wine from Florence out. Your uncle said it's the best he's ever tasted. If we don't get a sip now, it'll all be gone."

I had been curious about this wine too, for it was so expensive that Grandfather had traded one of his bulls for it, but I did not have the same confidence as Dáire that we would get any. Already light seeped over the eastern horizon, which meant the morning servants would be up soon to clear away the leftover food and drink. If they spotted what me and Dáire were up to, they'd most certainly tell my father.

"Maybe we shouldn't, Dáire. What if we're caught?"

Dáire shrugged. "Doubt it. Most of the warriors are passed out. The others are dancing. You should see them. They can hardly stand."

"Come on then," I said, Dáire's infectious grin worming its way inside of me. "Whoever gets the first sip is the winner!"

The two of us snuck closer to the feasting hall, holding in our laughter as we tried to stay hidden in the shadows, and gripping each other's tunics so the other couldn't take off and get to the wine first. As we approached the door, Ruaidrí staggered out of the dun, swaying and unable to walk in a straight line. The two of us stilled as he made his way to the guest house, sniggering into our sleeves and hands as he grinned and slurred his words of goodbye to those left inside the dun.

"He's not even the worst," Dáire whispered.

Once Ruaidrí had disappeared into the shadows, we entered the feasting hall, and I realised very quickly that Dáire was right. As well as the warriors passed out by the doors, there were more asleep inside, flopped over the tables and wooden benches. Those who were dancing were spinning and laughing as they tried to keep to the rhythm of the pipes and drums. It seemed strange to see such behaviour upon the death of my grandfather, but it was not merriment or joy that I heard in their laughter. It was release.

My father, however, was not dancing or sleeping. He was awake and talking to Osán at the top table, so I tugged at Dáire's arm, and we dropped to the ground. Crawling under one of the wooden tables, I glared at my friend. "I thought you said everyone was asleep? Both of our fathers are awake. If they see us drinking the wine, they'll…" I stopped speaking. Something rumbled outside the dun. Thunder perhaps? Though I had noticed no storm clouds on our way over.

Dáire licked his lips. "Still might be worth it."

"No, wait." I grabbed him by the tunic. "What's that sound?"

Dáire held his breath. At first he looked set to argue, but then he heard it too, though like me couldn't work out what it was. "Drums?" he guessed.

"No. Shh." I crawled closer to the table leg by the wall. The sound was footsteps, lots of footsteps, and I shrank to the floor, fearful that my mother had sent out a search party and I would be in trouble for sneaking out this late at night. But as I looked out from under the table, I could see it was Uncle Ruaidrí who had entered the feasting hall. He was no longer swaying. No longer grinning.

"Did you not have your fill, brother?" My father laughed from the top of the room. He had not yet noticed the change in Ruaidrí.

"I must say I didn't care much for the wine at all," Ruaidrí returned.

My father sat up straighter. He saw the difference now, just in time to watch as twenty warriors poured into the feasting hall. I didn't recognise all of them, but a handful of them were my father's men who guarded the dun. The men and women who had been dancing stopped and staggered to the side of the hall to get out of their way. Some of them gathered around the table I was underneath, and I crawled further along to see what was happening.

"So, you've come to fight, Ruaidrí," my father said as he set down his cup. "Our father's body is still warm and the oaths you swore to me are not yet a day old. I was warned you would do this, and I did not believe it. I will not make that mistake again."

"You won't have the chance to make a mistake like this again."

My father stood and slowly walked forward, his sword in hand. I looked at him, awestruck at the sight. Uncle Ruaidrí was half a foot shorter, and though he took out his sword too, it was not so long or as heavy as my father's. *How could Ruaidrí even think of winning?* My father would cut him down without even trying.

"Now!" Uncle Ruaidrí shouted.

Ten, no fifteen of the men lying asleep on the tables sprung to life. These were all my father's men – those charged with guarding the feasting hall – but instead of guarding it and driving Ruaidrí away, they took out their swords and began to circle my father and Osán.

"Men of Dúnmór, put down your swords," my father said to them. "Whatever Ruaidrí has offered you, I will offer more."

The man closest to the table I was hiding underneath clutched at his sword, eyed the man beside him, and then gave a firm shake of the head. Together, the group of men moved forward, closing the circle that my father and Osán found themselves in.

It was then I realised that Ruaidrí didn't mean to fight my father for the kingship. He simply meant to watch while other men did his work for him.

"Father!" I crawled forward, desperate to help, though my hands and voice shook. It was shock and despair and anger all rolled into one. How could my uncle do this? *Where was his honour?* "Fight, Father! I will help you!"

"No." Dáire sprung forward and grabbed hold of my legs, then tried to wrap one of his hands around my mouth. "Don't."

"Let me go, Dáire. I need to… need to help."

"They'll kill you too."

"Cowards, all of you!" my father shouted as I struggled out of Dáire's grasp. "Ruaidrí, this is madness. How can you be a king if you cannot fight for yourself?"

Wriggling free, I crawled to the table edge, but Dáire still had a hold of my foot. He pointed to the door, but I shook my head, for I could not leave my father. Dáire, all mischief gone from his face now, crawled away and dashed outside. Now that he had left, I rolled onto my stomach. A meat knife that had fallen to the ground during the feast was right in front of me. It wasn't so sharp, but sharp enough. I reached out to take it.

The men were moving closer to my father, and I jumped out from under the table and struck the man closest to me in the thigh. Blood spurted from the wound, and my father roared. He charged into the group of men, Osán at his side.

"Don't kill them," Ruaidrí shouted. "All three must be kept alive."

My father roared again and stabbed the man beside me. As the man fell, my father grabbed me by the arm and threw me behind him. "Stay there, Cuan," he shouted. "Stay back."

But I couldn't stay back. The knife in my hand, covered in blood, was all I could see. All I could think of. How dare these men turn on my father? I charged forward and struck another, this time in the shoulder, and the man fell.

Before I could strike again, two men grabbed me. The taller of them prised the knife from my fingers while the other wrapped his arm around my neck and squeezed. Dragging me to the back of the feasting hall, I struggled to break free, kicking and twisting with all my might. I had to get back to my father. To save him.

As the men pushed me down, the rest of the warriors swarmed around my father and Osán, using their numbers to disarm them. The men at the back of the hall threw ropes to those at the front, and the warriors began to bind my father and Osán with them. Arms first. Then legs. Then necks.

"The kingship is not yours, brother," my uncle said. "It was never meant for you." He walked toward my father and pulled a sharp knife from his belt.

My father struggled against the men who held him. "Coward! Fight me one-on-one, like a man!"

But my uncle didn't flinch, and as he reached my father, the warriors tightened their grip and held him firm. With no hesitation, my uncle brought his knife down onto my father's eyes. The man holding me turned my face away. I could no longer see my father. Only hear as he screamed.

But his scream was not the only one to fill my ears. By the doors, a flash of silver caught my eye. It was my mother. She had come into the feasting hall, tears falling down her face as she saw what was happening. No one else noticed her standing there, for everyone was watching what she was. *My father and the kingship being taken from him.*

My mother's hand slowly reached upward, shaking uncontrollably. "No," she sobbed. "Not this." With this sob, a bolt of fire shot out of her hand. I blinked, sure I had imagined it, but one of the tables at the back of the hall crashed against another with the force of it, and the flames caught quickly, fuelled not only by the wood but by the wine and ale that had been spilled over it. *How was this possible?* I thought of the stories of Thor and Odin and Floki that my mother had told me. Was she a goddess? Did the old gods truly walk among us? As the fire flew out of her, she fell to the ground. The force of the fire pouring from her hands caused part of the roof to collapse, and a wooden beam laden with straw thatch landed on top of her.

The men in the room shouted as they noticed the fire and dropped my father to the ground. They rushed out of the feasting hall, Ruaidrí too, as thick smoke filled the air.

The men holding me let me go to make their own escape, and I stumbled forward. From here I could see Osán crawling along the ground, grasping for my father and then hauling him up onto his shoulder. I wanted to help, but I had to get to my mother first.

The men in the feasting hall ran past her, fleeing the fire that was spreading… all except for one. This man pulled back the wood and thatch, a knife in his hand that he pressed to her shoulder. "I saw what you did. A demon, you are! A demon from the pits of hell!"

I screamed as I threw myself onto him, trying to pull the knife out of his hand as he thrust it into my mother's shoulder again, this strike closer to her chest than the last.

I hated him. Hated them. Hated them with every bone in my body, with every drop of blood that ran through me. My skin tingled with this hatred, as if this emotion was a part of me now and could never leave. So much anger filled me that it burned my throat. My eyes. Then my body.

Fire suddenly burned along my palms and arms. *What was happening to me?* "Mother," I whispered as the fire surged over my skin. My mother opened her eyes and watched with horror as the flames moved over me.

Now it was the man who had attacked her who screamed as the fire from my hands jumped from me to him. The dark rage in his eyes turned to fear as the flames consumed him. He tried to crawl away, but the fire that danced upon me burned him so hot that his skin peeled from his bones.

Without warning, my mother threw herself on top of me, and her arms wrapped around me. "Calm, Cuan. Calm. Calm. Breathe deeply. Let the pain go. Let the fire go."

I tried to do as she asked, but the fire continued to burn. All over my skin.

"Control it, Cuan!" Mother's voice grew louder, harder. "If you don't, it will kill you. Do you understand? It will kill you."

"I can't," I screamed. "I don't know how."

Without warning, my mother's fist crashed down upon my face. My vision spun, darkness filling my mind with edges of light swimming through it. As I blinked through the pain, I was glad to see that the fire had gone from my hands.

"What happened to me?" I asked my mother. "To you?"

"You have the curse, Cuan." She wiped her mouth, streaks of black phlegm pouring down her chin, and tears and blood streaming down her cheeks. "I prayed that it wouldn't pass down to you. I'm so, so sorry. So very sorry."

WINTER 1169/1170

Cuan

Road to Connacht

Sleipnir walked slowly through the forest.

I hadn't the heart to make him go any faster.

I should. At this very moment, I should have been galloping to King Ruaidrí's dun. Toward Dúnmór. I was in Connacht, yes, but only just, and it would be safer for me to be with my uncle rather than alone on the western road. I wouldn't put it past King Diarmait to command his men to ride over the Leinster border to find me, even if it meant their presence was noted. Even if it meant the warriors of Connacht killed every one of them.

That thought should have urged me onward, but instead it made me still. Being with Ruaidrí was not safe for me either. Perhaps I would not be blood-eagled before a crowd baying for blood, but a knife in the dark was more than a possibility. No spectators to watch. No jeers. But blindness or death could come for me all the same.

What am I doing? Go back. Go back.

An inner voice that I had ignored for many years whispered inside of me. I didn't want to go to Connacht. I wanted to return to Isolde. To take her somewhere nobody knew either of us.

"Come on, Sleipnir. Keep going."

Sleipnir was clever, clever enough that he'd run into the forest during the attack at the ráth, and once Isolde had healed me, I'd been able to follow his tracks. Grateful that I had found him, I patted his neck and urged him forward. He trotted for a few steps, then returned to his slow walk. There, he was being clever once again. He could tell my call to go faster was no true command. No true wish.

This hesitancy was most unlike me. Usually, I made a decision and saw it through with all haste. *Speed is good*, my uncle Godred had always said. *Less chance for your enemies to know what you are doing if you barely know what you're doing yourself.*

And perhaps that was part of the problem. I'd been avoiding thinking about what to do. Strategies of how to prevent blood eagles and knives in my eyes should be running through my mind, but they didn't capture my interest this evening. Instead, I found I could only look backward. Every so often I would turn in the direction of Seir Kieran and wonder if Isolde was alive. She had been shaking when I left her outside the monastery. Eyes closed and pale, lips black, splattered with the same dark liquid that had covered my mother's mouth. *What if Isolde was dying?* She had spent her energy saving me. I knew this now. *What if in helping me, she died in my place?*

Taking a breath, I held it. *No, Isolde was alive.* Her people, the Descendant healers, would save her as she had saved me. She was gone from *me* but not gone from this land. *Not dead.* How could she be? Isolde was too vivid in my mind for that to be true. When I closed my eyes, I forced myself to forget the way she looked when she was lying in my arms and close to death. Instead, I pictured her sitting under the tree at Kells. She was wearing her blue dress, her expression focused on the insects crawling along the soil, completely oblivious to the fact that the women working by the tents were staring at her. Completely oblivious to the eyes of the guards who watched her from afar. It had made me smile when I found her like this, perhaps the first smile that had been true for many years.

This memory made me want to go back to her all the more. To see her again. To watch her. To be with her.

Isolde did not want me though, I had to remind myself. She had said we could not be together, and now it was on me to accept that. Isolde was alive, yes, *she had to be*, and a whole life awaited her.

A life that would be better than any I could give her. For, even if our ancestors were not enemies, what happiness could she derive from a man who more wanted to kill than see alive? What joy could I give her when I didn't even understand what I was?

Staring at my hands, I curled them into fists. Fire had burst from my skin on two occasions now. First when I was a child at Dúnmór and second when I was trying to escape King Diarmait. I had killed men on both occasions. Burned them.

Keep your emotions tight, Cuan. If you don't, the curse will kill you, my mother had said to me once.

And now I had to pull in my emotions once again. I was almost of an age with my mother when she died. Losing control of our emotions was what caused the fire to come, and it was this fire that killed us in the end too. Indeed, if I had not been with Isolde, I would already be dead. I had to make sure not to let that happen again, though this was easier said than done. The love that I had felt for Isolde had stretched the threads I had coiled tight around myself, and they needed to be tightened once more. Not for long, and perhaps that made it easier. Death was coming for me whether I wanted it or not, for I had sworn oaths to my father three years ago, and soon I would have to make a move against Ruaidrí.

The memory of making these vows moved me back to stillness. Back to ridding myself of emotions. Once I returned to Dúnmór, my father's plan to make me King of Connacht would be set into motion. Then I would die, for there were many men who would strike me down if I killed Ruaidrí. I was sure, had been sure ever since I'd made this vow, that this would be how I met my death – not with a sickness that ate me from the inside out, but with a sword deep inside of me. The way men were supposed to die. Other men feared the blade. Ran from it, but if they had watched my mother dying, they would embrace it. They would know, as I did, that there were worse ways to go.

*

Once I was far enough away from the Leinster border, I dismounted and led Sleipnir to a narrow river. It was shallow here, slow-running, and Sleipnir walked a couple of steps into the water and swished his tail as he nibbled at the grass along the riverbank. The forest was thick here, and the smell of moss filled the air, though this deep into the forest, the smell of rot filtered through too. I crouched down, wanting to splash some water on my face, to feel something cool and living upon my skin, but before my fingers touched the water, I paused, catching the reflection before me.

Scarless. Unbroken. I knew Isolde had healed me, but somehow, I had not expected this. I ran my fingers over my left eye and nose and then over to the right side of my chin, feeling for the scar that should be there. *It was gone.*

The memory of the man attacking me, axe pressing against my skin, had not left me. It was Conchobar, of course, who had paid someone to take my eyes last year. He'd wanted to give me the same punishment that his father had given mine, and just like his father, he had been too scared to do it himself. However, this mercenary had failed to take my eyes, instead he had left me with a scar that crossed over my face. Now that deep scar was gone. And it wasn't just the scar on my face. The scars on my arms had vanished. Every wound, every broken bone, every fracture, even the blood inside of my left eye… all as if they had never happened.

Slowly, I took out my sword. I couldn't return to my family like this. They would know there was something wrong with me. Something *unnatural*. I set the blade against my eyebrow and carefully pressed the sharp blade against the trail of my old scar. From browbone to chin.

Blood ran down my hand and over my wrist, and the pain was sharp, but even so, I pushed the blade deeper. Only after I was satisfied that I had made the cut the same as before did I stand and clean my blade.

"Come, Sleipnir," I said. "Let's rest for the night."

I set up a shelter in the forest, knowing that I needed to let the scar heal over for a week or two before I continued my journey.

It looked too fresh right now, and I needed the scabs that would form over the cut to fall away.

Days of hiding like this were never easy, for it was never easy to be alone with my thoughts. They were dark, full of screams, full of death. My mind would move to memories of my mother dying. Of my father losing his eyes. And now, of Isolde dying in my arms.

Enough, I told myself. *Enough*.

On the tenth night, my final one of hiding in the forest to wait as my cut healed over, I lit a small fire then settled down for the evening against a tree. I was not tired enough to sleep, though I knew I should try to get some. In two days, I would be at Dúnmór, no matter how slow Sleipnir walked, and then I would need my wits about me. Chewing on the winter berries I had scavenged, I wrapped my cloak about my shoulders and closed my eyes.

"Excuse me." A gentle tap on my shoulder pulled me out of my sleep.

I tightened my grip on my sword, only to find a boy, of maybe ten or eleven, standing in front of me. He had a missing front tooth, and his hair was long and matted, but there was flesh on him that spoke of a gentler past.

"Do you have any food?"

I stood, then glanced at Sleipnir to make sure no one had tried to steal him or was close to him. There was no one. At least, not yet. Cursing myself for letting myself fall into such a deep sleep that I had not heard a stranger approaching, I walked away from the boy.

"No."

I mounted Sleipnir quickly and moved him into a walk, glancing about me, waiting for any men who might be hiding behind the trees to run out. Sleipnir, feeling my feet at his flank, was ready to bolt forward, but when no one else appeared, I stared once again at the boy. "Where are your parents?"

"Dead," he answered. "There was a fire."

A terrible thought occurred to me. There had been people in the ráth that Isolde and I had fled to. Could this boy be one of… no, I was too far away from Ferns for that to be possible. But the sudden jolt of guilt made me reach into my bag and throw him a leaf wrapping I had made and filled with berries the day before.

The boy caught it in his hands and opened it, salivating as his teeth pierced through the berries. He was hungry indeed.

A man came out from behind the trees. Too loudly to be attempting theft or murder. He was tall, slim, wore his hair short, and was using a long stick to beat away the low branches. If he'd come out earlier or with any attempt at stealth, I would have urged Sleipnir onward, but this man was no more threat to me than the boy.

"Meallán!" he said. "I told you not to speak to strangers."

"Don't worry, Brother Angelo. I've come to no harm."

A monk? I stared once again at the man approaching us. Through the dimming sunlight, I could see he was of an age with me, or perhaps a little younger. He had an odd look about him, though I couldn't decide why that was. Perhaps it was merely the strange styling of his hair, or the golden colour of his eyes that put me in mind of a cat.

"You're related?" I asked the boy.

"No," Brother Angelo replied for him. "I am a monk from Rome, looking to spread the word of the Lord. I found this boy alone and hungry. I was hoping to take him somewhere where he could be provided for. Do you know if a monastery is close by?"

I knew of one, but I could not say it out loud. It was no good anyway. It was several days away for a man and boy on foot. There were several other churches closer now. But even closer was Dúnmór.

"I am on my way to the king's dun. If you bring the boy there, I will see he finds work and somewhere to stay."

Brother Angelo bowed his head, and the young boy, Meallán, gave me a wide grin.

"It's a two-day walk from here, but there is a bruidean along the way. If you keep walking, you'll reach it before the sun sets tomorrow. There will be plenty to eat and drink, as well as a warm fire."

"May the Lord shower his blessings upon you," Brother Angelo said, making the sign of the cross.

I bowed my head, preparing to kick Sleipnir onward.

"You are travelling? But it will be night soon," Meallán said. "Mightn't your horse go lame if it falls in the dark?"

I shook my head and pointed up at the sky. It was cloudless, and so the sky would soon be filled with the moon and stars. "Good luck, Meallán. Good luck, Brother Angelo. I hope to see you both at Dúnmór in a few days."

I pushed Sleipnir into a trot and drove him back toward the path.

If Isolde were here, she would ask if the boy could climb up onto Sleipnir or to let them travel with me… but I was not Isolde and could not afford to be so kind. Already, the veil of detached coldness was pulling around me, and now that I was returning to Ruaidrí's dun, I had to keep it there and hold it tight. Kindness and mercy were not attributes that I could afford to have.

As Sleipnir plodded onward, howls rose with the wind. Wolves. Hunting. Sleipnir's hind legs jittered. He wanted to gallop, and while it was safe to walk in the moonlight, it was too dangerous for him to run with the light so low. I glanced backward. A thick spire of smoke was rising upward. My fire, but the monk and boy had put too much fuel upon it. It would attract notice. Fuidir lived in the forest and might come to see if they had anything of value. And if it was the wolves that came and not men, would Meallán and the Roman monk know to climb the trees?

Yes, I was cursed, but there had to be a way to retain something of who I was. It was my uncle Ruaidrí who I could show no mercy to. Not these poor people who had lost so much.

Turning Sleipnir, I returned to the camp. The monk and the boy were holding their hands over the fire. Meallán was shivering, though he still had a grin on his face.

"Here," I said, picking up some fallen branches. "Let's make the fire bigger, but only sticks, not leaves or gorse, otherwise the fire smokes too much."

The monk, Angelo, smiled at the boy. "I told you he would come back. God is good."

The boy clapped his hands and threw more branches onto the fire. "God is good," he repeated as he reached out to feel more of the growing heat.

"This man is like the Good Samaritan. Do you remember I told you about him, Meallán? The story from the Bible."

The boy nodded, his face now serious.

The monk, however, smiled as he turned to look at me. "What did you say your name was?"

"Cuan."

"Well, Cuan. I believe God has put us in each other's path. Perhaps one day I can return the favour and be of use to you." He held out his hands to the fire, the flames shimmering in the gold of his eyes. "Or perhaps it will be you who helps me again. God is mysterious, is he not?"

I had not thought of God in a long time, but this monk from Rome was all fervour and devotion, so I nodded as I threw another stick onto the fire. "Yes, I suppose he is."

Gormflaith

Chepstow

"Hurry, Alys," old Ranulf said. "The birds get agitated if you take too long to put on their hoods."

The falconry at Chepstow was quiet today, so I gave Ranulf the sweetest smile I could muster as the hawk continued to wriggle his head, hoping that he would come and do my work for me.

My smiles usually worked. Ranulf was old, but not so old that he didn't like to come close to me when chance permitted. Ranulf, dependable as ever, walked over, and with his big oafish hand, shoved the hood over the bird's head.

"Is Strongbow hunting today?" I asked.

"No. Le Gros is, though. And his friend. William Ferrand."

There was something about the way he said the name *William Ferrand* that caught my attention. A faint whiff of disdain. Coyly, I peered up at him. "Who is he?"

"You haven't heard talk of William before?" Ranulf asked, a smile curling at his lips, enjoying the power of knowing things I did not.

"No."

"I only say…" He trailed away and came even closer to me, so close that I could smell the stale stench of last night's ale upon his breath. "I only mention it because he is a leper. I would hate for you to catch the disease from him. When he comes out, keep a good distance away."

"A leper?" A shiver moved through my body. Leprosy was a sickness that terrified all. From the Pope himself to the humblest of peasants, all prayed never to be afflicted with it. "How can Strongbow permit him inside the castle with such a sickness upon him?"

"William is very careful. He wears his helmet and armour at all times. He doesn't even take it off to sleep or eat."

"Does that truly stop it spreading?"

Ranulf shrugged. "I suppose if I wake up one morning and half my nose has fallen off, we shall know."

I made the sign of the cross, more out of something to do with my hands than anything else, for God could not cure those afflicted with this pestilence any more than he could stop its spread.

Ranulf put a friendly hand on my shoulder. "That's all very well and good for me. I'm old. You are young. When he comes out, let me deal with him. You stay back."

I nodded, though I was not as afraid as another young maid might be. Could Fomorians catch such a thing? *No, surely not.* There had been an outbreak once when we travelled through Athens, eighty years ago now, but none of my kin had caught it. The thought of it, however, the thought of skin and flesh crumbling like dust, was enough to make me feel sick.

"I still wonder that Strongbow allows him here," I muttered. "The presence of a leper will make everyone uneasy."

"William Ferrand is a legendary fighter and fought in the Crusades. Strongbow means to make use of him in his war against the Irish, mark my words." Ranulf tapped his nose. "You don't get to my age without learning a thing or two."

I nodded, lowering my eyes as I pulled the hood further down the hawk's face. *So, Strongbow does mean to invade Ireland then.* With Donnchad and Angelo gone, and Strongbow still here, feasting night after night, it was easy to forget that plans were underfoot. There was a patience to these Normans that the Irish did not possess, and I envied them for it. Indeed, I was learning much from their ways and was determined to learn more. If this leper warrior William Ferrand was here, there must be a reason.

He wasn't just another knight to make up the numbers, for Strongbow had plenty of those.

"Do you wish to go, Alys?" Ranulf asked. "If you wish to leave, I will say you're unwell."

"No. If Strongbow has invited William here, he must be confident that the leprosy will not spread." I made the sign of the cross one more time. "And I have faith that God will protect me."

Ranulf gave me a bucket of chopped fish. "Be that as it may, stay back. How about you feed the hawks instead of the eagles? That will keep you out of the way."

I stole a glance at Olaf. My wretched former lover, who was now in the form of a beautiful golden eagle. He watched me closely when I came here. When I fed him, he would gently peck at my hands, his way of begging that I transform him into a man once again and give him my love. I would need him soon, I was sure of that, and so I would have to give him what he wanted sooner rather than later. Not today, though. Not yet.

I took the bucket and walked over to the hawks, scattered the contents into the birds' cages and filled up their water bowls. The bones of dead mice and rats from yesterday's bucket littered the floor of their cages, and I brushed them up and into the corner. Cecile had almost vomited when I told her about this duty, but I didn't mind. It was interesting to see the little skeletons, stripped of flesh and skin.

It didn't take long for Le Gros and his friend to appear.

This knight, William Ferrand, walked into the courtyard first. From head to toe, he was covered in steel. Not just the ringed chain-mail that the Norman warriors usually wore, for this was only visible over his arms. On top of this, whole plates of armour covered his torso and upper legs, and a large helmet covered his face. Again, this was different. This helmet didn't just protect the scalp and nose, but covered his entire head, with only two holes for his eyes and a slit for his mouth, which I supposed allowed for the passage of food and water. A sudden rumbling of laughter moved into my throat as I pondered how he managed to piss and shit if he never removed any armour, but I pushed that aside. Some things were too depraved even for me.

Le Gros spoke with William but kept his distance. Le Gros was a boisterous man, given to slapping his men on the shoulder and pulling them into headlocks when he was drunk. I suspected that even deep into his cups he would not do this to William.

William, hands clasped together behind his back, moved along the cages to look at the birds. As he reached the end of the row, I turned to face him. "Do you wish to take one out to fly, my lord? The hawk at the far end is very well-trained."

The knight, surprised that I had spoken to him, shook his head. "No. I do not partake in falconry anymore, though I enjoyed it in my youth."

"Then why come to see them?" I asked.

Le Gros sniggered. "All men like to see pretty things in cages, Alys. Have you not learned that already? Why else do you think Strongbow allows you to work with Ranulf?"

I lowered my eyes as if trying to conceal my blush, but there was no blush. Of course I knew this. I knew it better than anyone.

"This is David's woman," Le Gros said by way of introduction. "Alys. Her father is Norman, but her mother is Irish, and she and her brothers are helping us with the invasion."

"You are married to David?" William asked me.

"Not yet," I replied. "My brother, Donn, must prove his worth first."

William laughed, the sound dulled against the steel of his helm. "If I were a young man and of good health, I would marry you anyway." He turned to Le Gros. "What is wrong with your cousin? Does he have no passion?"

"David is a good boy, and he listens to his lord."

William gave a small nod. "Well, I hope your brother does well and that you marry soon, Alys. I should like to toast a wedding before I die in battle."

The tone of his voice caught me by surprise. There was delight when he spoke of his own death. Joy, even. "You wish to die in battle?"

William nodded. "I wanted it to be in the Holy Lands, but if not there, Ireland will do just as well. I am here on God's work, to spread his word. Death in his name will be an honour."

He turned away from me then, moving back along the row of birds and listening to Le Gros as he spoke of who owned which bird, and which bird was the best, and just for a moment I saw the grey skin behind the slit over William's eyes. The swelling and crumbling and pockmarking of the skin on his brow. There was something about the pallor of his skin behind those slits that dredged up a memory I had long thought buried.

My mother, when she had come to see me before she died, had withered away like this. Her long black curls had turned to thin white strands. The skin under her eyes sagged. Her cheeks were hollowed out, her nose and chin pitted and swollen. That was how we died. For hundreds of years, we lived in the bloom of youth, and then we rotted in plain sight over the course of a few months. So quickly did our lives fade. How old had my mother been when this happened to her? *Three hundred years*, she had said. Back then, that had seemed like an unfathomable amount of time. Not anymore.

How old was I now? Over two hundred years. One day, this rapid decline would happen to me. What fate would I choose? My mother had gone to a nunnery and paid the nuns to look after her. Uncaring, cold hands. Silent lips. A death in a grey building filled with strangers. And here was William, willing to die in a foreign land to escape the misery of falling apart piece by piece.

Well, neither would be my fate. I was Gormflaith, a queen. A High Queen once, and I would be a queen again. Death would come for me, but not like it had come for my mother or would come for William. In the company of strangers, or else with a sword in my stomach. Mine would be death by fire, glorious and all-consuming. A death of my own choosing.

*

"Alys! Alys!"

David came running out of the castle. Hands covered in old feathers, I crawled out of the cage to speak with him. He was in a state, whatever had happened. *Might he be angry with me for speaking to William Ferrand?*

"I am sorry, David. I promise—"

David shook his head, cutting me off from what I was about to say. "Maurice de Prendergast and his men have just arrived. Your brother is with them. Come!"

Helping me brush the feathers off my dress, he then took my hand and pulled me into the castle. "Hurry. Get changed. We need to go to the feasting hall as soon as possible."

"You need to get ready too, David," I said, once we reached my room. "You must be close to Strongbow and Le Gros when the news from Ireland is being said. Wear your finest clothes so that Strongbow will notice you and give you his favour."

David's eyebrows knitted together. "It is not my place to be at the front, Alys. Besides, that's not why I'm excited. It's that Strongbow can give us permission to marry now if your brother has done what he promised. How can I think of anything else but us? How can you?"

"I didn't want to assume that your heart was still mine." I smiled, lowering my chin as he gave me a gentle kiss on the cheek.

"How could anything sway my mind from you, Alys?"

What a sweet man he was, but his words also troubled me, more than they had before. *What use was a man with this much love but such low ambition?*

"Then let me wash and change, David. Come back to collect me within the hour."

"Very good, but quicker if you can." David kissed my hand, a wide grin on his face, cheeks flushed like a virgin bride on her wedding day.

I closed the door and quickly rushed to the water basin. Despite David's lack of ambition, things were finally moving, and ambition could always be worked upon. Now was the time to focus on my son. Donnchad would have much to say to me, no doubt, but…

"Miss me?"

Turning to my bed, I found Donnchad sitting on my blankets and leaning against the wall. The grey of his armour almost seemed to blend into the stone.

"Where is Cecile?" he asked, not waiting for an answer to his first question.

"Working in the kitchens. Don't worry, you shall see her later."

"And where have you been?"

I opened my arms and gestured to one of the feathers that was still stuck to my dress. "Working in the falconry."

He nodded, his face giving nothing away, and lazily looked about the room. "I don't suppose you have anything to eat?"

"I'm afraid not, but there is to be a meeting soon, or so David just told me. There will be plenty of food there."

My son sighed and lay down on the bed, setting an arm over his eyes.

"Well… speak to me. What did you find in Ireland? Anything interesting?"

I paused in what I was doing, truly interested in what he would say. He knew I could see in my dreams, so he knew that I might know some of what happened. But would this be enough for him to tell me the truth? All of it.

"I found a land ripe for the taking, Mother. A land of many kings, each of whom wants to be High King to the detriment of their own people. It's a land of men who have become so greedy and so treacherous they would willingly cut off their own arms if it meant their enemy lost their arm too. They make my father appear a saint. They make even Sechnall and Máelmórda appear like saints."

I held my tongue as he spoke his news, for it was nothing I did not already know. Men, kings especially, had always been like this in my opinion. Brian, Sechnall, Sitric and Flaithbertach. Not content with what they had, they had always sought to be greater than the other. Donnchad had been like this too when he was a king. He had been like this as a prince, and so if anyone could be described as treacherous, it was he.

"You think this Anglo-Norman army can take any land?" I probed. "Outside of the ports, I mean?"

Donnchad nodded. "They are organised. Singularly focused. When they fight, it is a sight to behold. They are so… unified. They do not splinter and follow their own clan leaders or family members. No, they follow the hierarchy of the army. They follow orders exactly. It is strange."

This was good. Very good, though I shouldn't be too excited yet. Donnchad was being honest, but he had something else to tell me. I could see it in his eyes.

"And so now," he began, "we must decide who to push forward and how we can work together."

"What do you mean?"

"The failing of the Irish kings is in their inability to work together. We cannot let that failing be ours too. The four of us need to work as one, each of us playing our parts."

Ah, I could see very clearly where this conversation was heading. "And what part would you play?"

"The part I've been playing. Translator for the Anglo-Normans so I can push them into making the decisions I want them to."

"What about the rest of us?"

"Once I have spoken to Strongbow, I will know more clearly, but I do have thoughts."

Oh, the arrogance. He'd only apologised to me a few months ago and swore that he wanted to go to Ireland to kill Fódla's daughter to protect me. Back from Ireland only a few days, already he was treating me as his subordinate. His servant. I suppose poor Angelo had suffered this role while they were in Ireland together. It dawned on me then that my grandson was not here.

"I suppose it is best to have this conversation when we are all here. Where is Angelo?"

"He remained with FitzStephen at his camp in Carrig."

"You left Angelo all alone in Ireland?"

What a fool Donnchad was. Angelo, though clever, was mute. Alone, he'd be vulnerable, and we still did not know for certain if all the Descendants were gone. Was this part of Donnchad's plan? *Was his heart so dark that he'd be willing to use his own child as bait?*

"He is stronger than you think, Mother, and he asked to stay. It is best this way. When I return to Ireland, he will know what has happened in my absence."

"What about the Descendants?"

"They are all dead, Mother. We killed them at Rathlin. If any had survived, they would have come for Angelo and me."

I nodded and smiled at my son. Yes, Isolde was dead now, and so were those who had tried to protect her. I had to allow my fear to fade away.

"I suppose the only reason you left Angelo was because you wish to marry Cecile?"

He looked a little surprised that I had guessed so easily, but at least he didn't deny it.

"She doesn't love you, you know. You'll have to win her over."

"Don't you worry about that... but it did make me think, if she comes with me to Ireland, you should stay here. Out of danger. Just as you wanted."

Out of my way, was what he really meant.

I shrugged as I shook out a clean dress from the box at the end of my bed. "You'd better go then, *Donn*. You've got an important meeting to prepare for. If you want Strongbow to do your bidding, you need to start planting seeds of ideas in his head now. And if you want Cecile to marry you, that might take more than a compliment or two."

That was an understatement. With Cecile having fallen in love with Strongbow himself, it would take a lot more than sweet words to turn her from such a prize. A kinder mother might have warned her son about the perils that lay ahead, but not I. Not until it suited me, anyway.

Donnchad smiled and stood. A strange sort of look on his face. Pride, I thought. Pride that finally he had found his place above me and that I was willing to follow his lead. Satisfaction that everything was falling into place. I waited until the door closed behind him before I rolled my eyes.

I had promised myself I would wait until I punished him, but perhaps I had waited too long. Whereas David had no ambition, Donnchad had an abundance of it, and ambitious men were never short of knives to throw into those who moved against them. I felt my stomach for a moment, remembering the knife that he had plunged inside of me at Clontarf. Perhaps it was now time to push him back down before he rose too high.

Isolde

Seir Kieran

I fell to my knees.

My stomach throbbed and as I looked down, blood poured from the open wound there.

All around me were the ruins of a great building. The walls of the inner houses were burning still, the thatch and wood scattered over the ground. The outer walls, made of stone, were collapsed and destroyed.

I looked to my side, wiping the liquid running from my mouth. Not the red of blood, no, but black. Thick. So thick it covered my teeth and tongue. The foul taste clung to the back of my throat, and I tried to spit it out, though to no avail. That's when I saw the dead body lying beside me. Long brown hair covered the grass, but I could not make out her face, for it was turned away from me. A thick layer of blood had pooled under her head.

What had happened here? I couldn't comprehend it… though this was not the first time I had seen this. Yes… I had walked these very steps once before. Continuing to scan the grounds, I looked over the many bodies lying on the grass. I had seen them like this before too, knew already where they'd be and that many of them were women and children. All dead.

"You did this."

Lying on the grass beside me was a man with black skin and pale white hair. His grey eyes stared at me. A sword pierced his chest and blood seeped from his body onto the grass.

"No... No, Colmon. How could I do this?" I crawled over to him, one hand over my wound so that I could move. I expected more blood to pour from my stomach, but none came now. I stopped crawling, prised the fabric open, only to find that the skin had already knitted over. The wound, gone.

As I reached Colmon, I tentatively reached for the sword.

"Don't," he said. "It is too late."

"I don't understand." I sobbed then. Sobbed to see him like this. "Who did this to us?"

"You. It is you who did this, Isolde. Look at the dead. It is all you. I told you that you must learn to control your gift, and you did not listen."

"I am sorry, Colmon. I'm sorry. Please let me save you. Please let me try."

He took my hand in his and shook his head as tears fell from his eyes and down his cheeks. "It is over, Isolde. Your strength has left you and we have failed. They will come for you now. You should run."

"I can't." I wiped the tears spilling from my own eyes, too many to catch. "I cannot... what if I do this again?"

Colmon closed his eyes and as he did so, he turned his head from me. With this final effort, his last breath left him, and I had no answer to my question.

"Isolde? Can you hear me, Isolde?"

My eyelids fluttered as the dream vanished and the colours of red and black faded to grey and blue. Opening my eyes, I squinted at the ceiling. There was no fire. No blood. No corpses. Just the edges of a dream that was fast disappearing.

"You are awake, Isolde. Oh, I'm so glad."

The voice pulled me more fully from my sleep, but my mind was at a loss for why I was lying on a bed.

Memories came to me slowly. At first, I was lying in the forest with Cuan. Blood covered us. Despair. But then another memory replaced it. One of waking up in a grey stone room. Of walking along a corridor, and finding Colmon asleep, caught between the effects of the potions of death and life and unable to wake. The same Colmon of this dream. A dream in which he was dying… because of me.

I pushed that thought aside, for there was no point in getting lost within something my imagination had conjured when there was so much confusion already at hand.

I breathed deeply, letting more of my memories come to me. More truths. I was in Seir Kieran. This was my room. The same grey wall surrounded me now as when I had woken before. The same heavy oak door partitioned the room from the hallway. There was, however, a new person in the chair beside my bed this time. The owner of the voice which had told me they were glad to see me awake.

Shifting to the side, I ran my gaze over this woman. She had a friendly smile. Rounded cheeks and light brown eyes. Not elegant in the way Affraic had been or the way Báine was, but she was beautiful too, in a softer, sweeter way.

"My name is Siobhan," she said after a few moments, and she tilted her head so I could see her better. Now I was fully awake, I could take in her voice properly too, hearing it as it was, rather than through the haze of sleep. It was light. Not determined the way Affraic's had been. Not sharp like Báine's or deep like Broccan's. It was as soft as the rounded features of her face. Kind.

"Hello, Siobhan," I answered. "What…? Why…?"

"I've been healing you," Siobhan said as my questions ran into each other. "And I've had to tend to you twice now, even though we've not yet been introduced. I'd almost be tempted to call you rude."

She spoke with humour, and the sweetness in her voice should have brought me to laughter, but none left my lips. There was something hard and joyless that resided in me now. In my heart, in my head. In my arms and legs. It weighed me down. Fighting this feeling, I sat up and ran my hands through my hair. "Was I sick again?"

"Yes. After you woke Colmon, you collapsed. Waking someone

after they've been in a coma for over a hundred and fifty years will do that to a healer who doesn't know how to control their gift."

A healer? No. I wasn't a healer, was I? Affraic had told me I was a witch. I had summoned storms and hailstones and saved myself on Rathlin Island by calling them. Then I had saved Cuan by summoning a storm to Ferns so we could escape... *but I had healed him afterward, hadn't I?* King Diarmait had taken his eyes, and I had given them back. *How was that possible? How was it possible to hold two gifts at the same time?* My mind ran to my dream, of the wound in my chest that had disappeared... but that was just a dream... was it not? *A dream... or a vision?*

"How is Colmon?" I asked, for I did not want to think about myself. Not yet.

"He is well, but tired. He grows stronger by the day, though, and that is all due to you. I could not believe it when I saw him sitting up. I tried, believe me, I tried to heal him many times over, Affraic too. What a gift you must have."

Once again, she brought the conversation back to me. There wasn't just sweetness in her voice now. Expectation tinged her words too. Curiosity. I could only disappoint her. I had no answers to her unspoken questions today. Secrets, they were what I had instead. They swirled inside me when all I wanted to do was close my eyes and lie down and not think of anything at all. Siobhan, however, didn't move her gaze from me. She stared at me as if I were an object of absolute interest.

Sitting up straighter, I inched backward so I could lean against the wall. In times past I might have spoken to ease away the awkwardness, but I could not bring myself to do it this time. It was the weight inside me. It held down my tongue too.

"Your mother was a healer, as was Affraic, as you know," Siobhan said, filling the silence. "Both were much stronger than me, though I was pleased that I was strong enough to heal you. It has taken a few weeks this time, though."

"A few weeks?"

"Twenty-two days, to be exact."

"I've been asleep for twenty-two days?"

"I'm afraid so. As I said, I'm not as strong as Affraic. I can only do so much at a time before I become too weak to continue. When you are trained, you will understand this and know when you're putting yourself in danger by using too much of your gift."

I bit my upper lip as my mind struggled to understand everything she had said. She was so convinced I was a healer. So certain. I wished I were certain about something. About anything. "Where is Colmon now?"

"He's up, although… well… perhaps that's not important right now. I can take you to him if you like? He's eating breakfast with Méabh."

I thought on this new name, repeated it in my mind. *Méabh*. I felt as if I'd heard it before but couldn't remember where. Was she a Descendant? She must be if she was looking after Colmon.

"She's a cupbearer," Siobhan said, seeming to sense where my thoughts had gone. "She's keen to talk to you. We all are."

"I am eager to talk to you all, too."

This was both the truth and a lie, for while I had travelled here for months to find Colmon and the other Descendants, I didn't feel like talking just yet. What would I say to them? What would they say to me? And what of Colmon now that he was awake? He was a famous warrior. My mother's cousin. Broccan's mentor.

I'd have to tell him about the dream I'd just had. Of him lying on the ground, a sword in his stomach. *You. It is you who did this, Isolde. Look at the dead. It is all you. I told you that you must learn to control your gift, and you did not listen.*

What would he think of me if I told him this? Would he ask me to leave?

And with that thought, another came to me. *I was supposed to be the Descendant who destroyed fire*. Colmon, as a warrior, had sworn to kill all Fomorians. What then would he want to do to Cuan? The secrets multiplied within me. Cuan had been with me almost from the moment I left Rathlin. He was the one who had brought me here. He had been a stranger at first, then a friend, and then the one I loved. What story could I give the Descendants in which he did not exist? Because I couldn't tell them about him. I wouldn't.

Siobhan leaned back in her chair, then stood, the kindness upon her face growing rather than abating. "I'll have hot water brought to your room now. Food and fresh clothing, too. Take your time. Colmon and the other Descendants can wait until you are feeling better. We are all impatient, you see. You'd think after living for hundreds of years that attribute would have left us by now."

She gave me a last smile, looking for a moment like she wanted to say something more and then thought better of it. As the door closed behind her, I was left with silence, and this was somehow worse than anything. The weight inside pulled harder. Not on my limbs this time, but deep inside. My head. My heart. My chest. My bones.

It was perhaps as well that I wasn't left to my own company for long. The breakfast and hot water that Siobhan had promised me materialised not long after she left. Two young girls and an older woman came back and forth with buckets of water that they poured into an iron basin. All three spoke to each other in Irish, but the older woman muttered to herself in the Saxon language too. They were all kind and did not ask me questions other than if I liked the food and if the water was warm enough. They spoke instead of the coldness of the winter air that had blown in from the north. The ice on the grass that morning. Of the berries they were going to pick before the frost finished them off.

This chatter did much to revive me. I asked for the name of the berries they spoke of and wondered if they were similar to those on Rathlin. They also spoke of the gardens and the work needed to harvest the last crops before the ground became too frozen. "You will help us?" one of the girls asked.

I nodded.

"Can you spin wool?" asked the older woman. She came in this time, not with water, but rather a parcel wrapped up with rope, which she set on the table at the far end of the room. Through the corners of the wrapping, I could see the armour that Broccan had given me, and she set down a clean dress on the chair beside it.

"A little." My reply seemed to satisfy her, and as the tub of warm water was now ready, the three of them hurried off to collect the berries they'd spoken of.

"Enjoy your food," they said before they shut the door.

"The salmon is good," the closest girl, the one with the straight brown hair, added. "And the butter with the garlic is nice too. I made it myself!"

"Thank you," I said. "I'm sure it's delicious."

The smile I gave her felt odd on my face, but I kept it there until the door closed.

Once I was washed and felt more like myself, I went over to the table and examined my possessions. Carefully opening the wrapping, I took out my pendant, the name *Isolde* engraved within the silver. *Fragarach*, my knife, was next. The knife I could use to point at the throat of another so they could only tell me the truth. The blue dress Dáirinn had given me, and finally Broccan's bull-hide armour. Four things. All that I owned. All that I was.

Running my fingers over each of them, I began to dress. First, I put on the clean shift and dress, then my pendant and armour. Using a piece of rope that had bound the clothing together, I made a belt and placed *Fragarach* through it. Only then did I make my way outside, deciding there was no point hiding away any longer. As I left my room, I walked toward the sunlight and the icy sharpness of the winter air. The grey walls inside the monastery loomed down on me as I walked along the hallway, oppressive and cold. Outside was better. Familiar. The sky was grey, but there was no rain in the clouds. Not yet, at least. It was damp, though. It would rain soon, and once it came, it would rain for a long time. A flock of sparrows flew overhead as I thought this, moving south and away from the gathering clouds and the winter that would soon be upon us. Not all the animals were so aware of the seasons and how they passed. The goats by the gardens bleated as they chewed at the grass, and the dogs lying under the trees snored as they slept.

Yes, it felt better to be outside. To watch rather than be watched. To be among the animals I knew so well.

"Do you want some garlic?"

The young woman with the long brown hair, who had brought water to my room, handed me some freshly picked herbs from her basket. Now that we were closer, I could see she was close in age to me, perhaps a couple of years older.

I took a bunch and smelled the leaves. "Is this what you used in the butter?"

She nodded. "My name is Leofwynn. And yourself?"

"Isolde."

"Did you escape too?"

"Escape?"

"Your masters?"

"Oh." I understood her meaning then. She had once been a slave, like the people on the longphort in Dublin. I glanced around at the others working in the gardens and wondered if perhaps they had all once been slaves. "No. Did you escape your masters?"

"Yes, a year ago. I tended to the cattle for one of the kings in Bréifne. Hated it. Too many wolves for comfort." She moved a little closer. "There were quite a few of us to start off with. The wolves got one. Three others went missing."

"Did they run away?"

Leofwynn shook her head. "They were taken."

"By whom?"

"Men. They came from the forests sometimes, looking for food to steal and sometimes wives as well. Or else looking to sell the girls on to those with gold and cattle. I didn't want to stay there any longer. I didn't want to disappear, to be a wife, or to be food for the wolves."

The girl set the garlic back into her basket, a hopeful smile growing on her lips.

"You prefer it here?"

"This is paradise compared to where I've been. Look at it. What is there not to like?" Leofwynn gestured at the grey stone walls of the monastery that I already detested. "There is food and warmth and company." She glanced upward at the sky, the smile on her face fading a little. "It rains, but not as much as it did in Bréifne… and we work, but not to the bone… and at least here there is time to sing. Sometimes there is even time to dance."

"And that's good?"

"Oh, yes. I love to sing and dance. Don't you?"

"Sometimes."

Leofwynn gave me a curious look, then a gentle smile. "Even better, Siobhan is teaching me the names of the herbs that heal. Honey for sore throats. Cabbage leaves for swelling. Blackberries or dandelion leaves for the stomach."

"You want to be a healer?" I asked.

"Yes. Wouldn't you want to help those in need if you could?"

Leofwynn's earnest gaze made me think of myself, the Isolde who had existed on Rathlin Island. In those days, I had run along the beach with my friend Móirne, catching fish and searching for eggs. Perhaps if someone had suggested that I learn to become a healer, I would have embraced it with the same enthusiasm as Leofwynn. A mortal healer was not the same as a Descendant, but with the right herbs and knowledge they could do a lot of good.

Before I had a chance to reply, Báine came into view and waved me over. She was so like Affraic, my heart stuttered a little on seeing her.

"Oh," Leofwynn said. "Are you one of *them*? Like Siobhan?"

"What do you mean, *one of them*?"

"The order of monks and nuns that are in charge of the monastery."

I glanced back over at Báine, who was waving once again. I supposed there was no point in denying it. "Yes. I'm one of them."

"I should not have kept you back. I apologise." Leofwynn bowed her head, her voice now hushed with reverence.

"There's no need to apologise, and you have not kept me back. I enjoyed our conversation. Perhaps the next time you see me, you will come and talk to me some more? I should like to learn about herbs and healing too."

Leofwynn straightened awkwardly, nodded, then made her way to the other end of the garden, where two men were pulling up leeks and onions from the ground.

Leofwynn said something to them as she passed, then made her way to the garden fence. Once again, she reminded me of the way I used to be on the beaches of Rathlin. So carefree. Free to run and skip whenever I wanted to.

The weight returned then. It had lightened talking to Leofwynn, but now she was gone, and once again, I had curious eyes staring at me. And it wasn't just Báine now. When I turned to look at the monastery doors, I saw that Colmon had walked outside. He used a long stick to help, and his back was bowed ever so slightly. Another woman came out next. She had short dark hair. Slender face. Beautiful, as all the Descendants appeared to be. Siobhan followed, then another woman I did not know. This woman was tall with long fair hair that reached the back of her thighs. She seemed to be singing a song, and I found it lifted my mood. But this shift in emotion caught in the back of my mind. *Harpist.* That's what she was. I knew it.

Stop it, I shouted inside my head.

The fair-haired woman turned toward me, her eyes narrowing momentarily. Colmon muttered something under his breath to her, then the group of them walked toward me. Báine came first, arms swinging, so self-assured. Colman was at the back, one hand on his stick, the other leaning on the woman with the short hair. Siobhan and the harpist walked between them.

"Do you wish to talk inside?" Báine asked once she was within earshot. She glanced up at the sky and the darkening clouds. "The rain will be in soon."

"No, let's stay outside until it comes. Over by those trees looks like a nice place to sit." Perhaps I should have agreed to go inside and made it easier for them, but the full harshness of the winter would be upon us soon, and then the frosts and storms would trap us inside the grey walls until spring.

Báine gestured for me to lead the way, and so I did. The trees around us were oak, their trunks thick and strong, the leaves above us swaying gently with the breeze.

I sat first, and they followed. They all stared at me, expectation building once again, but I waited for one of them to speak.

"Isolde," Báine said, once Colmon had settled. "You know me, Colmon and Siobhan, but these are the other Descendants who are still with us." She pointed toward the first woman, the one who had linked arms with Colmon. "This is Méabh. A cupbearer." Her hand moved along the line until it reached the woman who'd been singing. "This is Gisela. She is a harpist."

I nodded a greeting to each of them, keeping my eyes on the harpist a little longer. Why had she used her gift to alter my mood? Had she done this for a particular reason or was this simply part of being a harpist? Just as a healer wanted to care for people, a harpist might want to make others happy.

"This is all of you?" I asked.

Báine nodded. "Shae passed away a short while ago. Echna, a druid, passed before him. Étain, who was my sister, is gone too. We are all who remain."

"Did all of you know my mother?"

"Yes," Gisela answered. "All of us loved your mother. Whatever you want to ask, please ask it."

There it was. So easy. On Rathlin, I'd thought on this moment constantly once Broccan had revealed what I was. I had so many questions. Hundreds. I had come here with the purpose of asking them all, but now I was here, I found myself drawn to the darker ones. The ones I never would have dared to ask Broccan.

"Was my mother loved by all, even when she was with Tomas? What about my Aunt Rónnat? Why was she banished and forced to live out her life all alone?"

The Descendants stilled.

"There is anger in your words, Isolde," Colmon answered. "And I do not blamc you. In the past, the Descendants did not act as we should have. We grew afraid. Many things happened that I now regret, and we have suffered for it. When I was your age, there were hundreds of Descendants. Now there are only the six of us. It is our fault this has happened. My fault."

My breath caught as I listened to Colmon. His voice was just as it had been in my dream. *You. It is you who did this, Isolde. Look at the dead.* There was no pain in his words now, though. Only kindness.

"But let us apportion blame later," Colmon added. "For now, let us talk of your mother. And of the Descendants who are gone to the otherworld. You are a mystery to us, and we are a mystery to you, and together we will unravel them." Colmon lowered his gaze to catch mine. "Are you willing to do that with us, Isolde?"

I nodded, even though I knew I could not tell him everything.

"Good. Then I will begin and tell you about your grandfather, Ciarán. Then I will tell you about your grandmother and their two daughters, who none of us understood or helped enough when they were alive."

Donnchad

Chepstow

The hall was full when I entered. Strongbow, as well as the other knights he had summoned to Chepstow, were anxiously awaiting what Miles and Maurice had to say. Rumours were already being whispered in the hallways and courtyards. *Victory. Wexford. Osraige. Ghost armies in the Irish forests.*

I ignored the whispers and walked over to the table around which the men were gathering, deciding to stand behind Miles rather than Maurice, who was closest to Strongbow. I also made sure to stand beside the knights who had fought in Ireland rather than the archers. This was wrong in terms of my position within the army, but my rank had never been clear in any case, and none of the archers I pushed in front of raised their voices or told me to step back. On the other side of the room stood the knights who had not gone to Ireland. David was among them, and he gave me a hopeful smile. Mother stood beside him, gazing up at Strongbow, no doubt trying to work out what he was whispering to Maurice.

One by one, other knights, new ones who I had not met before, trickled into the room. I watched them, noting how they acted at such a meeting. There was no laughter, no grumblings or whispers. They all came in with serious expressions on their faces, and when they bowed to Strongbow, it was with complete subservience. They were knights, but they knew their place, for everything here was so structured and orderly. Nothing like Ireland at all.

The only man who was in any way different was the one who remained at the back of the hall. He had come in with Le Gros, and clearly was a knight, and yet stayed apart from everyone else in the room. *How strange.* I watched him a moment longer than the others, fascinated by the design of his breastplate which contained Moorish motifs upon a Moorish style of armour. I'd seen them when we travelled through Libya, and it seemed odd that a Christian should wear a style of armour used by the Muslim people that he must have fought against.

This curiosity, however, did not captivate for long, for Cecile entered the room next. She came into the hall with a group of serving women, all carrying cups of watered ale and wine. It was a tragedy to see her like this. The other women's faces were lined, with heavy jowls, pox scars and missing teeth. Cecile was a vision among them, even with her headscarf that did such a good job of concealing the fullness of her beauty. She did not belong here, covered in dowdy woollen clothing and a broth-stained apron. She knew it herself, for while the other women chatted and winked at the men they served, Cecile remained silent and kept her eyes on the floor.

Mother said Cecile had no feelings for me, and perhaps in Paris that was true, when Máelmórda bought her silk dresses and men lined up to pay her compliments, but I felt sure that would change. Perhaps when she saw me standing here, a smile would grow on her face. Not love yet, no, but familiarity. A knowing that I was better than the other men in this room.

It was as I watched Cecile give the final cup of wine to Strongbow, that Strongbow raised his hand. Without any need of command, his men rolled out a map of Ireland on the table and the conversation around the room fell away. Some of his knights, the ones who hadn't come to Ireland, weighed down the edges with small stones, and once this was done, Strongbow gestured for Miles and Maurice to approach. The knights gathered closer around the table, some of them even standing on the benches to get a better view. I pushed forward and edged to the left so I could see the table between the shoulders of two knights.

It was all neatly arranged, the map not accurate by any means, but I could still make out the shape of my homeland within it. On the edge of the table were miniature wooden carvings of ships, knights on horseback, archers, castles and a maiden. Strongbow moved one of the wooden ships over to where we had landed at Bannow Island.

"After you landed here, you took Wexford. Is that right, Miles?" Strongbow asked.

"Yes." Miles moved another piece, this one of a knight on horseback, toward the black dot on the map that marked Wexford. "After a short siege, Robert and his brother Gerald were granted lordship over the city, while Hervey was granted the farming lands around it. However, it is my opinion that these titles and the granting of land hold no weight. Robert was not even allowed to enter. Before I departed, Robert told me he intended to claim it properly, and that he wanted to build a castle somewhere close to Wexford as a base from which to do this."

"That is true," I said, adding my voice to the conversation. It was important that I did so early, for Strongbow needed to notice me from among his growing number of men. "The fort he built is on the Hill of Carrig. Two miles outside the city." I moved forward, and the two knights I stood behind parted to make way. I pressed my fingers against the map to show everyone where it was.

Strongbow nodded, and he placed another marker on the map. This time of a castle. "Strange that FitzStephen has built his fortress outside the city. The King of Wexford did swear vows to FitzStephen, did he not?" Strongbow removed his fingers from the map. "It was sworn on the Bible, or so Hervey's letter mentioned. Why will the king still not allow him in?"

"The King of Wexford did swear his vows on the Bible and agreed to fight for Diarmait," Miles said, "but as I said before, these vows regarding power and lordship mean nothing. The Irish kings' words, even when sworn on the Bible, are empty."

Strongbow grunted. "So, you won, or thought you won the city of Wexford, but quickly moved on. Where to?"

"We marched into this land here, south of Leinster. Osraige, they call it." Miles pressed his finger roughly to where Osraige was, and one of Strongbow's knights placed a carving of a knight on horseback there. The location was a little too far west to be Osraige, but it was not a bad guess considering how meandering the forest paths were. "The dun we raided after the battle was full of gold and silver, though neither the dun nor the land around it was given to anyone. Not even Diarmait claimed it."

Strongbow digested this information slowly, his eyes switching between Miles, Maurice and the map. "So… you fought here at the behest of King Diarmait, but no land was gained, not even by Diarmait? Why did Diarmait want to fight in Osraige if not for the land?"

Miles shrugged. "Some sort of blood feud." He turned to me, forehead furrowed.

"The King of Osraige blinded Diarmait's son, is what I heard, my lord." Once again, I addressed Strongbow and spoke clearly so the whole room could hear. "This raid was for revenge."

"Even so… a king would risk his army and yet not bother to take the spoils of war?" Strongbow frowned.

"The land is not owned by the king. It's owned by the clan," I said, even though Strongbow had not expected an answer to this question. Still, my words had the desired effect. All eyes were upon me now, and I paused, trying to think on how to explain it. It had taken long enough for me to elucidate Robert FitzStephen, and he had been in Ireland to see the Irish customs for himself. To explain it in a Norman hall – in Wales – to men who had never set foot in Ireland would be harder again.

Moving forward, I took the string that had been used to wrap up the map, and using a small meat knife, I cut it into eight pieces, and using the cut string, I marked the lines between the main kingdoms. Leinster, Munster, Connacht, Osraige, Ulaid, Meath, Bréifne and the Kingdom of the Northern Ó'Neills. "These are the main kingdoms of Ireland, my lord. To redraw the borders of any of these kingdoms, you would need to convince the clan who lives there it was in their interest, and they rarely comply with change. In truth, it is only a High King that can really enforce the splitting of kingdoms or else the taking over of one, and even then, this rarely holds for long. And so, King Diarmait invaded Osraige and raided one of their duns, but the taking of land, that never even would have crossed his mind."

Strongbow's eyes widened as if the story I was telling him was madness. His fingers reached out and touched the wooden knight with the sword and shield. Slowly, he took it away from the map and replaced it with a wooden carving of an archer. Both were symbols of battle, I realised. The knight symbolised the taking of land, while the archer did not.

"The Irish are a strange people." Le Gros sniggered, grinning so widely that his fat cheeks pushed up against his eyes. "Are all these kings so lacking in ambition they cannot think of how to use their power?"

I disliked how Le Gros spoke of Ireland but did not interrupt him. There would be time to put him in his place later. For now, I wanted to see how Strongbow reacted to what I had told him.

"What about the battle itself?" Strongbow asked Miles as Le Gros' laughter fell away. "Hervey wrote to me of it and said it was a great victory."

"Yes. It was," Miles answered. "The Osraige warriors are skilled and brave, but they lacked tactics and good armour, and we were able to use our archers and cavalry to good effect."

"What were their numbers compared to yours?" Strongbow asked.

"They had the bigger army by far. Five to one, maybe more."

"And after the battle, you went to Ferns?"

"Yes." Maurice pointed a finger over where he thought Ferns was. A little too close to Dublin, but again, a good enough guess that I didn't correct him.

Strongbow drummed his fingers over the map as his eyes moved into Leinster, and then toward Ferns. The home of King Diarmait. A black mark was placed there, and another marker was moved, this time of the maiden. That was right. He was engaged to marry King Diarmait's daughter. The beautiful Eva, a distant descendant of Máelmórda. Angelo had liked to watch her. *I had liked to watch her too*. She had no Fomorian fire, but she had the look of our kind about her, with her dark curls and pale skin. It made me uneasy to think of Strongbow having her.

"What happened while you were in Ferns?"

"At first, we rested," Miles said. "Then High King Ruaidrí sent us a letter, telling us he would gift us much gold if we abandoned Diarmait and sailed home. We thought about it, but Diarmait, perhaps knowing this would happen, told us that he had forbidden the Wexford Vikings from sailing us home. Proof, if it was needed, that Wexford was never truly ours. King Ruaidrí and his army then rode to Ferns, and Diarmait swore oaths of submission to Ruaidrí. During these vows, he promised to send us home."

"And this was when you and FitzStephen decided to split the army? Risky, no?" This time it was the knight at the back of the hall who spoke. The one dressed in the Moorish armour. His words echoed around the hall, and the people stared at him, almost seeming to hold their breath.

"It was Donn's idea," Miles answered, holding out his hand and placing it on my shoulder.

Strongbow turned to face me. His eyes took me in properly this time, examining rather than merely looking. "You know the Irish customs best, Donn. I am glad you were with us. Tell me, what was your reasoning?"

"I know the Irish ways enough to fear that Diarmait might have killed your men once he had achieved his objective of retaking his kingdom, especially considering he had promised to send you home and pledged his own son as hostage to Ruaidrí. By splitting the army, he had no choice but to keep Robert FitzStephen at his side in case Maurice attached himself to a rival king. This also gave FitzStephen the power to insist Diarmait ride out to Dublin."

Strongbow reached for another carving of a knight on horseback and placed it over the black mark that indicated Dublin on the map. "Hervey told me that the King of Dublin submitted to Diarmait, but given what you have told me so far, I would guess these vows are meaningless too?"

I nodded. "The vows were said to get rid of Diarmait, that's all."

Strongbow pressed his lips together and moved a ship toward Dublin and stared at it. *This was a sign that he still meant to invade.* Good. This was what I needed him to do. Once he and his men took Dublin, and then Leinster, I could take this land from them.

"That is enough for now. I need to think over what you have told me." Strongbow glanced around the men, his face serious at first, then breaking out into a smile. "Let us eat, my friends. Let us enjoy this night and the fact our kinsmen are returned to us."

The knights responded by saluting the men who had returned from Ireland, then dispersed around the hall to sit at the various tables and take part in the feast. The serving girls were already bringing in platters of bread, roasted meat and stewed vegetables. Nothing compared to a feast in Ireland, but at least the food was plentiful.

I ate in silence, listening to the men around me. They spoke of the challenges ahead, and more rumours of the battle of Osraige were discussed. One of the knights who had fought at Osraige said he'd seen a woman with a mane over her back like a horse, while others spoke of watching the Irish remove the ears and noses of their enemies.

It made me smile, the talk of this savagery. I couldn't wait to return to Ireland and use it to my own ends.

"Donn." Le Gros walked up behind me and slapped his hand on my shoulder. "Strongbow wishes to speak to you."

I raised an eyebrow, acting surprised, though in truth I wasn't. I was sure he had more than a few questions he couldn't ask in front of the others. Walking with Le Gros, we made our way over to the top table and I took the vacant seat beside Strongbow. Here, a fresh plate of food was readied for me, as well as a glass of wine rather than ale.

"Yes, my lord," I said, once I had sat.

"I would like a few minutes of your time, Donn. I hope you do not mind?"

"Not at all."

"I can see that FitzStephen has done well. The advice you gave, for him to stay with King Diarmait and for Maurice to leave, was risky, but intelligent, though I do have some concerns. On my first hearing of what happened, it appeared that the campaign was a success, but if the lands FitzStephen and Hervey won are not truly theirs, then perhaps there is no success at all. This begs a question. What will happen to FitzStephen if I do not go to Ireland? Can he hold onto, or even gain control over, Wexford?"

"No, I do not think so. His fort in Carrig will protect him over the winter, but he cannot conquer the city with so few men, at least not without Diarmait's army at his side. But if you do not go, Diarmait would never agree to fight for him. I would go so far as to say Diarmait would probably prefer it if the Wexford Vikings fought and defeated FitzStephen if you don't sail to Ireland."

"You think Diarmait is as traitorous as that?" Strongbow glanced at me, half smiling. "I suppose you must do, given all you have said. Well, if I were to go, how likely is it *I* will be able to gain the land I want?"

"It will be hard to gain land in Ireland, that is the truth… but if I were you, I would not delay."

I was on shaky ground here, to say what I were to do if I were a lord. I was not a lord. To Strongbow, I was the son of a poor trader who was already acting above his station. But I could not stop. Strongbow did have to invade now if he was to be of any use to me.

"King Ruaidrí will punish Diarmait for going against his oaths and riding out to Dublin, and so war is brewing in Ireland whether you go there or not. King Ruaidrí will seek to destroy Diarmait in the spring, and so Diarmait needs you. This is your strength. But know this, if you do not help Diarmait, Ruaidrí will win, and Diarmait will either be killed or he will flee to England once more, and all the advantages you have now will be lost."

"Which means I must decide and decide quickly." Strongbow

lifted a piece of bread to his lips and bit at the crust. "Final question, Donn. Is Dublin the prize we have been told it is?"

"Dublin is the kingdom that can make kings or destroy them."

Strongbow nodded. "I thank you, Donn, for answering my questions. You have given me much to think on. If I can ever help you, you only have to say."

"Of course, my lord. There is only one thing that I would ask in return."

"Yes?"

"To marry Cecile."

"Ah, of course. Miles told me of your wish to marry your cousin."

I nodded, smiling.

"But that is now two weddings I must approve for your family. One between yourself and Cecile and the other between David and your sister, Alys. I don't know if I can do that."

Strongbow stabbed his meat with a sharp knife, the tone of his voice somewhat sharp too. Why would that be? He could hardly be worried about my marriage to a kitchen maid, which meant it had to be my mother who had displeased him. I glanced over at her, watching as she laughed at something David said. A nightmare she could be, but she usually knew how to behave herself when seeking to elevate her status. *What had she done while I was away?*

"I hope that Alys has not been too much trouble, my lord," I said, keeping my voice light as if not noticing his displeasure. "Alys has been a good sister to me. I am sure she will make a good wife to David."

"Then I will allow it." He raised a cup to this, his sharp eyes staring into mine. "But you are in my debt, Donn. For rarely is a woman like Alys elevated to the wife of a knight."

"Debt?" I found this word strange. Moments ago, he expressed that if I wanted something, I only had to ask. Now it was I who owed him again.

"Do not worry. As I rise, so will those in my service." Strongbow gave me a curt nod, then his eyes roved to the man standing behind me. One of Maurice's knights. "Tell Maurice I wish to speak with him now."

That was it, my audience was over... but he hadn't answered my question. *My request*. Not properly. As I stood, I set down my cup. "I am delighted you have approved my sister's marriage, my lord, but what of my marriage to Cecile?"

"I will think about that and give you my decision tomorrow." He waved his hand then, a final sign of dismissal, and I had no choice but to bow and walk away.

It was not as I had wanted it to be, but I guessed Strongbow couldn't be seen to be giving away too many favours at once. I had been the same when I was a king myself. The wedding between Alys and David was the bigger one, the one that needed the goodwill of a returning army to approve. My marriage to Cecile, a kitchen maid, could happen at any time. *Yes, that was it*.

I moved back over to where I was sat before, a broad smile on my face as I told the knights that Strongbow had given permission for my sister and David to marry. Good news travelled fast it seemed, and once Le Gros heard of it, he clapped his hands and roared with approval, and soon many in the hall were offering their congratulations to David and Alys.

David called me over to drink with them, and so I did, even though I had wanted to find Cecile. But it would be folly to refuse such a welcome, and Cecile was gone anyhow, back into the bowels of the castle, where no doubt she was washing dishes and awaiting rescue.

Perhaps it was best to let her remain there a little longer, so that when I liberated her, she would be all the more desperate and all the more grateful.

Cuan

Road to Dúnmór

Dúnmór was not far away now.

It was strange to think I was returning to my old home, but that my uncle Ruaidrí was king there rather than my grandfather. Since my return to Ireland, Ruaidrí had never stayed at Dúnmór. He hadn't even visited. He usually stayed at one of the stone castles my grandfather had constructed before he died. They were more modern, more like how kings lived in England and France, and this appealed to Ruaidrí, although having seen the stonework in England when I had fought for Uncle Godred, I knew the castles of Connacht were poor fare in comparison.

I couldn't fault Ruaidrí's reasoning for wintering at Dúnmór this year, though. It made sense that he would want to retreat to the heart of the Ó Conchúir clan lands with his most important hostages – the son, grandson and foster-nephew of King Diarmait. Perhaps my uncle had known too, that trouble brewed on the horizon, though even with his eye for trouble, I knew he'd be shocked at how quickly Diarmait had broken his oaths.

As Sleipnir continued along the path to Dúnmór, the hairs on my arms stood on end. Many years had passed, and yet I remembered everything so clearly. I'd probably ridden along this path with my father a hundred times. I'd climbed these very trees looking for eggs, and I had jumped into the river flowing past me on many a hot summer day. Usually, it was with Dáire at my side, but sometimes my mother would swim with me, her long white-golden hair streaming out behind her.

"Are we nearly there?" Meallán asked. He wriggled into a new position, sore from two days of being on Sleipnir's back.

"Patience, Meallán," Brother Angelo chided. He, as usual, was resolutely cheerful and still surprisingly energetic, even after walking the entire way. I'd offered to let him ride Sleipnir a few times, but he always declined. *I am a servant of God*, he would say. *The Lord will give me the strength I need.*

"I'm only asking." Meallán frowned.

"Fear not, Meallán," I returned. "The dun is just over this hill. We'll be there in time for dinner."

Meallán's eyes widened at that. Perpetually hungry, the berries I'd been able to scavenge throughout the day had not been enough. In my grandfather's time, there was always a stew cooking at Dúnmór so that unexpected guests could be offered food. I hoped my uncle had kept this tradition going. In my memories, my grandfather, even though he was the king and ailing, came out to personally greet his guests, no matter who they were.

Pulling Sleipnir to a halt, I bit my lip.

"What is it?" Brother Angelo asked, coming to a stop beside us.

"I need to let Sleipnir drink. We'll go straight to the dun after. I promise."

Brother Angelo glanced at the river flowing beside us, which was wide and deep. "Is it clean enough for us to drink?"

"Not here, no." I handed him my water skin. "There will be plenty of water in the dun. Don't worry about saving what's left now."

Brother Angelo accepted the water skin, his long, thin fingers wrapping around the leather. He took a small sip, then held it out for Meallán to take. Meallán slid from Sleipnir's back and took some of the water, thanking Brother Angelo once again for finding him and excitedly asking what he thought the dun would be like.

While they took turns drinking the water, I led Sleipnir over to the river, where I let go of his reins so he could drink his fill and nibble at the long grass growing along the bank.

Crouching over as if to splash my face, I stared at my reflection instead. The water moved slowly, but my reflection was not as clear as I would have liked. Still, I could see that the cut I had given myself was healing, the scabs already fallen away. They had left behind a long red line, but it was a ghost of the scar that had once been there. I had cut too straight along my chin, I realised. Not deep enough. My blade was too narrow, which meant the skin around my mouth wasn't puckered and the muscle there had not been weakened. The blood that had once filled the white of my left eye was gone too.

What would my family make of this?

It was hard for me to conjure what their reaction might be.

Over the last few days, I'd trained in the way my uncle Godred had taught me. Practised distance. Control. Detachment. It was as if even my curiosity was dampened now. But I could not let myself be incurious about this. Too much was at stake.

Taking a deep breath, I finally splashed the water over my face. The scar I had cut into my own flesh was enough. *The scar had healed*, was all I needed to say. Scars faded. Everyone knew that, and they hadn't seen me for a month. Time moved on for us all. It aged us, made us wither, but it mended us too.

Pushing my fears down, I took hold of Sleipnir's reins and walked toward the path. Even if they noticed, what would they say? They had no knowledge of Isolde and what she could do. They had no thoughts of the Descendants of the Tuatha Dé Danann walking among us. The old gods, the Morrígan and the Dagda, were stories now.

As Sleipnir and I reached the path, Brother Angelo stood waiting for us, while Meallán had run on ahead.

"I think he's grown tired of riding your horse," Brother Angelo said. "I didn't have the heart to make him wait."

"Riding all day isn't easy if you're not used to it."

Brother Angelo nodded, then lifted his hands and held them out wide. "The more I see of this land of yours, Cuan, the more I can see God at work. In the greenness of the leaves and the blue of the sky."

"Your faith is strong, Brother."

"No." He shook his head, his pale face suddenly very serious. "My faith wavers as it does for all men. This is the sin that lives within mankind. I merely understand this sin and fight against it. Here, in Ireland, the fight is easier."

"Easier than in Rome?"

"Oh, yes." He bowed his head. "You cannot comprehend the depravity that lurks in the heart of the Holy Kingdom. Evil is everywhere, Cuan. You must remember that. In the darkest of places and in the lightest."

"I suppose you are right."

"Oh, I am. Every man has a vice. Mine was always women, and I find myself tempted by the flesh still. What about you, Cuan? Did you ever love a woman so much that she drove you toward hellfire?"

"No, Brother."

He looked up, his golden eyes holding my gaze, as if he was expecting me to confess then and there to all my sins. Well, I had many of those, and none I wanted to talk about. Not that I was only returning to Dúnmór so that I might take the Kingdom of Connacht from my uncle and avenge my father. Not Isolde. Not the fire that lived inside of me.

"Come on, Brother Angelo!" Meallán shouted as he breached the top of the hill. "We're nearly there. Look, you can see the dun from here!"

"I'd better ride on ahead," I said, grateful for the interruption. "I'll make sure there is food and drink ready for you both."

"That is kind of you, Cuan," Brother Angelo said, laughing gently, the seriousness of our previous conversation falling away. "I think poor Meallán will collapse if he doesn't eat something more than berries soon."

Mounting Sleipnir, I urged him into a gallop. The time for thinking was over. Onward was the only direction for me now. Onward to Dúnmór.

*

The dun loomed large in the distance, and I rode Sleipnir hard for this final push. As I approached the path that rose to the dun wall, guards congregated around the gate until one of them recognised me and shouted my name. The rest of the guards parted to make way for my arrival.

Once I was inside the walls, I pulled Sleipnir to a stop.

"Cuan?"

Cathal rushed out of the feasting hall. His eyes were bright, but as his gaze ran over my face, puzzlement, then disbelief replaced it. "We heard you were dead… I cannot… I cannot believe you are here." He placed his hands behind his head, then turned to face the door of the feasting hall. "Ruaidrí! Róisín. Gráinne. It's him! Cuan is here!"

"You thought me dead?" I asked, once Cathal had stopped shouting. "Who told you that?"

"A messenger from Dublin. He said that Diarmait's son, Domhnall, had pursued you into the forest outside Dublin and captured you. The messenger then said Domhnall took you to Ferns, where Diarmait killed you." Cathal smiled, but as he stared at me, his eyes narrowed as if perhaps I were a ghost, and his eyes were deceiving him.

All this worrying over my scar when it was news of my capture that I should have been afraid of. This news led to a different set of problems. A different set of questions I might be asked by Ruaidrí. Not of scars that had healed over, but of how I had escaped. To answer these, I needed to know exactly what Ruaidrí had been told and who the messenger was. Someone Ruaidrí trusted or just one of Asculv's men? Did they know that my eyes had been taken? *Did they know about the fire?*

Cathal came closer, and gently he touched my arm as I dismounted. "The messenger told us that Diarmait had blinded you. He said he'd seen it being done himself. I don't understand?"

There was no judgement in Cathal's voice. Nothing in his words was calling me a liar… yet.

I opened my arms wide and pulled Cathal into a hug. "Do not

fret, Cathal. There has been a misunderstanding." Pushing down the panic that had risen within me, I gave him a warm smile. "Now, who was this messenger? As you can see, I'm not blind."

"I can't remember his name," Cathal said, head shaking. "Was it all a lie?" There, his relief was already turning into something else.

"No. Not all. Some."

Cathal nodded and gave me another hug. He was used to me, more so than the other members of the O'Conchúir family. Not that he remembered me from when he was a baby, he was too young for that, but still there was a connection between us, and it had grown during our travels before the Tailteann Games. In some ways, he was like me. An heir to the kingship of Connacht and therefore a rival to Conchobar. Being younger than me and Conchobar, and having been brought up within Ruaidrí's household, had saved him. He was more deferential and boyish, exempt from the isolation I had endured, but now that he was becoming a man, he was beginning to understand that the danger following me, followed him also.

As Cathal pulled away, I realised some warriors and servants had come out of the feasting hall, as well as the other houses. All staring at me and whispering. Feeling uncomfortable under their watchful gaze, I moved over to the dun gate to where one of the guards stood. "There is a boy and a monk coming to the dun. Meallán and Brother Angelo," I said. "They are friends of mine. Can food be readied for them and a seat by the fire in the feasting hall?"

The guard nodded, and one of the serving women began to stir a pot of stew that was bubbling over the fire, her gnarled hands reaching for a clean bowl.

"You must be hungry too," Cathal said. "Why don't you—"

"Cuan!" My uncle's voice boomed from within the feasting hall. Footsteps followed. This was it, the real questioning was about to begin. I took a deep breath and pushed down my fear. I was nothing. Nobody… and a nobody could not feel.

My uncle came out of the feasting hall, his arms opening to embrace me. His wife, Queen Gráinne, and their children Róisín and Conchobar followed. Róisín had tears in her eyes, and she steadied herself by holding onto her mother, who was on the verge of crying also. Conchobar stood slightly apart and stared at me. Amazement in his eyes. Then annoyance.

Conchobar had never been able to hide his emotions, but at least they were truthful. Despite Ruaidrí's embrace, I was sure he was more frustrated than relieved by my reappearance. He did not want me at Dúnmór any more than Conchobar did. I was his nephew, and therefore he could not deny my living in his dun. I had won the sword-fighting at the Tailteann Games and so was part of his fianna, but he did not like me. My father had wanted me to gain Ruaidrí's trust. According to him, that was how my quest to become king had to start, and to an outsider it might look like I had succeeded in doing this. I, however, knew better.

"Cuan," my uncle said as he moved out of our embrace. "We heard such terrible things. We had prayers and a funeral mass said for you only last week, and now you are here. What happened?"

I began with the truth. At least what truth I was able to give.

"Some of what you heard is true. Domhnall did take me captive while I was on my way here from Dublin."

"What of Isolde? We heard she was killed," Queen Gráinne said, her chin trembling.

"Isolde?" I cocked my head to the side. "She was not there, aunt. I have not seen her since I left her in Dublin. I'm sure she is well."

Relief flooded Gráinne and Róisín's face, but my uncle Ruaidrí gave me a hard stare. This meant he had heard of Isolde's death, and I had made a liar of whoever this messenger was. But I could not have said anything different. What if they came across Isolde one day, alive and well?

"It seems we've been misinformed," Ruaidrí said, his relief at seeing me alive already fading. "Tell me then, what *did* happen when Domhnall took you?"

"I was taken to Ferns and held prisoner. I was told I would be blinded and given the blood eagle, but I was able to escape before that happened."

"You escaped King Diarmait's dun?" This time it was Conchobar who spoke, disbelief embedded within every word.

"I did, cousin. I am part of the High King's fianna after all. It was difficult, but when such a fate awaited me, what choice did I have? I would rather die fighting than have my back opened by a Leinster axe."

King Ruaidrí smiled at this. "But of course, the warriors of Connacht have always been the most fearsome. It does not surprise me that you bested the warriors of Ferns."

"Thank you, uncle. It was made easier by the fact they were drunk and there were no Norman knights in the dun."

My uncle started at this. Ah, there. *Something he didn't know.* Hopefully, the movements of the Anglo-Norman knights would now occupy his mind.

Conchobar snorted. "We're supposed to believe that you escaped King Diarmait's dun without so much as a scratch? I don't believe it. Diarmait must have let you go. He let you come here to spy on us."

"And why would I want to spy on my own family?"

"Because you are not a part of this family."

"Conchobar," my uncle snapped. "Enough."

A silence grew. My uncle had never chastised Conchobar publicly. Not ever.

"I can attest to what Cuan has said."

I turned around. It was the young monk who had spoken. Brother Angelo. He had come into the dun while my uncle had been speaking. Meallán stood behind and peered around his side.

"I am only a humble monk, but I would not tell a lie to anyone in this world. God may strike me down if I ever stray from this vow."

My uncle looked at the two new arrivals, his eyes quickly fixing on the monk.

"And you are?"

"Brother Angelo. I have come from Rome to travel across Ireland. The Pope, the Holy Father himself, asked this of me."

"The Pope sent you?" Conchobar asked. "How is it that you know our language?"

"We study the languages of all Christian kingdoms in Rome."

Conchobar, not convinced, stared at the monk. "If the Pope really did send you here, where is your finery?"

"Ah, young prince," Brother Angelo said, his voice turning soft, "our Lord Jesus came to Jerusalem on the back of a donkey. He spoke with the poor, healed the sick, offered friendship to all. If the Son of God lived such a humble life, why should his servant try to surpass him?"

Conchobar, only moments ago filled with bluster and outrage, deflated. I remembered these biblical stories well. The monks had taught them to me as a boy. No doubt Conchobar knew them too.

"These are wise words, Brother Angelo." King Ruaidrí, usually impatient with monks and priests, gave Brother Angelo a warm smile. "Tell me, then, how can you vouch for my nephew."

"As soon as I landed in Ireland, I travelled west. The Irish have a reputation for kindness, and I must tell you I have found it to be greater than I expected. During my travels, I have had to take shelter several times, and many people have welcomed me into their homes. One night, I was travelling, and a great storm blew in. A kind man, Ultán, took pity on me and gave me food and shelter. As we ate, the man's brother came into the ráth and said that a third brother and their niece were dead. All of us rushed off to see if anything could be done. I would not have intruded on their grief except I felt it was my duty to say prayers over the dead.

"When we arrived at the ráth, indeed there were two dead bodies. Ultán and his brother wept to see them, but quickly their grief turned to anger, for the death handed out to these two poor souls was not natural. Added to that, their ráth had been burned to the ground."

Conchobar stared at me, but everyone else was entranced by the young monk and his story. I crossed my arms, keeping my face blank, but inside my heart pounded. What had Brother Angelo seen? What was he about to say?

"As we dug their graves, a man came out of the forest. A fuidir. A clanless man, I was told this meant. Ultán and his brother tried to drive him back, but he would not go. He told us he knew what had happened."

King Ruaidrí cleared his throat. "Which was?"

"That a young man, an enemy of Leinster, had escaped King Diarmait's dun. He had entered the ráth seeking clothing and food, but did not stay long, for the warriors and hounds of King Diarmait were not far away. The fuidir said the young man escaped, but the warriors of King Diarmait could not make out the tracks for some time. He said that while King Diarmait waited for the hounds to find the trail, he had the young man and his daughter slain for the crime of helping his enemy, and their ráth was burned to warn others of what happened to those who worked against King Diarmait. I departed shortly after and continued to make my way west. As soon as I heard Cuan tell you his story, I knew that he was the young man who had escaped the clutches of King Diarmait."

"Is this true, Cuan?" Ruaidrí asked. "Is this how it happened?"

"Yes, this was the manner of my escape. I had Sleipnir so I was able to outride them at first, but as Brother Angelo said, I had to steal clothing and food. I did not know that Diarmait had killed the man and young woman who lived in the ráth." My voice trailed away then. I knew there had been people living in the ráth and that they had run away when Isolde and I arrived. Were these the dead people that Brother Angelo spoke of? If they had lost their lives as a result of my escape, I was sorry for it. *Calm, Cuan. Calm.*

Cathal shook his head. Queen Gráinne too. "It was not you who lit the fire," she said. "That was Diarmait and his men. The shame is theirs. Not yours."

"My wife is right." Ruaidrí nodded. "And I am sorry to hear that King Diarmait was so violent to his own people, but that is the sort of man he is." He turned to Brother Angelo. "Tell the Pope that when you next speak with him. Tell him that Diarmait Mac Murchadha is a king who kills his own people and shows them no mercy."

Brother Angelo's hand reached up to touch his cross. "The wicked of this world have the devil sitting upon their shoulder. It seems to me that King Diarmait has many devils upon his."

The wicked of this world have the devil sitting upon their shoulder.

Was that true?

I was grateful to Brother Angelo, but his story was not wholly true. It was I who had burned the ráth. Once again, I tried to focus my mind the way Uncle Godred had taught me. To desire nothing. To feel nothing.

"You've had a terrible time, Cuan," Queen Gráinne said, holding out her hand for me to take. "Why don't you come and eat? I'm sure you are cold from riding in the forest for so long."

I agreed, glad that the examination had come to an end, and together we walked into the feasting hall. King Ruaidrí and Conchobar made straight for the top table, while Queen Gráinne brought me over some food. Róisín followed her mother's example and made up a cup of honeyed milk. I was glad to see that Brother Angelo and Meallán had been brought inside too and given a seat beside the fire. Young Meallán shovelled the food into his mouth so quickly that he barely seemed to chew it before he swallowed.

He put me in mind of myself when I was his age, back when my grandfather was king. Back when my father was expected to be king and I king after him. Before I knew that fire could come out of my hands and kill those who tried to help me.

Gormflaith

Chepstow

I watched Strongbow talk with my son. Watched as Strongbow approved my marriage to David, then listened to Donnchad talking of Cecile. I didn't need the warrior gift to hear this. I could see it in the way their lips moved, in the way Donnchad's eyes lit up when my marriage was agreed, and then in the way they dulled when marriage to Cecile was denied.

What to do though? *What to do?*

First, did I want to marry David? That seemed to be the most important question, and my answer was dependent on whether or not Strongbow was serious about invading Ireland. However, it was not a pressing issue. I could always say yes tonight and change my mind later.

The second, more important question, was whether to let Donnchad move ahead with his plans or not.

It would be easier to let him try, and he might even see them through. My son was confident of his position now that Máelmórda was dead. I could see this in the way he held himself, and he was not without experience, for he had clung onto the kingship of Munster for fifty years after Clontarf.

But it was this very confidence that irritated me so, and the same anger rose inside of me as when we had spoken in my bedroom earlier. He was so certain of being our leader, so certain he knew best, and I had finally come to my own certainty. I didn't want *him* to win this victory in Ireland. I wanted it myself. Ireland was mine. Not his.

But how? How could I do this? How could I oust him from the position he had climbed into?

"David!" Le Gros shouted. "Have the women fill your cups! I have news!"

Saying nothing, I smiled at David, trying my best to appear infatuated and angelic, as if I thought a kiss on the lips could convey the entirety of a woman's passion. It wasn't too hard to play the part of innocent virgin. I had only to lower my head demurely and laugh when the others did so. *What could the news be?* The knights asked each other. *Has an invasion been approved?*

Le Gros, who was currently speaking with Miles, clasped his friend on the shoulder, then the two of them walked over. I rearranged my hair and sat straighter, making sure to place my hand on David's arm.

"I have news for you, David," Le Gros said, chuckling, the red veins on his nose particularly virulent this evening.

David jumped out of his chair. "Did you speak to Strongbow for me? What did he say?"

"He said yes. You are to be married. To any girl of your choosing."

The men around us cheered, each of them raising their cups and toasting Strongbow's decision.

Le Gros raised his cup higher than any of them, tilting it toward David and then toward me. "When you first asked me if you could marry Alys, I was not convinced, but well, we have all witnessed your love for each other, and I believe she will make you happy. God knows I cannot bring you to war without knowing the love of a woman."

Giving a girlish giggle, I kissed David on the cheek. That was all that was required of me in any case, for the men spoke of the wedding and when it might be. Of which priest should say the mass. The church. The day. The time.

I nodded along with all their ideas, but of course, I had work of my own to do this evening.

Donnchad had already set himself up to take control of our

plans in Ireland. To change our direction required a gamble and a risk… and I had not truly rolled the dice in quite some time. Fear had held me back. Fear of Isolde, and the prophecy that said she would kill me. But it was she who was dead. Not I.

And so I watched Strongbow and made a vow to myself. If he left the hall alone, I would gamble. If he stayed here with his men all night, I would let Donnchad have his time to further our ambitions and make my move later.

"What do you think about a dowry, Alys?"

I turned my head toward Le Gros, who had asked the question.

"Do you think your brother will provide anything for you?"

"Oh… I… You will need to ask him."

David tutted. "That is for me to worry about, Le Gros, but it doesn't matter. I do not care for a dowry."

"Then who is going to pay for the new armour you need? Me again, is it? Your poor uncle, who is never done spending coin on you."

The two of them argued back and forth, not seriously, for it was obvious that Le Gros was going to purchase whatever David needed.

"Donn!" Le Gros shouted after a while, giving David a sly wink. Waving over to my son, Le Gros asked him to join in our celebrations. Donnchad came over, all smiles, and he shook the hands of David, Le Gros and the other knights in our company, and gave me a kiss on the cheek.

It was then that Strongbow stood. He nodded goodnight to his two natural daughters, then to Miles, and walked toward the courtyard. Alone.

This was it then. My sign.

I leaned toward my husband-to-be. "David, I will be back in just a moment." I pressed my hand over my stomach to indicate I needed to pass water and left the hall. David blew a kiss after me, and I grinned as I pretended to catch it. He was happy, this man of mine. His eyes were sparkling. His laughter was loud. Joy was something I had not felt much of in my life, but if I ever had to describe it from now on, I would think of David in this moment, for his happiness was unbridled by the shadow of loss or despair. It filled him entirely.

Turning, I moved toward the outer door and left behind Le Gros talking once more of dowries, this time conversing with Donnchad. I followed Strongbow along the corridor and out into the courtyard, and then into the small garden. He was alone, taking a moment of solitude now that the men were too drunk to so loudly crave his attention. Wrapping my scarf over my face and shoulders, I transformed into Cecile as I walked into the garden, though I pretended I had not noticed anyone entering it before me. In this garden there was a statue of the Virgin Mary, and I stood in front of her, made the sign of the cross, then touched her foot.

"Cecile?"

I stepped away and stared at Strongbow, wide-eyed as if he had startled me. This show of fear was not so hard to do, for much uncertainty ran through me. *How did Cecile act with Strongbow?* She was sullen with me, had been childish with her father, but perhaps with a man like Strongbow she was a wild seductress and would kiss him passionately when he reached her side. I decided to err on the side of caution and let him be the one to move first.

"How are you, Cecile?" Edging closer, he touched my hand lightly, as if even for his skin to brush against a woman's was sinful, and yet he couldn't make himself pull away. Ah, so that was how they were. In love but separated by piety.

"I've been asked…" he said, his voice close to a whisper. "Donn has asked if he can marry you."

"What did you say?"

"A match between the two of you is not in my power to refuse. It is not like David and Alys, where David is my kin."

I lowered my gaze.

"It was, however, a shock to me to discover he is your cousin, not brother." His hand slid away from mine.

Ah yes, Donn had changed our story during his travels in Ireland. This put me, or rather Cecile, in an awkward position, for a man like Strongbow would dislike lies coming from the lips of the woman he loved.

"I've lived with him since I was a young child," I said. "He is like a brother to me. That's what our relationship has been and what I've always called him. His sudden wish to marry me is a surprise to me as much as it is to you."

Strongbow glanced my way, some of the annoyance in his brow falling away. "You don't wish to marry him?"

"No, but he will be difficult to refuse. If I say no, and he casts me aside, I'll have nowhere to go. I will be alone in this world. Alone and unprotected." I lowered my face, crestfallen, the picture of a star-crossed lover when fate had turned against them.

"There is nothing I can do, Cecile," Strongbow said, his hand gently moving to my cheek. "I am promised to another, and I would not make you my mistress. I have two natural daughters from a woman of low morals and cannot bear to make you like her. To have men and women gossip about you."

"Then send Donn away."

Strongbow breathed deeply, eyebrows knitting together as he thought.

"Don't you have a message to give your kin in London or Normandy? Please. Think of something. Send Donn away. I cannot bear the thought of marrying him. If I cannot be with you, I don't want to be with anyone."

Strongbow nodded, his thumb brushing my cheek again. "I will think about what to do, sweet Cecile. I do not wish to see you unhappy."

"I would be your friend, always."

"Don't you think that would be difficult? I've rarely seen it exist when love flows underneath."

"Why should that be? Friendship is a just and true kind of love... perhaps it's not the way I want it to be, but I will take it if it means I can remain at your side."

I moved a little closer to Strongbow and kissed his hand. Soft, but not so soft that he could not feel my lips against his skin. Was this like Cecile? I was tempted to turn his hand around and kiss his palm, but no, I could sense from the way Strongbow's whole body stiffened that even this contact was more than he was used to from Cecile. He wanted her though. Oh yes.

Stepping slowly backward, I turned away from him only once I reached the wall of the garden, then ran back inside the castle. There. I had done enough. Told him what I wanted and given him enough temptation that he might actually do it. Quickly, I transformed back to myself and removed the headscarf from around my shoulders.

On returning to the feasting hall, I found David seeking me out. Rather than waiting for me to come to him, he rushed toward me. He had a silver bracelet in his hand as well as a gold ring. "The last time I gave you money, did you buy yourself a new dress?" he asked, his voice so breathless, I could hardly make him out.

"Yes."

"Then put it on."

"Why? Where are we going?"

"To the church. We are to be married."

"Now? Tonight?"

He wrapped his arms around me and kissed me on the lips. "The priest is already there. As soon as you are ready, come down."

Halting, I stared at the ring.

"What is wrong, Alys?" David asked. "You seemed happy earlier on."

"Oh, I am happy. It is just... are you sure? I am so beneath you in rank that I—"

"Hush, Alys. Don't say it. Listen to me. Strongbow has just given Le Gros and his men a mission." He lowered his voice. "We are to be part of an advance invasion into Ireland. I have to be married to you before I go. I can't bear the thought of waiting a moment longer. Don't talk of rank and things that don't matter. Do you love me? That's all I want to know. Do you wish to be my wife?"

I glanced once more at the ring and bracelet, my smile widening. David must have paid good money for them, though the craftsmanship was not up to Irish standards, but while they were beautiful, that was not what made me so happy. If David was going in as part of the advance, I could go with him. Once in Ireland, I could put my plans in motion, and the Fomorian conquest could truly begin.

"I cannot believe it," I hushed. "I prayed and prayed for this day to come, but I did not believe that God would answer me. He has done it, David. He has given me you."

David grinned. "Go then. Hurry. Your brother has been told. He will be at the church along with everyone else."

Hurrying to my room, I slammed the door shut behind me. Cecile was lying on the bed, exhausted after working in the kitchens all day and serving all night. Even the noise of the door didn't stir her.

"Hurry, Cecile. We've a wedding to attend."

"A wedding?" She pried open one eye. "Whose?"

"Mine."

Cecile rolled over. "David is so desperate he has to marry you this very night?"

"I suppose."

"Gods almighty, what a sop he is." She stood then and picked up our comb.

"Talking of sops, I spoke to Strongbow tonight."

Cecile's smirk faded. "You spoke of me?"

"I'll tell you more tomorrow. For tonight, don't speak to either Strongbow or Donnchad. After the wedding, leave. Do you understand?"

She stared at me, a glint in her eye. That was good. She was more sceptical than she used to be. She might even be useful one day. "Believe me, if you don't want to marry Donnchad, this is what you must do."

"What did you say to him?"

"I don't have time now to tell you. Tomorrow. Now lace me up and come with me to my wedding. Wear my blue dress. It will suit you."

Cecile, mouth tight, looked set to argue, but once I mentioned the dress, she could not resist. She desired Strongbow. Even if she couldn't speak to him, she wanted him to see her in something pretty, rather than the rags she wore in the kitchens.

Once we were ready, together, we rushed to the church.

Both of us gasped as we entered.

It was full of the people of Chepstow, all of them smiling and clapping their hands with joy. Smiling back, I walked down the aisle and toward David.

What words could I use to describe this wedding? Beautiful. Romantic. I'm sure if I had time, I'd have conjured more. My mind, however, was more preoccupied with the contrasts and contradictions of it all. This was my first time marrying a man with no wealth or title, and yet it was the most pleasant one of all.

The church was decorated with winter holly. The maids blew kisses and cheered me on. Some of David's friends attended too, and they each gave us their good wishes and a gift. William Ferrand did not enter the church but stood watching from outside, and Ranulf gave me a silver coin as a present. The kitchen girls, who I had long forgotten, gave me a basket, and when I looked inside, I realised they had parcelled up some breads and salted meats, along with a bottle of imported wine. Not the best wine, no, but still, it was wine rather than ale. Such plain presents. No chests of gold and silver. No dowry. No crown. Only friendship, trinkets, and genuine wishes for happiness.

Even Cecile smiled as she watched me and David hold hands. My son played the part of a devoted brother well and told everyone how proud he was of me. Laughter was the music of the night. Leftover wine, ale and bread were our feast.

David stared at me as the priest spoke. In his eyes there was lust, not that this was unusual, for there was always lust in the men I seduced, but today there was love too. *Adoration*. He blushed when the priest spoke of the sanctity of marriage. He kissed my hand. Told me I was the fairest woman he had ever seen and that even if he were a king, he would choose me over all others. *I believed him*.

After the priest had finished the ceremony, David lost no time in leading me toward his bedroom.

If I'd always endured my weddings in the past, it was because fate had made it so. When I was younger, I married who my father told me to, then who my brother told me to, and then who my son Sitric wanted. I had been married to Amlav and Brian, my first two husbands, then Sigurd the Stout had become my intended. All were arrangements to allow my kin to hold or gain power. There might have been lust from these men but not love. There had *never* been lust or love on my part. Both emotions had to be conjured from the edges of my imagination. In the years since I'd left Ireland it had been much the same. I'd married for money or for safety, and that was why I always dreaded what came after the wedding feast. In these moments, I prayed not for love or tenderness, but speed. That it might all be over soon.

I knew that this bedding would be different.

The first one where my imagination would not be needed. Thoughts of pleasure came to me. David was not a virgin, but he was inexperienced compared to me. I, for once, could be in control, could demand, could play. Could destroy.

But throughout the pleasure and the joy of our bedding, there was one certainty.

I had no intention of being married to David for long.

Isolde

Seir Kieran

The image of my mother that I'd had in my youth was as if she were an angel. Broccan had drawn this picture for me oh so well. He had told me of her kindness, her sweetness, her loyalty. When I used to picture her in my mind, her smile was pure and filled with joy.

The other Descendants had given me new perspectives. They told me of how Tomas had captivated my mother, Fódla, then controlled every aspect of her life. They told me about Fódla's love for my sister, Aoife, who aged like a mortal because she was giftless, and of my mother's grief when she died. Finally, they told me about my mother's loyalty to Rónnat when everyone else had turned against her, and of course her love for the mortals once she came to know them. She had been afraid of them before that. *Broccan had never told me this.*

It was a different version of my mother, of course it was, for Colmon had known her since she was a baby. He had watched the fear grow inside her. Watched as she hid herself away in the fortress, scared of the people who lived beyond the safety of Fennit Island. And in this confinement, she remained in the shadow of Tomas, shielding Aoife from both him and the world.

Once Colmon, Báine, Siobhan, Méabh and Gisela had finished their stories, I excused myself and left their company.

For the next few days, I walked the grounds of Seir Kieran alone, finding solace in the animals and birds, trying to rediscover the girl I had been on Rathlin, but when I closed my eyes, the mother I had once seen so clearly in my imagination no longer looked at me with wide-eyed adoration. Her joy had vanished. When she looked at me now, I saw worry. I saw pain… and disappointment.

Today, I tried to banish this new image of my mother. The morning air was cold, the wind sharp, and I wrapped my cloak tight around myself as I walked toward the stables. *I was being watched.* Not by Leofwynn, who sometimes stared at me from afar, too nervous to talk to me again, but curious enough to follow. I did not mind her eyes. They were kind. Laughter lived inside them, and I found solace in the fact that even though she'd once been enslaved, it had not destroyed her spirit.

But it was not her today. No, another was watching.

Colmon.

After our last conversation, he had gone back to his bedroom to sleep. Ageing was tiring, Siobhan had told me. He would sleep often and for long periods, and so even though I wasn't ready to speak to him, I decided it was time. I could not remove myself from the other Descendants forever, and there were many things he still had left to tell me. Many things I had to tell him. The vision of him dying, I had kept a secret, but that was not fair. Even if he hated me because of it, he deserved to know.

Where could we talk in private?

The answer to this question was an easy one. The same place as our last meeting. Out in the open and away from the grey walls that pressed down on me whenever I was inside. Grabbing an extra blanket from the stables, I made my way toward the hawthorn tree that was situated behind the monastery, sat on one of the logs, and waited.

It wasn't long before I heard his footsteps, slow and uneven, his walking stick helping him along. I turned my head after a while and smiled as he approached. Méabh, the cupbearer, watched him from the door but walked back inside the monastery once he reached me.

"This used to be easier," he said, his knees clicking as he lowered himself onto one of the logs.

"I'm sorry."

"Don't be sorry. It is the way of life. We must all grow old at some stage. I'm only grateful that I have woken and can say goodbye in the way that I want." Now seated, he used his stick to help straighten his posture, and once his gaze found mine, he grinned. "I'm also glad to be able to speak with you, Isolde."

"Are you?"

"You doubt me?"

"I doubt everything."

"Why is that?"

"Because I don't understand what is happening to me. Everyone is being very kind, and I liked that you all spoke of my mother, but there are so many things I feel distant from. There are secrets here too. I don't like that."

"No. I suppose you don't." Colmon sighed. "I never liked secrets either. Why don't we make a promise to each other? Let us always tell the truth."

I didn't react to this, which made the openness in Colmon's expression fade. By not agreeing to make this promise, I had revealed that I carried secrets of my own. I could not tell him all of them. I could not tell him about Cuan. *Not ever.*

"You go first," I said, speaking before he could. "Who are you? What do you want from me?"

The old warrior ran his hands over his face, his fingers coming to rest once they reached his beard. This was greying too, though not as much as his hair.

"I am Colmon, the warrior. My father was a warrior, too. My mother was a mortal princess from Egypt who he fell in love with. She was very beautiful. Loved to sing and dance, but as with all mortals, her life was short, and my father brought me to Ireland once she passed. He died not long after, at the great age of four hundred and thirty."

I felt as if I should convey my sorrow at the loss of his parents, but I didn't want to interrupt him. Unsure of what else to do, I remained silent as a look of sorrow swept over his face.

"At the fort of the Tuatha Dé Danann, I trained under the guidance of your grandfather, Ciarán. He was my uncle, my father's brother. Together we fought off the Fomorians who attacked us. We met them at Ráthteas monastery so they could not find our fortress, and though we won, your grandfather died not long after that battle. We thought we had killed all the Fomorians, and for a time, we lived in peace. That was always my greatest wish. Peace."

"Strange for a Descendant with the warrior gift to want peace. Surely it is war you crave?"

"Perhaps it was at first, and yet I realised very quickly that when I used my gift, it meant my family and friends were in danger. I never liked that... and we live such long lives that after a while I had come to know death too well. That was why I tried so very hard to keep our lives... steady... calm... but it was not to be. War and death came for us all the same."

"What shattered the peace? The Fomorians?"

"No." He shook his head. "We shattered the peace ourselves. Our numbers dwindled, you see. Most of the children we had were giftless, and if not giftless, their gifts were weaker, and we fought among ourselves as to the reason why. Tomas, who was our leader at the time, thought it was because we were having children with mortals, and so we removed ourselves from their world. That was the beginning of our undoing. We grew too proud and thought ourselves better than those we had once loved, and our numbers continued to decline all the same."

I thought of Aoife. She had been giftless. What had her life been like? That my mother had felt the need to protect her indicated that she'd not been treated well. I didn't like that.

"Did you ever find out why our numbers declined?" I asked.

He glanced at the monastery and cast his eyes over the mortals tending the sheep. "I suppose the reason doesn't matter now. We will never recover. Perhaps that is our destiny. Either way, it is no longer a question that matters to me."

"What does matter?"

"You. You are the only thing that matters."

He didn't know me. Why would he say that I was the only thing that mattered, when he moved so quickly toward death? The prophecy was the only answer I could think of. I was the daughter who was supposed to *conquer fire*. This surely was who Colmon wanted. A fearsome woman who would destroy his enemies.

"Do you know, on Rathlin, Broccan thought I was giftless. So did Affraic. It was only when the Fomorians came to the island that I was able to summon the storm. I don't even know how I did it. It just happened. I'm afraid I am only going to disappoint you."

"Disappoint me? No. Never."

"You know the prophecy, don't you? If so, you know that I'm the girl who is supposed to conquer fire. How can I do that if I didn't even know I was a Descendant until a few months ago?"

"Let us not worry about the prophecy for now. Instead, let us talk about you, as you are now. I know Broccan raised you, and it's clear you loved him very much. I am not him, but I loved him too. Please let me help you." Colmon sat up straighter, no longer leaning on his stick, and something of the warrior gift seemed to move through him. "Could you tell me what happened? I haven't wanted to push you, but I cannot help unless I know."

He spoke with such earnestness that I agreed to tell him my story. There was sadness in his voice too. Sadness for Broccan, and perhaps it was this emotion that allowed me to begin.

"When the Fomorians attacked Rathlin, Broccan went to fight them while Affraic and I were supposed to sail to the mainland, but I couldn't leave him. I ran to where Broccan and the Fomorians were fighting and drew two of them away. Affraic found me as I was running through the forest, and the two of us tried to run back to Broccan's land where the spells would protect us but… but a Fomorian caught up with us and trapped us inside a circle of fire. He came into the circle and hurt Affraic. It made me angry. So angry. And with this rage growing inside of me, a great storm arrived. The hailstones were so big that the Fomorian was thrown to the ground and his fire disappeared."

"Did you see the storm in your mind before you called it?"

"No."

Colmon nodded. "What happened next?"

"Again, we tried to make it to Broccan's land, but Affraic couldn't. She was too badly hurt. We both were hurt by the hailstones, and she insisted on healing me. She… she pretended she was healing my lip when she poured a liquid inside my mouth. It was the potion of death that Echna had brewed for her."

Colmon's eyes widened. "Affraic gave you the potion of death?"

"Yes, followed quickly by the antidote. She pushed me into the lough, then told me to get to Seir Kieran once I woke up. My mind drifted then, but before I faded, I heard her screaming. When I woke, she was gone. So was Broccan, and for days and days I shook and shook."

"I am sorry, Isolde."

Brushing away the tears that were falling down my cheeks, I gave him a nod to show I accepted his sympathy. I felt a deep sadness for him too. I had known Broccan for eighteen years and Affraic for only a couple of weeks. He had helped raise Broccan and had known Affraic for hundreds of years.

"Before Affraic gave me the potion, she said I had the witch gift, and that I was powerful. She told me I had to survive so that I could make it here and be trained. That was why she sacrificed herself, though I wish she hadn't."

Colmon sighed, the sound letting me know he understood. "So, you left the island? Alone."

"Yes."

"And?"

"I wasn't long on the mainland when four men took me captive. They heard me speaking Norman French to a stranger in a church and then Latin to a priest. They thought I was a spy."

"Norman French? Why would someone be speaking that language here?"

"It is the language the English nobility speaks."

Colmon's brows inched closer together. He had been asleep for over one hundred years, and I supposed the politics of England had not been high on his list of things to learn.

"Around one hundred years ago, a Norman duke invaded England," I explained. "William the Bastard, the people called him. He was the heir to the king, I think, but one of the Saxon lords said *he* was the heir. Anyway, there was a battle, and the Norman duke won. He brought lots of warriors with him and gave them lands and titles, and so the English nobility all speak Normandy French now. The poor people still speak the Saxon language, though. Or at least, that is what Broccan told me."

Colmon ran his hand through his hair. "Being asleep for this long, many things change."

"And now the King of Leinster, King Diarmait, has invited some of these Anglo-Norman lords to Ireland to fight for him against King Ruaidrí, who is the High King of Ireland and King of Connacht. That's why these men were so suspicious. They fought for King Ruaidrí."

Colmon closed his eyes for a moment. I thought he was going to ask more questions about the Normans, but instead, he moved back to me.

"What did the king say to you when you were brought before him?"

"He said he believed I was not a spy but still would not let me go. The truth, or what I came to believe, was that he did think I was a spy and wanted to watch me."

"Then how did you get away?"

My heart raced. I was moving closer to Cuan's part in my story. Closer to the strange things that I had done. Soon I would have to tell him about the storms and the knight slitting my throat and me healing myself. *Then I would have to tell him about the vision.*

"I told a story to his wife, Queen Gráinne. It was one that Broccan had told me about Cú Chulainn and Fand. About how they loved each other but were separated, and about how Cú Chulainn's wife Emer loved him too, and how devastated she was to be betrayed."

Colmon smiled. "I told Broccan that story."

"Did you?"

"And it was your grandmother who first told it to me. Many years ago." Colmon leaned forward, his fingers picking at the tall grass by his leg. "But while the story is sad, I'm not sure how it induced the queen to let you go."

"I told her that just as Cú Chulainn was lost without love, so was I. I told her that Broccan was dead, and I had to find someone else who knew of him. She cried when I told her this. I cried too. Strange, I know, but it worked, and she spoke to the king on my behalf."

"I see. What next?"

"Then I made it to Dublin."

I knew leaving Cuan out of this story was wrong, but it had to be this way. I skipped over him, pretended that he was not there and not a part of my life. "King Diarmait and his Anglo-Norman army came to the city while I was there, so I ran away before the gates were closed. While I was travelling, King Diarmait's men captured me… and they… they slit my throat."

"What?"

"I know it sounds unbelievable, but it happened. I swear it. They opened my throat and blood spilled down my dress. I had tried to conjure a storm to stop them, but it came too late. When I woke, my throat was as if it had never been cut open, but I was soaked through and covered in blood. The shaking came to me again, as it had done when I woke up in Rathlin, and black phlegm filled my mouth."

"That is from using your gift without training. The power inside of you eats at you if you cannot control it."

That was what Affraic warned me would happen. I thought of all the times when the shaking and the black phlegm had come to me. After the storm on Rathlin. During the fight at the bruidean when I had thrown a man against the wall. Then after I told the story to the queen, and after I had healed myself and Cuan, and also after the vision. *So many times*.

Colmon examined me, face full of confusion.

"You are as confused as I am, Colmon. I can see it. Affraic told me I was a witch, and yet I have done things that are not of the witch gift. I don't understand how that is possible. I have summoned storms. A man slit my throat, and I did not die. I woke you up when Affraic and Siobhan could not… and before we met, I had dreams of you."

"Dreams?"

"A dream, no, that's not right. A vision. Wherever we are, it is on fire, and you have a sword in your stomach. Before you die, you tell me it is my fault and that they are coming for me. You tell me to run."

I told him about the vision in as much detail as I could. I didn't hold back. Told him about the dead bodies and the wound I had in my stomach that disappeared. I had removed Cuan from my previous story, but when it came to this, the vision of Colmon, everything I said had to be the whole truth. It was his life that my vision had shown me. His death.

Colmon listened intently, and once I was finished ran his hands down the long grey strands of his hair again. "So you've summoned storms, made queens cry, healed your own body from bleeding out and you've glimpsed the future?"

"I don't know. Yes. I think so."

"Did Broccan ever tell you about Lugh and how he came to win the Battle of Moytura against the Fomorians?"

I nodded. "Lugh took up his spear, and it flew through Balor's eye and out the back of his skull, killing Balor. The fire that flooded out the back of his head destroyed the whole Fomorian army which had lined up behind him."

"Yes. That is true, but why was Lugh the one who took on such an act? Why not the warriors? The witches?"

"Because…" I fumbled for the right answer.

"Because Lugh had *all* the gifts. The only one of our kind who has ever held all the gifts. Until you."

I could only stare at him. All the gifts? *Me?*

"You have come to us when once again we need to drive back our enemies. That is how you will conquer fire, Isolde. This is how you fulfil the prophecy. I couldn't understand it before, but now it is so obvious."

He spoke with such wonder and clarity, as if I were a puzzle he finally understood. I, however, did not share this sentiment. If anything, I felt more confused than before.

"But how can I learn it all?" I stammered. "There is so much to learn for even one gift, and there isn't even a druid alive who can teach me, or a weapon-maker."

"Those of us who remain will teach you everything we know. You will stay here with us and learn. More than that, there are other things that can help you too."

"Like?"

"You have *Fragarach* in your belt for a start. If you point it at the throat of another, they must tell you the truth, and there are other weapons in our possession. A spear that does not miss and a sword that lights the way to your enemies. They are yours now."

These were the gifts of the Tuatha Dé Danann. Broccan had mentioned them in his stories, back when I thought they were only stories. "Where are they?"

"They, believe it or not, are on Rathlin Island. I hid them while I lived there with your mother and Broccan. I wanted to keep them hidden from Tomas. Don't worry, they are safe, and once the winter passes, we will travel there."

He smiled as he spoke, looking north with hope in his eyes, while I filled with fear and confusion. How would he manage such a long journey through a land on the brink of war when he was ageing? But other thoughts came to me too. In his excitement at discovering my gifts, he had forgotten the vision.

"But what about the vision, Colmon? I kill you."

"We will think on that, Isolde. When you described me, you

said my hair was white, yes? It means I am older than now. Once my hair starts to turn more white than grey, we will all leave this place. The others can find another monastery to take them in. We will travel north. The Fomorians cannot kill us if we are not here."

He looked so confident when he spoke. I was glad, for he needed enough for the two of us. While he spoke of the northern path we would take, I let what he had told me sink in.

I had all the gifts. He wanted me to stay here, to train and learn all that I did not know… which was everything.

The girl inside me, the one who had lived on Rathlin with Broccan, would have agreed with this. But the Isolde who had been born after the fire and on the road with Cuan, found her heart sinking. I knew then that any thoughts of Cuan had to leave me now. Wherever he was, he was lost to me.

I had kept him safe by removing him from the story I had told Colmon. That then was all I could offer. Not love. Not friendship. Just life.

"You don't look very happy, Isolde. Is there something wrong?"

I shook my head. "I'm just worried that I will not be able to learn everything."

"Don't worry about that," Colmon said. "Your training begins today." With a sudden burst of energy, he stood and threw his stick toward me. The speed and strength of it startled me, and the long wooden staff clattered on the ground by my feet.

"I am still a warrior, Isolde," he said, smiling. "And I can draw on my gift when I need to. So, without wasting another moment, let us begin."

I picked up the stick, moved into a fighting stance, and pointed it at Colmon.

"Good," Colmon said. "Now, try to hit me."

Donnchad

Chepstow

I awoke the next day, a smile upon my face.

With my mother now married, everything was moving along nicely. Strongbow planned to use me in the Irish war, yes, but I would use him too.

The high kingship would come to me, not through birth or marriage, but through fear. If the Descendants were all dead, why hide the fact I was a Fomorian, a warrior and a cupbearer? I was a god among men, and it was time the mortals of Ireland saw this, for if a poor man in Jerusalem could persuade half the world that he was the Son of God, what could I convince them of? He raised the dead and cured lepers, but I could part rivers and scorch the earth.

If... if the Descendants were all dead.

This thought caught on me. *They had to be.* Broccan had fallen off the cliffs. The girl, Fódla's daughter, was dead, and so was the witch who had tried to protect her. I had promised my mother they were all dead and left Angelo behind feeling that this was right... but I had also known that if any did lurk, they would find my mute son all alone and unprotected first. Leaving him behind had not been easy, but to obtain greatness, tough decisions had to be made. The Spartans had left behind the weak in pursuit of victory, and to become High King, that was what was required from me too.

I pushed thoughts of the Descendants finding my son away,

letting myself move toward logic. If there had been any more Descendants, surely they'd all be protecting the girl. No, they were dead. They had to be. When I returned to Ireland, Angelo would be alive, and my walk along the path to kingship would begin, the sacrifice I had been willing to make, not required.

When I closed my eyes, I could see it. See me once again walking toward the dun at Killaloe. See me sitting on Sitric's throne in Dublin. I could have let myself dwell within these dreams all morning, but as glorious as these pictures were, I was not king yet, and many things had to go right before I was. My first step was to win followers from the Anglo-Norman army, for I could not conquer Ireland alone. A single man, no matter how powerful, could not hold a throne. Toir had proven this when he ousted me from Killaloe.

No, to make myself king and keep hold of it, I needed men at my command. Men willing to die for me and drive back my enemies when they came from all sides.

This would not be so easy. To steal an army, I needed to surpass FitzStephen and Strongbow in the minds of the knights, which meant I needed to be seen as a key part of the invasion planning. The warriors needed to know that my mind was as sharp as my blade. Then when I had them in my grasp, I could reveal the Fomorian I had hidden away for so long.

Today was the first step.

However, lowly as I still was, I couldn't go straight to Strongbow with talk of politics and strategy. I needed to find another way in. *That was easy enough.* He'd told me at the feast we would talk of my wedding to Cecile soon. Now that my mother was married, today was the perfect moment to have such a conversation. After he said yes, I was sure I could give him some more information about Ireland. Describe the dun at Ferns. The layout of Dublin. Draw a map of the rivers that Sitric and my father had once dominated.

Perhaps a wedding today might be possible if a priest could be prevailed upon to say the mass? Miles had given me a little silver as payment for my services in Ireland, more than enough to bribe a lazy priest to get out of bed.

I got up and dressed, making sure that my clothes were clean and in good order. In Ireland, I had been a common foot soldier, then a translator. At the meeting with Strongbow, I had advanced to adviser. Things were on the up, and it was time to ensure everyone knew it. I wrapped my hands around the silver coins and put them in my belt pocket. A new tunic and fur cloak was needed for me, a dress for Cecile for our wedding, and then I should have enough left over to pay the priest, but first, before I bought these garments or arranged a ceremony, I had to find Cecile. She had disappeared after the wedding last night, tired from a hard day working in the kitchens, she had told my mother. That was the first thing I would change. Cecile was Fomorian. Not a servant.

My stomach fluttered a little at the thought of talking to Cecile about marriage. I'd had many wives during my life, but none of whom I'd had to woo. These had been arrangements made with their fathers or brothers. Asking for Cecile's hand was different, for she was an equal to me.

I didn't have words of love for her such as David had for my mother. No poetry, no declarations of ardour. That was not my way. My way was to show Cecile what I could give her. My hopes for the future could become her hopes too. More than that, the survival of the Fomorians depended on this union. I was certain that Cecile wanted this too. And while I was not fashionable, I was a kind man. Had always been good to my wives, never hit or scolded them. Always bought them gifts to their liking when they pleased me. Cecile would come to see these qualities. *Perhaps she already saw them.*

Making my way to the feasting hall, I expected to find Cecile serving breakfast with the other kitchen maids. However, she was not there. *Where could she be?*

"Donn!" David shouted over to me, his smile wide and eyes bright as he walked my way. "I was hoping to speak with you."

"Yes?"

"I wanted to say thank you. I should perhaps have waited longer to marry Alys, and properly asked your permission, but—"

"Don't worry, David. I understand." I smiled back and offered my hand for him to shake. David was a key part of my plans, and establishing our friendship as soon as possible was paramount. If he had any ambition at all, his marriage to my mother could be beneficial to him too. Unlike Sitric, I had no plans to annoy my mother with arranged marriages and forced unions. As long as she was out of the way, she could marry where she chose, and David was as good as any other.

"I'm glad. It's just with us leaving soon, I didn't want to wait."

"You're leaving?"

David paused, then cleared his throat. Oh, interesting. *He'd spoken out of turn.*

"I will not repeat anything if that is your worry," I said as the pause lingered. "We are family now."

"Yes, well, I suppose I can tell you… if I have your word that you will keep it to yourself."

"You have my word, David. Of course."

David leaned in, lowering his voice to a whisper. "A scouting party is heading over to Ireland. Not just yet. In the spring. I am to be part of it. Alys was delighted when I told her, but I know it was an act. For my part, I do not wish to be separated from her so soon either, but I cannot refuse Le Gros."

I patted David on the shoulder. "She'll be upset, but she loves you."

David was relieved by my quick assurances and our conversation moved back to the wedding, and I happily let him talk to me of his love for Alys, but all the while my mind whirled. *A scouting party*. I should be part of that. If David was going, then this was my way in. I was his brother-in-law now. *Family*.

"Have you seen Alys this morning?" David asked.

The question brought me back to our conversation. "No."

David rolled his eyes. "No doubt she's off to see that damned eagle of hers. I'd better find her. See you later, Donn."

I gave a nod of farewell, then quickened my step toward the tables closest to Strongbow. Sitting down, I took a piece of bread and covered it with honey and berries.

I did not have to wait long for Cecile to appear. I watched her carefully. She was dressed once again in poor woollen cloth, her hair covered with a blue shawl. Her face was so beautiful, even with such drab attire, that I didn't know how all the other men paid her so little heed. She no longer limped either. This was good, and I was glad for her that this injury from Rathlin Island would not mark her always.

I raised my hand and waved.

"Donn!" Strongbow stood before she could even take a step in my direction and beckoned for me to go over to him.

I smiled as I walked his way, then bowed. Cecile could wait. "Yes, my lord."

"I have been thinking long and hard about what you, Miles and Maurice have told me. I've decided that I would like you to go to London and speak to King Henry on my behalf. You can more aptly describe the situation in Ireland than anyone else. This might finally make him see sense and grant me permission to invade."

My smile dropped. "But I am not worthy to speak on your behalf, my lord. Not to a king."

"You are if I say you are," Strongbow replied. "Believe me, Henry will be most intrigued by you." He nodded over at the knight who stood behind him. An old man with a hollow cough and a broken cheekbone. "FitzHubert will go with you. The two of you will deliver my message, and you will both await his reply."

I looked at the old knight, who gave a low bow to Strongbow. The task excited him. I could tell by the way his feet shifted and his back straightened. An honour this might be for him, but it was not an honour I wanted. I needed to return to Ireland at the earliest opportunity. Not just for Angelo's sake, but for mine. If Strongbow left for Ireland before I returned, my chance to move him as I wished was gone.

"FitzHubert, if you could go to the stables and have them ready one of my horses for Donn. You will take care of Donn on the way to the palace and make sure he is welcomed into court alongside yourself."

FitzHubert bowed, then promptly left.

"A word of warning," Strongbow said, once FitzHubert was gone. "Henry likes to speak in riddles and can be difficult to understand. You should not try to argue with him. A vague answer in some ways is what I'm after. Also, FitzHubert is Henry's man, not mine. Now off you go."

He waved his hand to dismiss me.

"What about my wedding to Cecile?" I asked.

"Oh, the wedding? Yes. Once you return, Donn, of course. But right now, I need this to be done, and I want you and FitzHubert to leave today. Before winter hardens and the roads become difficult to pass."

Giving as agreeable a smile as I could manage, I moved away from Strongbow's table and sat on one of the benches to finish my breakfast. What had just happened? Why had Strongbow done this? I had no knowledge of Henry's court. No rank. No title. I was the worst person he could send to speak with the English king.

"Why so sad, sweet Donn?"

My mother gave me a sly smile as she sat beside me.

"Strongbow sends me to the court of King Henry."

My mother reached forward to grab one of the boiled eggs from the middle of the table and slowly peeled the shell. "Tis no bad thing to see where the true power lies behind all of this." She waved up at the castle. "Strongbow is Earl of Pembroke here. It is not so at Henry's court. There he is merely the Lord of Striguil."

I took a long drink of watered ale. It was foul stuff, and I had never taken to it in the way that Máelmórda had. Still, I drank longer and deeper than usual. My mother had not told me this yesterday. What else had she withheld?

My mother watched me drink, a smug smile twitching at the corners of her mouth.

I almost laughed then. Gods, it was so obvious. She was the reason Strongbow had chosen me to go to England. While everyone else had been celebrating her wedding, she'd been scheming to get me out of her way. She might be a genius if she'd been able to conceal it, but she'd never been very good at hiding her feelings.

This was her downfall. She was so very easy to see through. Even Sitric at times had divined her true nature.

Once I'd drunk my fill, I set down my cup and returned my mother's smile. "You should be careful, Mother. One day the cat will eat you, and then the devil will eat the cat."

She snorted. "What you fail to understand, Donn, is this. We are the devil, not the cat."

Biting the inside of my lip, I composed my features. I couldn't let her see my annoyance. That would only feed her joy. "So, when did you speak to Strongbow to arrange that I should leave?"

My mother laughed.

"Perhaps you find all this funny, but I meant it when I said that we needed to act as one," I said, keeping my voice smooth. "The Irish kings are going to lose this war because they cannot unite. They'd rather bicker than help each other, and it will be their undoing. And here you are, doing the same thing. And what for? You asked me to kill the last of the Descendants, which I did for you. Why have you now decided to push me away?"

"I? Push you away?" My mother tilted her head. "It was not I who came begging forgiveness of you. No, it was the other way around. When I found you in Rome, poor and filthy with a child scurrying in an alleyway, Broccan was hard on your heels. I saved you, even though you once tried to kill me. And you talk of us uniting and yet you have never spoken to me once about your plans. Rather than I pushing you away, it is quite the opposite."

To my shame, I could not conceal the red flushing along my cheeks. I thought this would make her laugh. Perhaps it did inside, but if so, she held it in. Indeed, rather than further admonishing me, when she next spoke, her voice had softened.

"I want to speak to you properly now, Donnchad. I've had my fun and shown you it is wise not to forget me, but there is another reason for all this."

"A reason to send me away?"

She nodded, her smile completely faded now. "Years ago, I spoke to an Irish traveller in Venice. He told me you had two other sons, older than Angelo."

It pained me to think of my two older boys. They were good boys, though they were both without fire. I had wondered over the years what had happened to them, though less and less as time had passed. They'd be long dead by now, even if they'd lived to be the oldest of men.

"The traveller told me that you were so despised, that both sons were banned from holding the kingship of Munster, as were all of their male descendants. That has never happened before. Never has a legitimate candidate been barred from staking his claim." She took another egg from the table and began to peel its shell, even though she had not eaten the one on her plate. "I do not say this to pain you, simply to apologise because it is I who failed you."

An apology from my mother? My breath left me, and it took much longer than I wanted to regain it. "*You? You* failed me?"

Mother nodded. "With Sitric, I primed him to be king from the day he was born. I had the best fighters train him. The wisest in the city taught him. When he was older, I forged connections and relationships. First with his older brothers and the significant men of Dublin. Then Sigurd the Stout of Orkney and Brodar from the Isle of Man. I taught him about the importance of connections and friendships. It's a softer type of power, but it is every bit as important as commanding an army and defending a dun." She twisted her lip, a flash of sorrow moving over her face. "I never did the same for you."

"That's because you loved Sitric more than me."

"I used to think that was true," she answered, her voice still soft. "When Sitric was a young man, I thought he would give me freedom, but he took that from me when he married me to your father, and yet, I could never quite bring myself to acknowledge this. I would somehow forget his betrayal and remember the boy who had once saved me."

My heart raced as she spoke. Old emotions bubbled into my chest. Ones of envy and bitter regret. I had hated Sitric at times. Just as I had hated Murchad and Tairdelbach. I had loved

Tairdelbach too, but so much jealousy had built up inside me that I had killed him.

Doing my best to keep this emotion from my voice, I took a bite of the bread on my plate. "Why do you tell me this now?"

"Because I'm rectifying my mistake. King Henry is the King of England and also rules over Normandy, Anjou and Aquitaine. He holds these vast swathes of land, some of which he gained through his mother's line, and has kept control over them. You must go to him and learn. One day, when you are king, he will be your rival. Perhaps an ally. Perhaps an enemy. You must take this opportunity to learn how to be king in this century for I cannot teach you any more. Go now. While Strongbow and his men gather their strength over the winter."

She was right. I could speak with Henry and be back before the spring advance that David had told me about. My marriage to Cecile could wait.

"When you return from London," she continued, "you will go to Ireland, *as you wish*. Cecile will be yours, *as you wish*, and I will help you in both causes."

Mother's words were tempting. I constantly expected her to diminish me and to make my life harder, and here she was offering her help. A twist of suspicion kneaded at my guts. There had to be something she wanted in return. "What about what Strongbow wants?" I asked, keeping my voice low. "Apparently, I've to convince King Henry to allow his invasion into Ireland. What do you think of that?"

"Strongbow going ahead with his invasion is important to us, and so it would be best that you get Henry's permission. Charm the king while you are there. Make him think this invasion is a good idea. Strongbow is a strangely pious man. Though he says he will go, he might change his mind if he thinks leaving these shores breaks one of his precious vows."

"And what will you do while I'm away? What plots are you working on?"

"No plots. I shall merely listen to what is being said so that when you return, you will know every plan that has entered Strongbow's head, and together we will figure out what to do."

I stared at my mother. She had always been manipulative. Knew the right honey to pour in the right ear, and I'd played the part of pauper for so long, a stint at Henry's court intrigued me, and yet, the knot of suspicion had not receded. What if she was lying? What if she used the time I was away to poison Strongbow against me?

"You doubt me?" she whispered. "I understand you so well I can see your thoughts as they pass through your mind, but think on this: if I wanted to truly undermine you, I would have married Strongbow, not David."

This was true. If Mother had wanted more power, surely Strongbow would have been her target. Perhaps Le Gros or one of the FitzStephens. Not a lowly bastard-born knight.

She stood then and held out her hand. "Do we have an accord?"

Taking her hand, I kissed it. "Yes. I will do as you ask."

"Good. I am glad we are friends, Donnchad. United in common cause and working together to retake Ireland. No more knives in my stomach. No more betrayals. Promise?"

"Promise."

I smiled at her as she walked away, deciding I would go to visit King Henry as Strongbow had asked. Mother was right, it would be advantageous to see who Strongbow's master was.

But did I truly believe her reasoning? Did I believe that she no longer schemed for herself?

I was still torn. She could be planning something… though there was so much truth in her words I found it hard to understand what that might be. And yet… if it was all lies… sooner or later she would come unstuck. She seemed to always forget how much she'd needed Máelmórda to get her out of her scrapes. He wasn't here now. I was.

Yes, I was sure of it. The next time we spoke, it would either be her relaying messages from Strongbow as she had promised, or else she would be begging for help, tangled up in a web of her own making.

To know which it was to be, all I needed was patience.

And as everyone knew, patience was a virtue, and perhaps the only one I had.

Cuan

Dúnmór

"Diarmait is a reckless bastard, that's what he is," Conchobar seethed. "An oath-breaker who has brought a foreign army onto our shores. They'll turn on him. He must know that. He must."

The men sitting along the table murmured their agreement. None of them were quite as fiery as Conchobar, though their hatred for Diarmait was still plain to see.

My uncle had called a dawn meeting in the feasting hall, which perhaps accounted for why everyone was so subdued. It was either that or the small number, for my uncle had not invited many to muse over how he should deal with the wayward King of Leinster. Only six. Cathal and Conchobar, who sat to Ruaidrí's right. Eoghan and Tóla, Ruaidrí's chief warrior and his brehon, sat to his left. Fearghus sat beside me, the two of us on a bench that ran along the opposite side of the table to the others.

The list of Diarmait's crimes had been recounted already, mostly by Tóla. From the abduction of Derbhfhorgaill Ua Ruairc to his riding out to Dublin with his Anglo-Norman knights and demanding Asculv's vows, his crimes were great indeed. My imprisonment, to my amusement, had not been mentioned.

"What shall we do with him, is the question?" King Ruaidrí leaned back in his chair, his fingers tapping the wooden arms. "His time as King of Leinster is over, we know that, but how do we go about it? When I ousted him last time, he travelled to England, met with King Henry, and then recruited these knights."

"We go to battle with him. That's what." Fearghus slammed his fist against the table. I raised my eyebrows at this, for he had hardly spoken the whole meeting.

"I agree." Conchobar's cheeks flushed. "Diarmait rode out to Dublin with his army only a matter of weeks after he swore obedience to you. We should go to war, and before we leave, kill his hostages and send Diarmait their heads."

Ruaidrí pressed his lips together, deep in thought.

"We should not do that," I countered.

Conchobar rolled his eyes.

"Connor is the only legitimate heir Leinster has now," I said. "To kill him would be folly. However, I do agree we should go to battle. We should do this now. No vows this time. Only war. When Diarmait submits, send him to one of the monasteries in Connacht where the monks can keep an eye on him. Then have Connor crowned king and married to Róisín. That way, Leinster falls under your sway once again, uncle, and the Anglo-Normans can go home, tail between their legs."

"That sounds like wisdom, except you forget one thing," Ruaidrí answered. "The winter is hardening, and to fight in the ice and frost is a death wish. I will lose my own men this way, and I will not risk that."

"Then we will fight in the spring," Conchobar said. "Wait until the frosts thaw, then ride to Leinster. Let's give ourselves the winter to prepare and gather up the clans."

"And what if Diarmait strikes before we do?" I asked. "Then we will be on the back foot. And what if more Anglo-Normans decide to come over? It's best to destroy them now before their numbers grow. Show them, before they gather a fleet and an army of a significant size, that there is nothing for them here."

Tóla pressed his lips together. He knew I was right but was too scared to say so. Eoghan was scared to speak too. Scared of being blamed lest they declare for a plan that later failed.

Fearghus was the first to shake his head. "Conchobar is right. We should fight in the spring when we are prepared and have more men. With the full might of Connacht, Munster, Ulaid, Bréifne and the Northern Ó'Neills with us, we'll have the numbers to shatter theirs. We must trust in that."

"Yes." Ruaidrí nodded. "That is the correct path. I'll tell the kings who have sworn their oaths to me to gather here for the spring equinox. When they come, we will have thousands. Tens of thousands of men, and we will flatten whatever army Diarmait is able to cobble together. Conchobar, see that done. Have messengers leave this afternoon."

Conchobar smiled, glad that Ruaidrí had chosen his plan, and walked toward the doors.

"Tell the women to bring the food in, too," Fearghus called after him. "It's time for breakfast."

Once Conchobar left, the serving women came in with platters of food, while the others who lived within the dun entered. Róisín and Queen Gráinne came in first. The hostages from Leinster followed, and they sat alongside the hostages Ruaidrí had taken from South Munster and Ulaid.

What an array my uncle had collected over the last two years. It meant that inside the feasting hall, when the warriors were guarding the dun, there were more hostages than Ó Conchúirs. They were not allowed to carry weapons, of course, but even so, if they had a mind to unite against us, they could.

I found it sad that so many sons and grandsons were required to hold these Irish kings to their word. There should be no need for young men's lives to hang upon the word of their fathers, uncles and grandfathers. So easily their lives could be forfeit, as Conchobar had proven this morning. So quick had he been to suggest cutting off the heads of the Leinster boys.

I looked over at these hostages for a while, one a son, one a grandson, and the other a foster-nephew of the man who had tried to kill me. Diarmait's son, Connor, picked at his food. He didn't look much like his father or his half-brother Domhnall, which was good. When I closed my eyes, I could see both watching me as I was tied to the post at Ferns, laughing as a sharp knife was heated over the cooking fire. Connor's face didn't inspire any dread inside of me; no ghosts whispered in my ear. He was close to manhood, fifteen or sixteen, but there was something quite childish about the way he acted. Perhaps it was that he was so quiet, or perhaps it was the way he stared at Róisín with such obvious fascination.

"Morning, Connor," Abbán said as he sat down. "How are you today?" Abbán was a nephew to King Odhrán of North Munster, and like all the men of Munster, he had the confidence of a cockerel.

"I'm well, and yourself, Abbán?" Connor replied.

"Oh, I am as lonesome as the dawn, for I have no princess to smile at me and keep me company."

Abbán, who was of an age with me, nudged Connor with his elbow, which produced a shy smile from Connor. "Don't worry, I'm only teasing. I'm jealous, is all."

Abbán of course referred to the marriage pact between Connor and Róisín, which I guessed was common knowledge now. The children of two enemies had been brought together to do what their parents could not, for redemption and forgiveness were sometimes gifts that the next generation could provide. Curious, I watched them. *Surely this plan would fail.* Surely hatred and revenge festered in this boy's heart if he was anything like his father, and yet this appeared not to be true. When he spoke, he was kind. When he looked at Róisín, there was no reluctance or sullen politeness. The other Leinster hostages, Caomhán and Olcán, kept more to themselves and cast dark looks at the Connacht warriors in the feasting hall from time to time. I understood this. They were strangers. Worse than strangers, they were kin to Diarmait Mac Murchadha, and everyone in this dun hated him. But Connor did not join in with them.

Was it an act?

I kept watching, hoping to find out. Róisín was taken with him. I could see that from the way she glanced at him when she thought he wasn't looking at her.

"Would you like more to eat?" Róisín asked him when the serving women set some new plates of food on the table. She smiled as she said this, her eyes hopeful that he might say yes.

"No, thank you. I'm too full, but the venison was very good." The edges of Connor's lips curled upward a little.

"Do you want to ride out with me and my mother to see the abbey at Cong?" Róisín asked next. "My father has added some new buildings to it. We can stay at one of the other duns or even a bruidean overnight, and then we'll be able to spend the whole day there tomorrow."

The young prince nodded his head, his smile growing.

"Abbán, would you like to come to Cong?" Róisín asked.

"You know me, princess," Abbán said, leaning back in his chair and running a hand through his long curly hair. "I love nothing more than a good tour of an abbey."

This made Róisín laugh, though she was wise enough to smother it before Gráinne heard.

"If I could be so bold as to ask, may I accompany you?"

Brother Angelo, who had been sitting at another table with Meallán, stood and stepped a little closer. "Forgive my asking out of turn, but I've already heard much about Cong Abbey and would like to see it with my own eyes."

Queen Gráinne clapped her hands together. "Of course, Brother Angelo. We should enjoy your company very much, and I would love to hear your thoughts on the new construction. I'm sure the holy buildings in Rome are much finer, but I hope you'll find Cong to your liking."

"I'm sure I will, Queen Gráinne."

"What a fine idea, Gráinne," Ruaidrí said as he ate the last of his stewed salmon. "Why don't we all go? A last trip out before the winter takes hold."

My uncle's eagerness to impress this monk was understandable. The monks and priests from other countries rarely had nice things to say of the Irish, for I'd heard what was said about us when I lived with my uncle Godred. *Like beasts, we were. Lazy. Savage. Lustful.*

They didn't understand why we divorced or why many of the kings had more than one wife. Christian doctrine had not overtaken the Brehon laws the way it had superseded the old legal systems in the rest of Christendom, and it drew much criticism from those who visited.

Uncle Ruaidrí appeared to want to rectify this reputation. He wanted Brother Angelo to see that these old ways aside, we were a kingdom of honour, of courage, and followers of Christ. A new abbey was the perfect way to showcase this.

"What about you, Cuan? Do you wish to come with us?" Brother Angelo asked, turning his attention to me. "Perhaps after the hardships *you* endured, you would enjoy the comfort our Lord has to offer?"

I lowered my gaze, thinking on how to politely say no.

"Thank you, Brother Angelo, I—"

"Cuan, your eye!" Róisín shouted, her finger pointing at my face. "All the blood has gone from it."

"Has it?"

"And your scar has healed too." She gestured to the skin below her lips, to where the original cut had severed my muscles.

I shrugged as if I hadn't noticed.

"Oh, yes," Queen Gráinne said. "Now that you've pointed it out, there is a big difference from before."

"It seems you had a restful time at King Diarmait's," Conchobar said. He had just come back into the hall and sat down on the wooden chair by the fire. *My grandfather's old chair*. "Why, you've come back to us in better condition than you left. Perhaps I should ask to be King Diarmait's hostage next, then I too will return home with all my ailments gone."

"Scars heal over time," I said. "That is all." I tried to keep the annoyance out of my voice, but I could hear it there all the same. Scars healed. Bodies healed. Everyone knew this. There was no need for me to worry. They couldn't know that Isolde had healed me. They wouldn't even believe it if I told them.

"So, what happened? The truth now." Conchobar leaned forward and stared at me, not smirking this time, but frowning.

"I told you the truth. Whether you believe it or not has nothing to do with me."

"Oh, but it *is* to do with me. Traitors and spies are not welcome here." He glanced at Brother Angelo and gave a gracious nod. "I do not question your story, Brother Angelo. No doubt King Diarmait and Cuan planned the whole escape and set a ráth on fire to give their plot some credibility."

Before Brother Angelo could answer, I stood. "You think I am a spy? Really, Conchobar?"

"Yes."

"And what do you think I'd be finding out here that I don't already know?" I gave him a small smile, trying to keep the conversation light, but failing to do so. My uncle had not yet interrupted him, which meant he wanted to hear my answer too. "What I'll tell you is this. When I was in Dublin, King Diarmait asked for me to be given to him. Asculv agreed. When I heard of this request, I escaped through the monk's gate by the river, but Domhnall and his men pursued me and beat me until I could no longer stand. I was then taken to Ferns and tied to a post where I was told they would take my eyes and give me the blood eagle. Why would I spy for that man? Why would I spy for a man who has sworn a blood feud upon me?"

Conchobar shrugged, his smirk growing. "You don't look like a man who was beaten until he couldn't stand."

My temper flared inside me. I could feel it, the heat rushing to my face. *You are nothing. Nobody. You are nothing. Control yourself. You are nothing.*

"It is a miracle."

Everyone in the feasting hall turned to stare at Brother Angelo.

"When I first met Cuan, he had blood in his eye, as you said. He was sleeping by a tree, weary from his escape. When Meallán and I approached him, he thought we were thieves and rode away, but on seeing that Meallán had suffered so much, he returned and gave Meallán his food and built us a warm fire. Wolves howled in the distance, and he kept them away from us."

"This is true," Meallán said, coming forward to stand beside

Brother Angelo. "Cuan came back and showed me how to keep the fire going. He let me ride on his horse when I was tired, too."

Brother Angelo smiled at the young boy. "When we travelled the next day, it was then that I realised that Cuan looked revived. Stronger. His wounds seemed to fade away before my eyes. I knew then it was a blessing from God. A reward for showing pity to the poor. A miracle. That was why I followed him here."

Blushing at this depiction of my generosity, I lowered my gaze. Confusion filled me too. Brother Angelo had not seen any blood in my eye. Why then had he lied? Was it merely gratitude? Or did he, like so many others, want something from me?

"I don't know about miracles," Connor said. I turned to find the young Prince of Leinster staring at me. "But I know my father. He has a blood feud with Cuan and has vowed to kill him. Everyone in Leinster knows this. There is no way he would make a pact with him and allow him to escape. That is not my father's way."

Surprised that the prince had spoken for me as well as Brother Angelo, I remained silent.

It was Tóla who spoke first. "You are to be commended, Cuan. Not just for following the teachings of God, but for being a true member of the king's fianna. If God has blessed you with a miracle as Brother Angelo has said, we should be grateful that He has seen us and deemed you worthy of His Grace."

King Ruaidrí smiled and clapped his hands. "Then off to Cong Abbey we go. We must thank God that he returned Cuan to us and also brought Brother Angelo and Meallán to our dun. Now, let's try to be quick, otherwise we won't make it to the bruidean before dark."

While the others got ready, I calmed myself by walking around the dun. Conchobar had caused an anger to rise inside me that I thought I'd already subdued. The fact he so easily riled me up meant I had more work to do.

Familiarising myself with my surroundings was the first step.

I needed to discard the memories associated with them. To see wood and straw rather than the home of my childhood. I went to the stables first. Memories of my father holding me by the legs struck a pain in my heart for a moment. That was wrong. I had to push that out of my mind. It was only a stable. Nothing special. Just wood and thatch. The same way that the old chair in the feasting hall that my grandfather had used to sit upon was just a chair.

Before his death, I was destined to be a prince. Now I was nobody. Nothing. I had to remember that. If I was nothing, then I would feel nothing... and the fire would stay away.

"Visitors," one of the guards called. "Musicians. Two horses."

The stable boys ran out to take the horses from our guests, looking a little more excited than if it were a visiting king or queen. But of course, music was for everyone. Even the stable boys were allowed in the feasting hall when musicians played in the king's dun.

The other stable boys were working to ready the horses for our visit to Cong Abbey. Sleipnir had already been saddled and snorted as he saw me, then walked over to the wooden gate so I could stroke his nose. He might still be tired from our last journey, but the trip to Cong would not be so bad. A day's walking, a day's rest while we visited the abbey, and then a day's walk home.

"That is a beautiful horse."

A man with a long white beard came into the stable. He wore a patched cloak and thick boots lined with fur.

"Thank you," I replied.

The man came over and stroked Sleipnir's nose. "Though I hear I've come at a bad time. The king is leaving for Cong Abbey. I doubt I'll have the pleasure of playing for him tonight."

"Ah, well, I don't think we'll be away too long."

The old man's hand moved along the side of Sleipnir's neck. "I suppose tis no bad thing to have a night of rest. The winter is already upon us, and my bones ache more and more in the cold with every year that passes."

He smiled and moved his hand closer to mine. A piece of

parchment appeared from between two fingers, and he held his hand still as I took it from him.

"Good boy," he said, still talking to Sleipnir in a slow, soothing voice as he patted his nose. "There now, I'd better be off. The smell of food is calling."

He walked away, back out to the other musicians, who together made their way into the feasting hall.

Quickly, I opened the parchment. It was my father's hand.

My son, the time approaches when we will make our move. Until then, remember what I told you; Ruaidrí must believe you are loyal to him. A knife can only twist in flesh that is warm.

I quickly scrunched the parchment in my hand and walked outside to the fires. Leaning closer as if to warm my hands, I threw it onto the flames and watched as it burned. I could feel my heart thudding against my chest again. Could feel my anger and rage rising.

Not for the first time, I felt that betraying Ruaidrí was not what I wanted to do anymore. When I was with Isolde, I had so desperately wanted to take her away with me. Perhaps to the Isles, but maybe not even there. Somewhere we could be safe and away from all of this.

This time my reluctance sprang from my own feelings. Talk of twisting knives did not feel as good as it used to. Ruaidrí, yes, I was happy for him to suffer, but not his wife or daughter. Not the Kingdom of Connacht, which was heading toward war, and which would be weakened by the loss of its king.

I took a breath by the fire. As I did so, I glanced at the house where I used to live. Memories flooded my mind against my will. I could almost imagine my mother walking out the door. As her tall silhouette formed in my mind, a shadow appeared. My mind played a trick on me, and I thought I saw her, the silver orbs shining in her hair. But the image faded, and in its place stood my cousin Conchobar.

He stared at me, face sullen. "This is my house now."

"I see."

Another burst of rage came over me, though I was quick to push it down this time. *The house was just a house. Just like my grandfather's chair was just a chair.*

"I don't believe you, you know," Conchobar said as he walked over to me. "I know you are up to something. You see, I hear things. Hear whispers. Your father visited you in Dublin is what I heard. What does that blind fool want with you?"

I was tempted to deny it, but I had to be careful. I had lied so much on my return that I couldn't afford to be found out on something like this. "What does any father want with his son? Simply to ask after my health."

"You aren't allowed to see him."

This was true. I wasn't. It was why I had gone to so much trouble in Dublin to meet him in secret, though apparently that had not been as successful as I had hoped. My eyes moved to the fire, watching for traces of the parchment burning there. What would Conchobar say if he knew that not only had I met my father, but that he was sending me messages and plotting his father's downfall?

"It wasn't my choice, Conchobar. It wasn't even my choice to go to Dublin. Your father sent me there to deliver a message to my uncle Godred. My father simply happened to be close by, and once he realised I was there, he came to me."

"That's irrelevant. My father has commanded that you are not to meet with him, and as a member of his fianna, you must obey him."

"What you say is true, and I will tell my uncle of my father's appearance in Dublin when we next speak. To be honest, I had not thought of it since. So much has happened."

Conchobar clicked his tongue. "See that you do. And remember, I'm watching you. Everyone else here might buy that monk's story, but I don't. A miracle. For you? You're the last person who'd ever deserve such a thing. And as for being held prisoner by Diarmait and escaping, I've heard more convincing lies from our slaves when they pretend not to have drunk my father's wine."

Conchobar pushed past me and walked over to the stables.

I took a deep breath and pushed down my emotions. I did not like Conchobar, but I could not fault him. I *was* keeping secrets from my uncle, and my healing was no miracle.

Most of all, he was right not to trust me.

All those earlier misgivings regarding my plan to betray Ruaidrí, I pushed aside now.

I had made a vow to avenge my father, and it would be done. This meant that very soon my uncle would be dead, and it would be my doing. No, I could not fault Conchobar for his distrust of me.

I was only welcomed into the dun because of my name, Cuan Ó Conchúir, and custom dictated that they could not turn me away.

But the truth was, I was nothing. Nobody.

And now, I was a traitor.

Gormflaith

Chepstow

The walls were high. Stone. The sky above was black, clouds half obscuring the stars and moon. Even though it was night, men still walked about. Some were in armour, though others wore silks and furs.

At the edge of the dun, the people knelt, and a monk wearing a brown robe with a hood covering his face, spoke words of Christ to them. An early morning mass, perhaps. A call to prayer before the dawn.

"Beloved, never avenge yourselves, but leave it to the wrath of God, for it is written, 'Vengeance is mine, I will repay,' says the Lord." The monk held his hands wide as if trying to embrace his growing congregation from afar.

The people on their knees made the sign of the cross, but I could not see an Anglo-Norman among them. Where had my dream taken me? I had wanted to find Angelo, but I could not see him. Was this Carrig? Initially, I had assumed yes, for the Anglo-Normans were pious enough to hold nighttime prayers, but now that I had inspected my surroundings more closely, I realised it could not be. The walls were both too high and too well made for this to be a new fortress.

But if not Carrig, where?

In my dream, I moved behind the crowd of people praying, searching for my grandson. Still, I couldn't see him. My witch-magic, the magic that allowed me to travel in my dreams, should have brought me to him, and yet, he wasn't here.

"The Lord is not slow to fulfil his promise as some count slowness,"

the monk said, his voice rising, "but is patient toward you, not wishing that any should perish, but that all should reach repentance."

Once again, the crowd murmured their agreement or else asked for forgiveness, but their words blurred. The colours around them turned darker… which meant I was waking. Desperately, I tried to hold myself within the dream; to move past the haze, but alas, the people before me faded to nothing, with Angelo still nowhere to be found.

When I woke, frustration flooded through me. What had Donnchad been thinking, leaving Angelo in Ireland? Mute and odd, he would not do well alone, and it frightened me that I could not find him. *Had he been hiding?* Too scared to be among the other men and women who knelt before the monk. Angelo was clever, yes, I could see that in him, but he was not quite of this world either. And what about the Descendants? I'd had no dreams of them and Donnchad swore they were all dead, but what if one still lived? What if they had found Angelo?

By all the gods, I had to find him and find him quickly.

An idea quickly formed in my mind, and I dressed in all haste. If my dreams couldn't locate him, Olaf would. He was becoming agitated locked up in his cage anyway, even more since I had married David. This would give him something to do as well as set my mind at ease.

Skipping down the stairs toward the falconry, I halted just before I reached the courtyard. Voices drifted in the air, and when I peered around the corner, I found a group of men had already gathered by the falconry and were readying their birds. I recognised them all. Le Gros. Miles and Maurice. Leaning against the wall, I pressed my body tight against the cold stone.

"FitzStephen has sent another letter," Maurice said.

"Oh?" Le Gros murmured as he petted his falcon. "What does it say?"

"King Diarmait has asked them to join him in another battle. They are going to Munster this time. Fighting for Diarmait's son-in-law, a King Odhrán, against one of the other Munster kings. Odhrán wants to retake the city of Limerick, and Diarmait means to use this as an opportunity to lure King Ruaidrí out of his dun. Unbeknown to the High King, a trap awaits his army."

Le Gros snorted. "This King Diarmait is a sleekit man, but I suppose he may as well use FitzStephen while he can. Once Strongbow lands in Ireland, it will not be so easy for Diarmait to use our knights."

"You aren't afraid that this will lead to FitzStephen gaining more land, while we are all still here, waiting, and with nothing to show for it?" Maurice's words were sharper now. Fearful. Jealous.

Miles grunted. "I must confess, this worries me too. I thought I was returning to Wales to gather up an army. It disturbs me that Strongbow is delaying until late next year. If we leave it too long, FitzStephen will be King of Ireland, mark my words."

"What say you, Le Gros?" Miles stood beside him, watching Ranulf take the birds out of the cages for them. "You've been asked to make up an advance party. What exactly has Strongbow said about that?"

Le Gros stroked his falcon, unruffled by the serious tone in Miles' voice. "We are to set out in the spring. We are to be a small enough group that Strongbow can say to King Henry that we went of our own accord."

"That will be dangerous," Miles answered. "Not quite what he promised at the feast when we returned."

"It will be dangerous, yes." Le Gros pulled the hood from his peregrine falcon and gave him a bloody cut of meat. "Whoever decides to go could lose their heads, for Strongbow might have to punish those guilty of *disobeying him* to placate the king. Henry could also order it done himself if he was to hear about our exploits during one of his dark moods."

"If the king is unhappy," Maurice said, "his wrath will be great indeed."

A hush fell over the group as they contemplated this. *How curious.* I knew little of this King Henry that Donnchad was on his way to visit, but it was interesting that the men spoke of him with such reverence... such fear. I had wanted Donnchad out of the way, but perhaps fate had worked with me for once and given truth to the words that I had fabricated to make him go. A king that men feared was worth watching. Donnchad was arrogant and vain, and no doubt many of these lessons would be lost on him, but they would not be lost on me.

Miles sighed as he furtively glanced at the castle. "Is that why you have brought William Ferrand here? If he were to be part of this early expedition, I suppose even the king would find it hard to order his execution given his renown."

"Ah, Miles," Le Gros gave a low and rasping laugh, "you play the virtuous man, but truly you are as corrupt as the rest of us."

"I'm not as corrupt as you."

"How then do you know what I've been plotting?"

Miles seemed set to deny this assault on his character but then paused a moment, his expression moving from indignation to stillness. "I must say, I enjoyed my time in Ireland. It is wild there, Le Gros. How I imagine Chepstow was before William the Conqueror came to this land. Even wilder, perhaps. I tell you it is there for the taking, and it worries me that after everything I've done, Strongbow may decide not to go."

"I think..." Le Gros began. "No, I *believe* Strongbow will go."

"Are you willing to gamble everything on that?"

"Obviously not, otherwise I would not have volunteered to lead this early excursion. I've put my head on the block now, haven't I?"

"What is your plan once you reach Ireland?"

"I will land close to Wexford. I suspect FitzStephen could do with more men to bolster his numbers. Donn said he's building a fort at the Hill of Carrig, close to the city. We will be safe there and can plan out what to do next."

"That is sound," Miles agreed. "You can see for yourself what Robert is up to."

Maurice agreed too, and then Ranulf appeared with the final bird, and their conversation moved back to falconry and where they would fly the birds.

I lingered by the wall, going over their words. *Ah, curse these men with so little imagination.* How could Le Gros not see that sailing straight to Robert FitzStephen would only place him beneath him in status? More to the point, Wexford and the land around it had already been pledged to FitzStephen and Hervey. Le Gros would be better sailing somewhere else and laying claim to that land instead.

But *I* couldn't say this to Le Gros.

It would be too forward, too violent for a woman to contemplate war and death. I knew these Normans well enough by now. David had shown little aptitude for politicking so far, but perhaps now was the time to see if he could be swayed. If the message came from him, a man and kinsman, it might go down well with Le Gros.

Resolving to speak to David later, I walked around the corner and pretended to be surprised to see the men gathered there. "You are taking your birds out too?" I asked no one in particular.

"Yes." Le Gros was the one who answered and held up his bird that was perched upon his gauntlet. "Are you going to join us?"

"No, not today." I gave the group of men a timid smile. "I'm training Olaf. I won't be venturing too far away from the castle."

Moving away from the men, for I didn't want them to think I craved their company, I walked into Olaf's cage.

"Olaf. I'm going to take you out to fly today. You'll like that, won't you?" Petting him, I gathered the leather gauntlet for my arm and set some pieces of meat into a pouch.

Old Ranulf chuckled. He was watching me now that the others had left. "You speak to that bird as if he's your child."

"Perhaps he is."

"Not for long. David will have a pup in your belly before long, and then poor Olaf will be left to pine in that cage for you, only you will never come."

"What careless women you must have known before me, Ranulf. Can a woman not love more than one thing at the same time?"

"Only a fickle one, and a sensible man should avoid them at all costs."

"Harsh words, Ranulf, and to think I thought you were my friend."

Ranulf laughed again as I took Olaf out of the cage. "I'm only going down to the river. I'll be back later."

Already tidying the hawks' cage, he grunted as I left the falconry and waved goodbye.

Past the river and deep in the woods, I transformed Olaf. First, to a man. Old, scarred, dishevelled and reeking of bird. Next, I reached out with my witch gift and made him look as he had as a young man. I preferred him this way, could just about stomach the pleading and unfettered desire when he looked as he had when I had once desired him.

"I need you to help me, Olaf."

Olaf, who had been ready to beg for me to be with him, closed his mouth. He wanted me to need his help. This pleased him.

"What do you need, Gormflaith? I'll do anything for you. Anything."

"To further my plan, we must go to Ireland soon. David does not want me to go, but don't worry, I will convince him."

"How can he stop you?"

"He's my husband now."

"You married him?" Olaf put his head in his hands. "Why? Why would you do such a thing?"

"You know I had to. It is how we survive. And I've told you my plan. It is to return to Ireland. To be queen. You promised to help me, or are you already planning treachery as you did once before?"

Olaf fell to his knees. "I will never betray you, Gormflaith. You know I'd rather cut out my own heart than hurt you."

"Then enough of making me feel guilty. I don't intend to stay married to David for long. He is a stepping stone, that is all. I told you when we last lay with each other that it's you I want by my side. Only you."

I ran my finger over the coils of the snake that was tattooed on his arm. Tracing the lines around his forearm, then his wrist. His eyes, wet with lust, watched my finger. I allowed him to kiss me on the cheek. I don't know why other than I valued him at this moment. David was like a pup, enthusiastic but in want of training. Donnchad was full of schemes, few of which were to my benefit. Cecile was useless. Angelo wasn't here. That meant Olaf was the only person I could rely on.

It was the love potion that I had given him all those years ago that held him tight to me, but if anything, this only allowed me to trust him even more. No one he had loved was still alive, thus there was no way the spell could ever be broken. There was something comforting today about this unbreakable devotion.

"Will you help me, Olaf? Help me as you promised when last we lay with each other?"

He nodded.

"Then find Angelo. Donnchad said he agreed to stay in the Carrig fort close to Wexford, but I do not believe it, for I cannot see him in my dreams. Do not return to me until you've found him." I held out my hand, and slowly the serpent wrapped around his wrist faded and turned to feathers.

My mission accomplished, I returned home. Tears wet my face as I told Ranulf that Olaf had flown away and not returned.

He consoled me, told me that Olaf might return in a few days once he got hungry, which moved me to a fresh wave of tears, and I ran to David's room.

My husband was there when I entered and moved toward me with alarm once he saw that tears wetted my cheeks.

"What is wrong, my love?" he asked.

"Olaf flew away."

David pulled me into a hug, though I knew he was delighted with this outcome. He had never liked me working in the falconry, and as soon as we married, my working there stopped. I was married to a knight now. Bastard-born, yes, but a knight, nonetheless, and nephew to the famous Le Gros. I spoke with the other ladies during the daylight hours instead, playing the part of devoted wife and joyful bride. I embroidered, recited poetry and listened to them singing.

On occasion, when the boredom became too much, I would go to the falconry. Not to work, but to check on Olaf. It was infrequent, for it was not ladylike to fly birds the way the men did, and David found it curious that I would prefer this pastime to being with the ladies of Strongbow's household where there was an endless supply of sweet apple cakes and all sorts of musicians to entertain us.

"Do not worry, Alys. When you found him, he was injured. Now he's flying in the sky, hunting and happy, I am sure."

I nodded, wiping my nose with a handkerchief.

"I'm sure very soon you will have other things to occupy your mind."

"Like?"

"A baby."

I set down the handkerchief and gave my husband a small smile. *Talk of babies already?* I had hoped the thought of bedding me would occupy his mind a little longer. The smile he returned was shy, but full of hope.

It was a shame that I did not want to give him a child. He would have made a good father. Patient and kind, I could see him holding a babe in his arms and teaching him to ride a horse and shoot with a bow.

A younger Gormflaith might have pandered to such notions, but no longer. My own plans were all I could think of. Isolde was dead, and the threat from the Descendants was at an end. Donnchad was out of the way too, which meant it was time for me to return to Ireland. The advance in the spring, I had to be a part of it, and so keeping in David's good graces was key, but a child in my belly would only ensure I was left behind.

"A baby? Are you sure you want one, David? It will take my attention away from you."

"Not a bit. We'll be a family."

"A family is a beautiful thing if it is provided for." I lay back on the bed and smiled at my husband. "How do you plan to provide for us?"

"I fight for my uncle," he replied, his smile fading. I was testing him, and no man liked to be tested by their new bride.

"That is all well and good, but opportunities are on the horizon. Land in Ireland is on offer. Should you not wish to have your own land? Your own wealth?"

"Alys, if I am fighting for Le Gros, any land that is won will be his."

"What if you were to fight under your own banner? I tell you, there is plenty of land in Ireland. I could help you. The language is—"

"Alys." David said my name. Not snapping, but sharp. "How about you leave the advance into Ireland to me? You don't have to worry about me providing for you. Le Gros is my uncle. His success will reap rewards enough."

I smiled again, knowing I had pushed him far enough, but this continued lack of ambition might become a problem. How could I convince him to take me to Ireland if he had no desire for power?

"Now come here," David said, falling onto the bed beside me. "Let me have you one more time before I go out to train."

I complied. Giggled. Removed his clothing. For now, that was all I could do. We had several months over the winter during which I could persuade him, and I always got what I wanted when it came to men. I wasn't about to start failing now.

Isolde

Seir Kieran

I fell to my knees.

My stomach throbbed, and as I looked down, blood poured from the open wound there.

All around me were the ruins of a great building. The walls of the inner houses were burning still, the thatch and wood scattered over the ground. I recognised the gate and the gardens behind it this time. Seir Kieran. Yes, I was certain. It was the monastery that burned, the out-houses and stables too.

I looked to my side, wiping the black liquid running from my mouth. The foul taste clung to the back of my throat, and I tried to spit it out, though to no avail. That's when I saw the dead body lying beside me. I inched closer, dragging my body with my arms. Pushing her hair away, I revealed a face. Báine. I looked over at the other bodies this time. Siobhan and Méabh were lying by what was left of the garden fence, holding hands, as if they'd been shielding the mortals behind them.

"You did this."

Lying on the grass beside me was Colmon. A sword pierced his chest and blood seeped from his body onto the grass.

"No… No, Colmon. How could I do this?" Crawling over to him, I placed one hand over my wound so that I could move. I expected more blood to pour from my stomach, but none came. Oh yes, I had all the gifts, so of course the wound was gone. I had healed myself. Perhaps that was why I was shaking so hard. But perhaps not. Colmon had

told me this was my fault, which meant I had done something wrong. Something else. Something I could not yet comprehend.

As I turned to Colmon, I tentatively reached for the sword that protruded from him. The handle was made of silver with a spiral gold engraving, while the blade itself was wide and sharp. It had pierced him through, and I paused as I thought how best to remove it. Fast and straight. Back out the way it had gone in. *Then I could heal him. Slowly, I tightened my grip around the handle.*

"It is too late for me," Colmon said, pressing his hand over mine. "But you must take the sword. Hide it. Don't let them find it."

"I don't understand," I sobbed. "Who did this to us?"

"You. It is you who did this, Isolde. Look at the dead lying on the grass. It is all you. I told you that you must learn to control your gift. You tried, but not hard enough."

"I'm sorry, Colmon. Please let me save you. Please let me try."

He shook his head as tears fell down his cheeks. "It is over, Isolde. Your strength has left you, and we have failed. They will come for you now. You should run. Take the sword, though. Promise me you won't let them have it."

I wiped the tears spilling from my own eyes, too many to catch. "I cannot run… what if I do this again? And the sword… where can I hide such a thing?" Another thought filled me. Perhaps I should simply throw the sword in the river and then let the Fomorians kill me. If I had done this and killed everyone, what good was I being alive in this world?

Colmon closed his eyes and, as he did so, he turned his head away from me. With this final effort, his last breath left him, and I had no answer to my questions.

I collapsed beside him. Smoke filled my lungs, so did the foul stench of rotting flesh. The Fomorians were coming for me now. He was right. I could smell them everywhere.

Already another fire burned in the distance, and the monastery, rather than burning out now the wood and thatch were gone, burned even brighter. I watched as the flames danced. Something made me stay. Something anchored me to the ground, and it wasn't long before, from the smoke, a man walked toward me. I recognised him. He was the Fomorian who had attacked me and Affraic on Rathlin. The one who had entrapped us in a circle of fire.

Wearing a plain brown robe, his hair shorn short, he came closer, his eyes burning yellow and a smile upon his lips. Pressing his hands together, a ball of fire grew between them.

I woke up trembling. It was the same vision that I'd had before, but it had changed. Some of it was clearer, and this last part was new. I had known that the fire was Fomorian fire, but now I knew which Fomorian it was… and I knew the names of the dead. Báine. Méabh. Siobhan. The others lying dead in the grass were the mortals who worked at Seir Kieran. They had come here to find peace and refuge. And here I was, about to bring them death.

I needed to speak with Colmon.

Rolling out of bed, I quickly dressed and made my way to his room.

When I opened the door, Méabh was sitting on the chair beside his bed. Siobhan sat on another chair, close to the far wall, with a piece of embroidery on her lap. An image of them lying on the grass holding hands came to me, and for a moment I stepped back.

"Come in, Isolde," Siobhan said.

I did as she asked, and while Siobhan smiled, Méabh only stared.

"Colmon is sleeping," Siobhan added, her voice low.

"I need to speak with him."

"Not yet," Méabh answered. "Later."

"No," I said, finding my voice and my strength. "Now."

I returned her gaze, the power struggle between the two of us moving back and forth in silence.

"What's wrong, Isolde?" Siobhan asked. "Why do you need him?"

"Colmon told me to wake him if I had a vision."

"I'm sure he did." Méabh stood. "Nonetheless, he needs to rest, or he will be no good to you."

I wanted to tell her then that I had seen her lying dead on the grass. Perhaps then she might understand my urgency. Instead, I looked at Colmon and reached out to touch him with my hand.

"It won't work," Siobhan said. "Healers can do many wondrous things, but we cannot stop the ageing of our kind, and it is the ageing that makes him tired like this."

I let my hand hover over him, then set it down on his arm. Siobhan didn't know for sure, did she? She hadn't been able to wake him from his coma. Perhaps I could do many things she could not. "Colmon, wake up. I need you." I closed my eyes, trying harder to bring him back to wakefulness.

"Come, Isolde."

I turned to find Gisela at my side. I hadn't even heard her enter the room. Gently, she pulled my hand from Colmon's arm. "Why don't I work with you for an hour or so? Colmon needs a little more rest." She turned to Méabh. "You will come to fetch us when he wakes, won't you?"

Méabh nodded, her finger gently smoothing over the fabric of Colmon's sleeve where I had touched him.

Gisela linked her arm in mine and led me out of the room. Embarrassed, I marched quicker than she wanted to, though she quickened her pace to match mine. It was rude of me to do this, but I couldn't make myself slow down. I was too angry. Angry at whom was a harder question to answer.

The grey corridor loomed over us, and I changed direction so that we moved away from the chapel and instead walked outside to the stone courtyard. My stomach suddenly churned. Ached. Bowing over with the pain of it, I vomited a black sticky substance onto the ground.

I was not surprised by this reaction. I had tried to use my gift without understanding it – tried to wake Colmon up when Siobhan had told me it was impossible. In my vision, Colmon had chastised me for not learning to use my gift, and here I was proving him right. My anger faded, leaving behind only shame and regret.

Wiping my mouth, I glanced up at Gisela. "Sorry."

"Don't be." She rubbed my back and pulled my hair away from my face. "Visions are frightening things. Colmon will waken soon, but you must understand that when Descendants reach this stage, they become tired as their ageing progresses. Colmon's rests will become longer and more frequent."

I nodded, straightening now that the sickness had left me. The shaking would come next, and I rubbed my hands over my arms as if trying to keep it at bay.

"We do what we can to help," Gisela continued. "I sing to him sometimes to ease his sorrow. Siobhan heals cuts and bruises. But that is it."

"What about Méabh? What does she do?"

"She's his friend."

I eyed Gisela, wanting to know more about the woman who had stared at me so coldly. "They are close?"

"Yes. I do not like to gossip, but I feel there is no harm in telling you that once they were lovers."

"But not now?"

"No. Not for many years before the attack on Fennit. We all told you there would be no secrets, and so I will not lie, though I only give you my opinion in this case. I believe Colmon grew weary after so much death, and he pushed her away. Many of our kind suffer from this melancholy, but it was always the warriors and weapon-makers who suffered the most. My father-in-law was a weapon-maker called Fiachre. When he was young, his laughter filled the hall. When he was older, sorrow consumed him and he laughed no more."

"Oh."

"And…" Gisela took a deep breath. "There was always something between Colmon and your mother. Not romantic love, but a deep connection. She was his cousin, you see, and he loved her very much, more than any of his other family. Méabh was never able to understand why his heart had hardened toward her and not Fódla."

"So that's why she doesn't like me."

"She doesn't not like you, Isolde. I would say that she doesn't like that Colmon has woken only to be called to duty once again. Even in his final days, he cannot rest, and so he suffers, and she cannot bear to see it."

"I would gladly leave this place if it meant he could find peace."

"I know. She knows that too."

I felt myself on the verge of walking toward the boundary wall of the monastery. Perhaps once I got that far, I would continue walking. Wouldn't that be better? No one would die if I left. I shuddered again on remembering the vision. The only consolation was that Gisela had not been one of the dead.

"Colmon would not want you to leave, Isolde. You're his family. Do you understand that?"

I didn't like that Gisela had been able to read my mood so easily, but still I nodded. She was right.

"Don't worry about Méabh. Once you get to know each other, she will thaw." She paused then, holding her stomach. "Love, the having of it, then the losing of it is hard to bear. All of us here have lost. I know you have too. We must remember that and be kind to each other."

Gisela held out her arm, and we continued to walk. This time, we made our way toward the gardens. I peered over the wall and saw that two of the young men were pulling up the last of the crops. This was the garden that burned in my vision. Squeezing my eyes shut, I turned away from it.

"What's wrong, Isolde?"

"Nothing."

"Look, there's Leofwynn," Gisela said, "coming from the orchard."

I focused on Leofwynn, who was talking to a young man, laughing at what he had just said, but she was shy, and once she had finished laughing, she became quiet again. However, seeing her happy like this, realising that I had not seen her in my vision either, gave me an unexpected burst of joy.

"She wants to be your friend," Gisela said.

"I know."

"Do you want to speak with her?"

"I thought we were training today?"

"Yes, and this is the next step."

I looked at Gisela, not quite understanding what she meant.

"You struggled when I trained you yesterday, and I realised it's because you need to remember the feeling of laughter inside of you. It is hard to conjure emotions if you cannot remember them. That is the truth of being a harpist. That is why you so easily made the queen cry. You are filled with sorrow, Isolde."

Gisela lifted her arm in the air. "Leofwynn," she called, "I wish to speak with you!"

Leofwynn ran over to us, grinning. "Do you want a wreath?" She removed two woven circlets made of holly from her arm.

"Yes," I replied, taking it from her and examining how she had woven the leaves together. "Are they difficult to make?"

"Oh no, it is easy. You must make sure the branches are all the same length, though." Gently, she pulled apart the leaves, showing me what she meant. "I was going to bring one to Cinnia, Gisela. Do you think she would like it?"

"I'm sure she would," Gisela replied.

"Who is Cinnia?" I asked.

"She lives over the hill. Her son is sick often, isn't he, Gisela?"

"Yes."

"Can Siobhan not help him?" I asked.

Gisela raised an eyebrow at this, which made me flinch. That was right. Leofwynn was a mortal and did not know about our gifts.

"Siobhan is good with herbs, isn't she?" I added, trying to smooth over my mistake.

"Oh, yes," Leofwynn agreed. "She is teaching me all about them. Honeysuckle to cure people with yellowed skin. Watercress for bleeding gums. Buachalán for coughs and colds."

"Ah, but with this ailment, her herbs are no good," Gisela said. "This is an ailment of the mind. A melancholy that the young man cannot escape. We spoke earlier of it afflicting the old, but the young can suffer with it too. Leofwynn and I visit the family sometimes, Siobhan too, and we give them food and gifts and good company. Cinnia has two little girls too, and they both love Leofwynn. I'm sure they will enjoy these wreaths."

Leofwynn fixed the leaves, moving the red berries into a more pleasing position. "Next time we visit, I'll bring them one each. I've already prepared a basket of apples and hawthorn berries for them."

"How about I leave you two to make some more wreaths? Isolde, I'll find you once Colmon is ready."

Gisela unlinked her arm and walked away, giving me a knowing smile. Reluctantly, I smiled back. She was right. Already I felt happier in the company of Leofwynn.

"See, Isolde. I told you how wonderful it is here. Gisela and Siobhan are the best teachers I could ever wish for. I love them both dearly." Leofwynn led me over to a wooden bench, sat, and smiled as she worked. She gave me a couple of holly branches to work with, but when she wasn't weaving or helping me, I noticed her eyes roving over to the man she had spoken with earlier. He was tending to the horses now, alongside another man who was old and bowed over.

I followed her stare the next time she did this, which made her laugh.

"What do you think of him?" Leofwynn asked.

"Which one?"

"What do you mean, which one?" She gave me a look of disgust. "There is only one worth looking at unless you like men older than your great-grandfather."

Glancing to the side, I examined the man in question. He was handsome, and the way Leofwynn stared at him reminded me of the young princesses at King Tigernán's dun who peered out the door to stare at Cuan and Cathal.

"What do you mean, what do I think of him?" I teased, knowing exactly what she meant.

"I mean… do you think he is handsome? His name is Aznar. Haven't you noticed him before?"

"I've seen him once or twice but never thought about him in that way. I suppose he is."

Leofwynn blushed. "I think he is. Do you think he's ever noticed me?"

"I'm sure he has. Why don't you speak with him again?"

Leofwynn shrugged as she gave him one more fleeting look, then stared back at the holly in her basket. "I haven't decided myself yet what I want. There's no point in speaking to him until then."

Now this I didn't quite understand, and looking at the frown working on Leofwynn's face, I didn't think she understood it either. "When you say you haven't decided on what you want, what are the options?"

Leofwynn glanced up at Aznar again. "Marry him. Have his children. Grow old with him and them around me. It was the life my grandmother had, and her mother before her."

"That's a good option."

"It's a hopeful option. I am not sure if it can happen for me though."

"Why do you say that?"

"I've been helping Siobhan and Gisela tend to many families that live around the monastery. There is one woman, Teafa, who we help. Her first husband used to argue with her all the time, and then he divorced her. After this, she married another man. Teafa had six children with him, but two of them died young, and then her second husband died too. She's always sad. She tries to hide it, but I can see it. I think this is perhaps the truth of marriage and bearing children. Loss and grief and strife. I don't know whether I want that. Also… it was my mother who sold me to the slavers. When I was younger, I was so angry, but now I see that she must have been desperate. I cannot bear to think of having to do that."

Reaching out with my gift just as Gisela had taught me, I could feel a deep grief inside of Leofwynn. Anxiety too. Frustration. I could try to take these feelings away. I could make her see more joy, less sorrow. Perhaps then she would speak to the young man, and her imagined vision of happiness would have a chance to flourish, but it would be wrong of me to do so. She had to make up her own mind. It was not my place to meddle in the thoughts and desires of others.

"What's the second option?" I asked. "If not a family, what else do you want?"

"I could stay here and let Siobhan train me in the use of herbs. Help people who suffer. To continue to be the person who visits those in need and lessens the burdens of sickness and fatigue."

"Do you think that would fulfil you?"

"Yes." Leofwynn looked more certain when she said this, her chin firm. But then she pulled me closer so that her lips were almost touching my shoulder. "It is only when I lie down to sleep that sometimes I feel lonely… but then I think that will pass. That I will not always feel this. What do you think? Are you ever lonely?"

"Sometimes, but as you said, it passes in the daytime when I am busy and with company."

Leofwynn nodded, comforted by my words, and set herself to weaving the holly branches.

The lie felt heavy. Oh, I understood this loneliness she spoke of, more than I had let on, for I felt it often, not sometimes. When I lay down to sleep, I remembered Cuan and the feeling of his hands upon me. Of his lips on mine. That feeling of desire had not passed. I missed more than that, though. I missed talking to him. The sound of his voice. The knowing of his moods when he was silent and wouldn't speak. Watching him. The knowing that he was watching me.

"Isolde!"

Méabh came out of the side door of the monastery, gesturing that I should follow her.

"Sorry, Leofwynn, I'd better go. We'll speak more later."

Leofwynn nodded, happily weaving her wreaths, while I hurried over to Méabh.

"He's awake, but not strong," Méabh said. "I'll take you to his room."

As we walked, I thought of apologising for earlier, but there was no chance. Méabh marched onward, her head firmly fixed ahead.

Colmon was sitting up in bed when I entered his room. His eyes were tired, the skin around his jowls sagging as his shoulders hunched forward. Méabh didn't speak as I sat on the chair, and without a word she left the room, closing the door behind her.

"I think training me took too much out of you."

"Not at all. I'm ageing. I'm often tired, and that will only get worse, I'm afraid." Colmon tilted his head, smiling, though the tiredness in his eyes had not yet left him. "Now tell me about this vision."

"It was the same as before, only parts of it have become sharper. I could make out the dead this time. They were the mortals who live here. Báine too. And Méabh and Siobhan. You said the same words as last time, only you wanted me to hide the sword that had pierced you. Once you… once you had died, a man came out of the fire. It was one of the Fomorians who attacked me on Rathlin, the one who caught up with Affraic and me. He hated me. Hated me with every fibre in his body." I shuddered as I remembered the heat of the fire between his hands. "I am a danger to you. To everyone here. I think I must leave."

"No."

"But I must, Colmon. My being here will destroy the monastery. All the people were dead on the grass beside us, and you said it was my fault. Everything was on fire. It was awful."

"We cannot let this happen, no, but the answer is not you leaving." Colmon paused. Staring at me, his dark grey eyes seemed to pierce my very soul. "These visions, Isolde, do not always come true. Things can change if we work to change them. You must put everything into learning your gifts so you can control them. That is the first thing the vision is showing us."

"Really? You think that will work?"

"Yes. We also have time to get the mortals who live here somewhere else to stay. If the Fomorians do come, they will not kill the people here. That I promise you."

"What else?"

Colmon bit his lip. "Tell me, what did the sword look like? The one I told you to hide."

Rubbing my head, I tried to remember.

"Did it have a silver handle?"

"I think so? It… yes, it was silver and had a gold spiral engraved upon it."

Colmon sighed. "Tell me, what did I look like? Still the white hair?"

"Yes. Your hair was white. Almost silver. Why?"

"I had thought to take you to Rathlin Island sooner rather than later, but that is the wrong move. This is the second message the vision has given us. It is too soon for you to have the sword and spear of the Tuatha Dé Danann, for it is this sword that has killed me, and we cannot let it fall into Fomorian hands."

I nodded. This made sense.

"And so instead of travelling north, you must learn to use your gifts, but we must focus our attention going forward."

"On the warrior gift?"

"Yes, and no. In the vision, the Fomorians have already attacked us, that is why the monastery is on fire. But it doesn't seem like they are responsible for killing everyone. That was you, according to my words, so we must attempt to school you in the most dangerous of the gifts. Warrior, cupbearer and witch."

"You, Méabh and Báine." I muttered these names, trying not to let the disappointment cloud my features. I didn't know Méabh and Báine so well, both being colder than Siobhan and Gisela, but I would not complain. The vision had been too devastating. Too awful – and so I would do whatever it took to bring my gifts under control.

Donnchad

Road to London

The road to London was a good road – well maintained and full of travellers and traders. The weather was turning though, and the people we passed were in a hurry to get where they were going. I was in a hurry too, and thankfully, after four weeks of riding, FitzHubert and I were approaching London. Already wooden houses were lining the road, and in the distance, the Norman castles loomed over the rest of the city.

This morning was especially cold, and ice crusted at the edges of the puddles on the ground. I thought this would put FitzHubert in a foul mood, for he often complained of sore bones and aches and pains, but instead, he seemed almost jubilant. So jubilant that for the first time since we'd ventured out from Chepstow, he asked me a question.

"You speak French fluently, yes?"

"*Oui. Je parle français.*"

"Where did you learn it?"

Still speaking French, I told him that I had grown up close to Caen when I was younger, and he appeared satisfied that I knew the tongue well enough to please King Henry. Enough to be considered more Norman than Irish, which in his eyes was almost as bad as being a Moor.

"What about Latin?" he asked next.

"Yes, I speak Latin too. Why?"

"Henry speaks to commoners in these two languages, so it's best you are prepared. He, however, understands a great many languages. More than anyone knows, so do not think to speak or mutter to yourself in Irish in the hope that he will not know what you say."

"The king speaks Irish?"

"It is a barbaric language, no offence, so I doubt it, but when it comes to Henry, who knows? He is clever and likes to surprise his subjects from time to time. He enjoys playing games with them too. Keeps us all on our toes." He chuckled and then quickly wiped his mouth with his sleeve. "If he hears Strongbow is sending an Irish messenger to him, he might find it amusing to converse with you in your mother tongue. No doubt he'll speak it better than you."

I didn't react to this. There was no point. When FitzHubert spoke of his king, it was as if he were a god. In his eyes, King Henry was the greatest man that ever lived. A man who seemingly could learn an entire language in a few days and then speak it better than a native.

"Tell me more about the king," I asked, taking advantage of his good humour. "How many times have you met him?"

"Many," the old knight said. "I fought for his mother, Queen Maud, before him. Henry was just a boy then. He is very good to those who fought for his mother, always remembers them and grants them favours when he can. I am but a humble soldier, but he made me a knight. Many other kings would not do such a thing. They would not raise a commoner from the grass. Henry is different. A king of the people."

I nodded along, letting myself look impressed as he explained Henry's many virtues. Thankfully, he moved on to the Anarchy and Henry's part in that. Now, this was a story I was interested in. It was a mighty war, for even I had heard of it when we came back from Libya and travelled through Greece. No one had thought Maud could win against her cousin Stephen, but finally, once she agreed to step aside for her son, Henry, the barons of England fought for her line.

"You must understand, Donnchad, Queen Maud never gave

up. Not even when Stephen took her half-brother, Robert of Gloucester, captive."

"What was it really like fighting a war like that?"

"Hard and long. There was many a time I thought we would lose. Persistence was key. Waiting for the right time. Picking which fights to fight, you know? Stephen de Blois was clever too. All Norman lords are. Schooled in war from the time they can walk."

"How then, may I ask, did you end up under Strongbow's banner? He fought against Henry and Maud, did he not?"

"Aye, he did. Poor Strongbow. He picked the side of Stephen, the king who never should have been, and has suffered for it. It is not fair, perhaps, but the world is not fair, and Strongbow still suffers because of this decision."

This was interesting too. Mother had told me in Chepstow, Strongbow was an earl, but in the English court he was only a lord. I was finally getting to the bottom of why this should be.

"How does he suffer? He seems to me to be a great man."

"Ah, just as Henry raises those who helped his mother, he lowers those who helped Stephen, and that in truth is why I have been sent to watch over Strongbow. He holds too much land for King Henry to take it all away, but the king is wary of him, and so I must act as a conduit between the two."

And so you watch Strongbow and report what he does to your true master.

That meant Henry was afraid of Strongbow.

I did not say this aloud. I did not have to. When I was a king, I feared my nephew Toir, and so I'd had him watched too. In the end, it hadn't helped me keep my kingdom, but it had enabled me to escape to Dublin before he reached my dun.

"The Anarchy was fifteen years ago," I mused. "Tell me, what sort of man is Henry now?"

"He is honourable. Clever, as I told you before. At present, however, he is preoccupied with archbishops and successions. This gives him dark moods."

I raised an eyebrow.

"There was much talk of the Archbishop of Canterbury when I was last with the king. Thomas Becket, he is called, and he and the king have fallen out. Apparently, Becket has fled from Henry's court, but the king needs him to return to England so that Henry the Younger can be crowned as king."

"King of where?"

"England."

"But King Henry is not dead. How can his son be crowned King of England?"

"Henry the Younger will not rule; it's just the king's way of splitting his territories and having his sons in agreement over what happens when he dies."

"You mean to ensure his sons don't fight over his throne?"

"Indeed. We've just left one civil war. There's no need for another, and the sons of King Henry are not called the devil's brood for no reason. Not yet men, only thirteen and fourteen the oldest two are, and already they vie for their father's and mother's attention and for their own power. Henry was much the same, and he quarrelled with his own brothers often. This is why he tries to prevent his sons from repeating these mistakes and is gifting them their territories while he is alive."

I could see some sense in this plan. By allowing his sons some power over their individual holdings, it allowed them to become ingrained in that land and earn the loyalty of the lords beneath them. Still, it meant King Henry gifting away some of his own power, which was unusual. It was something I would never do. As for an archbishop having so much sway that he felt he could defy a king, that was curious too. Indeed, with so many feuds and tensions, I was finding Henry more and more interesting.

The image FitzHubert had drawn was exaggerated, yes, but I found I was beginning to get a sense of the English king. Henry was a ruler who valued legacy and who planned not just for himself, but for the generation ahead. I had not done this. It had never entered my mind to plan for my sons and their sons after them. *Perhaps that was why I had failed.*

*

As we reached London, the roads toward the castle and royal houses by the river loomed ahead, and we steered our horses in that direction. The streets were busy here. The houses and shacks built ramshackle and on top of each other. Coins swapped hands, traders with carts of fish and vegetables shouted for custom, and dirty children ran with buckets of piss toward the tanners. In truth, it was the worst possible place imaginable. It reminded me of Paris a little, though I had rarely gone into the parts of that city where the poorest people lived. Here, everyone seemed poor.

"It smells bad by the river," FitzHubert warned. "But unfortunately, the river is where we must go."

"Is there no other way into the castle?"

"No castle for you today!" FitzHubert laughed as if I'd said the most hilarious thing. "A ship. We go to Normandy. Look, the king's flag is not flying over the White Tower. Henry isn't here."

I frowned. A voyage to France would lengthen this journey by weeks.

"Why are you so sad, Donn? You must remember the women of Normandy," FitzHubert said. "Angels they are, compared to the beasts sired here. Tis the cold and the rain – it breeds the pox, I say. Rots the teeth too."

I shrugged, neither agreeing nor disagreeing. I'd travelled the world over, and the angelic could be found in every corner. So could the most wretched of hags, and I had no need of any women anyhow. I was here on a much greater mission.

My mother, flawed though she was, was often right. Strongbow was cautious, too cautious, and needed the king's permission to fight in Ireland. And so, while I waited to speak with King Henry, I would watch him and see how he held so many men in the palm of his hand. It was a humbling lesson for a man who had once been king, but I would prove myself worthy. This time my mother would see me for what I was, without the light of Máelmórda or Sitric to get in the way.

Broccan

Toraigh Island

The wind howled around me. I tried to close my ears to it, but I could not, for I was too weak to even raise my arms above my head. I ached everywhere. Every bone, every muscle, every bit of skin felt as if it were on fire, but the sound of the wind somehow made it worse.

Looking around me, I tried to work out where I was. Oh yes, I was on a rock. The cliffs of Rathlin rose above me while the sea crashed against them. The tide was coming in and soon I'd be washed away, but I couldn't let that happen. Isolde needed me. Isolde. Yes, she needed me at her side. Using my warrior gift, I tried to move but couldn't. I couldn't turn… or even feel my legs.

Broccan.

It was my mother's voice. I knew it was her. But where was she? I had held her as she died. Watched as the air left her lungs, and yet somehow, she could speak to me on the wind in times of need. Why only then, though? Why could she not speak to me always? She wore her hair wild on the crannog. I remembered that.

Broccan.

The wind was wild too. How many voices were upon it? Sometimes I heard others speaking. Whispering.

Broccan.

"Mother?"

I love you, my son.

I loved her too, but rather than these words giving me comfort, a swell of bitterness filled my mouth. A pain that built up from the inside. Why did she not speak to me always?

"Where are you?" I asked.

The water tells lies, my son. I had to see the truth, and I gave myself to the wind. Fire is coming. I've seen it devour everything. You need to find Isolde before it finds her. She is the only one who can stop it.

I lay still, for what else could I do as the wind blew around me, but as with the last time, once the message had been given, my mother's voice disappeared.

Why could she not speak with me always?

"Wake up, Broccan." A hand pushed against my shoulder. Gentle at first, then harder. "Wake up."

Senna's face loomed into view, her long, dark hair falling over my face.

"What is it?" I asked, my mouth feeling so very dry.

"You told me to wake you up if you slept too long."

Shifting to my side, I took a drink from the cup beside me, then fell back to the ground, exhausted from even that small movement. My body was a mess, and my head was now a mess too. That dream I'd had, it had made me think I was back on the rocks of Rathlin, but that had been months ago. Now I was in a cave on Toraigh, another small island off the north coast of Ireland and many miles from where I needed to be.

"Are we going to try again today?" I asked her, forcing some urgency into my voice. "I need to get to Isolde."

"We can if you wish." Senna gave me a stern look. "But you must be honest about your pain this time. Transformation into an animal takes getting used to, and you are not a witch. The times we've tried when you couldn't take—"

"I know. I know." I shook my head, wanting to forget the times she'd transformed me into a crow and my body had ached so much that I'd passed out. Those times, she'd transformed me back into human form to find me unconscious, and I'd slept afterwards for days. She may as well have transformed me into a worm for all the use I was. "I feel much better. My burns don't hurt as much as they used to, and the pain shooting up my neck has gone."

Senna didn't look convinced by my words, and I couldn't blame her as I stared down at my body. I was covered with burns. No longer just the scars from Clontarf, but fresh welts covered my right shoulder and arm. My lower back was broken, and I could no longer move my legs. My ankle was broken too. Senna had done her best to set it, but given that I couldn't walk, there had probably been little point in her doing that.

Muttering to herself, Senna turned my face and looked me over. "The burns over your neck and shoulder, they don't look better." She bit her lip. "If I could get you to Seir Kieran, Siobhan could fix you... which is why I've been thinking of trying something different. Transforming you into a crow isn't working."

"No. Not the cart idea again."

She'd suggested only last week that she could find a horse and cart and drive it to Seir Kieran, but that couldn't be. We had no money, and I could never trust anyone to take care of me on the road. Not even Senna. There was war on the mainland, which meant roving armies. They could easily take a witch, and an injured warrior like me. And the Fomorians, they were still out there too.

"Try the crow again. Last time, I was able to flap my wings. I'm sure this time I will be able to fly."

Senna shook her head. "When I transform you, you have no feathers where your burns are. And while the spine of a bird is shorter than a human's, meaning your back isn't broken any longer, the broken bones will be in your tail. I don't think we can make this work. You need feathers to stay in the air, and to land, you need both your legs and your tail to balance." She brushed her hand over my ankle, and though I could not feel her touch, I saw how the bones protruded oddly under the skin. I understood her concerns. If I tried to land as a crow with a broken ankle, I'd probably snap my leg.

"Landing doesn't matter," I said, trying to sound determined rather than desperate. "Even if I shatter my leg, once I reach Seir Kieran, Siobhan can heal me."

"What if you don't make it to Seir Kieran, Broccan? It's too risky… but there is another way. Another animal I could try, though I've never attempted it before."

I didn't like the sound of this. Keeping the mind intact was key when transforming, or so Senna had told me. This was why witches often transformed into crows or eagles, who were clever and had their own language. It kept the mortal mind alive and allowed the witch to retain her memories and communicate with others. Other animals, slow and stupid, or those with no brains at all, were always a risk. It had been known for witches to transform into cows and sheep and even insects, and when they transformed back, they were no longer themselves.

"I will try harder this time."

"You cannot try harder, Broccan." Senna sighed. "Your body has been damaged beyond what is normal for a body to endure. Time is what you need."

"I don't have time." These words came out short. "Sorry, Senna. But I must leave here. Now. Isolde needs me." I closed my eyes and took a breath. "Or… or you could fly to Seir Kieran and tell Siobhan to come to me."

Senna shuddered. "I have not been in crow form since your mother saved me. I cannot… what I mean to say is… I cannot bear it. But still, I would do it… I would return to the darkness if—" Senna trailed away.

"If what?"

"If your mother asked it of me. But she has not. All she said was that I was not to leave your side until we reached Seir Kieran. I cannot go against her wishes. Not when she sees into the future."

It was strange to see Senna look so despondent. Usually, she was trying to cheer me up. I wondered then what else my mother had said to her.

"Do you always do what my mother asks?"

Senna nodded.

"Have you ever paused to consider that it's not in your best interest to do so? If it makes you unhappy, you don't have to."

Senna inched closer to me and didn't move for a while. There was a deep sadness within her. A sadness I could see because it was so like mine. "Perhaps it is not in my best interest, but it is in *our* best interest."

"What does that mean?"

"It means your mother sacrificed her own life, her own joy and hopes, to listen to the wind. It drove her to madness, and she knew it would do that to her, but she wanted to save the people of Ireland. All of us."

"She saw our destruction?"

"Yes. And she's doing everything she can to stop it." Senna stared at me. "It has been hard for you, I know. To have lost her so young. I loved my mother too. I wish every day I could see her just one more time, but you are a warrior. The only one left. You must be strong. Strong like Rónnat."

To my shame, Senna was right. I was thinking too much of my own suffering. It made me forget that Senna had suffered. That my mother had too. Shifting my weight with my left arm and using my warrior gift, I pulled myself up into a sitting position against the wall of the cave. "My mother didn't tell you what animal to try by any chance?"

"No, but I'd already had an idea. I think it's time to try it."

I closed my eyes and took a deep breath. "What animal?"

As if in answer to her question, a wolf howled in the distance, and Senna gave me a small smile.

"No," I said. "I cannot be a land animal that big. My back and ankle are broken. I'll be too slow."

"You'll be slow, yes, but you will get there. The broken bones of your back will be in the wolf's tail, but a wolf doesn't need its tail to balance if it's only walking. As for your broken ankle, you'll manage."

She reached forward, touched my arm, and I felt my body

change. The world became dark, leached of colour. I felt my back bend. It was agony at first, but as the broken discs of my back disappeared into the tail, once again I felt my legs. But with this came a fresh wave of pain as the break in my ankle became apparent.

"Try to walk," she said.

Using all my strength, I stood. Four legs. Three that were working. I limped forward, unable to bear any weight on my back left leg. An inch, that was all I moved. Tilting my head at Senna, I said, "I'll be too slow," but of course words did not come out, just a howl.

Senna stared at me and then walked to the boat. "Come on, Broccan. It's time."

Slowly, so very slowly, I hobbled toward her. Toward Isolde. And toward the fire that was heading her way.

PART II

1156

Cuan

Dúnmór

(Thirteen years ago)

My mother lay on the ground, gasping for breath. Every time she exhaled, more of the black liquid filled her mouth and trickled down her chin. I knelt beside her, using my body to haul her up and pressed my hand against the knife wound in her shoulder, but all the while, I tried to understand what had just happened to me. *To us*. My mother had summoned fire, and then… so had I. How? *How was that possible?*

"We need to get away from here, Cuan," my mother said.

I pushed my confusion and questions aside and tightened my grip around my mother's waist, using all my strength to keep her steady on her feet. The man who had tried to kill her was lying on the ground beside us, though I couldn't bring myself to look at the burns covering his body. *The burns my fire had given him*. "Come on, Mother. Hurry. The hall is going to collapse."

"I'm sorry, Cuan. I didn't want this for you."

I couldn't answer. We needed to get out of the feasting hall and find bandages for her wounds. Then we had to get away from Dúnmór. Away from Ruaidrí and his men. That was all I could think about for now. Though I struggled to hold her weight, we finally made it outside.

My mother fell forward and vomited, blood and the black

phlegm mixing on the ground. With this sudden movement, blood spurted from the stab wounds in her shoulder, and the upper part of her dress quickly soaked through.

"You need the healer." I glanced around the dun. Men and women were running back and forth with water to save the outhouses, but over by my father and mother's house, I could see Osán and Dáire. The healer was with them. The healer spoke with Osán for a moment, then rushed inside. "Look, Mother. Osán is over by our—"

"No." Mother shook her head, took a deep breath and wiped her mouth. Using me as a crutch, she stood again, but the words she spoke were drowned out by the sound of screams. It was Father. Whatever the healers were doing to him, I guessed to the place where his eyes had once been, it sounded like the hounds of hell were ripping him apart.

"Use my belt and tie it over my shoulder." My mother shook me, drawing my attention back to her as she shoved her leather belt into my hands and leaned down so that I might do as she asked. While I tied the belt tight around her shoulder, she ripped the fabric along the hem of her dress, and once I was finished, she stuffed the fabric between her wound and the belt.

"We need to leave." She winced as she pushed the fabric further in. "We need to go to Dublin."

I turned to stare at my father's house. His screams were rising again, loud and high-pitched like the banshees in my grandfather's stories. I didn't like to think about what the healer was doing to warrant such a noise, and so instead focused on what my mother wanted. Dublin… we had to get to Dublin… but how? "I don't think Father will make it so far east. At least, not so soon. Is there nowhere else we can go?"

"Your father isn't coming with us, Cuan. Osán will take him to one of the monasteries in Connacht. I need to take you to my brother, Godred."

"What?"

She didn't want us to be with Father?

Amid the panic and screaming, I stilled. Mother was struggling to breathe, to form words, but her expression was serious. She meant what she had said.

"Why would we not go with Father?"

"I saw you," my mother panted. "I saw the fire in your hands." She reached up to touch my face. "You are like me. I'm sorry, Cuan. I'm so sorry, but this changes everything. You cannot stay here. We cannot."

"What… what is wrong with us?"

"I don't know. My mother called it a curse, and it killed her. I am scared it will kill you too, but my brother, Godred, he knows a way to help us, and he is King of Dublin. We will be safe with him."

Tears filled my eyes. "No. No. We can stay with Father. I promise everything will work out if we do. He can help us."

"You know that is not true, Cuan. I need my brother. You need him too, or else the curse will come back."

The curse will come back.

That phrase made me feel sick. Whatever I was, whatever evil was inside of me, had made me kill a man. *Burn him.*

My mother gasped for breath, her hand clutching the belt over her shoulder and then her stomach. "We need to leave. Now. We need to get to my brother's fort while I still have some strength left."

I looked about me. The feasting hall was still on fire, and the roof was on the verge of collapsing. Through the noise of the flames and falling wood, Osán called my name. "Cuan! Where are you?"

"Get a horse," my mother said. "We need to leave now. Don't talk to Osán. He'll only try to take you from me."

I didn't want to leave my father, but I had to help my mother, and if her brother could help, then that was where we needed to go. We could meet up with Father later. Yes, that was it. Quickly, I ran to the stables, saddled my horse, then led him outside. Using all my strength, I pushed my mother up and onto his back.

"Hold onto me," I said as I mounted the horse. Mother wrapped her arms around my waist, and sagging against me she pointed toward the gate. "Ride east, Cuan. And don't stop until we reach Dublin. Promise me you won't stop."

"Promise."

I pushed the horse forward. A walk only, for we could not run while the dun was so crowded, but slowly, we edged our way toward the gate.

"Cuan. Where are you going?"

Through the smoke, I made out Osán standing by the door of my father's house.

"We are going to Dublin," my mother hissed at him. "Stay away from us, hound."

Osán stretched his hand out toward me. "Your father needs you, Cuan. We need you to help us against Ruaidrí."

He nodded at my grandfather's house. Ruaidrí stood outside it, watching the chaos as the men and women tried to put out the fire. Through the smoke, his gaze shifted to stare at us, but he didn't move.

"Don't listen to Osán, Cuan. Listen to me. We must go to my brother. It is not Ruaidrí who can hurt us now. Just the fire."

My mother shook, her eyes closing, and more of the black liquid oozed from the corner of her mouth. Without saying a word, I urged the horse forward and rode out of the dun and toward the rising sun.

When I first spotted the walls of Dublin, I didn't know what to do. My mother had slipped in and out of consciousness during our journey east. For the first six days, she had spoken to me, but for the last two, she'd barely woken at all. She appeared to be saving whatever energy she still had to hold onto my back, while I did everything I could to make sure my horse kept to a steady pace so she wouldn't jolt from her position and fall.

I worried that she was dying, but when we stopped to let my horse drink and to rest, I carefully checked her wound. The skin around it was not hot and did not weep with pus. Whatever illness she had, she said she needed her brother, and so my fear changed. It was no longer of death; it was of how to find Godred. Where would he be in Dublin? *What if the guards didn't believe who we were and wouldn't let us through the gate?*

Despite the fears growing in my mind, I kept going. I had to get in. Once we found him, the ordeal would be over. Mother's brother was the King of Dublin. That meant he was wealthy and would see that we were both looked after. He would find her healers, and then she would get better.

It was with this surge of optimism that I urged my horse toward the distant stone walls.

My first fear, that the guards wouldn't let us in, turned out to be unwarranted. They let us through without so much as a second glance, even with my mother slumped against my back. That led me straight to my next worry. How would I ever find my uncle in a city of this size? The city smelled strange, disorienting. Pots of orange and red spices and black herbs sat in bowls along the market stalls. As the wind blew, like grains of sand, these spices blew up, and the strange smells grew stronger and made my nose itch. Thousands of people competed for my attention. They shouted at me, trying to sell goods and food. I recognised some words, for my mother spoke to me in her own language from time to time, but there were other languages here too. Words and sounds I had not heard before. It was the noise of it all that struck me the most. Everything together was so loud that I couldn't even hear the caws of the seagulls flying overhead.

Moving slowly through the market, I finally came to a row of houses. An old woman sat outside one, threading wool into a loom, humming a tune and tapping her feet.

"Where is the king?" I asked her.

The woman raised her head, looked at me and then at my mother. "What sickness ails her? Is it the bloody flux?"

"I don't know. I don't think—"

The woman rushed inside her house, slamming the door shut behind her. Those close enough to hear our conversation also eyed us with suspicion and moved away.

"Mother." Gently, I turned around and shook her arm until she groaned. Her lips were black, I realised. They hadn't been like that yesterday. "Mother, we are in Dublin. I need you to wake up. Where do I go?"

She opened an eye and raised her head an inch. Even this slight movement caused her to wince. "The king's fort is by the sea. By the longphort. Keep going. Once we get there, you… will need to help… me stand."

I did as she instructed, and once we reached the fort, I dismounted. Slowly, she wrapped her arms around my neck, slipped down the horse's back, and fell against me. Using whatever strength she had left, she straightened, placing only one hand upon my shoulder.

"Where is the King of Dublin?" I asked the guards. "Tell him his sister, Tora, is here."

We stood there waiting until a thin man with shoulder-length brown hair came out. I stared at him in silence. He didn't look like my mother, not even a little. "Mother," I said. "What's going on?"

"I think… I think that is Brodar Mac Torcaill," she whispered, "but my vision is not so good."

"Where is King Godred?" I shouted up to the man.

The man, whoever he was, walked down the steps that led into the fort, and came closer. He stared at my mother's face, frowning as he took in her black lips and pale skin, then beckoned for his slaves to come and help her. "Tora. I hardly recognised you."

My mother gave a weary nod. "Brodar. I thought that was you. Where's my brother?"

"Your brother is no longer King of Dublin. We fought over the kingship only last week, and now he has gone."

"Where?"

"To the Isles."

My mother's hand tightened around my shoulder. She was struggling, and I moved closer to her so that she might lean against me too.

"You must ready a ship for me, Brodar," my mother said. "I need to find him."

"The sea is not safe to cross. Storms are blowing in, one after the other. Please stay here as my guest. Whatever feud there is between me and Godred, it does not extend to you, and I can see you are unwell." Brodar looked beyond us then as if expecting more men to be with us. "Where is your husband? Let me welcome him into my hall too."

"He isn't here," my mother said, but her words were now less than a whisper.

"My father isn't here," I repeated for her.

Brodar moved a little further back, staring once more at her lips. "Is there a sickness in Connacht? Has it killed Bardán?"

He had been all politeness before, but now his words turned sharp. Men feared the sicknesses that blew in from the south. I knew that from the stories my grandfather told.

"I'm unwell, Brodar, but I do not bring the bloody flux with me," my mother said, her voice stronger this time. "As you can see, my son is well, and my husband is alive in Connacht. Please, I need my brother. Take me to him and I will give you these orbs." She removed a pouch from her cloak pocket and held it out. They shimmered in the sun, just as they had when she'd put them on to welcome Ruaidrí to Dúnmór.

Brodar studied the silver hair decorations, gave me a once-over, I supposed to check that I truly did not suffer from my mother's ailment, then gave a curt nod. "I perhaps could find a ship for you in the next few days. But your son belongs with his father, no? I don't want a fight with the High King because I've helped remove his grandson from Ireland."

"Ah," my mother said. "Now we get to the reason why you don't want to help me. It is not my health that concerns you, but an army from Connacht riding toward your city."

"Forgive me, Tora, but yes, that does worry me. We've had to fend off many armies over the last few years. Munster snaps at us from the south and Meath from the north. I don't want an enemy coming at us from the west."

"Well, you need not worry," my mother replied. "The old king is dead. My husband has been blinded. His brother, Ruaidrí, did it and has made himself king. Believe me, no one will come looking for my son."

Brodar stared at my mother, something like pity sweeping across his face. "Very well. Come inside, Tora. I'll have my healers tend to you."

I followed my mother into the fort and helped the slaves lay her on the bed. Her face was pale and covered with a sweaty sheen, her black lips had turned even darker, and each time I gave her water, I noticed the strange dark substance congealing over her teeth. The same black liquid that she'd spat out after she'd summoned the fire.

Two days passed, then three. Still, there was no word of a ship.

On the fourth day, Brodar sent a messenger who asked me to speak with him in the hall. I had not ventured out yet, preferring to stay with my mother, for despite several visits from three different healers, she had grown weaker.

Ready to plead our case once again for a ship, I walked out of our bedroom and into the feasting hall. A large wooden chair was at the centre of the long table, and Brodar sat there. His wife was beside him, and beside her sat another man with beady eyes and a sharp nose.

"Morning, Cuan," Brodar said, pointing to the man with the beady eyes. "This is my nephew Asculv."

"Hello, Asculv," I said, remembering to be polite.

"And this is another friend of mine. His name is Viggo." This time Brodar gestured toward a tall man who stood by the fire. He looked to be broad, but I couldn't clearly make out how much of his bulk was due to his shoulders or his cloak. He was a sailor, I knew that, for I could smell the salt on him. The bone underneath his eyebrow was broken, and there was a chunk of flesh missing on his right cheek. It gave his face a strange look, but for all that, I liked the look of him. Asculv, on the other hand, reminded me of a rat. Even his nose twitched as he waited for the conversation to start.

"Viggo will take Tora to your uncle," Brodar said.

"Thank you."

"Your mother can go, but not you."

"Why?"

"Your uncle Ruaidrí sent a message," Asculv said. "He says his brother wants his wife and son back. If Tora takes you away, Bardán will divorce Tora for disobedience, and she will no longer be welcomed into Connacht. If, however, she complies and brings you back to Dúnmór, she will be allowed to visit you and granted a home and three servants to tend to her needs."

"This is a generous offer," Brodar's wife said. "We think you should accept."

I thought of my mother and of how she had suffered during our journey here. There was no way she could go back. If my uncle could save her, as she said he could, we needed to leave as soon as possible. But she wouldn't leave without me. I knew that.

"I don't think my mother wants a house in Connacht. She wants to go to her brother."

"And she is free to go," Asculv said. "You, however, are the grandson of the late King of Connacht, and your father wants you with him. We cannot go against his will."

Arguments ran through my head. So did anger. I was so angry. Angry at this man who looked like a rodent. *Who was he to tell me what to do?* I could feel it then. The feeling that surged through my body when the fire came to it before. I bit my lip and tried to push it down, looking away from Brodar and Asculv in case they said something to provoke me further.

My gaze landed on Viggo. He gave a small smile and then winked. Somehow this unexpected gesture made the tingling in my hands fade away.

"Come, Cuan," Viggo said. "Listen to Brodar and Asculv. Say goodbye to your mother now. I must leave before the tide turns." His expression was serious now, so serious that I felt I might have imagined his wink. But I hadn't. I was sure of it.

I turned heel and rushed into my room. "Mother." I shook her gently. "Mother, there is a man called Viggo who says he will sail you to your brother."

"Good."

"But Brodar won't let me leave. He says Father and Ruaidrí have asked for my return."

She opened her eyes and rolled to the side. Spitting into a bucket, a ball of black phlegm and blood hit the bottom.

"You should go," I said. "You aren't getting any better here. Once Uncle Godred has helped you, you can come back for me."

She shook her head. "No. You must come with me." Taking a deep breath, she wrapped her hands around her stomach and tried to stand. Blood stained the bedsheets, her fingernails, and also the skin under her nose. Groaning, she made it onto her feet, though she needed the chair to lean against. "What does Viggo look like?"

"Long black hair. Broken brow bone. A big chunk of flesh missing over his cheek. He winked at me… I think."

A small smile flashed across Mother's face. "Listen to me, Cuan. Viggo is my brother's friend. I trust him, so you must do what he says."

My mother gestured to her cloak, and I grabbed it for her and set it about her shoulders. "Help me to the ship, Cuan."

I did this, and we slowly made our way to the longphort. Viggo's ship was easy to spot. It was huge, much bigger than I expected it to be, and the sternpost was shaped into the head of a wolf.

Viggo stood by his ship and offered my mother his arm once she approached, gesturing for a couple of his slaves to come and assist her on board. "I'm sad to see you so unwell, Tora."

"I am saddened to be this unwell, but I am glad of your help, Viggo. For me and my son."

Viggo smiled and placed a hand on my head. "You're a good boy to help your mother, Cuan." He ruffled my hair then in the same way I would pet a dog, and he laughed at the affronted look I gave him. Play-wrestling with me, he pulled me into a headlock. The unexpected move caught me off guard, and I wriggled around to escape. "Say you want to go back to the fort," he whispered in my ear. "My man will be in your room. Do what he says."

Letting go, he laughed loudly. "You are a fighter, Cuan. Just like the famous warriors of Connacht! Now off we go! The tide waits for no man. Not even me."

Brodar, Brodar's wife and Asculv were waiting a little further along the longphort, and I made my way over to them, and together we watched as my mother was helped onto the ship.

Brodar set a hand on my shoulder. "You'll see her again one day."

"When will I see my father?" I asked, smiling up at him.

Brodar returned my smile. "His man Osán will be here tomorrow. Not long to wait, little one. And as you are a guest, you can come to my feast tonight. I'll even let you drink the ale."

"Can I sleep in my mother's room tonight too?"

"Yes. If you wish."

"Good." With a spring in my step, I turned around and began to walk back to the fort.

"Don't you want to say goodbye to your mother?" Brodar asked.

"I've already said my goodbyes. I'd rather go to the fort steps so I can see the ship sail away."

"Ah, yes." Brodar's wife smiled. "There is a good view from those steps, to be sure. It's where I stand when Brodar sails away."

Scampering along the longphort, I ran up the fortress steps and made a point of waiting on the top one so that both Brodar and Asculv could see me. I waved at my mother, who was now lying on a bed of furs at the far side of the ship. She waved back.

As soon as Viggo started saying his farewells to Brodar and Asculv, I ran into my room.

Just as Viggo had told me, a man was waiting there for me. He stood by the door with a large axe strapped to his belt, and his moustache and beard were so bushy that I could hardly see any skin below his eyes. A boy stood beside him. Roughly my height and with hair the same colour. "Come," the man said to me. "We must hurry. Give this boy your cloak."

I did as the man said and took the threadbare one the boy offered in exchange.

As the boy ran back out onto the top steps, the stranger and

I made our way to the side door that the slaves used. An empty water barrel was there.

"Get in," he said. "And not a word."

I climbed inside, hunched over as he pressed the lid down. Suddenly everything was dark, and I closed my eyes, pretending that I was in my bed at home.

The pretence was short-lived, for soon I was flung forward as the stranger picked up the barrel and set it on his shoulders. Bouncing around, we moved back toward the longphort.

"Is that the last of the water?" I heard Viggo shout.

"It is," the man answered. Suddenly, I was turned about again as the barrel was set down. I bit my lip and steadied my body so that I did not make a thudding sound that would give away that there was something other than water inside.

I waited then, hunched in the dark as men shouted around me. I was afraid, and yet I couldn't let myself give in to that feeling. My mother needed me. She needed me to be brave and to do what I was told, but still a panic grew inside of me. I did not like small spaces like this. My ankles ached. So did my knees. I wanted to get out.

"Well done, boy," a voice said as the lid was lifted. Squinting as light poured into the barrel, I yelped as Viggo hoisted me out of my prison. But I didn't care for the pain of the light hitting my eyes nor for the numbness in my legs. All I could think of was Mother. Finding my balance, I turned and saw that she was still lying on the makeshift bed of furs.

"Thank you," I said to Viggo.

"Don't thank me," he replied. "Thank your mother for being clever enough to seek me out. Thank the slave who carried her note. Thank the gods that your uncle Godred saved my life once when he could have taken it."

I gave him a nod, then rushed over to my mother. She placed her hand on my cheek. "We will be with Godred soon," she said. "He's on the Isle of Man. 'Tis not far away."

"How soon?"

"Tomorrow."

Relief spread through me, and I hugged my mother. She hugged me back and closed her eyes, and soon she was asleep.

The ship tossed and turned throughout the whole day, but as the night approached, the sea calmed. After moving over to the stern to watch the waves, and checking that Brodar had not sent anyone to catch us, I made my way back to where my mother was sleeping. The makeshift bed of furs and blankets was holding up, despite the swell, and I pulled the blanket up over her shoulder.

"How are you, Mother?" I asked.

My mother took my hand in hers and pulled me onto the bed beside her so that her mouth was close to my ear. "*Keep your emotions tight, Cuan. If you don't, the curse will kill you.*"

"What do you mean?"

"The only way to stop it is to turn your heart to stone. I tried. I tried. But I loved your father, and when Ruaidrí blinded him, I couldn't control myself. The fire came out of me. Poured out of my heart."

I placed my other hand over my mother's and squeezed it tight.

"If I hadn't hit you, the fire would have kept pouring out of you too. Do you understand? You cannot use it. It destroys you."

Mother did not need to tell me this. The black liquid filled her mouth as she spoke, and blood seeped from her gums. Her hands were covered in blood too as it leached from the skin around her nails. It was like the fire was still burning her on the inside.

"What can I do, Mother? What do you need once we reach Godred?"

"I am not here to get better." Tears seeped from the edges of her eyes as she said this. "I am sorry I lied to you, but there is nothing that can help me now. There was never anything that could help me. I came here for you."

"Don't say that."

"Godred is my brother. He knows what is wrong with me,

which means he knows what is wrong with you. He's the only person I trust to keep it a secret, and it must stay a secret. Godred will train you. Keep you safe."

My body shook as she spoke. I didn't want to believe it, but it was true. She was dying… and she'd known it the whole time.

"Father would have looked after me. We could have trusted him."

My mother shook her head. "Oh, Cuan. If anyone found out you had the gift of fire, they would use you. Even your father. He would use you to destroy his brother and would convince himself you could be saved. But you can't use the fire and live. It is a curse we have. Nothing more, and so you must distance yourself from him. I've done what I can for you."

"What do you mean?"

"I sent him a letter before I left Dublin… saying that I wanted you to be King of Dublin. Not of Connacht. And that is why I brought you to my brother. That's why he thinks we left."

She rolled onto her side, the black liquid spluttering over the blanket. "Promise me you will not speak of our curse with anyone apart from Godred. Not your father. Not Ruaidrí. No one. Promise."

Overwhelmed by both sorrow and fear, I nodded.

She wheezed again and rolled back. Her energy had left her, and her eyes closed, so I moved closer and rested my head against her shoulder. Despite the horror of what she had said, the night was dark, and soon I found myself drifting off with it. In my dreams, we reached my uncle's house, and my mother was already well. She walked off the ship and embraced him and introduced me as a prince of Connacht, but when the dawn approached, I reached for her hand. Her skin was cold, and I knew then that she was dead.

I cried, buried my head in her cloak, and didn't move from her side, barely noticing that we had reached the Isle of Man. Nobody spoke to me either, not even Viggo, though he came over to place a flower in my mother's hair.

Hours had passed, perhaps more, when a man boarded the ship and sat beside me. He was well-dressed, with long, light brown hair. He didn't look like my mother, but the way that he tilted his head to the side as he looked at me reminded me of her. He didn't speak but kissed her hand and removed a piece of parchment from her cloak. Quickly, he read it. Once this was done, several men who had followed him onto the ship began to wrap my mother in a pale cloth until her face was hidden from me.

I touched her hand one last time before the cloth covered it. Her fingers were cold, colder than they had been before, and I pulled back quickly. I didn't want to remember her like that.

"We are taking her to my fort," the man said.

"Are you Godred?" I asked.

"Yes." He stared at me, his face emotionless, and I brushed my tears away for I didn't want him to see them. Silently, I stood and followed the slaves who had now lifted my mother so as to carry her off the ship.

"Where are you going?" Godred asked, pushing me back down.

"With my mother," I answered.

"Tora is being taken to my fort to be prepared for the afterlife because she was the daughter of a king. Who is your father?"

I looked at him blankly, unsure of his meaning. He knew who my father was. "Bardán O'Conchúir," I said at last.

"And who is he?"

A silence fell between us as I reached for the answer he wanted.

"I'll tell you who he is. He's a nobody." My uncle said this quietly. "A man who failed to be king when it was all but given to him. A man who could not keep his wife alive. You are his son, and that's all you are now, too. Nobody." He rubbed the parchment in his hand a moment. "Now, my sister tells me you are like her. For her, I will train you. Teach you what her mother taught me about their sickness, but until you prove yourself, stay out of my way." He turned then and stormed off the ship.

I shuffled slowly to the wooden plank that led onto the longphort and then stopped. There were hundreds of torches that led up the path to his fort, and many guards stood outside the entrance, though they stepped aside as the servants passed the door with my mother. I could hear singing from inside the fort, and by the shore a great funeral pyre was being prepared.

"Cuan," Viggo shouted at me. "Come."

He was standing on the path and waved for me to come to him.

My mind and body, weary with grief, did as he asked.

"You are to sleep with the slaves who we are training to fight," Viggo said, pointing to a large outbuilding. Twenty or so boys sat outside it, mostly warming themselves by the fire and eating stew, though a few were watching the building of the funeral pyre.

"Your uncle has told me I've got to train you so hard you will not be able to keep your eyes open come nightfall," Viggo added. "That means you will be trained twice as hard as anyone else."

I nodded, everything about me still numb.

"You must be brave, Cuan. Like your mother was."

I knew then that I would be, and that I would not disgrace her memory. In silence, I followed Viggo over to the slave building where I sat and took a bowl of stew.

"Cuan."

I was surprised to find my uncle walking toward me, and without ceremony, he handed me a wooden training sword. "There. That is the last thing you will be given until you earn it. Remember who you are. Nobody. And what does a nobody feel?"

I shook my head, once again lost for words. Some of the other boys laughed.

"Nothing," Godred said. "A nobody feels nothing. That is your first lesson. You'd do well to remember it."

"I will."

"Answer me then. Who are you?"

"I am nobody."

Godred nodded, then walked toward the funeral pyre which was already burning.

Spring 1170

Cuan

Dúnmór

The spring frost was thick this morning, and the women around the cooking fires stood close to them, their woollen scarfs bundled around their heads and shoulders. The walls of the dun kept the worst of the wind out, but gusts still swept through the gates to nip at uncovered noses and fingers.

Winters in Ireland were not as vicious nor as long as in the Isles where I had grown up, but the air was damp and seemed to permeate all but the thickest of furs and warmest of fires. Today at least there was no rain. The sky was clear. Blue. The sun shone, and though it offered no warmth, it rendered the dun less gloomy. Spring was not even a suggestion yet. Just a hope.

"Hurry, Ailill," I heard Eoghan shout. "Training starts whether you're ready or not. Where's your shield? Where is your winter cloak? Hurry, boy."

The chastisement made me smile. As well as being weapon-master, Eoghan oversaw the training, which was supposed to whip the boys and men into shape for battle. He was good, but not as good as Osán had been. Not as good as Viggo either, for while Eoghan was an excellent warrior, his bite was weak compared to the two men who had trained me. Osán would have clipped me around the head for coming to training without a shield. Viggo would have made me train the whole day with two shields strapped to my back. Eoghan merely shouted, never punished, and as a result his training sessions always started late, and the younger warriors did not focus as they should.

Walking over to the gate, I stretched out my arms and legs, wiggled my fingers and toes; anything to force the stiffness from my body that would slow me down. Eoghan's training was not difficult, and I would do my own practice later, but I was part of my uncle's fianna. That meant I had to set an example and help the men. It wasn't an unpleasant task, and I wasn't the only one charged with helping Eoghan. Fearghus had been called in too. Laughing loudly, he was currently standing by the cooking fires with Cathal and trying to convince one of the women to give him a ladleful of fish broth. A few of the other warriors were gathered by the stables, stretching as they spoke or else breathing into their hands.

Taking hold of my training sword, I walked through the gate, then practised my footwork. The wind was so sharp here it made the guard's teeth chatter. I didn't feel the cold the way others did, but I did feel the bite of the wind when it blew. When I'd had my scar, I'd felt it even more, a sort of pressure that made the skin either side of it ache. Now that pain was gone. As I moved back to my original stance, I ran my hands over the fresh scar I had cut into my own face. It was a line now, fading more with every month. There was no pain when I touched it, no muscles numbed around my mouth. No relentless itch every time I blinked.

Though I tried not to think of her often, Isolde came to my mind as my finger touched the once-scarred skin. *How had she fared over the winter months?* Was she staring up at the same blue sky? If so, what would she be thinking? She might be looking at the birds that were making their nests, and at the buds that would soon come into bloom. If she were here, she wouldn't be in the dun; she'd be walking by the stream or else through the trees. I imagined that it was true for a moment, that she was here and I was not alone.

"Who is that?"

The guard standing behind me stepped forward and pointed at

something in the distance. There was a man riding toward us. As he came out of the forest and up over the hill path, sweat glistened on his horse's coat, which meant it had been riding through the night.

"I'll tell my uncle a messenger is coming," I said to the guard. "Make sure the horse is tended to once it arrives."

Making my way inside the feasting hall, I found Róisín and Connor eating breakfast at the long table, but not my uncle. Not my aunt either.

"Where's your father?" I asked Róisín.

"Getting dressed," she replied. "Why? What's wrong?"

"A rider is coming."

Brushing crumbs of breakfast from her mouth, she stood. "I'll fetch him."

She gave a shy smile to Connor as she ran off, leaving the young Leinster prince to watch after her.

"She's got you hooked like a fish, boy," Conchobar said, laughing as he sat in his chair and readied himself to eat the bowl of stew that the serving women had just brought over.

"Ah, leave the boy alone," Abbán answered. "Sure, isn't he in love?"

"If we are to be married, that's no bad thing." Connor gave a small shrug, then leaned back in his chair and dared to hold Conchobar's gaze. He was growing in confidence, this youngest son of Diarmait Murchadha. A part of me was glad to see it. Being a prisoner of that man had been the worst night of my life, but I suspected being his son had its own challenges.

While Conchobar and Abbán teased Connor about his growing love for Róisín, I returned to the gate to wait for my uncle. The rider was almost at the dun now, but who was he? Not any of Ruaidrí's warriors, that was for certain. Not a rider from Dublin either, for I felt I would have recognised any of Asculv's warriors from this distance.

"What do you reckon, Fearghus?" Cathal asked. "An invitation to a feast or bad news?"

Fearghus pressed his lips into a thin line. "Bad news, pup. Only a man with ill-tidings travels that fast."

The rider reached the dun hill just as my uncle came out of his house. Ruaidrí walked as if there was no message the rider could give him that would perturb him, but that was all for show. The quiet winter months had been full of planning and discussions over what steps we should take with Diarmait. So far, my uncle had been reluctant to commit to anything. The kings of the smaller kingdoms under his sway were due here at the spring equinox, and he'd set his mind on reorganising the dun so that we might accommodate these numbers. Waiting to act was a foolish thing to do, and I had said as much many times over, but my uncle continued to ignore my advice. The rider coming toward us spoke to my fears – that Diarmait had made his play before us and thus set up how the war would begin.

The guards took hold of the horse's reins, spoke with the rider, and then gave him space to dismount. As this happened, the first guard walked toward my uncle.

"The man's name is Finnén. Cousin to Cormac Mac Carthaig, the King of South Munster."

Ah, so it was a man from Munster. They had not yet involved themselves in the wars between my uncle and Diarmait Murchadha. They were too consumed by infighting and the split of Munster into North and South. Cormac was King of the South, while his distant cousin, Odhrán Ua Brian, had declared himself King of North Munster. I wondered what had happened to make this man ride as though the devil was on his trail. More infighting, or something more sinister?

My uncle gave a nod to indicate that the messenger was to be allowed through, though before this happened, Ruaidrí quickly turned to Fearghus. "Ensure none of the hostages are in the feasting hall when Finnén enters. Abbán especially."

Fearghus nodded and disappeared to do as my uncle had directed.

"Good morning, King Ruaidrí," Finnén said as he approached.

The guards spent a minute searching him for weapons then, removing two long knives and a sling from his person. Once they were satisfied this was all he had, they stepped back.

"Greetings, Finnén," my uncle replied. "Please, come into my hall and eat and drink with me, then you can give me your news."

Finnén nodded and walked silently into the feasting hall, which was now emptied of people. He was shivering, though he tried to hide it. His cheeks burned with wind chill too, and his nose and eyes still streamed from riding so fast.

The serving women rushed into the hall after us, platters of food in their hands, as well as a thick blanket for Finnén to place over his legs. Upon these platters, there were bowls of hot stew, steamed fish, milk, cheese and garlic-buttered skirret. Roasted venison was also put out on platters, with more garlic and bog butter to flavour it. It was too much for only one guest, but this was the dun of the High King, and my uncle wanted to ensure that his hall was always spoken of as being generous. Feeling that this day would not merely consist of training, I ate my fill.

Only after Finnén had finished his bowl of stew did my uncle lean forward. Conchobar sat to his right, with Cathal and Fearghus also gathering around the king. I found a seat beside Fearghus, and then Eoghan came in and sat beside me.

"So, tell me, Finnén. What has happened?" my uncle asked.

"King Odhrán has invaded the Southern Kingdom of Munster and has declared war on my cousin, King Cormac."

"The feud between the two kingdoms of Munster is not my business, Finnén. I desire peace, yes, but I cannot stand over every dispute between the north and south of Munster, otherwise I'll have no time for anything else."

"I suppose that is true, but let me tell you this. There was a skirmish between King Cormac and Odhrán only a few days ago. As we rode away, Odhrán asked us to give you a message."

Ruaidrí sniffed. "Why didn't he tell me himself?"

"I suppose he might have feared losing his own head if he did that."

Ruaidrí raised his eyebrows and gestured for Finnén to relay the message.

"He told us he no longer recognises you as High King and has withdrawn his oaths from you. He says if the north of Munster and Leinster are against you, that you are no true High King."

"They are bold words," Conchobar said.

"They are indeed," Finnén replied. "King Odhrán also told us he planned to invade the south and unite the two kingdoms. Cormac told him that could not be as it is against your ruling. However, Odhrán made good on his word and has invaded our lands. And so, I've come to you. This is not just a skirmish between North and South Munster anymore. As our High King, we are asking you to enforce the boundaries we agreed upon at the Tailteann Games."

"I see. Thank you for giving me this message."

Finnén nodded as he wiped his mouth. "Now, if you don't mind, I would like to rest before I ride back to my king. The Southern Kingdom of Munster has many battles to prepare for. King Odhrán and his men have already raided along our borders. We believe they will ride to Limerick next so as to take the city from us. If you could have someone wake me at midday and have my horse readied, I would be grateful."

My uncle opened his hands. "I will do as you ask, Finnén, and I will give you one of my own horses, a fresh one, so you can reach your cousin with all haste."

Finnén gave his thanks for this offer, then walked out of the feasting hall with a servant who led him to a guest house at the far end of the dun.

Only once he had left the hall did my uncle slam his fist against the table. "This is Diarmait's doing."

Conchobar frowned. "What has the fighting in Munster got to do with him?"

"The clans in Munster are always fighting over Limerick," Feargus added. "Surely there is nothing more to it than that."

"It is not their infighting that concerns me. It is that King Odhrán has cast off his oaths so easily, and believe me, it is no coincidence that

Odhrán is married to Diarmait's eldest daughter. I believe Diarmait has asked his son-in-law to agitate, and now I must respond or else the kings of other kingdoms will throw off their oaths to me too."

Ruaidrí wiped his mouth as he contemplated what this meant. "I wish I had killed Diarmait and his whole clan when we rode to Ferns last year. Tigernán told me to do it, but I, the fool, would not. It was not kinglike, I thought. Well, I'll not be so merciful the next time I meet Diarmait."

"What are you going to do?" Conchobar asked, voice hushed.

My uncle ran his left hand over his right, twisting his rings about his fingers.

The best thing for him to do was nothing, for King Odhrán's words had not been said to his face. *But was this the advice I should give him or not?* My father wanted me to get Ruaidrí to trust me, and so far, he'd ignored everything I'd said. It might be best simply to agree with him to earn his favour? However, as I looked out the doors of the feasting hall, I realised I could not do that. How could I weaken my own kingdom? Revenge on Ruaidrí should not impact those who had nothing to do with him. So instead, I thought about what I needed to say and how best to convey my meaning so that Ruaidrí might, for once, heed my thoughts.

"Be patient, uncle, and do nothing is my advice. It is Diarmait who seeks to force your hand, and so it should be he who suffers. You can deal with Odhrán later."

"Can I?" my uncle snapped.

I knew then I had spoken too truthfully, too decisively.

"What would you know about being a king? What would you know about my ability to bear insults? Besides, you were the one only a few months ago who was telling me to strike."

"Aye, to strike first. Now you're reacting." I leaned closer to my uncle, for it was too late to change tack now. "Let the north and south of Munster fight. It might be that Cormac puts Odhrán in his place for you. It is Diarmait you need to sort out. If he is behind King Odhrán breaking his oaths to you, then he's doing it to distract you. Don't fall into his trap."

My uncle waved his hand as if to brush away my words, but the skin under his eyes and lips had turned white. He glanced around the feasting hall, eyes narrowing. "Where is Abbán?"

I gently bit the inside of my mouth. If Abbán, the hostage taken from King Odhrán to hold him to his word, was in my uncle's mind, that was not good, but I could not question my uncle again. Cathal glanced at me, then at Conchobar, who was resolutely staring into his hands.

"Still asleep, I think," Eoghan said. "I have not seen him—"

"He was here earlier with Róisín and Connor," Fearghus interrupted. "When I ushered them all away, he said he was going to light the fire in his house and play his pipes."

Ruaidrí tapped his fingers against his leg. "Fearghus, Cathal, Eoghan, gather the men. Once you are armed, Abbán is to be taken out of his house, wrists and ankles bound, and then taken to the river. Do it now before he hears of Finnén's appearance."

Fearghus left first, quietly calling up the Connacht warriors who guarded the doors to the hall, while Eoghan and Cathal made their way outside.

"You're going to execute him, uncle?" I asked, after Fearghus, Eoghan and Cathal had left.

"What else can I do? King Odhrán gave him to me as surety, as a sign that he was willing to keep his vows to me. It is not I who has decided to forfeit Abbán's life, but he."

"What of Diarmait's hostages?" Conchobar asked. "Shall I have them taken to the river too?"

"Yes, but not to kill. To watch what happens when kings disobey me."

"You should kill them too," Conchobar said. "It is Diarmait's doing, and so he should suffer the consequences as well."

My uncle shook his head. "Connor is useful to me for now. Keep the Leinster hostages close though, closer than before. No more visits outside the dun. Cuan, siphon off ten warriors to guard them while we are at the river."

I nodded and together we walked outside. I did not like what was about to happen, but my uncle would not listen to me, and so to argue further would only antagonise him. Hardening my heart, I made my way to the hostages' houses. Men died all the time. Through sickness, ill-fortune and war. This was another way. To be a hostage and your king to break his oaths. It was cold though. To be struck down when your hands and legs were tied.

Already the warriors had gathered outside Abbán's house, a house he shared with hostages from Meath and Ulaid. I gestured to a group of the warriors standing a little further back.

"Keep your eyes on the Leinster hostages," I whispered to them. "If they run, catch them. Do not injure or kill. Understand?"

All of them agreed, their eyes hardening as they stared at the house the three Leinster hostages shared.

Conchobar came out of their house then, he and a group of his friends dragging Connor, Olcán and Caomhán out. The Leinster hostages' hands were bound, and cloth covered their mouths. They stared at the Connacht warriors gathered, and Olcán, thinking they were there for him, lost the feeling in his legs and sagged between Connor and the house.

Fearghus and Eoghan moved closer to the door of Abbán's house, waiting to be given their orders. Once the Leinster hostages stopped moving, my uncle gave Fearghus a sharp nod.

"Abbán," Fearghus shouted, his fist banging the door. "The king has asked to speak with you."

Abbán came out, eyes widening once he saw the crowd that had gathered, but before he could move, Fearghus had swung his sword so that the tip was pointed at Abbán's throat.

"Don't move," Fearghus said. "You must come with us."

Three more warriors rushed to Abbán and bound his hands. Abbán struggled, all animal instinct, even though he knew he could not escape. Not now. A hundred warriors or more stood between him and the gate, one hundred blades all ready to strike him down should he decide to fight.

I could only watch as my uncle's warriors pulled him out of the dun. I should try to speak to my uncle again. Try to persuade him that this was a bad idea, but my father's voice whispered in my head. *Keep the king on side. Make him trust you.* So instead, I watched Abbán until he'd been dragged to the river.

Abbán, stoic at first, shook as Fearghus unsheathed his sword.

"Don't," Abbán said to my uncle. "Don't do this."

"I've not done anything," Ruaidrí said. "It is your king, your own uncle, who has given your life so little thought. King Odhrán has decided he would rather break his oath to me than keep you alive. That is why you are here."

Abbán took a deep breath. "You are no High King then. That title is gone from you."

My uncle stilled at this, the skin around his eyes and lips blanching once more, and any thoughts I'd had of trying to stop my uncle from doing this left me. My uncle would not take an insult like this.

"You cannot be High King if both Leinster and North Munster have now moved against you," Abbán continued. "If you kill me, it's for nothing."

"No. Not for nothing. I will not have it said that I do not keep my word, and any king who stands against me will learn this lesson today."

Fearghus strode forward, his blade sharp and shining in the morning light. Five warriors, using the ropes that bound Abbán, forced him to his knees.

I remembered this feeling so well. The humiliation of being forced to kneel as your enemies looked on. I had tried to bear it without showing signs of fear. To bear the indignity with bravery.

Abbán lowered his head, trying to do the same. To fight and scream would do him no good now. "I hope Odhrán takes it all back," he said, his voice sharp and breathy. "All of Munster. And then I hope he rides north into your lands and splits Connacht in two, so your descendants know the pain of having their kingdom divided."

Ruaidrí stood very still as Fearghus set the blade across Abbán's throat. "My judgement is decided. I offer death to the hostages of kings who break their word, and only death."

Fearghus pulled his sword and opened Abbán's neck.

It was only once Abbán's blood had stopped gushing over the ground that my uncle raised his hand. "We go to war, men. We ride to Munster to show King Odhrán who is High King. Call the warriors up from all over Connacht. We leave in five days."

The warriors rushed up the hill. Eoghan gave each of them a dun to visit, so each of the lesser kings of Connacht would call up their men to fight for King Ruaidrí. Cathal helped Eoghan organise the men alongside Conchobar. As brother and son of the king, they were not expected to play the part of messenger. As a nephew, that was not my job either. My uncle had already given me my job. To watch over the three Leinster hostages.

The men I'd told to guard them were doing as I bid, and I walked over to them. From here, the hostages, all fifteen or sixteen, looked like boys, and were horrified by what they had just witnessed. The death of another hostage whose king had dared to defy King Ruaidrí must have been hard to watch, for his death could so easily have been theirs.

"Take them to their house for now," I said to the men. "You can remove the ropes then, but best keep them confined for today."

If the boys had any sense, they'd be thinking of escaping as soon as possible. That's what I would do. If I were them, I would not stay in this dun, not for all the gold of Dublin. Not even for a princess.

The men pulled the three boys up the hill, while I watched as Abbán's body was wrapped in cloth. It made me think of another whose throat had been cut before a crowd.

Isolde.

This morning, I had wished she were here, and now I was glad she was not. What a terrible sight she would have just witnessed. No, she was safer where she was, away from the world of men and the evil we inflicted upon each other.

Away from me. The man who had watched and done nothing to stop it.

Gormflaith

Pembroke

Le Gros and his men lined up in the courtyard, making their final preparations before setting sail to Ireland. After so much waiting over the long winter, suddenly everything was happening. We had left Chepstow Castle only two weeks ago, had finally made it to Pembroke Castle yesterday, and today the ships were leaving.

Strongbow had said to his servants in Chepstow that Pembroke offered better hunting and fishing, but the real reason we were here was that this was the closest port in Wales to Ireland. The river that led to the Irish Sea was in view from the castle walls, as were the ships that would sail us west.

Of course, among Strongbow's knights, it was an open secret that Strongbow had travelled here so as to receive any messages from Le Gros as quickly as possible. I was glad of this, for it already showed that Strongbow was prepared to take *some* risks to further his own ambitions, though I wished he would take more.

There were not as many men in the courtyard as I would have liked. Despite the fact it was an open secret, this delegation still had to claim they left without Strongbow's permission. To have too many men involved would pour doubt onto that narrative. I counted the warriors as I stood on the steps. Only seventy archers and eight knights. That was it. They were all skilled warriors, yes, but skill could only go so far if an Irish king sent hundreds, or even thousands of their warriors to drive them back.

I could only think of the numbers that came to Máelmórda and Sitric's aid at Clontarf. Thousands and thousands of Viking and Leinster warriors had rallied to their cry, and Brian had still won the day. If thousands hadn't done the job, how could fewer than one hundred even dream of winning so much as a blade of grass? Part of me longed to go to Ireland, but another part dreaded it now that I realised Strongbow was sending so few. *Dreaded that after working so hard to send Donnchad away, I might fail.*

Not that I should be so confident of making it to Ireland just yet. David had not given me permission to go with him. I'd thought with a winter to bed and persuade him, he would relent, but this had not been the case. He had remained resolute in his desire for me to stay behind, and no number of sweet words or kisses could undo it.

Today was my last chance, and I was determined to change his mind. Dressing carefully, I had put on my most beautiful gown and adorned myself with all the trinkets he had bought me.

There he was coming into the courtyard now. I gave him my sweetest smile, but clearly knowing what I was about to ask, he moved past me, his eyes focused on Le Gros and the men gathered in the courtyard.

"You would rather leave me here, my love, than have me by your side?" I called after him, tears springing to my eyes and my chin trembling in the hope that he might turn and witness my performance of heartbroken grief. "I cannot be parted from you, David. We are only just married. How can you do this to me? How can you leave me?"

"Hush now, Alys. No more of this."

"David." I caught up with him and pressed my hand against his face. "David, please take me to Ireland. I will be desolate without you."

David stopped, the expression in his eyes as wretched as I had portrayed myself to be. "It is safer here, Alys. You are *safe* here." Gently, he wiped my tears with his thumb. "We have lain with each other many times. You could be with child, and I would not risk you or our baby by bringing you to war." He kissed me, first my lips, then my hands. "As my wife, you can stay at Pembroke as one of the ladies of the castle. Wouldn't you like that?"

"No." I wiped my tears and pulled my hands from his. "It's not that I am ungrateful, but I know you will be safer with me. I know the language of the land you go to. Without me, you are like a flock of lambs to the wolves. I can't bear it. I won't be able to sleep for a second while you are gone. I shall weep myself dry."

"Alys, do not fret so. Le Gros and William Ferrand are seasoned warriors. They know what they are doing. I know you want to go, but it cannot be. At the harbour tomorrow, you will give me a kiss of farewell and then return to Pembroke Castle with the other ladies. That is my final word. I am your husband, and you must trust that I know best in these matters."

He smiled, kissed my hand one final time, and then walked toward the stables where his horse was being readied.

With his leaving, I felt the strength of my argument fading. I had played my part too well. Sweet. Chaste. Gentle. It was no wonder he couldn't see me at his side in Ireland. He wanted to dream of me at home. A babe in my belly and sleeping inside the castle beside a warm fire. If anything, my trembling chin and sudden tears had only made him more determined to leave me behind.

This was a problem.

Frustrated, I sighed. If lust would not work, then I had to find some other way to convince him.

Or someone else.

I waited for my chance and followed Le Gros when he next left the courtyard. He was my last hope. A Norman knight and trusted by Strongbow, he also drank to excess, had affairs with women and had brought a leper into his fold. He was shrewd too, and ambitious. If anyone was going to defy David and bring me to Ireland, it was him.

Walking slowly, I made my way to the falconry and watched as Le Gros fed his falcon.

It would have been an easy place to meet with him if I'd still had Olaf. Alas, Olaf was still searching for Angelo, and so instead

I pretended that my affection for these birds I had once looked after had led me to visit their cages.

"What are you doing out here, Alys?" Le Gros said as I walked over to the eagle cage. "Surely you are not looking for work? Is my nephew not keeping you in the fine silks that you deserve?"

"You think I must work to *earn* my coin?" I tutted. "You have mistaken me for a whore, Le Gros. What a shame. I remember saying my marriage vows only last winter, which means you are blind or a fool." I glared at him. "You're not blind, so a fool you must be. A fool who is bringing my husband to war with only eighty men."

"Sweet Alys, I jest." Le Gros' voice was softer this time, kinder – even though I had just insulted him. Despite his smile, he didn't want to linger in conversation and instead cooed at his falcon, which in turn ruffled its tail feathers. The knights thought this was a sign of affection, but really it was food they longed for, and for their wings to be unclipped.

"Will you take your falcon to Ireland?" I asked.

"No." Le Gros scoffed at the suggestion. "War is no place for birds such as these."

"David says war is no place for women either, though I disagree."

"Disagree? A lover's tiff already? Surely not."

"He can't bear to see me hurt, and I can't bear to be without him. What can we do then but argue?"

Le Gros gave a sympathetic nod, but his interest had now faded entirely. Turning, he took a step back toward the courtyard.

"I've told David, I understand the language of Ireland. I can be of help. I can even tell you what Robert FitzStephen has said to his brother at Carrig because..." I broke off and moved closer to the cage.

"What did Robert FitzStephen say at Carrig?" Le Gros stopped walking.

"I'm not supposed to repeat it. I swore I wouldn't."

"Swore to whom?"

"My brother, Donn." I bit my lip. "If I have not told David, I should not tell you. I'm sorry I mentioned it."

My words lacked subtlety, but Le Gros, all ambition, could not turn away. Like a fish on a hook, he came closer to me, his mind already whirling with potential schemes and whispers. "If you truly wish to see David succeed, you must tell me, Alys. We are family now, are we not?"

Wrapping my arms around my body, I lowered my face. "FitzStephen and his brother are building a fort outside Wexford, on the Hill of Carrig."

"Yes. I know this."

"But what you don't know is that they are going to attack Waterford this summer. They will stake a claim on that city too. The longer you wait, the more land they will take, and Strongbow will have less to give his supporters. This hurts David. I know it. There will be nothing left for your family. But I don't know how to help him. He won't listen to me when I tell him that treachery is afoot."

Le Gros sighed. "I half suspected what you've told me, Alys. Robert and Gerald FitzStephen have done much of the hard work and deserve their just rewards, however it is worrisome that they think to lay claim to so much. Robert never mentioned Waterford in his letters to Strongbow."

"Donn said it was to be a secret. That they would attack and ask for Strongbow's forgiveness after. It is why… I thought perhaps… you should not go to Carrig right away… though I am ignorant in the ways of war."

"Where do you think I should go?"

"Waterford. You should stake your claim first, no?" I ran my hand through my hair and shrugged. "But I don't know about these things. Perhaps I'm wrong."

Le Gros tilted his head. "Tell me more of your thoughts. They might help me conjure ideas of my own."

Taking my time, I ran my hands over the bird cages in front of me. "Well… I just thought… if you sailed straight to Carrig, you would be subservient to the FitzStephens. Robert and his brother are entrenched in Ireland already. They know many of the kings.

They have all the connections, and if you go to Carrig, you will join *their* army. You will be their knights and archers to do with as they will, but if you go to Waterford, the land they so desire, then you can say that you must lead the invasion into that city." I gave a small smile. "Does that sound as silly to you as it does in my own head?"

Le Gros took a deep breath. "I must confess, this was something I had mulled over myself, but I decided against it in the end because I have no knowledge of the land. In a way, I am reliant on Robert because of the relationship he has built up with Diarmait, the Leinster king. There's no getting around that."

"But that is where I could be of help." I gave him my brightest smile. "If I went with you, I could be your translator and help you set up your own fort close to Waterford. Even better, I know Waterford. I visited it as a girl."

Le Gros shook his head. "David would not thank me for it."

"He will when you win land in Ireland. He will when he has a title and a place in this world." I stepped forward and bowed my head as if in prayer.

To touch Le Gros' hand was tempting. Both these things I might have done with men like Sigurd and Amlav, but Le Gros was not like these men. The women he wanted to chase were pure, chaste, virginal, not the wife of his nephew. And so I took out a handkerchief that I had embroidered and dabbed my eyes, allowing my gaze to meet his for only the briefest of seconds. "Please let me come with you. Please let me stay with my husband. You know he can hold no land in England or Wales, but he can win it in Ireland. Let him become the great man he was destined to be. You are his uncle, and you have paid for everything. I know you see greatness in him too, or else you would not have done all this for him."

Le Gros stared at the castle for a moment, looking over the new stone tower and turrets, then nodded. "You will accompany us to the harbour, and you will tell David that you plan to return to the castle once the ships set sail. However, you must board the ship just before this happens, and if you come, you must be able to carry all your possessions yourself. More than this, you cannot tell David what we plan until the ship is out at sea. Do you understand?"

"I understand."

Le Gros smiled then, his fleshy lips curling over his small grey teeth. "Then welcome to my army, Alys."

Without another word, he walked away, arms behind his back, and I took a moment to breathe. I had found my way onto the ship at the very last hour and needed to ready my possessions quickly... but first, I had to find Cecile.

Rushing toward the servants' quarters, I searched for my niece. Cecile was a lady's maid now, working for Alina, one of Strongbow's natural daughters. Dressed in plain clothing, she already dazzled the court, and many of the knights looked her way in the feasting hall at night. I was sure that if she tried, she might convince one of them to make an offer of marriage, but alas Strongbow's interest in her was already more than a rumour. Over the winter months, he hadn't been able to help himself when she was in his company. He sought her out, asked her to sing, and conversed with her like no other.

"Cecile, I need you," I said once I spotted her arranging a basket of cloth and thread. "Come."

She set down the basket and followed me outside. "What is it?"

Linking my arm in hers, I led her away from the castle and toward the market. "I'm leaving," I said in a low voice. "You will stay here. You will answer any letters that I send, and if Strongbow does come to Ireland, you will go with him."

"What if he doesn't want me to travel with him?"

"You will find a way." I stopped. Pulled her closer. "You are a Fomorian, Cecile, and you have stolen the witch gift. You are *not* a powerless maid, though you play the part so well."

Cecile sighed.

"How is your practice coming along?"

"I cannot do any of the witch things you can. You're right. I'm useless."

Well, I could hardly dispute that, but now was not the time for harsh words. I needed her, and if I wanted to keep her on my side, I could not be dismissive. "You just need time, Cecile, and I've had little time to help you. When we are in Ireland, it will be easier. Perhaps being there… perhaps being a part of our own land will help you."

"When do you think that will be?"

"I hope not too long. Strongbow has said he will set sail in the summer. If not, then it will be too late."

"What if I don't want to go?" She bit her lip. "Strongbow goes to Ireland to take a new wife. I don't think I can bear to watch."

"Ah, Cecile. Who knows what will happen in Ireland. You think just because a half-hearted promise has been made that it will be so? No. You will do everything you can to get on the ship with him, and once we have Ireland at our command, he will beg for you to be his wife."

"You speak of dreams, Gormflaith, but I must live in reality. He will be married to another. It's all arranged. I can't bear even to think of it!" Tears streamed down her cheeks and sobs took hold of her chest. Cecile, usually so poised and calm, could no longer hold in her emotions. "He's already pulling away from me. I know it. He hasn't asked for my company any evening this week."

"You have to bear it. You are strong."

Cecile shook her head. "I'm not."

"Then know this, if you stay behind, Donnchad will claim you. I'll be in Ireland and no longer able to save you."

Cecile wiped her eyes, her face the picture of misery.

"These are your options. Come to Ireland and see what destiny has in store for you, or you can marry Donnchad when he returns, bear his children, and pray that some of them are Fomorian."

"I wish… I wish all the time that I were normal. A mortal. Why can I not be like everyone else?"

"Oh, Cecile, you are young, and I know what it is like to want to be someone else, but you *must* listen to me. These young women, whom you envy so much, will be married soon. Maybe to a man of their choosing, but likely not. Either way, the same fate awaits them. With marriage comes children. If they survive the birthing of the first ones, then they will bear many more. Ten. Twelve. Sometimes as many as twenty. Their husbands and the children they give her will feed upon her youth and joy and laughter until there is nothing left but a withering husk. And then what will their husbands do with them? Love them? No. How can a man love a woman who has grown old? How can a child truly love a mother who has had to raise so many? Out of loyalty or a sense of gratitude, they might grant her a seat by the fire where she can watch over her grandchildren, but they are just as likely to send her to a nunnery to live out her days in silence. Is that truly a fate you wish for? To be normal."

"It is not that way for everyone, Gormflaith."

"No? Whom here has it better?"

"The ladies who are married to the knights are happy."

"They are happy because their husbands are often away at war and do not pester them with their needs or inflict too many children upon them. It is not love they have. Just time."

"Strongbow's daughters are well looked after."

"Yes, but you are not his daughter. You wish to be his lover. Tell me, where is the mother of these natural daughters? I cannot see her anywhere."

"Strongbow says she was a whore."

"And that is the final word the world has for us. Maid, mother, crone and whore. That's what he will make you if you are not careful."

"I don't wish to be his whore. I wish to be his wife."

I didn't laugh, as sometimes I was wont to do when Cecile said something stupid. Instead, I became quiet and still. "And as I said before, perhaps one day you will be. But you must learn to be patient. Games of love can last ten seconds or ten years. It's up to you how to play this one. Once I am away, I will not be here to help you. Donnchad intends to marry you, and he will do that by force if he feels he has to. But I assure you, Cecile, I do care for you. Máelmórda was my brother."

"You fought with each other all the time."

"Yes. We did, and yet he never left my side, and I never left his. Think on that."

Cecile cleared her throat and brushed the last of her tears away. "Do you need my help to get ready to leave?"

"No. I cannot bring much with me. Anything I leave in the room is yours. All my dresses and furs. But listen, Cecile. It is time for you to embrace who you truly are. I go to Ireland to further our cause, but also to find Angelo. We can be great again. No longer running and hiding. We can be kings and queens. Men like Strongbow will beg us for the merest of touches. Will you help me? Please say you will."

Cecile nodded. "I will, and I will do as you say, Gormflaith. Thank you."

I gave my niece a smile as I turned away from her, glad that she'd been more pliable than David. Her use to me was minimal, but still, if she had any sway over Strongbow and if I could use her to manipulate Donnchad, then keeping her happy was worth the effort.

Once I reached my room, I packed. All my gold and silver that could be used for trade, my warmest dress, and finally my old cloak. I ran my hands over it, feeling for what I had sewn into the lining along the collar. I'd given the last of my gold and silver to Máelmórda when we'd arrived at Bristol, but there were still some secrets hidden away.

Two vials were sewn into the collar. Unbroken. These were the last of the potions Tomas had made for us. We'd used them recklessly at first. I'd used up all the sleeping potions to escape boorish husbands. Máelmórda had used the love potions at the brothel houses to satiate his lust. But the potion of truth and the potion of forgetfulness, I'd hoarded away once they had dwindled, knowing that one day I might need them. Rubbing my hands over them as I put my cloak about my shoulders, I closed my eyes and gave thanks for my prudence.

Once I was ready, I made my way down to the courtyard, tying my bag of spare clothes underneath the fabric of my skirts so David wouldn't notice it when he saw me.

David was standing in the courtyard with the rest of the men, now all ready to leave. His horse and the horses of the other knights were being led to the ships first so they could make it across the Irish Sea with their masters. It was not an easy journey for them, and their heads were covered to conceal them from what was about to happen.

"Alys!" David grinned as he noticed me standing with the other ladies.

I returned his smile. "I've come to say goodbye, my love."

He ran over, pulled me close and kissed me on the lips. "It's time for us to go."

"I know. I will walk with you to the ship so that I can wave you off." This time it was I who kissed his hand. "Already I cannot wait for us to be together when you return."

The ship was ready to depart when we arrived at the harbour. The horses walked over the gangplank first and were led into specially built cages so that they could not move while the ships were at sea. The archers followed, and the sailors began to remove the ropes that bound the ship to the port as servants brought the final provisions for the voyage on board. I waved at David as he left my side, blowing him kisses as he boarded the ship. Le Gros, who stood beside him, gestured for David to help him to do something, and suddenly David disappeared from sight.

This was my chance. Quickly, I pulled the hood of my cloak over my head and picked up a bag of grain. Following the servants who were carrying the last of the provisions onto the ship, I walked up the gangplank. Glancing to my side, I saw David was wrestling with one of the sail ropes at the back of the ship, and so I moved to the front and crouched down between two water barrels.

I stayed there with my eyes closed until the ship set sail, opening them in time to watch as the land slowly disappeared against the horizon. More hours passed and still I did not move, not until darkness began to fall. It was only then that I stood and walked toward the centre of the ship where David was sitting.

"Alys?" David stood as he took me in, face paling. "You disobeyed me?"

"Yes. I did."

Face turning red, he marched over to Le Gros. "Turn the ship around."

Le Gros blinked, then shrugged. "No. She can help us."

"Oh, so you knew she was here?" David snapped. "You betrayed me too?"

"Come, David. She speaks the language. We need all the help we can get."

"She's my wife!" Spittle flew out of David's mouth, and his hands clenched into fists. "You would put her in danger to satisfy your ambition. No! Turn the ship around. We are taking her home."

Le Gros stood up, his face red now too. "I am your uncle, lord and master, and I say no. Sit down and do not speak to me again until you have your temper under control."

David, holding his breath, took a step back and walked past Le Gros, then past me.

"David," I whispered as he passed me, but he didn't stop. He wouldn't even look at me. It was sad that the first person who had ever truly cared for my life should be the one I betrayed the quickest. Alas, it could not be helped.

Staring at the floor, I walked toward the side of the ship where there was a space and sat down. I noted then that William Ferrand was sitting on the seat beside mine, which accounted for why there was a vacant seat here at all.

Leper and woman. *The two outcasts.*

But I did not care. I was on my way home. On my way to regaining what my ancestors had lost.

Angelo

Dúnmór

I knelt at the foot of my bed as I did every morning. With the door open, the people saw me and sometimes asked to pray with me. Over the winter, when food was plentiful and war a distant concern, it happened once or twice a week. Ever since Finnén's message and the death of Abbán, it had been every morning. And not just one or two people, but dozens.

Such was the sudden rise in devotion to the Lord, I had started to pray outside the dun, and on those occasions, many came to listen to me. I spoke of Jesus and Barabbas. Of tax collectors hiding in trees. Of men trying to stone a woman to death and Jesus saving her. I spoke too of hellfire, and Satan, who tempted even the Son of God with his wickedness. The people loved this the most. Not tales of turning cheeks and blessings. No, they loved to hear of anger and punishment. It was the way with all mankind. Nothing roused people's imaginations more than the thought of their neighbours suffering while they rose to eternal glory.

On the day the army of Connacht was to ride to Munster, it was a prince who visited me. Young Connor, the son of Diarmait, came in just as the dawn had broken and knelt beside me.

"Morning, Brother Angelo. I hope you do not mind my praying with you?"

"Not at all."

Connor smiled, then knelt. I had not spoken to him much since my arrival, for he and the other Leinster hostages had met me in Ferns, and I had worried that they might recognise me. This worry turned out to be unwarranted. Brother Angelo was a different being to the mute son of a foot soldier. My hair had been long and untamed then, my gaze always lowered. Here, I spoke loudly and to all. I kept my hair short and wore the plain tunic of a monk. Strange that people with eyes in their head should be so blind.

"I am afraid of dying, Brother Angelo," Connor said, as he knelt beside me. "Am I a coward to admit such a thing?"

"No, young prince. Never. God put us on this earth to live before we die."

"He has other purposes for us too. At least, that is what my father said. He sent me here to convince Róisín to share a bed with me and make a child so that her father would marry us quickly… but I cannot do that."

"Why? Why do you not follow your father's orders?"

"It is a sin to be with a woman before marriage, is it not? I do not want Róisín to sin and be cast into hell. Nor do I want that for myself."

The young prince pressed his hands to his lips, his chin trembling. *What sweetness there was within him.* If I were this boy, I'd have a child made with Róisín already, willingly or not. The word of God was truly powerful – so powerful that it made men act against their interests and even stripped them of their instinct to survive.

"While we are away at war, I suggest you pray, Connor. Pray to God that he will have mercy on your soul and on the souls of all men. Blessed are the peacemakers, for they shall inherit the earth."

The young prince closed his eyes and blessed himself.

"And know this, I will do my best to help you, Connor. You have a friend in me. You have a friend in God too. He is always watching."

Connor smiled, some of the weight falling from his shoulders. "Thank you, Brother Angelo. Thank you for your kindness."

"Now come," I said, "the army is getting ready to leave, and I am to leave with them. You must wave us off, let everyone see you are strong and that you do not fear them."

The prince opened his eyes and stood. "Yes, you're right."

"You could help ready my horse," I suggested. "You are better with them than I am, and that way the men will see you are cheerful despite all that is happening."

Connor walked out of my house, glad to be given a task. That was another thing I had observed with these hostages. They were so bored. Dying on the inside, while an endless supply of food and drink was set at their table. While the poorest of men might crave their jewels, fine swords and silk tunics, these rich men and boys craved the work of the poor.

While Connor hurried to the stables to ready my horse, I watched as the Connacht army assembled within and outside the dun. I observed the weapons they brought and the armour they wore.

It was a sight to behold. Not just the sheer number, but the way those inside the dun, the closest kinsmen of Ruaidrí, jostled for a moment of his time. Like flies to shite. Outside the dun, the poorer warriors gathered along the riverbank. At least a thousand of them. So many of them had come to fight, and yet they were nothing compared to the Anglo-Norman army I had fought with last year. It seemed to me that this Irish way of fighting, the numbers, the horses, the old style of armour, it was like stepping back in time. As if the rest of the world had progressed and Ireland had not.

It was not that these men were not good warriors. They were, and the men understood war well. It was their way of life, yet still they all seemed utterly unprepared for it. Their armour was mere leather, or the chain-mail tunics that I remembered my father wearing when I was a boy. No archers. Only swords and spears. It was as if this were a game. As if their time on this earth had no true meaning, and death on the battlefield was of no consequence.

But war always had consequences. How could they not see that? How could they fail to see that they should not be looking south toward Munster because of some petulant insult, but rather east toward the Anglo-Normans and King Diarmait? They were their true enemies. They were the ones who wanted to destroy what Ireland was and make it anew. But Ruaidrí was blinkered by pride. My father had this fault too, and so perhaps I should not judge them so harshly, and yet I did.

Ireland had been left alone too long; that was the problem. Rome had not come here. Neither had armies from the Saxon lands. Only the Viking people had attempted to take Ireland, and rather than conquer, they had rather quickly become a part of it. But the Anglo-Normans were different. They desired land more than wealth, and soon the Irish would learn that these men had come to take everything from them.

Experience is the teacher of all things, Julius Caesar had once said, and this was true. The Irish had no experience of conquest, but they would discover what it was before long. Before the summer, I suspected. As I looked around the warriors, I almost wanted to tell them. What a waste, I wanted to say. What a waste that your king cannot see what is so obvious. What a waste of death for it to be on a wet, ugly plain in Munster.

"Are you sure you wish to come, Brother Angelo?" King Ruaidrí walked over to me.

I bowed and smiled. A monk should always be delighted that a king would wish to speak to him, even though I'd much rather continue to watch. That was the old Angelo inside of me. Wanting to observe instead of talk.

"Of course, King Ruaidrí," I said, forcing my tongue to move. "The Holy Pope has sent me to see your country. All of it. I cannot stay within your walls forever, no matter how well you treat me."

"Then please stay at the back where it is safe and wear your holy garments and cross always. I will order some of my men to guard you, but war is a dangerous business, and I fear I cannot strike down every spear or arrow that flies your way."

Indeed, he could not. He was not a god, not a Fomorian or a Descendant. *Just a mortal*. Already I wanted to be away from him and among the men before death came to them. That was always the most delicious part of death. Watching the joy in people's hearts before they realised it was coming.

"Thank you for your concern, King Ruaidrí. Now, before we leave, I will say prayers over the men." I moved toward the crowd of warriors who stood beyond the gates. They had come inside to eat, but the serving women had not yet given them anything.

"Not those men, Brother Angelo," the king said, placing a hand on my shoulder. "Why not come and bless my family? It would be an honour."

I glanced once more at the group of men. They were rough-looking compared to those in the upper echelons of the Ó Conchúir clan. I could see the hard look in their eyes and their weathered skin. Thick and rough like their leather vests.

"Of course, King Ruaidrí. I would be only too happy to bless you and your family, but is there something wrong with those men? Should I be on my guard?"

"They are fuidir. Clanless. Criminals."

"And they fight for you?"

"They do. I need men like them sometimes. War is a cruel mistress, and there are some tasks I am loath to send good men to do. Do you understand?"

Oh, I knew very well what he meant. Some men were men, and others were animals. These were the latter. Depraved and evil and willing to do anything for a bit of coin, or perhaps even the joy of watching others suffer more than they.

"Yes, it makes sense, King Ruaidrí. Isaiah says, *The wicked are like the troubled sea, when it cannot rest, whose waters cast up mire and dirt.*"

"That is the truth of these men, yes. I fear the dirt that they would cast up would infect others, but perhaps the Holy Father would not agree with me?"

These questions made me smile. The High King had blinded his own brother to win his kingship. Surely he knew sin as well as the next man.

"The Holy Father would say that all men can be forgiven, but he is a shepherd who guards his own sheep fiercely too. I believe he would understand your concerns."

The king nodded and then moved to speak with his son, taking me with him.

I opened my hands and said prayers and passages from the Bible in Latin. Sometimes Italian when I was minded to. The language I had first heard as a boy had always fascinated me. How the words flowed like water along a stream.

More of Ruaidrí's family approached as I spoke, all wishing for a blessing before they left. Cuan was one of them. I watched him as I prayed, using the lowness of my hood to conceal my gaze.

What a curiosity he was. So quiet. So still.

That was how he had survived. How he kept the fire locked deep down inside of him. I had tried to talk to him during my time here, but he rarely said anything other than to ask after my health and Meallán's. He didn't speak of King Diarmait, or of the girl who had escaped the dun with him. *Isolde*. I had thought repeatedly of new ways to ask about her. A friendly monk might enquire about marriage prospects for the young men they preached to. He might enquire about friendships, but Cuan repelled all such questions with little more than a polite nod or shrug.

But why had he left her behind? If I knew someone who could give me new eyes, I'd always keep them with me. I'd never let them go. He had to have hidden her away somewhere. Somewhere close to the dun. Somewhere safe… and yet, he never left the dun. Had not visited this girl with life in her hands.

Yes, Cuan was a mystery indeed, one I had not yet worked out, though I had learned something important during my time here – an answer to one of my questions. *Where had his fire-magic come from?* The answer was now obvious, for as soon as I enquired about him, I was promptly told he was descended from Sitric Silkbeard. *Gormflaith's first son*. And I would have assumed that his fire-magic had skipped Sitric and turned up in his progeny, except for one thing. Cuan looked so very like Olaf. The same flaxen hair. The same high cheekbones and pale blue eyes. This wasn't a child born from Sitric's line, no, but Gormflaith's other son. The one she'd had with Olaf. *Godfrey*. She's swapped Sitric's newborn baby with her own, that was what she had told me. Like a cuckoo, Sitric and his wife had raised Gormflaith's son as their own, and here was the result of it. Another Fomorian. But one who had no idea how to use his power.

I continued to watch Cuan as I spoke the words of Jesus and Matthew and Mark. He bowed his head, just like the others. Stood still as always, unlike Conchobar and Róisín, who fidgeted, and the queen, who kept touching her hair. Conchobar didn't listen to my words at all. He spent his time glaring at Cuan from under his heavy-lidded eyes.

King Ruaidrí listened, but only with one ear, for he was also listening to the men in the stables who complained that there were not enough horses. Once this argument had ended, his gaze roved over his family, and for a moment, he stared at Cuan too.

We were all watching the same young man. King and prince and monk. I wondered if they could sense there was something strange about him… something not quite right. They were afraid of him, the two of them. Was it his Fomorian strangeness or perhaps the rumours that followed him? He had escaped King Diarmait's dun unscathed, and the bloodied eye and long scar that had once marked his face was all but gone. I had added fire to these rumours by giving one of my own – that God had blessed him and taken away his red eye in exchange for helping me. A miracle. I found that men, above all, feared miracles. To be touched by God was not a blessing, but a curse, something that belonged to the dead rather than the living.

I was not afraid of Cuan. He was like me. Fomorian. Only I understood what I was and could use my fire at will. His fire was burning inside his flesh, crying to get out. One day soon, I planned on bringing it out of him.

A horn blasted. "Warriors of Connacht, it is time to leave,"

Fearghus shouted. "We take the southern path. Eoghan and Conchobar are taking the lead."

Conchobar brightened as his name was called, and mounted his horse. He and Fearghus pushed past the other warriors and made their way out of the dun. Like ants, the other warriors followed.

I gave one final blessing over the king and his wife and daughter, though I was eager to be away. I wanted to keep close to the king and, by extension, close to Cuan. "Keep safe, princess," I said as I blessed her, then I turned to walk away. Connor was standing by the stables, with my horse at his side.

"I will. You keep safe too, Brother Angelo," she replied. "You are the one riding to war."

"Have no fear, princess. God will keep me safe." I walked toward the stables, but annoyingly the princess followed, and so I had to keep my pace slow and expression open, as if walking with her was a pleasure.

"That is good," she replied, "because I heard you wanted to visit other monasteries while you were here and I had a request."

"Oh?"

"I've remembered where a friend of mine is. I thought if you visited where they were, you could give them a message."

I raised an eyebrow. "A friend? And who is this friend? A lover, perhaps."

She scoffed at this. "Of course not. She's a friend, and her name is Isolde."

My heart thudded. Isolde was an unusual name, to be sure.

"Who is she?"

"I met her at the Tailteann Games, but she left to go to Dublin with Cuan once it was over."

An Isolde who was with Cuan just before he was captured. *It had to be her.*

Trying very hard to remove the excitement from my voice, I shook my head. "I do not plan on going to Dublin, princess."

"Oh, she isn't there. At least, I don't think so. It was the monastery of Seir Kieran she was travelling to. In Leinster. When I overheard you say to my father that you will not stay with us for long. I just thought, if you don't come back here after the battle that is, that you might visit and see if she's there? I'll remember the story she told me about Fand and Cú Chulainn until the day I die, and how passionately she wanted to find her family. If she's there, tell her I send her my love and that I pray for her good health."

"I will indeed, princess. I shall call at Seir Kieran, no matter what. You have my word."

For the first time in months, I touched the Descendant knife I had stolen from my father. The knife that could steal gifts. *I might get to use it sooner than I thought.*

The princess smiled as I gave her a nod of farewell, as did Connor when I thanked him for readying my horse. Following the other men, I made my way out of the dun. However, I didn't move to ride close to the king and his entourage as I had originally planned. No, I found the men with the leather skin. The fuidir.

The king had use for men like this, and now, so did I.

Isolde

Seir Kieran

I stood among the oak trees, dressed in my bull-hide armour, and with a training sword in hand. The forest behind the monastery had become mine and Colmon's sanctuary, a place where we could talk and train and fight with no one watching us. Not Méabh and her cautious eyes, not even Leofwynn and her playful spirit. It was only in this seclusion that I felt safe enough to draw on my warrior gift. Here, there were no buildings to burn. *No people for me to destroy.*

"How are you, Isolde?" Colmon asked as I stretched my sword arm.

Colmon liked to begin every training session with this question. Sometimes I answered and spoke to him of Broccan. Sometimes I spoke of the birds that soared above us, or of my travels from Rathlin to Seir Kieran. I never spoke of Cuan, though. I had buried him deep inside of me where he was safe. Only on the long, cold nights did I let myself think of him, and only when I was alone.

"I am well, Colmon," I answered, deciding that I did not want to talk about myself today. "How are you?"

Colmon shrugged, but he was leaning on his stick more and more these days. Even when drawing upon his gift to train me, he used his stick between bouts. His hair was grey, with only a few strands of black still speckled within his beard. Age was moving swiftly, but for now, his hair was not white. We still had time.

Not enough, a voice whispered inside my mind.

"You are learning from your teachers," he said. "I am pleased that you are trying so hard."

I smiled at this, for Colmon did not give compliments that were unearned, and he was right. I *was* learning. Báine had taught me to move the grass, and Gisela had taught me to sing songs that gave happiness to the mortals working here. I had once made Gisela cry, and I could do all these things without the black phlegm flooding my mouth or shaking. Even better, I could move fast, so fast that I seemed to move with the wind.

During all those training fights I'd had with Broccan over the years, I'd always been so hopeful I would win. These memories made me smile now. There was no way I could have ever defeated him. Not one chance in one thousand. But of course, Broccan had done such a good job of pretending he was a mortal that I had not noticed how little he'd needed to try.

"Méabh says you are struggling," Colmon added after a pause.

Ah, so not all compliments today. I was not despondent, for I knew this was coming. Colmon did not try to protect my feelings in the same way Broccan might have done, and he was right. I was still nowhere near as good as I needed to be. I could not change form. I could not summon laughter or jealousy. My warrior strength was hard to find, and I'd made no progress at all during my sessions with Méabh. The water did not want to dance to my commands, no matter how hard I tried.

"I struggle with the cupbearer gift, yes. I'll try harder."

Colmon gave a curt nod. "It takes Descendants years to learn how to use a single gift. Here we are asking you to learn them all and so quickly. It is unfair, and you must remind us. We are old and do not remember being a novice as well as we should. Years ago, we could learn from ten or twenty different teachers, and each teacher gave us different methods and tricks. I will ask Méabh to think about this. Something that didn't work for Méabh might work for you."

"Maybe." I stared at him, taking in his grey eyes that were so focused on me, and the shoulders that were slowly rolling forward. We had only been in the forest for a short while and already fatigue was creeping in. It was time to get started. "For now, Colmon, tell me how I might improve in the warrior gift. My warrior strength is hard to find. Why is that?"

"You are learning quickly, Isolde. Broccan was your teacher before me, and I can see his technique in your movements, but you are right. Your strength is lacking."

"Should I try lifting more rocks? On Rathlin, I didn't really understand the lessons Broccan was teaching me, and my gift had not presented. Perhaps if I lift more, run with them, move my feet..."

"Enough, Isolde. You are focusing on the wrong things. Technique and training will help you, yes, but they are not what the warrior gift needs."

"Then what am I missing?"

Colmon held out his stick. "Young warriors, myself included when I was a novice, make the mistake of thinking their skill resides within their weapon or, if not that, then the arm that wields it. That is not true. You are the weapon, Isolde. That is why you must be so careful. That is why we must move slowly. The vision you had speaks of a sudden loss of control at a time when your gift is growing."

"You think I draw upon my gift too quickly and then cannot control it?"

"Yes. On Rathlin, you summoned a hailstorm without knowing how. But what if you knew how to? What if you knew how to summon a storm and felt a battle rage so strong that you drew your sword, and then you couldn't hold all this power you had called upon? That's what is in the vision, I'm sure of it. This is what we must focus on. Not skill with the bow and arrow. Not posture. *Control.*"

I nodded, for I wanted this more than anything.

"Then let's begin." Colmon threw down his walking stick and took the training sword from his belt. He straightened suddenly, the movements in his arms becoming fluid. He was drawing upon his own gift, channelling it so that he was once again a true warrior.

"Now, when you fight, you must draw on your gift slowly. It comes from inside you. You will have felt it already, a feeling that something inside is burning you." He pounded his fist against the centre of his stomach. "And when you don't know how to use your gift, you will feel this sensation spreading through your body. You must *not* allow this sensation to spread. It must stay as if it is a knot inside the centre of your being. It is from your core that your power must flow. Your focus must not be on arms and legs and swords, but on keeping that knot tight. The smaller the better."

He closed his eyes, and I knew this was what he was focusing on. This was why, for now, he didn't need his walking stick.

"Hit me, Isolde. Strike harder than before. And when you call on your gift, focus on this sensation in your stomach. Not your arm. Not the sword. Not me. Only on yourself and stopping the burning from flowing through you."

"But how can I do that and fight? How can my mind focus on two separate things?"

"Practise, Isolde. Soon, focusing on your gift will be the same as breathing."

I held out my sword, and Colmon did the same.

"What if I hurt you?" I asked.

Colmon grinned. "While we are fighting, I am not the old man you pity. I am not even Colmon, warrior of the Tuatha Dé Danann. I am the Fomorian in your vision. The one who has come to kill you. It is he you must train to fight. Now hit me. As hard as you can. *If* you can."

It was late morning by the time we had finished. Covered in blood, cut, bruised, and with ribs and nose broken, I finally felt I understood what Colmon had tried to teach me. The knot, I felt it. Sometimes I had been able to keep it tight, other times the heat spread through my body. It was unnatural to hold the knot, as if I was fighting against all instinct, and as a result I lost focus on the fight. But not every time. On one occasion, my sword had touched Colmon's skin.

"Time for lunch," Colmon said as he wiped his sword.

"Agreed." Using my gift, I healed the cuts and bruises on my body, then I walked over to Colmon, reaching out with my hand.

"Do not waste your gift on me, Isolde. You are tired. I can bear a few bruises and cuts well enough."

He was still standing tall, for he had not released his gift, but soon he would have to let it go and I could not bear the thought of him being in more pain than he needed to be.

"It is not a waste, Colmon. It is an honour. Please." I reached out with my hands and touched his arm.

Colmon nodded and let me heal the wounds I had given him. Was it wrong to feel pride that I had fractured one of his ribs when I blocked him during our fight? Perhaps. I felt guilt too, though this feeling softened as I mended him. I tried to use the lessons he had taught me in the warrior gift for the healing one. When I watched the cut on his arm healing, it was as if my gift wanted to flow through my arms and into my hand. But this was wrong, wasn't it? I held my gift tight this time. Deep inside. Closing my eyes, I pictured all the wounds on his body healing. There. It was done. Quicker this time than any other time I'd used the healing gift.

"Oh, I'm tired, Isolde." Colmon sighed as he sank against the tree we were standing beside. His eyes bulged, his body swayed, and his arms shook with the effort of not falling.

I rushed to wrap his arm over my shoulders. "We trained for too long. It's my fault."

"No. I am old, that's all. Old and tired. It is a terrible thing to have once run so carefree, and then to ache at the slightest movement." He put more of his weight on me until he stopped shaking.

"Come on. I'll help you back to the monastery." I gave him a reassuring smile, already knowing the look Méabh would give me when she saw him like this.

Colmon, eyes heavy, allowed me to help him walk toward the monastery.

As soon as we reached the monastery, Méabh ran over.

"The sweat is lashing off you," she scolded. "I told you not to push yourself so much this time."

Colmon waved her concern away, and the two of them walked inside. He would need to sleep now for a few days to recover, perhaps even a week. Already I mourned his loss in the days ahead. Méabh glanced back at me but didn't say anything. What was there to say? It was my fault that Colmon was so tired, and yet he had to train me. She knew the vision now. All the Descendants did. They knew what was at stake.

"Isolde! There you are!"

I turned to find Leofwynn rushing toward me.

"Hurry!"

"Why? What's wrong?"

Twirling where she stood, she clapped her hands. "The ewes are about to give birth."

Leofwynn and I ran over to the sheep pen. A group of the mortals living at the monastery had gathered to either help or watch. Aznar, the man Leofwynn liked, was part of the group. So was Ethel, the Saxon woman who had poured me a bath when I arrived, and Banu and Dolag too, though they seemed more interested in watching the men than the new lambs being born.

Leofwynn jumped over the fence to hold one of the ewes as Aznar gently pulled the lamb free.

While I watched, Gisela stood beside me, a grin upon her face. "It is a joyous thing to watch new life come into this world."

"Yes."

"If you close your eyes, can you feel everyone's joy?"

Even though I was tired from training with Colmon, I didn't want to waste this opportunity with Gisela, for I did not train with her often. Closing my eyes, I reached out to feel the emotions of those around me. I did feel joy. Love. Lust. The latter came from Leofwynn, who was watching Aznar. Recoiling at discovering something intimate, I stopped.

Gisela nodded. "You recognised Leofwynn's desire. That's interesting."

"Why?"

"Normally you can only sense emotions that you have felt

yourself." She gave me a sly grin. "Perhaps you met a handsome warrior on your way here?"

Trying not to react to her teasing, I shrugged. "There were several handsome warriors who fought for the High King. Even though I was naïve, I noticed that."

"What else do you feel from those around us?"

Glad that Gisela had not probed any further, I reached out again with my gift. But once again I pulled back. It felt wrong to pry.

"I will not ask you to do anything that breaks our laws," Gisela added. "I just want you to sense their emotions, not to manipulate them. A good healer should know where emotions stand before attempting to change them."

"Why?"

"The closer someone already is to an emotion, the easier it is to push them there. If you want someone to cry, one person might already be feeling sorrow. Another might be angry. Another could be on the cusp of hysterical laughter. If you made the one close to laughter feel sad, you would only move them away from your objective and have to work all the harder to make them cry. Whereas if you gave them joy or more happiness, you could easily achieve your goal."

I closed my eyes again. Aznar was happy but also worried. One of the ewes was taking too long to give birth. I sensed another wave of desire from Leofwynn, but also from Dolag, who was watching Aznar with unbridled interest. Ethel was happy, though an older grief shadowed it.

I reported my findings to Gisela, who gave an approving nod.

"Now, let us try one more thing. I want you to make one of them laugh."

"Isn't that forbidden?"

Gisela shook her head. "The two men beside Aznar are already happy. Many lambs have been born, and the ewes are in good health. See, the last one has now birthed her lamb. There are no secrets that you could bring out by letting them express their feelings. Do it now. Quickly."

I focused on my gift, holding it tight within me, and thought of a memory. One of Móirne and I skipping along the beach on Rathlin and skimming stones over the waves.

"That's good, but you are thinking of happy memories, not ones that made you laugh."

I dug harder into my memories, finding one of me hiding from Broccan and then leaping out at him when he didn't expect it. I was eight at the time, and oh, his expression of shock had made me laugh and laugh. Of course, now I knew that this reaction must have been false, for with his warrior gift, he would have known where I was. In retrospect, this made his reaction all the funnier.

"Nearly there," Gisela said. "Here." She pushed a smooth stone into my hand. "I have one too. I wear it as a necklace. Look." Pulling out her necklace, a thick woven thread which was wrapped around a smooth, circular stone, she smiled. "When I struggle to shift an emotion, I rub the stone with my thumb. Then I focus on the memory I need. Think of it over and over. Give it a rhythm."

I did as she asked and moved my thumb over the stone so that I moved it in time with the peals of laughter from my memory.

The man holding the newborn lamb chuckled. "What a glorious day it is," he said to Aznar. "What a beautiful day!"

Aznar agreed and then laughed too.

"There you are, Isolde," Gisela whispered. "Well done. Why don't we—"

A shout sounded from outside the wall. *Help* was the word, though no one else had heard it yet.

"Someone is in trouble," I said to Gisela.

The voice sounded out again, louder this time, and Aznar followed me, rushing past me toward the gate. I could not use my warrior gift in front of the mortals, so I let him reach the wooden post just before me.

As he opened the gate, a woman with a young child in her arms came inside.

"Please help me," she said, her face red with windburn and her arms shaking with fatigue. "My whole family is sick… but my little boy… he can't breathe. Please help him."

She held the child out, and I took him from her.

"Set the child on the grass, Isolde," Gisela said. "Let me see what's wrong."

I did as Gisela asked, then watched as she placed her ear against his chest, then as she opened up his shirt. His skin was red underneath the blue wool. Spotted and blistered.

Aznar stepped back and blessed himself. "Tis the yellow plague."

"No," Gisela said. "It's not, but it is infectious." She glanced up at the mother. "Have you met any strangers recently?"

The woman nodded. "Musicians passed through two weeks ago."

Gisela bit her lip and looked over the crowd that had gathered around us. "Leofwynn, go and fetch Siobhan."

"I can't. She left a while ago. To visit Cinnia."

"Oh yes." Gisela glanced over at the men. "Aznar, take a horse and ride after her. Tell her to return immediately."

Without hesitation, Aznar ran toward the stables. I could feel his relief that he was moving away from the sick child.

"Is your whole family like this?" Gisela asked the woman.

The woman nodded. "Except for me, they are all sick."

"Banu and Dolag, fetch me some fresh water and squeeze the juice from two apples. Give me a handful of hawthorn berries too. Ethel and Leofwynn, fetch me some blankets."

As everyone rushed away, I took off my cloak and wrapped it around the mother, whose shaking had grown worse. Her back and chest were covered in sweat, and her face was the picture of misery.

"Can I not help?" I mouthed to Gisela.

Gisela shook her head and then gestured for the woman to sit on the grass beside the child. "Give us a moment to get the help you need," she said. "And rest. You've come a long way, but you are safe now."

Pulling me a little away from the woman and her child, Gisela lowered her voice. "No. Do nothing for now. You should wait for Siobhan to return. Then you will see what she does."

"What do you mean? I can use my—"

"No. We must be careful, Isolde. One sickness being healed is innocuous enough. Two or three, a coincidence. Tens, twenties? Then we move into the territory of miracles, and with that comes a lot of notice. We cannot afford that. And so, we must move slowly. There must be other explanations as to why people are cured. Siobhan can use her gift slowly enough that it seems they get better gradually."

"But that means they will suffer needlessly."

"At least they live, and we can stay here to help others. Is that not better?"

I nodded, though I could not help but feel pain in watching the child moan and his mother cry. Gisela held my hand while we waited. I knew she felt the conflict within me. My desire to cure the child was overwhelming, but I was saved from my torments sooner than I expected. Siobhan and Aznar were on their way back; I could hear them in the distance.

When Siobhan came to the mother and child, she placed her hand on the child's head. "He's too warm," she said. "I'll need to fetch some water from the well to cool him down."

"My other children," the woman sobbed. "I was not strong enough to carry the others, but they are all the same."

"Then we will travel to them." Siobhan turned to Aznar. "Prepare the horse and cart for the woman and the child. I will take them back to their house and tend to the family."

Aznar and some of the other mortals, the men who'd helped with the ewes, ran off to prepare the cart, while Leofwynn, who had just returned with the blankets, offered her help to Siobhan.

"Can I come with you?" she asked.

"No, child," Siobhan answered. "Not when it's infectious. Better that I go alone."

"Come," Gisela said to Leofwynn. "Why don't we take the basket of food to Cinnia and her family now that Siobhan has had to come back?"

Leofwynn grinned. "Oh, yes."

"Let's go and take two of the horses and we will leave now. That way we will make it there before dark."

"What about getting home?" Leofwynn asked.

"We will stay over at Cinnia's house. Perhaps even stay with her for a few days. You know how she likes the company."

Leofwynn ran off to ready the horses while Gisela scooped up the basket of food that Siobhan had prepared for Cinnia and her family.

"Will I come with you?" I asked.

Gisela shook her head, nodding over at Báine, who was standing at the doors of the monastery. "You've got to train, Isolde. The witch gift and cupbearer gift are more important than harpist and healer." She held her necklace a moment. "See if rubbing it helps with their gifts. I knew a witch who used a stone once. She said the feathers of a crow had their own sound and the stone helped her find it."

Nodding, I moved back to the monastery and stood beside Báine. Siobhan and Aznar left with the horse and cart, the mother and young child bundled up in blankets as they rode away. Not long after, Gisela and Leofwynn left, baskets of food tied to their horses, and smiles upon their faces.

I watched them go, a sadness growing within me. I didn't like to see them leaving the monastery. A sickening feeling filled my stomach. Jealousy, I supposed, that they got to be somewhere else, while I had to stay behind.

"Báine!" Méabh came rushing toward us. "Come with me. Quick. You too, Isolde."

Báine and I ran after her. *She was going toward Colmon's room.*

"What is wrong, Méabh?" I asked, pushing past her to get into the room first.

But I didn't need her to answer me. It was obvious what was wrong. Standing beside Colmon, I picked up the braid closest to his face. The hair here had turned completely white.

"The ageing up until now has been slow," Méabh said in a hushed voice. "It is going to get much quicker now."

I knew the true message within these words.

We were running out of time.

Cuan

Road to Limerick

The ride south was hard and fast. My uncle wanted to catch King Odhrán before he retreated to his dun, and thanks to Finnén, we knew where he and his army would be. Limerick.

It had once been a great Viking city, or so my teachers had told me when I was young. That was until King Mathgamain and his younger brother, Brian Boru, had destroyed it and killed its Viking king. It had fallen into ruin for a hundred years or more, but in recent times the Vikings had reclaimed their city. These ports were lucrative, bringing wealth to whichever Irish king ruled over them.

King Cormac, as King of South Munster, currently held sway over the Limerick king, but now King Odhrán, whose family usually controlled the city, wanted to retake it and once again receive the Limerick king's vows and tributes. And so, this was what they were fighting over – not a crown or a kingdom, but gold and silver.

And no place had more gold or silver than a Viking city.

"We can't be too far away now," Fearghus said, breaking the silence at the front of the army.

"What makes you so certain?" Cathal replied.

Fearghus shrugged. "I can't explain it. I just feel that we must be close. The forests always feel endless, but haven't you noticed that the trees are less dense now? When I look upward, I can see the sky and feel the wind."

"That's wishful thinking," Eoghan replied. "There are just fewer oak trees and more willow now. The foliage is less dense, that's all."

Cathal sighed and moved in his saddle. He was a good rider, but even so, we'd been riding for five days now, and a prince such as he was not used to being so long on his horse without a feast or two to break it up. "What do you think, Cuan?" he asked, his voice still hopeful.

"We're close."

Cathal smiled.

"What makes you so sure?" Eoghan asked.

"I can smell salt in the air."

Fearghus laughed. "Trust the Viking to smell the sea. Is it calling you home, Cuan?"

I didn't respond to this. It was a jibe that Conchobar might have made if he were riding beside me. A way of saying I did not belong here. That I was not home. That I was an outsider. Fearghus had not taken to teasing me about this before. This sudden change caught my attention, but instead of arguing this point, as Fearghus might have expected, I turned my head away as if I was examining our surroundings – pretending that I hadn't heard the slight within his words.

After another hour of riding, it turned out that I was right, and we had reached the end of the forest path. Here, the trees made way for thick gorse and grassy plains. The ground turned soft, clay and sandy rather than hardened soil and rock.

"Look," Fearghus said. "Riders ahead."

At the crest of the next hill, a group of ten men were waiting for us. All on horseback.

Fearghus raised his hand, and the army halted. King Ruaidrí, who was not too far back, rode up to join us. Conchobar followed.

"Do you want me to speak with them? See who they are?" I asked my uncle, once he reached us.

"Aye," Ruaidrí said. "You ride ahead with Fearghus."

Fearghus and I approached the small group of warriors. We didn't have to go too far before I realised one of them was Finnén, the cousin of King Cormac, who had visited Dúnmór only a few weeks ago.

"We heard you were riding our way," Finnén shouted, his hand cupping the side of his mouth. "We thought we'd come to greet you."

"Thank you kindly," Fearghus said, once we had reached the group. He pulled his horse to a stop and smiled. "Where are you—"

"Has King Odhrán already taken Limerick?" I interrupted Fearghus, who I knew was about to ask where they were encamped, but we didn't have time for that. As soon as King Odhrán found out a Connacht army had arrived, he would retreat to his own land and hide away in one of his duns. Perhaps that was the point for Finnén – simply for King Odhrán and his men to leave Limerick, but for my uncle, it was to hold King Odhrán to the vows he had spurned. We had to find him before he disappeared into the Munster wilderness.

"Fool that he is, yes," Finnén answered. "He's had more than enough time to loot it, but he's kept his army there. To gloat, no doubt."

"He doesn't know we are coming?" Fearghus asked.

Finnén shook his head, a grin building. "As soon as we got word you had left your dun, we had our men keep a watch of who enters and leaves the city. We don't think Odhrán can know. Otherwise, he'd have left or would be preparing for a siege, and he's doing neither. If we strike now, we can attack while his army is unprepared, or else, you can come to our camp, and we can send a messenger to start the negotiations with him. I'm sure King Odhrán will be more obliging once he knows the warriors of Connacht are here."

"What is King Cormac's preference? Battle or negotiation?" Fearghus asked.

"He's happy to discuss both options with the High King."

Fearghus sat upright in his saddle, heartened by the deferential tone, but I was not so satisfied with what Finnén had told us.

"Are you sure King Odhrán doesn't know we are here?" I asked. "Have you kept an eye on the ships coming downriver?"

Finnén shrugged. "I suppose I cannot be completely sure, but if by some chance a messenger got through, Odhrán hasn't left. With our numbers combined, he's left himself in a vulnerable position. Come and see for yourself."

"Perhaps Odhrán wants a battle after all?" Fearghus mused.

"Perhaps," said Finnén. "And we are happy to oblige him, for we have come ready to fight. Have you?"

"The men of Connacht are always ready to fight," Fearghus said, chest out.

"What advantage would he have by fighting us from within Limerick city?" I asked, trying to keep Finnén focused on strategy a little longer.

"Very little. The walls are not strong enough to keep us out for long. Not like Dublin or Waterford."

"Then why would he—"

"Come, Cuan." Fearghus interrupted me this time. "Let us relay the news to King Ruaidrí. Then he can decide what to do."

I nodded, realising that I had acted out of turn by asking so many questions. And Fearghus was right. I should not be discussing strategy with Finnén. That was a conversation for Ruaidrí and King Cormac. It was my training with Uncle Godred that had made me so forward, for he always wanted his scouts to find out all the information they could before they returned to him, but this was not Ruaidrí's way.

Still, I did not like what Finnén had told me. *It didn't make sense.* Odhrán had wanted Limerick and had now retaken it, but if he could not defend his new city, why would he linger there rather than simply loot it? He was not stupid. He must know that he was in a weak position.

"The fun is just beginning, Cuan," Fearghus said as we rode back to my uncle.

"Fun?"

"Oh, yes," he said. "Battle is always enjoyable when you are in the bigger army. Perhaps you have not known what that is like – you having always fought for your uncle Godred – but it's been that way for my whole life in Connacht, and it's a glorious thing."

Once again, Fearghus was making a point of saying that I was an outsider and not of Connacht. This time, I decided to answer him.

"My uncle Godred often had the smaller army, but he usually won all the same."

Fearghus snorted, and he waved a hand at the Connacht army that stretched out before us. A thousand men on horseback and thousands more on foot behind them. He meant to indicate that with numbers such as this, we could not lose, and perhaps he was right, but still something niggled at me. Odhrán had to know the response his denouncement of Ruaidrí would bring. *He must suspect that my uncle would come to seek vengeance for the breaking of his vows. If he wanted to keep Limerick, why was he not preparing for a siege.*

"Well, who is it?" Conchobar asked.

"It is Finnén and his kinsmen," Fearghus answered. "They say King Odhrán and his men are still in Limerick. Finnén suggested that we can either go to their camp and begin the negotiations, or we can join with King Cormac and invade Limerick while King Odhrán and his men are unprepared."

"Odhrán doesn't know we are here?" King Ruaidrí asked.

"No," Fearghus said. "At least Finnén doesn't think so."

"There is something else you should consider, uncle," I added. "In Dúnmór, you said you felt Diarmait was behind this. You don't think he might join the fray? That his army might have marched to Munster as well as ours?"

"Diarmait?" my uncle sniggered. "Diarmait's a coward and always has been, which means he'll be holed up in Ferns like a spider. I've no doubt he's behind Odhrán's betrayal, but he won't send his men out to fight for anyone but himself." My uncle sniffed, straightened. "Come, let's find Cormac and get ready for battle. Before the day is over, I want to see Odhrán dragged out of Limerick like a dog."

The army moved forward slowly, as was the only way an army of this size could move after five days of marching. Once the front of it reached Finnén, we came to a stop.

"Greetings, Finnén," my uncle said. "I hear King Cormac has suggested we negotiate or we fight. I've come to tell you that the men of Connacht are here to fight."

Finnén smiled. "To fight is good for us. If you keep marching, you'll meet up with our army, and once we crest the next hill, you will see Limerick itself."

Ruaidrí moved his horse forward so that it could walk beside Finnén's as he led us toward Cormac's army. "Now tell me this, what size of army does Odhrán have?"

"I'd say a thousand."

"How many men fight for Cormac?"

"We have six hundred."

My uncle gave a curt nod. This was not as many as he would have hoped for, but still, if we had over three thousand and King Cormac had six hundred, that was more than a match for Odhrán's one thousand. Even my uncle Godred would have liked those odds, and he did not put the same faith in numbers as Fearghus did.

Once we reached King Cormac, he greeted us and showed us his army, who were all battle-ready and lined up behind him. My uncle gave Cormac a warm greeting and asked after the health of his family, but soon enough they got to talk of strategy. We were to attack at midday. My uncle and the Connacht army would attack the north side of the city, where the wooden wall gave way to an earthen one. King Cormac's men were to attack on the southern side and aim for a gate, which they said was rotten on the left side and could not be held for long.

I wanted to tell my uncle that he was being too slow. There was too much stopping and starting, and he was only gifting Odhrán more time to prepare. I also wanted to tell him to send scouts ahead to watch over Limerick and the forests to the east, for I did not like relying on Finnén's assertion that Limerick was not fortified for a siege or that no other army was coming to Odhrán's aid.

But I could tell my uncle was in no mood to listen. He was barking orders now, and everyone did as he asked without a word. He was the king, the *High King*, and I was but a warrior in his fianna who fought for him, and so I moved into line beside Fearghus and kept my mouth shut. This was what my father would want now. For me to gain favour and play the part of loyal warrior.

The readying of the army took a long time. Every man had to piss and shit, every horse had to be watered, and Eoghan had to line up each clan behind their chief warrior and tell them where in the shield wall they were to be. It was past midday when this was done, but eventually we moved forward. As we breached the hill, I stared down at Limerick city and quickly took in the terrain. The land around the wall had been cleared. Mostly this was for farming, but as with Dublin, it was always good to keep the trees a good distance from the city, lest an invading army thought to set fire to the forest, or else use it to conceal their numbers.

Within the city of Limerick itself, I could see warriors walking around, though not very many, and to my greater relief the wooden walls were indeed collapsed along the northern side, with only a low earthen wall to prevent our army from getting in.

Finnén was right then. Limerick was not strong enough to use a siege strategy.

"See," King Cormac said, pointing at the northern walls. "You will find it easy to get into the city. Why Odhrán didn't think to dig a trench there is beyond me, but he obviously didn't think we'd fight him."

King Ruaidrí murmured his agreement with this assessment. "Why don't you ride around to the south side of the city now? If we attack at the same time, we will break up their army. Whichever of us breaches the city first should open the main gate. That way our horsemen can enter too."

"Yes," King Cormac agreed. "That's a good strategy."

As King Cormac and Ruaidrí repeated their plan to make sure they understood what was expected of each side, I stared at Finnén.

"Do you have any scouts still in the forest?" I asked him.

"We did this morning, but they've been recalled to the army now. Why?"

"What about the sea and river? Has anyone checked for—"

"It's time," King Ruaidrí said, pushing his horse ahead of mine. "If we want to surprise King Odhrán, we'd better move."

King Cormac motioned for his men to follow him. Finnén, not bothering to answer me, rode off too, alongside the rest of their army, who made their way toward the southern walls of Limerick.

"Eoghan, ready the men," my uncle ordered.

Eoghan nodded, then rode along the front line. "Those on foot from every clan, come to the front," he shouted. "You are the first wave of attack. Move as a shield wall until you reach the earthen bank. The first and second lines should bring their spears out to repel any of Odhrán's warriors who attack us. Men in the third and fourth lines should throw their spears into the Munster army if an opportunity presents. Those behind them are to fight with sword and shield."

The more experienced spearmen lined up in the first four rows, while those who preferred shield and sword lined up behind them. Soon this first charge was twenty men deep.

"We will go slowly until we reach the bottom of the hill," Eoghan shouted. "Once we reach the plain, we will pick up speed. Warriors with spears in the third and fourth rows, you will keep an eye on the men along the walls. Take them down if you have a chance. Once we reach the earthen wall, we will try to breach it and once we are in the city, we will fight all who stand in our way. Warriors on horseback, you will put a stop to any retreat and once the main gate is opened, you will ride through. King Ruaidrí has offered a golden brooch to the first man who finds King Odhrán."

The men cheered at this last decree and my uncle gave the men an encouraging smile. "If you bring him out alive, I'll give you two gold brooches. One for you and one for your wife."

"What about me? I have two wives!" someone shouted.

This produced an outbreak of laughter, and my uncle clapped his hands together. "How could I put your happiness in doubt by only giving one wife a brooch? Have no fear, men. If you have twenty wives, each of them shall get a brooch… just as long as you bring me that traitor."

This stirred the men, and each warrior moved into position.

The rules were simple, but I couldn't help but note that most of the kings and princes on their well-fed horses were not really expected to fight. We were here to scare King Odhrán and his men into submission. *We were here to watch.*

Biting my lip, I lined up beside Fearghus and Cathal and waited for the warriors on foot to move down the hill. Their shield wall grew in length as they marched, twenty-men wide at first, then thirty, then forty, so that it was wide enough to cover the earthen part of the wall.

As they reached the plain, the warriors inside Limerick shouted insults. *Dogs of King Cormac*, they called them. *Fuidir. Cowards.*

Our men kept marching, ignoring the slurs, while those on horseback remained on the hill. From this vantage point, I could see King Cormac's men marching toward the southern gate. They were following a similar strategy to ours, with their sword and spearmen at the front and those on horseback staying further back.

Before long, our warriors had breached the northern side of the wall and entered the city. It seemed that there were no warriors there to stop them. Not even so much as a spear had been thrown.

"It's too easy," I said.

"What?" Cathal frowned.

"They are letting us in. Where are the spearmen on top of the walls? Where are the warriors behind the earthen wall?"

"They're too afraid to fight," Fearghus said. "They'll surrender long before we get anywhere near the city."

"No," I said. "This is all wrong. It's—"

A horn sounded then. Three long blasts.

I rode a little downhill and turned Sleipnir toward the eastern forest. Flashes of steel caught my eye as men on horseback rode our way. Out they came from the forest, the men fully covered in chain-mail, their horses too. Not Irish fighters, but the men who had come from Wales to fight for King Diarmait. This wasn't just King Odhrán trying to antagonise my uncle. This was King Diarmait trying to kill him.

"It's the Normans!" I shouted at our warriors on horseback. "Move into formation!"

The men behind me moved their horses into line, but not all had heard.

"Loose."

A command from within the forest soared into the air. *Arrows were coming.*

"Raise your shields!" I turned Sleipnir and rode along the Connacht cavalry line, lifting my shield to protect my head and body from the arrows coming our way. "Raise your shields," I shouted again. Fearghus, understanding what I wanted, repeated my command and lifted his shield high in the air so the warriors behind him could see.

The arrows hissed as they soared through the air, and they landed with a sickening thud as they pierced both the wood of our shields and the flesh of unguarded arms and legs.

My uncle, whose shield had been pierced with an arrow, turned his horse and rode back along the path toward Connacht with Conchobar. My father had always called him a coward, and this proved it. Kings were supposed to lead their men, not run at the first sight of hardship. Eoghan rode after him, as did a few of the older kings, but I was glad to see that the rest of the warriors stayed.

But I didn't have time to think of my uncle now. The Anglo-Norman cavalry was riding across the plain and toward the city.

"Spears!" I shouted.

The men on horseback with spears knew what I wanted and readied their weapons.

"Charge!" I screamed.

Together we rode down the hill and onto the plain, releasing our spears at the Anglo-Norman cavalry.

The Anglo-Normans had not only armoured themselves but their horses too. Thick steel armour covered their necks and shoulders, but their sides and flanks were still bare. Our warriors aimed for this unprotected flesh, and as they struck, eight horses crashed into the grass.

Hissing once again filled the air.

"More arrows. Raise your shields!" I shouted.

The Connacht warriors did as I commanded, lowering their spears and raising their shields instead. This protected most of our men from harm, but it slowed us down. Of course, the Anglo-Norman archers were doing this to distract us from their cavalry, but we had no choice but to protect ourselves.

"Look," shouted Fearghus, pointing at the earthen wall.

A few of our men had begun to climb back over. "There are thousands of warriors in the city," one of them shouted. "What shall we do?"

Ah, so King Odhrán had hidden his army from view. Rather than the one thousand Finnén had estimated, there could be many more.

"Regroup and form a shield wall," I shouted. "Then march in—"

"Retreat!" Eoghan shouted as he rode down the hill toward us. "Retreat!"

"No, Eoghan," I called back. "We should fight."

"Sorry, Cuan. It's the king's order. He wants us out of here."

Moments later our horns sounded. At first our men trickled out of the city, then they came out like a flood as smoke billowed up from behind the walls. Odhrán, so keen to defeat us, was setting parts of Limerick on fire to try and trap and kill our men.

Turning Sleipnir back toward the Anglo-Norman cavalry, I noted they had changed direction and were now heading south and toward King Cormac's army. His foot soldiers were retreating now too, and running toward the forest. My stomach sank as I realised the Anglo-Norman cavalry would catch most of them before they reached it.

I felt for King Cormac and his men, but the change in direction from the Anglo-Norman cavalry meant that our horsemen had not needed to engage in open battle. It had also allowed our warriors on foot to retreat. Over one thousand of our warriors had poured out of the city now and very few of them appeared to be injured.

But that didn't mean the archers were done with us.

The air hissed above us. "Shields," I shouted again.

This time, the arrows pierced a significant number of our warriors as they ran away. I realised then that they had discarded their shields, deciding to risk the arrows rather than be weighed down and not reach the hill.

"Protect our warriors," I shouted at our horsemen. "Get everyone back up the hill."

Fearghus once again was the first to understand what I wanted and rode toward the retreat. "Shields!" Fearghus screamed as he rode behind me. "Cover the men!" More of our horsemen rode toward our warriors, using their shields to protect the men who had none.

I rode back and forth along the plain, trying to ensure that the men at the back had some protection while keeping watch for another flurry of arrows. It didn't take long before I heard the hissing sound again.

"Shields," I shouted. "Shields up."

The men lifted their shields and this time I was glad to find only a few had hit their mark. The air, however, was filled with screams, and as I glanced south, I could see the Anglo-Normans cutting down King Cormac's men.

Once the last of the Connacht warriors had made it over the hill, I rode after them and then over to my uncle, who was on horseback by the edge of the forest. He and Eoghan were sending scouts out in all directions, making sure that an army aligned with Diarmait had not compromised the road home.

"We should return to Dúnmór now," Conchobar said to his father. "Now, while our losses are not many."

"No. We should fight," I countered. "The Anglo-Normans are

here and without Diarmait's army to support them. We can take them if we join with King Cormac's riders and—"

"And lose *my* men ridding Ireland of an enemy that affects *every* kingdom?" Ruaidrí shook his head. "Every rival king would be rid of the Normans without so much as lifting a finger while I'd be down two thousand warriors. The Ó'Neills, oh they'd love that. They'd have the high kingship wrested from me before the end of the year."

My uncle's words were not without logic. He was right, we would suffer if we fought the Anglo-Normans alone, and yet they were giving Diarmait all his power… and they were here. Now. And out in the open.

"So Dúnmór it is," Conchobar said.

"Not just yet." King Ruaidrí gripped his reins tight, the skin on his fingers turning as pale as his face. "If King Diarmait's Anglo-Norman army rode the whole way from Leinster to Munster, then it means nobody stopped them. It means that all of Leinster and over half of Munster do not recognise me as their High King. It means that once this failed battle is spoken of throughout Ireland, the other kingdoms will turn against me too. We cannot have that."

"Then what shall we do?" Cathal asked.

"If Diarmait wants to play games, we will play them," Ruaidrí replied. "If Odhrán wants to help take the high kingship from me with his treachery, then I will take what means most to him."

"Which is?" Cathal frowned.

Ruaidrí gave his younger brother a pat on the shoulder and then turned his gaze over the rest of us. "These are my orders. Eoghan and I shall ride home with half our army and call up the kings who are still loyal to us. Not just Connacht this time. I'm calling every king from every kingdom of Ireland to attend a feast at Dúnmór, and we, together, are ridding ourselves of Diarmait and his knights once and for all. Any king who doesn't attend will be our enemy, and we will deal with them in turn."

"What about the rest of the army?" Eoghan asked. "What are they to do?"

"They shall ride to Killaloe."

"Killaloe?" Fearghus repeated.

"Yes, go to Killaloe and set it alight. Burn everything. Destroy the home of their great king that they revere so much. Brian Boru fought and fought to save it. Let them see that Odhrán Uí Brian has fallen far from the tree. Let his men see that they have lost the very thing they swore to protect and that Odhrán's betrayal is the cause."

My uncle's gaze moved and rested upon his son, then me. "Conchobar, you are to lead that half of the army. Cuan, you will lead the raid into Killaloe. That won't be a problem for you, will it?"

"Why would it be a problem for me?"

"King Brian is your ancestor. I don't want to ask something of you that would make you uncomfortable."

"I have no discomfort when fighting for Connacht."

King Ruaidrí gave a nod. "Fearghus, Cathal, you go too. Take the Uí Maine, Delbna and Umall clans, and bring the fuidir."

"I'd rather not have them," Conchobar said.

"No?" King Ruaidrí replied. "Believe me, you should be glad they are joining you, for you won't want to do what I will ask of them. War is war, my son, and there are times when you have need of rats and wolves."

My uncle nodded at the group of fuidir that had come to us from deep inside the forests of Connacht. The clanless men who'd been cast out by their own families. Even looking at them made my skin crawl.

"Luchóg," my uncle said, gesturing for one of them to come over. "You and your men are to burn the monastery at Inis Cealtra. Take whatever gold you can find; that will be your payment. Spare none who get in your way."

"Isn't the abbot of Inis Cealtra the brother of King Odhrán?" Fearghus asked.

"Indeed," King Ruaidrí answered, smiling for the first time since our retreat. "Now off you go."

⋆

We rode hard toward Killaloe, burning and raiding along the way. This was a place famous throughout all of Ireland; the homeland of King Brian Boru, who defeated Sitric Silkbeard and King Máelmórda of Leinster. He was my great-great-great-grandfather through his daughter Slaine, and here I stood with a torch in my hand and with the order to set it alight.

I didn't like this command. To destroy what was a beautiful dun where great men had once trod.

"I can sense your hesitation," a voice said.

I turned to find Brother Angelo sitting on his horse behind me. He too stared at the dun.

"Should you be here, Brother Angelo? I'm not sure my uncle meant for you to join this part of the army."

"It is good then that King Ruaidrí has no power over me. I obey the Holy Father and the Holy Father alone, and he has charged me with exploring and understanding this land and your people."

Understand us? *What was there to understand?* All men were the same. I'd fought for two kings now and there was no difference as far as I could see. That was how I knew that Ruaidrí had given me this charge purely because he knew I would find it difficult. It was a test, and a test I promised myself and my father I would pass, but still, I could not find my way to giving the order to raid and set fire to the dun.

"What do you think the Pope would tell me to do, Brother Angelo?"

"You don't wish to follow your uncle's orders?"

"No."

"But the king of this dun, he has dishonoured your uncle, has he not? Broken his oaths."

"That is true."

"The Bible says: *and according to the Law, one may almost say, all things are cleansed with blood, and without shedding of blood there is no forgiveness.*"

It seemed a strange thing for him to say, for he had spoken of forgiveness and turning cheeks before, but perhaps I had misunderstood his meaning. My father had taught me the Bible, but

Godred had not continued this education, and I was often confused by the teachings of monks and priests.

"Did you ever hear of King Brian Boru?" I asked. "He was a great king of this land and an ancestor of mine. It feels wrong to burn down his home."

"That is because you reflect on worldly things, young Cuan, but a stone wall is not all we are. And you must also remember this: after King Brian, there was another king of this land. King Donnchad. King Donnchad was so unpopular that the Kingdom of Munster barred his two surviving sons from being king as well as their offspring. It seems that for every great man who was king here, there was a terrible one too."

"How do you know all that?" I asked, intrigued that he knew more about my ancestors than I did.

"I have my ears open, Cuan, and I ask the right questions."

The monk smiled at me, and though I found sense in his words, I found no comfort. Brother Angelo's words flowed too easily, his sentiments seeming to bend with whoever he was talking to, as if he had no true thoughts, but rather phrases he had memorised. Still, who was I to judge? He was telling me the word of God while I stood with a torch in my hand – ready to destroy the homes of the innocent.

Lowering the flame onto the thatch, I watched as the fire grew. The other warriors of Connacht saw my signal and rode toward the scattered ráths and the wooden walls of the dun and set it alight too.

It didn't take long for screams to echo into the night as the people ran to the river.

I imagined then Killaloe as it was during the time of King Brian and his wars with the Viking people. When the people had run from the river and to the dun. Now it was all backward. All wrong. Now it was the warriors of Ireland terrifying the people and making them flee their homes.

⋆

That night I could not sleep. Two of the men had been struck by arrows during our attack on Killaloe, and I knew they would not last the night. I took the first watch and sat beside them. As the night faded and the sun began to rise, Cathal came to take my place.

"You should sleep now, Cuan," he said.

"Not yet. Can you go and fetch Brother Angelo? I don't think either man has long left."

"He's gone," Cathal said. "We looked for him earlier, but he told the men he wanted to explore the monasteries along the river."

Taking a deep breath, I held the dying men's hands and waited until they passed over. I was no monk. I had no holy words to say over their bodies, but I would not have them die alone.

Gormflaith

The Irish Sea

I'd dreamed of Olaf often over the winter months, watching him as he flew over the Irish forests and duns, but I had not spoken to him. I had not wanted to distract him or to think I might recall him before he found Angelo.

On this voyage to Ireland, I dreamed of him again. He was perched on a dun wall, though I didn't know which one it was, and when I used his eyes to see, Angelo was not there. Where could he be?

Have you found him, Olaf? I asked.

From the way that Olaf shook his head, I knew that answer was no.

I am coming to Ireland, Olaf. I may need you soon, but until then, keep searching.

Olaf launched himself off the wall and soared into the sky, his keen eyes staring into the forests below. Staring into the endless green.

Waking from my dream, I pulled my blanket over my head to keep the sea spray from my face and sat quietly on my seat. I could do nothing for Angelo myself and so I pushed him from my mind and focused on more pressing matters. Glancing over at my husband, I smiled, but he turned his head. David had hardly spoken to me since our departure. He gave me food and water. He slept beside me and shared his warmth, but he did not make eye contact or answer any of my questions. I had disobeyed him. For a man like

David, who placed such stock on his name and his word, this had to be a hard blow to his ego.

While I acted contrite, I was not sorry for what I had done. Not in the slightest. It was my time to return to Ireland and to become what I was always supposed to be. *Queen*. David's sullenness therefore was not the punishment he intended it to be, and perhaps he realised that. That I was contrite but not desperate, and as such he grew all the colder as time passed. If I'd been a good wife, I'd be tearing my hair out and weeping. Begging for his forgiveness. But I was not a good wife. If I had been, I would be at the castle at Pembroke and embroidering by the fire.

To my relief, the voyage between Pembroke and Ireland was short. Only three days, and it was only as long as that because the wind was against us.

As Irish land came into view, Le Gros beckoned me over. A longphort loomed in the distance, and high wooden walls. It was like Dublin in so many ways, but an imitation only.

"That is the Kingdom of Wexford?" Le Gros asked.

I nodded.

"Waterford is further south and to the west, you say?"

"Yes, though it is not far."

Taking an apple from his pocket, Le Gros peeled the skin away with his knife. David did this too when he ate apples, though he was always careful and deliberate, using his knife to take only the skin. Le Gros performed the same procedure like a backstreet butcher. Piercing his apple with the blade, he sprayed juice all over his hand and wrist.

"What can you tell me about the land around Waterford?"

"It is lush and green, full of forest and not as mountainous nor as wild as the north. There is an outcrop of land just before you reach the mouth of the River Suir, which you need to sail up to reach Waterford. It's called Dun Domhnall, though there is no fort there now, and might make a good place to land. It's not too far from the city itself, and there are no strong currents in the bay. I remember swimming there as a girl."

Le Gros nodded.

I could have added some more strategic advantages. The land passage between this outcrop of land and the mainland was narrow and shaped like a finger that curled away from the mainland, which would make a land attack difficult, but a young woman called Alys would not know of these things. I would just have to let Le Gros come to this conclusion himself once he saw it.

"Anything else?"

"Not that I can think of."

Le Gros sliced a chunk from the apple and set it on his lips. While still chewing, he said, "Before I set sail, I wrote a letter to FitzStephen. I told him that we were landing here and to come to our aid. How long do you suppose it would take him to reach us?"

I mulled over the distance between Wexford and Waterford. It wasn't very far, and the forest path was fairly straight. "Two days, I think."

"Very good, Alys. If I have any more questions, I'll let you know."

Dismissed, I moved away from him and back over to David, devout little wife that I was still pretending to be, but I was worried. For Le Gros to stand a chance of winning land, he had to survive until FitzStephen arrived. That would take two days as I had said, maybe three if the Carrig army had to prepare for the march.

Three days would be a long time to hold out, for the small number within Le Gros' army would be immediately apparent to the Irish and Waterford Vikings, and while the site I had suggested would be easier to defend than anywhere else, I wasn't sure if it was good enough to endure a sustained attack. Even worse, the Waterford Vikings could sail around to the outcrop and fight us from the beach while another group of their warriors attacked us from the north.

Perhaps I had been wrong to suggest to Le Gros that this was the right course of action. Perhaps joining FitzStephen would have been best after all?

I sat beside David and stilled myself. This time I did not plead for forgiveness or beg that he speak to me. I was too afraid for that, and for the first time, the first time in truth, I lamented the loss of Máelmórda. Useless as he was, if he were here, I would know someone understood what had to happen and how to make it so.

"Do not be afraid, Alys," a low voice said to me.

I looked up to find William Ferrand staring at me.

"I'm not afraid."

"Oh, but you are, and you are right to be. You might be from this land, but the people here are your enemy now."

"Yes. I have betrayed them by helping you." I gave him a sad smile as if this was the first time I had contemplated my situation, but the truth was, I knew the people here were my enemies. The mortals of this land had always been the Fomorians' enemy. They had favoured the Tuatha Dé Danann over us for hundreds of years, fought for them. Loved them.

But now the Descendants were gone, we were all they had.

Perhaps in time they would come to love us too.

I huddled against the side of the ship, cloak pulled tight around my shoulders, and closed my eyes. Sleep was my friend now. Who knew how much time I'd have to rest once we landed.

I didn't know how long I'd been sleeping when the outcrop of land came into view. The men shouted with excitement, and I overheard Le Gros noting the strategic advantage of being able to defend it more easily than anywhere else he'd seen. He ordered the ship to land, and quickly the men set about gathering our provisions. Once we landed, the advantages of this site became even more apparent. Not only did the cliffs along the headland mean we could not be attacked from the rear, but a ditch had already been dug along the narrowest part of the peninsula. Some other army had once used this small outcrop as a refuge, and so all Le Gros had to do was enhance what was already here. Once all our goods and horses were removed from the ship, Le Gros ordered his men to cut down the trees to make wooden palisades between the trench and our camp.

I stared out at the land. Ireland. *My home*. A small smile crept onto my lips, enjoying the feel of the wind on my skin. The view was nothing special, the only thing between the camp and the endless forest beyond was a plain, and the only thing on that was a herd of cattle. They chewed the grass and stared up at us from time to time as if amused by our sudden appearance.

The men did as Le Gros asked without complaint, leaving me alone on the shore. It was with some sense of trepidation that I watched as the ship sailed away. Retreat was no longer in our gift. We had to stay and endure whatever came our way.

Quickly, I returned to my part of dutiful wife and made a fire so that food could be boiled up. Plenty of fish had been caught during our voyage, and a fish stew was not beyond my capabilities. I even remembered to pick wild garlic and skirret to improve the taste.

Two of the younger archers gutted the fish, while I did the best I could with the herbs and vegetables we had brought with us, and soon an edible dinner was readied. Le Gros was the last one to come over to the pot and took the final ladleful.

After eating, the men spent the rest of the evening readying their tents or else strengthening the palisade, but once the clouds blew over and the natural light faded, all they could do was rest and hold their position. Now it was a waiting game. Waiting to see if the Irish decided to fight us before Robert FitzStephen came to our aid.

Over the next two days, the Irish warriors from the local Munster clan, as well as the Waterford Vikings, had come to watch us. Perhaps confused by our low numbers, they had done nothing yet, but that would only last for so long.

On the third night, I heard horns sounding out from behind the Waterford walls. They were coming for us. I felt it in my heart. They had heard of the exploits of FitzStephen and knew already what befell kingdoms that did not have the stomach to fight.

At dawn, Le Gros, who'd obviously come to the same conclusion, had all the men dressed in full armour and ready for battle. It was then, just as the first rays of the sun shone over the trees, that we saw a rider coming toward us.

"Who is it?" David asked.

William Ferrand and Le Gros both walked forward, pulling themselves up so they could see between the gaps in the palisade.

"He's ours," William said. "The armour is Norman."

Five of our archers ran to the gate and untied the ropes that held the gate in the palisade shut. Next, they put down the wooden gangplank they had taken from the ship so the horse could ride over the trench and into our camp. As they did this, other archers put arrows into their bows and lined up along the palisade, ready to shoot at any Waterford or Irish warrior who tried to stop our rider from reaching the camp.

"It's Hervey," David said to Le Gros. "I recognise his helmet."

The excitement built as Hervey reached our palisade and rode inside. Even the cattle on the plain were excited by the appearance of a horse riding so fast, and they trotted out of the way.

"Hervey! How do you fare?" Le Gros asked once he reached us.

"I'm well, Le Gros." Hervey removed his helmet and pushed his hair, slick with sweat, from his brow. "You, however, have trouble heading your way."

"I've come to Ireland," Le Gros said, opening his arms. "Trouble is what I expect."

"I'm afraid it is worse than you are imagining." Hervey took out a piece of paper from his saddlebag and unfolded it. "I got your letter, but I'm afraid FitzStephen is not at Carrig. He and most of our men have gone to Munster at the behest of King Diarmait to fight against the High King."

"I thought that was happening earlier in the year?"

Hervey shook his head. "The weather's been too bad. We had to delay our march by at least a month."

"So FitzStephen and all our men are gone?" Finally, Le Gros seemed to comprehend the situation, and he stared out over the plain as if hoping that Hervey might be playing a joke and suddenly hundreds of archers would come out from the forest path. I don't know how he thought this might be. The Anglo-Normans, for all their wonderful armour and beautiful language, had no sense of humour.

"I'm sorry, Le Gros," Hervey said. "Robert left only a small garrison to defend Carrig, and none can be spared to come here. There are hardly enough to defend Carrig as it is."

"You have given us faulty information." Le Gros frowned. "How are we supposed to plan an attack if you are not honest with us?"

"The raid was delayed but not by much, and I would add, we were told you would be landing close to Wexford. Our fortress is secure, and we knew you'd be safe there. If anything, we left the garrison a little light in the belief that you would bolster our numbers." Hervey glanced around our camp, eyes narrowing at the flimsy tents and the wooden palisade. "You won't be safe here for long. There is an army gathering further north. I rode past them on my way here. Not just made up of Vikings from Waterford, some of them were Irish too. You should leave. Ride with me to Wexford right now and we might catch them unawares."

The mood turned sullen, and after further discussion between Hervey and Le Gros, they decided we would ride north as soon as possible. Everyone was ordered to get ready.

I ran to my tent and quickly packed up my possessions. *Damn it. Damn it all.*

"There," David snapped as he stormed into the tent. "Do you understand now why I did not want you to come?" Such disappointment filled his eyes as he finally looked at me. "I don't care if Le Gros said you could come. *I* said you couldn't. Do you understand? You are mine to keep safe. My wife. As soon as another ship comes over, you are going back to Pembroke."

"But I can help you."

"No, you can't. Even Le Gros has agreed that it was wrong for him to bring you here. It is decided."

My husband, always so sweet, was sweet no longer. He walked away from me and packed his bags.

What a fool he was. What a pretty fool. I would not be going back to Chepstow. Not now. Not ever. The Irish wind, the soil, the wildness of the sea, it was in my blood. I had run away from it for so long, pretending I hated it. But the truth was, I loved it more than anything.

*

Once David left the tent to ready his horse, I walked outside. Le Gros and William Ferrand were sitting by the fire, talking as they took their watch while their men got ready.

Le Gros turned to me, head tilted upward. "What is it, Alys?"

All pretence now gone, I spoke directly. "Do you want to go to Carrig?"

"No, but we have no choice."

I pointed east, toward the grasslands where the cattle were grazing. "You should steal them."

"Why?"

"To the Irish, cattle are their wealth. It is like stealing a chest of gold from a Frankish king."

"And why would we want to do that?"

"You think they are going to let you ride out of here? No. This land is theirs. There are hidden paths in the forest. They will watch us leave, take those hidden paths, and then suddenly their army will be ahead of ours and they will face us down. There is no way we will make it to Carrig."

"And you think taking a herd of cattle with us will help matters?"

"Whichever king owns the cattle will want them back. You can negotiate with them and ask for their men to give us safe passage to Carrig in return. At the moment, you have no advantage. This will give you one."

William Ferrand nodded. "She is right. I heard a horn in the wind last night. There are warriors out there, waiting for us to leave our protection. Riding out into the unknown is not the right move. Hervey believes we will catch them unawares, but I think they are already waiting."

Hervey shrugged, but as he stared out over the land, doubt crept into his expression.

"It's your decision, Le Gros," Hervey said. "What do you want to do?"

"Tell the men…" Le Gros said, standing and resting his hand on his sword. "Tell them we are going cattle raiding."

Donnchad

Château de Falaise

Normandy was a welcome change from England. The weather was milder; the buildings that FitzHubert and I stayed in as emissaries of the King of England – castles of various counts and lords – were made of stone and filled with the most exquisite furniture. Everything felt cleaner and more civilised. Finer in every way. Perhaps these opinions were merely the result of FitzHubert chirping in my ear for months on end, though now I was here I couldn't help but think he was right. I found myself smiling; smiling as I sat by the fire and ate my dinner, smiling as I was waited on by servants. It had been a while since I'd experienced such treatment. It made me remember what it was like to be a king.

Our journey through Normandy had been longer than I'd hoped. We had missed King Henry in Paris, as he had sailed back to England to oversee the crowning of Henry the Younger, and then on returning to Normandy, he had visited many of his castles. FitzHubert and I had found it difficult to establish his exact whereabouts, but on following his trail, it had soon become apparent that the Château de Falaise was where he'd decided to settle for the summer months.

As FitzHubert and I rode along the path, the Chateau de Falaise loomed large in the distance, its walls longer and higher than any I'd ever seen. Even from here, it was magnificent. Perhaps the greatest castle of its kind I had seen outside of Paris.

FitzHubert grinned and leaned forward in his saddle. "I cannot wait to be off this damned horse."

"Are you sure King Henry is here?"

"Oh yes. Look, his flag is flying over the castle. Even better, the queen's flag is flying too."

"Is the queen not always with the king?"

"She used to be, but it is not so anymore."

"Trouble in the marriage?"

FitzHubert, loyal to the bone, shook his head. "Between them, they have such large swathes of land to manage. This gives them much work to do, and it's not possible for them always to be together. For while Henry was at the crowning of Henry the Younger in England, Eleanor was at Poitiers for the investiture of their second son, Richard, as Count of Poitou."

"Ah, I see. Yes, I suppose it is more difficult to manage family life when the sea lies between your territories." I said this in the hope that FitzHubert would keep talking, but so enamoured was he with the castle ahead of us that he fell silent.

"If they are finally reunited, I hope King Henry will be happy?"

FitzHubert, always delighted to talk about his king, nodded as he dragged himself out of his daydream. "Oh, yes. The whole court will be in fine form. While you are here, there will be plays, poetry recitals, and music. Food for the soul, Donn. Food for the soul."

This gave me cause for hope. The king was more likely to agree to Strongbow's request if his mood was buoyed by the presence of his wife, though I didn't fully trust FitzHubert's assessment of their relationship. Given his inability to say anything ill of the king, I could arrive at Falaise to find the king and queen at odds with each other and the king in an ill-humour. Yet I had to admit, I was eager to meet Eleanor.

When Strongbow had first sent me here, I had not even considered that Henry's wife might be important. During our time in Paris, however, I'd heard snatches of conversation about the famous Eleanor of Aquitaine. Some adored her and said she had the face of an angel, while others were deeply suspicious and spoke of there being a curse upon her. From this gossip, muddled as it was, I could tell she was clever and wielded power in her own right. Indeed, it turned out that the queen was responsible for our dilemma when we tried to follow King Henry. Apparently, she had closed the ports to prevent any opposition to the crowning of Henry the Younger reaching London. Even stranger to me, the ports had obeyed, though it must have caused a considerable loss of trade.

"What's the queen really like?" I asked FitzHubert. "I've heard so many varying accounts of her."

"She is beautiful. Passionate. She almost caused a war after her marriage to the King of France was annulled, you know. Everyone thought her a woman scorned, and then suddenly she was married to Henry."

I raised an eyebrow at this, to which FitzHubert gave a reluctant grin.

"Some say she is cunning too," he added. "But that is no bad thing. It confuses those with simple minds to see a woman be both clever and pretty."

I almost laughed, for this description of Queen Eleanor put me in mind of my mother. She was beautiful and manipulative in equal measure, too. "So Eleanor was Queen of France before she was Queen of England? Why did Louis break with her?"

"Louis had it annulled on account of their being third cousins and too closely related, though it was really because Eleanor had given him no sons. She got her revenge by marrying Henry, who is her third cousin also, and then by giving *him* five sons."

"King Louis must have been furious."

"Oh, he was, but Henry and Eleanor prevailed. It's a great love story, is it not?"

I nodded, intrigued by all of this but wary of asking too much of FitzHubert. I should have kept myself more involved in the politics of Normandy during my time living in Paris, but we had not moved in royal circles, and my experience with kingship had left me bitter. Mother was right about me coming here, I knew this with certainty now. I had lived too long as a common man. To be king again, I had to change my way of thinking.

FitzHubert rattled on then about food, wine and a comfortable bed, but my mind moved to the king himself. I couldn't wait to see him and observe how he conducted himself and how he spoke to the men around him. How they reacted to his orders and who else in his retinue held any sway. Eleanor of Aquitaine seemed as formidable as her husband, a duchess in her own right, a former queen of France and now Queen of England, which made me wonder how many of Henry's triumphs were his own. Men liked to dismiss women in royal circles as merely being there to breed heirs. I knew better than anyone that this was not always the case.

As we made our way into the castle, FitzHubert introduced us to the guards and was promptly given directions as to where we should go.

"We've been given good rooms," FitzHubert said as he led me into the castle. "But first, I must introduce you to the king. He's in the hall of the Great Keep. Are you ready?"

Glancing about the richly decorated hallway, I followed FitzHubert, who led me into a large room, richly furnished with embroidered drapes and woven rugs. The king and his family were at the top of the room, surrounded by courtiers and friends. The king was sitting, while the queen stood beside him, playing with a boy of about four, who was laughing as he ran around her skirts.

Standing slightly behind FitzHubert, I watched as a servant spoke to Henry to tell him we had arrived. His eyes lit up as he greeted the old knight.

"FitzHubert, my friend," the king said. "I hear you've had quite the journey trying to find me. I hope you are well."

"I am well, King Henry. All the better for reaching Falaise."

The king smiled and leaned back in his chair. He was tall and stocky, with long auburn hair and pale, freckled skin. He had a neat beard and moustache, as was the Normandy fashion, and his eyes were quick, watching not only me and FitzHubert but also those who were talking behind us. Finally, his eyes settled on me.

"Who is your friend, FitzHubert?"

"This is Donn."

I walked forward and bowed low. "Greetings, King Henry."

"*Conas atá tú?*" King Henry asked, speaking the Irish words to ask me how I was, just as FitzHubert had told me he might when we left Chepstow.

"*Tá mé go hiontach, go raibh maith agat,*" I replied, telling him I was well. Smiling, I took a small step forward. "FitzHubert told me you would speak Irish, but I did not believe him."

"It is a hard language to learn, Donn, but seeing as you can speak both French and Latin, I thought I should try. I hope I spoke it to your liking?"

That he knew I could speak French and Latin spoke of secret letters reaching him from FitzHubert, or perhaps someone else from within Strongbow's retinue. I wondered then what else he knew about me.

"You speak my language very well, King Henry."

The king laughed at this, as did the men and women around him. His queen, however, eyed me with interest. She was as beautiful as the rumours suggested. Blue eyes set within an oval face and strands of auburn hair showing through her headdress. Yes, I could see how such a woman had captivated not one but two kings.

"What do you think of our guest, John?" she said to the little boy at her side. "We've heard ferocious tales of the men of Ireland. Your grandmother, Maud, thought them so savage as to be unconquerable. What say you?"

The little boy shrugged as he looked me over. Not bored, but unsure.

"You have a message from Strongbow, I believe," King Henry said. "It will have to wait, I'm afraid. The Bishop of Worcester is expected imminently, and I have no time to contemplate two problems on the same day. I'm sure you are tired. Feast and rest for a few days. I'll call you once I'm ready to speak."

FitzHubert, delighted with the offers of food and rest, thanked Henry and bowed.

I bowed too. "*Slán go fóill.*"

"What does that mean?" John asked.

"It means *goodbye for now*, little one."

John grinned and raised his hand. "*Slán go fóill.*"

Following FitzHubert, I glanced backward only once. The king was already speaking to a few of the men to his right, while the little boy, John, was playing with a toy. It was only the queen's gaze that had followed me. As my eyes met hers, she smiled a moment, then looked away.

Isolde

Seir Kieran

When I opened my eyes, I was surrounded by darkness. I was not within a place of stillness or memory… and I was not watching events unfold around me as in my visions… but rather standing somewhere real. There were scents of moss and rot. Leaves rustled in the wind. Birds cawed. When I moved, sticks crunched underfoot. It was cold though, and wearing only my nightdress, I had little to keep me warm. My bare feet recoiled at the feel of damp and mud, but still I smiled.

In my visions, terrible events were shown to me. Words came out of my mouth without me thinking them, and I could do nothing to change what was happening, but here, my mind was in control. I wriggled my fingers and toes. I stopped, walked, and then stopped again. I listened – my ears picking up the gush of a river flowing in the distance.

But if not a vision, what was happening to me? Where was I? I was certainly not within the grounds of Seir Kieran.

The edge of the forest was just ahead, and I walked toward it, drawing upon my warrior gift to give me stealth. Keeping the knot tight in my stomach, I moved as a ghost, swift and silent, until I reached the treeline. The river, the one I had heard from within the forest, was just ahead of me, and along the riverbank, there were hundreds of fires. Maybe close to one thousand men were huddled around them, all singing songs of battle and victory. Of

Cú Chulainn and the warriors of Connacht who had defied him. I smiled despite myself, for it reminded me of the Tailteann Games, but my smile soon faded. My harpist gift was telling me that these songs were not filled with merriment. No. There was bloodlust and battle fury in the men's voices. Pressing my hands around my stomach, I held the knot building there as tight as I could and reached out with my harpist and warrior gifts. Blood. I could smell blood, and plenty of it. Rage. Fear. Violence.

It was dangerous here and my warrior gift wanted me to leave, but I couldn't. *Not yet.* Not until I understood what was happening and where I had come to. Was this a dream? No, surely not. It was too real. Perhaps it was a vision, after all?

Avoiding the branches underfoot, I moved closer to the fires. Only an owl, perched on the branch above me, seemed to notice my progress, for its eyes followed me as I walked underneath its nest.

A sound caught my ear. Not an animal or the river, but a man. Even from here, I could sense that he was closer to me than the others by the riverbank. It was dark, but at the edge of the forest, there was moonlight. In this palest of light, I could make out the outline of a man leaning against a tree. He sat alone, away from the fires and the songs sung around them. Wrapped in a fur cloak, he cleaned his sword, his eyes glazed over as he did so, listening not to the men but to the sound of his cloth as it polished steel.

Cuan.

I rushed over to him. I couldn't help myself.

"Cuan. It's me."

His head turned in my direction, but he couldn't see me, for he looked through me, at the air behind me rather than my eyes.

"Cuan?" I whispered. "It's Isolde. Can you hear me?"

Cuan frowned, and for a moment I wasn't sure if he had, but then he leaned forward. "Isolde? Where are you?" He looked behind the tree, then held his breath, listening.

"I'm right in front of you."

Cuan turned back around. "I can hear you but not see you. How is this possible?"

"It's like I'm inside of a dream, except somehow, it's real. I don't understand it, though. This has never happened to me before."

Cuan's frown faded, and he smiled as he leaned back against the tree. My heart thudded, and for a moment all I could hear was the sound of it beating as I realised the joy on his face matched my own. After months of living at Seir Kieran, I'd made friends, but no one had looked like every wrong in the world could be righted by my presence.

"This is no dream," Cuan said. "If we are speaking, it is real." He looked ahead, his eyes searching for the exact location of where I might be. "I wish I could see you though. Touch you."

I moved closer and sat in front of him.

"Reach forward with your hand. Just a little."

He did as I asked, but his hand passed through my skin as if my body were air.

"I don't understand," I said. "It is like I am a ghost."

"Don't worry," Cuan said. "I'm just glad to hear your voice."

"Are you?"

Cuan nodded, another smile crossing his lips. "Of course. If you are here, it means you wanted to be with me."

"Maybe… or perhaps *you* were thinking of *me*, and this summoned me to you."

"I'm always thinking of you." He held out his hand, and I rested my hand upon it, even though I knew he couldn't see or feel it.

The smile faded for a moment, though he quickly fixed it. Using my harpist gift, I felt for his emotions, even though I knew it was wrong to do this. There was joy and happiness in his heart, yes, but a deep sorrow lay underneath it.

"What is wrong, Cuan?"

"I don't want to tell you. You will think less of me for it."

"Tell me. Perhaps I can help?"

Cuan breathed deeply and closed his eyes. "You cannot help me, Isolde. You know the path I walk."

I moved to my knees and crawled forward so I could sit beside him. He couldn't feel me, but I wanted to be closer to him. My sense of touch wasn't working, but my other senses were. I breathed in. A strange mix of scents filled my nose. The smell of Cuan, yes, but also the smell of Fomorian. The smell of burning from the fire he had made at the ráth. It had faded since that night, but still it was there. I didn't like to think of the fire or of Cuan having that power within him. It only made me think of the vision and the Fomorian who wanted to kill me. I inched back and rested against the tree.

"Then let us talk of something else."

Cuan smiled. "Like when I found you in the forest and you ran away? Now I look back on it, it was funny. The way you hit Scolaí, and he fell to the ground."

"You found that funny? You would never know. You scowled like an angry wolf the whole time."

"I did." He paused. Took a breath. "I wish sometimes that I had never left you. That I had stayed with you in Seir Kieran."

"You had to leave me. The other Descendants would not have understood."

"I don't care about that, Isolde. I wish I had stayed, and if they had taken my life, it would have been worth it."

"That is not a good wish, Cuan. We would not be together, and you would be dead. Why would you want that?"

Cuan shrugged, and I remembered this reaction of his so well. He did it when he didn't want to think about his past or his future. When he didn't want to talk about his father's ambition for him to become King of Dublin or Connacht, and that he had sworn to kill his uncle Ruaidrí.

"Tell me, Cuan, where am I? Who are all these men?"

"We are sitting by the River Shannon, and this is half of the Connacht army. We have been fighting King Odhrán of North Munster. We lost, Isolde. King Diarmait and his Anglo-Normans lured us to Limerick and defeated us. They are clever, those Anglo-Norman warriors. Too clever for my uncle."

That meant chaos was coming, for if Cuan could see King Ruaidrí had failed, so could others.

I felt the world around me fading then, the image of Cuan beside me paling.

"I have to go now, Cuan." I reached forward to touch his hair. Like a shadow, my hands moved through him, but I desperately wanted to touch him. Concentrating harder this time, using my gift and holding the knot in my stomach, I moved my hand over his cheek, and this time, when I touched him, I felt the warmth of his skin.

His hand brushed his cheek. He had felt it too. "No, Isolde. Don't go."

"I must, but do not despair, Cuan. I have to stay in Seir Kieran for now, but soon, one day, I will find you. Do not give up on me. Please. Please stay alive."

I woke, and heaving, I rolled over and vomited onto the floor. Black phlegm splattered over the side of the bed as well as the sleeve of my nightdress. *What had I just seen?* The past? The present? The future? Was it only a dream? Or had I travelled elsewhere in my sleep?

As my stomach settled, I sat up. It was still night, but I could not fall back asleep, not with what had just happened. I needed fresh air, to feel the wind upon my face and to know that I was a part of this world again. Quietly, I made my way into the hall.

As I walked, I tried to remember it all. The feel of Cuan's skin beneath my fingers. The warmth of his cheek and the sorrow in his eyes. It had to be real. It had to be.

Once I reached the door of the monastery, I opened it and walked outside. The wind blew over me, lifting my hair into the air.

Yes, it was real. I knew it. The sensation of the cold ground reminded me of the forest, and when I looked down at my toes, I saw the damp mud that had slid between them. I had fallen asleep and somehow my dream had taken me to Cuan.

What gift was this? Witch-magic? I would have to ask Báine.

But how could I ask Báine more about it without discussing Cuan? Who could I say I had spoken to that she might believe? I mulled it over, knowing that as soon as morning broke, I would find a way to ask her. I had to see him again. I had to see his eyes. His smile.

Are you listening, child?

I stopped in my tracks and turned around. "Hello?"

Reaching for my warrior gift, I tried to sense who was around me. *No one* was the answer. But I didn't trust in my gift enough yet to rely on it. I had heard a voice. Someone was here.

Are you listening, child? Do you hear the sadness in your song?

My stomach sank. I'd heard these words before. At the Tailteann Games. And on Rathlin too, just before the Fomorians came. *I'd thought it was Móirne calling for me.*

The wind picked up again, not just strong enough to tug at my hair, but almost lifting my body from the ground, and the hawthorn tree at the boundary line swayed as the wind continued to blow.

A part of me wanted to venture forward, to go where the wind was taking me, but I was frightened. Old dreams, dreams of the dark and living in the soil, came to me as the hawthorn branches groaned. It was as if the wind were not of this world.

Do you want to see, child? I can show you if you wish it to be so. I have given you a glimpse of the future. The fire. The Fomorian. The sword. But there is more. Much more. We can show you everything.

I… I… did not want to see. I did not want to see more. Did that make me a coward? Recoiling at my own fragility, I gritted my teeth. *How could I be a warrior if this was the character that lay underneath?*

"Will what you show me help me to save the people who live here?" I asked. "I would do anything to save them."

The wind blasted. The branches shivered, but this time, I heard a song within the noise. Then came a light.

A man lay dead, face down in the grass. Cattle tracks marked the ground where it was damp. Beyond him, there was crying. I turned my head. A group of men were tied up with ropes. Not just around their hands and feet, but around their necks. A woman was calling one of them forward. I tried to focus on the image, on the woman's hair and clothing, but it was a blur. All I could see were her thick black curls and the dark green of her dress.

Then there was the wolf with the bluest eyes. A woman walked beside him. A woman with pale skin and black hair. The wolf limped as he walked beside her, and she stared at the sky as if that was where she longed to be, but then she shuddered, and I knew she was afraid.

The image changed again. The sea. Dead bodies. Dead bodies with no heads. A battle had happened, perhaps? But why such savagery? No, I did not like this. I didn't want to see any more dead bodies. I didn't want to know of any more death or violence.

Holding the knot tight inside of me, I screamed. I wanted to be free of this vision, but I knew I had to see it. I had to see if there was a way to save my friends.

"Show me more," I shouted.

The images changed again. This time I was in a forest. A group of men were walking, stalking something ahead of them.

The wind stopped then, and I fell to the ground.

My body shook. My mouth filled with black phlegm, and I bowed over onto my hands and knees. All my strength had left me. I couldn't move, couldn't make it back inside. Vomiting again, I fell against the grass and my mind filled with darkness.

"Isolde." A hand shook me. "Isolde. What happened?"

I opened my eyes to find Báine kneeling over me.

"I..." I rubbed my head. It pounded, and even trying to sit up made me want to vomit. "The wind spoke to me. Showed me many things, but I don't understand them."

Báine stared at me, and I could see the conflict sweep over her face. Something sympathetic intertwined with confusion. "Well," she finally said. "Let us see if we can work it out. What did you see?"

I told her everything that the wind had shown me. The dead

bodies, the men tied up with rope, the wolf and the men stalking something in the forest.

Báine sighed. "I cannot help you with this gift, Isolde. I wish your aunt were here, but then again, her visions broke her mind, and you might have got no sense from her anyway." She shook her head. "There was a prophetess before your aunt. Gráinne. And she lost her mind too, and so as much as these visions may be useful, there will be a toll to pay for it. Perhaps you should not listen to the wind?"

Broccan had told me about his mother and that her gift had cost her everything. Was that my destiny too? To lose my mind and myself?

"Don't you think what it has to show me is important?"

"Perhaps, but I don't know. Not for sure." Báine came closer. "My mother believed in you, so much so that she gave her life for you. This prophecy, that you are the girl that will destroy fire, it is a burden. Part of that burden is that nobody can be sure of what these visions mean. Only you can decide."

I tried to process what she was telling me. That speaking to the wind would make me mad, but that I was the only one who could decide what to do. I had come to Seir Kieran wanting the Descendants to give me all the answers, but the truth was, they didn't know everything.

"Can I ask you something, Báine?"

"Yes."

"Is it possible to fall asleep and travel somewhere else? To visit someone somewhere else entirely?"

"Yes. That is dream magic. You think of who you want to talk to, and in your dreams, you will visit them, except you will not be dreaming once you reach your destination. Only powerful witches can do this, but of course you are very powerful. However, if it happens to you, you must remember to be careful."

"Why?"

"If someone on the other side wants to hurt you, they can."

I was about to ask her more, but the wind pulled at me. I could feel it tug at my fingers and my hair. The wind wanted to talk to me again; it needed to show me more.

"What's wrong?" Báine asked.

"The wind wants me to move closer to the tree."

Báine stared at me, then at the tree, which stood like a dark smudge against the horizon.

"Will you come with me, Báine? Stay with me while the wind speaks to me so I am not alone."

Báine took my hand and together we walked. The wind grew, and the branches and leaves crashed against each other as we approached. There was a voice upon the wind now too. A whisper. It swirled around me, hissing in my ear. *Are you listening? Are you listening, child? Can you hear?*

"Yes," I replied. "What do you want to say to me?"

The wind grew stronger, so strong that my hair lifted above my shoulders, and I felt myself suspended in the air. No longer on the ground. No longer part of the land.

A group of men were walking through the forest. Creeping. Stalking something or someone.

Then the vision changed and the Fomorian with the short dark hair was with Leofwynn. The group of men were now with him too. They were all smiling and laughing... but Leofwynn was dead. Face down in the mud. Skirts lifted so that her legs were visible in the light that sprinkled through the leaves, and blood saturated the soil around her. It stained her hands too. Her ankles and her shoes.

Screams. Or echoes of them. A man with long hair, tangled into clumps and half tied up with string, looked down at Leofwynn. He smiled as his fingers touched her cheek.

The Fomorian with the short hair, however, was not interested in Leofwynn. His attention was on another.

Gisela.

Gisela had a knife in her stomach and was lying on the ground too. She was alive but could not get away. The Fomorian moved closer.

*

"What did you see?" Báine asked.

Gasping as I collapsed to the ground, I tried to stand. *Oh no. Leofwynn. Gisela.* They had not yet returned from their visit to Cinnia. Had they tried to reach us though? Had this vision already come to pass? No… no… there had to be time.

"What did you see, Isolde?" Báine asked again.

"The men I saw in the first vision, they were following Gisela and Leofwynn. The wind just showed me… they are going to kill them. A Fomorian, *the* Fomorian from my vision, is there too."

I ran then, using my warrior speed to get to my room, and quickly I put on my bull-hide armour. The wind had shown me Leofwynn lying dead, of men standing over her and laughing, and Gisela with a knife in her stomach. Could it be tonight? Could the wind show me something like this and give me no time to change it?

I had to believe there was time. I had to act. Now.

As soon as I was ready, I hurried toward Colmon's room.

Méabh was sitting beside him, and I could see she was about to say that I should leave him, but I pushed past her and walked over to Colmon's side. "Colmon, wake up!"

"What's wrong, Isolde?" Méabh asked.

"The wind spoke to me. I need him."

Méabh stared, her lips pursed tight. "He cannot waken now. Not even if you screamed in his ear would he stir."

"It's important."

Báine came into the room, out of breath and eyes wide with worry. "Are you sure, Isolde?"

Méabh stepped to the side, eyes narrowed. "What did the wind show you?"

"Gisela and Leofwynn are in danger. A group of men as well as a Fomorian are going to kill them and it's happening now, or if not now, soon. I have to try and save them."

"You cannot," Méabh said. "You cannot leave these grounds. It's not safe. Perhaps it will not—"

"If you want to spend your life waiting, then so be it," I snapped. "I'm going after Gisela and Leofwynn."

"Isolde. Slow down," Báine said, catching my arm before I could run into the hall. "We need to think."

"No. All you do is think and think and think. But this is the end now. The Fomorians are coming. It's time to act."

"Colmon will be awake soon. Tomorrow. We should wait—"

"Colmon is dying, Báine. You're going to have to start deciding what to do without him to guide you. Now, I'm leaving. If you want to come with me, come. But Gisela and Leofwynn are my friends and I'm not going to desert them when they need me most."

I ran into the stables, leaving Báine and Méabh behind me, and readied a horse.

To my surprise, Méabh followed me. She eyed me again, her face like stone as she readied another of the horses.

"What are you doing?" I asked.

"I can't let you go alone, can I? If there is a Fomorian out there, you'll need a cupbearer with you. More than that, Gisela and Leofwynn are my friends too."

Mounting her horse, she urged it out of the stables and toward the forest path.

Glad that I would not be alone after all, I rode after her.

Angelo

The forest outside Seir Kieran

The fuidir were easy to tempt away from the Ó Conchúir army. Evil men always were the most susceptible to temptation. I'd discovered this many times over the years. These fuidir, banished except when the king had need of their depravity, were easier still. They had no pretences to maintain, no smiles they needed to show. They wore their vices as proudly as a priest wore his cross.

One might think that would make them hard to lure away, for burning the duns and ráths and monasteries along the River Shannon offered plenty of entertainment, but as soon as I told them that the enemies of God were alive and I knew where they were, they were interested, and when I promised them salvation in return for slaying these enemies, they were as compliant as a ewe following her lamb.

Of all the truths I knew, this was the first: there was nothing evil men loved more than the thought of playing a trick on God and winning. Just as Satan tried to tempt Christ in the desert, they wanted to meet with God, souls as unclean as they were, inside the Kingdom of Heaven.

The second truth was this: my words were sweetness. How could I not know how to speak like honey when my grandmother was Gormflaith? I had learned from the best, and after decades of watching, I was putting these lessons into practice.

The day after they had burned Inis Cealtra and killed the abbot, I watched the fuidir walk ahead of me. There were thirty of them altogether – all from different clans and countries. Three were freed slaves, one from Iberia, one from Croatia and another from England. The Croatian had fled to the forests after killing the old Irish king who had bought him. Another fuidir, one from Ulaid who had been banished by his clan, had confessed to killing his own mother and sister. Most of the others, however, kept their sins close to their chests. *No matter,* I had told them. *God could see their souls, and if they did as he commanded, he would forgive them, just as Jesus had forgiven Barabbas.*

Nothing truly bound the fuidir – no family ties, no clan, just that they had found refuge from the world in the forests of Connacht. They stole from the local kings, though never enough for it to be noticed. They stole from traders often, and I guessed sometimes killed them if their goods were valuable. The fuidir stole women too. Slaves or else women from families that could not properly care for them. They didn't seem to have any children though, which led me to believe these women didn't last long.

They truly were outcasts, and yet I found it amusing to observe they had not completely thrown away the structures of society, for if they had entered the forests hoping to find freedom from the clan system, they had not succeeded. After only a morning of watching them, it was obvious that they had a leader, a king in all but name. This man was called Luchóg. It was the Irish word for mouse, and it was a fitting name for him. He had sharp eyes that darted about, always watching, always listening, and long lank hair. That was why it was he I had sent to watch over the mountain path to make sure we were alone.

The rest waited with me, not wanting to listen to any sermons, for which I was grateful. They merely wanted to know that I offered something worth waiting for. Meanwhile, I contemplated what I wanted as I took out the Descendant's knife. I wanted a gift.

Not just any gift.

Isolde's gift, for she had died on Rathlin Island and now she was alive.

*

Making sure to keep the camp a good ten miles from the monastery, I told the men to make a perimeter. Tomorrow, I would send them to spy on the monastery, but today, we would rest and gather our strength.

I was surprised then when Luchóg returned not long after he left, eyes bright and cheeks flushed. The men with him were excited too. "Two women are riding toward the monastery along the mountain path," Luchóg said.

"And?" I asked.

"We could take their horses. It's been a while since I've tasted horsemeat."

Smiling, I gazed up at him. "And?"

"And… the women are both young. One has long brown hair, but the other… her hair is the colour of the sun. The most beautiful woman I've ever seen."

A Descendant then. Gormflaith had said that they were always beautiful. Neither were my red-headed Isolde though.

"They must live at the monastery, but they are not the ones I want. We should let them pass."

I was about to suggest walking closer to the monastery this evening instead of waiting until tomorrow so that we could spy on the people living there, except I felt the mood among the men shift. They wanted these women for themselves. Oh, but sins of the flesh really were the most prevalent and deep-rooted. I could sense from their scowls that they would not be dissuaded, which meant they would attack the women whether or not I permitted it, and then my plan would be ruined. A lesser man might be disheartened to have his plans change like this, but not I. Perhaps it was best to test these men here anyway. See how they performed before we reached the monastery.

"On second thoughts, these two women might be inflicted with the same evil. We should follow them and see."

The men smiled. Finally, I was making good on my offer.

"Let us go quietly," I said. "If they have the same evil inside of them as the woman with the red hair, they can summon powers from the devil himself."

"Will they use their powers on us?" one of the fuidir asked.

"Oh, they will try, but do not worry. God has given me powers too."

The men, more intrigued than actually believing my words, followed Luchóg.

I stayed at the back of the group, not wanting to be close to the women when the men attacked. Neither of them was Isolde, I knew that, but the Descendant might be powerful. The witch, who had summoned the hailstorm on Rathlin Island, had been stronger than I first thought, and I had learned the hard way that it was best to be cautious.

The men ahead of me sped up, then there were screams and shouts, and the sound of horses galloping away. Quickly, I rushed to the front. Given the screams were from both women, it had to mean this Descendant was weak. *Perfect.*

When I reached the front, the young woman with the brown hair was on the ground. Her head had been struck with a rock, and she was trying to get to her feet, but from the way she swayed, her vision and balance had gone.

The other woman, with long blonde hair, was extraordinarily beautiful, and she lay on the ground with a knife in her stomach. Her eyes rolled in her head, but she was not yet dead or dying, the embedded blade preventing her from bleeding out. She was a Descendant. I knew that just from looking at her, for her beauty was beyond compare. She wore plain clothes and a thick scarf over her hair to hide it, but no mortal could have such smooth skin. No mortal could look so like an angel.

"She's the one I want," I said to Luchóg. "Your men can take the other."

Luchóg glanced at the brown-haired woman. She was on her hands and knees now, trying to crawl away.

"Will Satan give her powers to strike against us?"

"Oh no, not that one. She's just a novice. No powers yet, but she is evil just the same."

Luchóg grinned and followed her. Grabbing her by the hair, he dragged her deeper into the forest, and the other men followed.

Her screams were a delight to listen to, only I could not savour them. I had another who needed my attention.

The Descendant woman lay on the ground. Whimpering, she tried to stand. As the screams rang out through the forest, tears streamed down her cheeks, but still, she could not get herself into an upright position. Not a warrior then. Not a witch either.

I knelt close to the oak tree opposite her. "You are a Descendant."

She eyed me, her eyelids fluttering open. Her body knew what had happened, that death was coming, and it wanted her to sleep. To drift away rather than suffer.

I walked over to her and twisted the blade in her stomach.

Adrenaline surged through her, and her eyes widened.

"Sorry," I said. "I only want to talk."

She looked at me, hatred visible in her glare. I took it all in, every flicker of her brow, every twitch of her lips. Trinkets to be savoured later.

"Where is Isolde?" I asked.

"I don't know… anyone by that name."

"That is a lie. I know she's at Seir Kieran."

The woman took a breath as the pain continued to surge through her.

"What gift do you have?" I asked.

This time she didn't speak. Turning her head, she wouldn't even look at me. The only movement was her hand gripping her necklace, her skin turning white as she tried to cope with the pain.

"I'll guess then. Not a healer. Obviously." I pointed at the blood oozing from her stomach, cheek and leg. "A healer would have closed these cuts by now, and you could remove the knife and heal the wound. Not a warrior, or else you would have defeated my men… or at least fought back… or fled. Not a witch, or you would have transformed into a bird and flown away."

"You should let me go," the woman said. "And you should let the girl go. She is not a Descendant."

"Yes, I know she's mortal, but I'm sorry, I cannot let her go. The men have helped me find you, and they must be allowed to have their fun. Do not fret. Her screams have already stopped. It is a shame, I know. A shame that men can be such beasts."

The woman did not answer this with words. More tears dripped along the sides of her cheeks. Water mingling with blood.

"You should let me go," she said again. Her voice was quieter this time. Even more beautiful. More beautiful than the screams, and I had not thought that possible before.

Should I?

Should I let her go?

Perhaps I should.

She had a weaker gift and not the gift I wanted. No. I'd come here for Isolde. This Descendant, so beautiful, should live. There was no reason to kill her.

"Let me go now," the Descendant said. "I would be forever grateful if you did."

Yes. This was right. *I should let her go*. Rushing forward, I placed my hands under her back so as to lift her without moving the knife.

Standing, she groaned and stepped forward. "Now, leave me. Don't follow either."

She took a few steps, and I watched her disappear into the darkness, then I made my way back to the men.

They were all laughing. The girl they had tormented lay in a heap on the muddy ground. Dead. Cold.

"Where is the other woman?" Luchóg said, sniggering. "Did you kill her, or is there some sport left for us? I wouldn't mind having a woman like her. Even if she's of the devil, she was more beautiful than any woman I've ever seen."

"I let her go."

Luchóg stepped closer to me, confusion written all over his face. "But she has seen your face. My face," he snapped. "A king might hunt us down for this."

A haze that I didn't even know was there seemed to lift from my mind. Luchóg was right. I should not have let her go. I hadn't wanted to let her go… and yet I had.

Oh. This Descendant was a harpist.

How interesting.

I had never considered this gift as powerful before, but to make people do what you wanted with just a few words, that was special.

These men had followed me here because I had offered them violence, but as soon as that promise faded or took too long, they would move on. They might even decide they would rather kill me than part ways peacefully. But to have them in my thrall, to move their moods to suit what I wanted, that was something worth having.

"I let her go because that woman is a devil. It will take three of us to destroy her."

"A devil?" Luchóg asked, brows pulling forward.

"Yes. The very worst. This is the work the Holy Father has sent me to do. To destroy the devil who roams this earth in disguise. Will you help me, Luchóg?" Carefully taking my hand out from my sleeve, I turned my wrist, so my palm faced upward. Moving so only he could see me, I let fire dance on the skin. "This is the power God has given me, and I have decided to reveal it to you first."

Luchóg licked his lips. His sharp eyes darted between my face and hand. At first not believing it but then moving closer. Not only could he see the flames, but he could feel the heat. He could smell it.

"What work is there in killing the devil?" he asked.

I let the fire recede, then took out my cross and held it up. "No work for you. Only for me, for the Pope himself has blessed me and this cross to do his bidding. But fighting this devil will be hard work. She will try to stop me again. Whisper words of temptation in my ear. And once I have killed her, a great weakness will come upon me. A strong fever, too. You will need to keep me alive, otherwise the devil will survive. Even more, you will need to take me away from this forest, otherwise devils like her will find us. Her death will summon them and then they will hunt us down. Only I can save you from them, and only you and your men can save me."

Luchóg stared at me.

"I need to keep you alive? How? Where would I take you?"

"Back to Connacht. Back to where you know. If you can, travel by water so they cannot follow your scent."

"Why me? Why my men?"

"God has chosen you, Luchóg. You are not a king, waited on by slaves and women. You are a man of the forest, and you know how to use it to keep me hidden. That is why God led me to you, and that is why he offers you salvation."

Luchóg nodded.

I walked after the Descendant. "Tell the men to follow," I said. "They will see God's power in me too and know that this is their calling."

Leaving Luchóg to gather the men, I followed my footsteps back to where I'd first found her, then followed the trail of blood that marked the ground. The woman was still walking, her hands shakily holding onto the trees as she slowly moved forward. A horse was just ahead of her, and she was whispering its name.

Holding out my hands, fire exploded against the tree she was holding onto. She screamed and fell to the ground.

Quickly, I rushed over to her and slid the magical knife out of my cloak. I had to get her gift before she could use her words on me again.

Turning her over, I held the knife over her chest.

"Don't," she whispered.

Don't kill her, a voice in my head whispered. *Kill the men behind you. They will turn on you if you don't.*

Screaming, I summoned more fire. More and more of it, so that the sound of it roared in my ears. I couldn't let her words stop me again.

"Stop talking," I shouted as I pushed my hand against her mouth and burned her tongue. With one swift strike, I struck the knife into her chest.

The white mist came from her body, just as Gormflaith had told me. Using my fire, I caught it, then pulled it into myself. Pain and nausea took me over immediately, and I felt myself falling in and out of consciousness when Luchóg came to me.

"We saw the fire," he said, his voice full of awe. "We saw God save you from the devil."

"You must help me, Luchóg," I whispered. "Keep me safe. God is watching."

Luchóg nodded and gently he lifted me from the ground and took me deeper into the forest.

Gormflaith

The camp at Dun Domhnall

"Men are coming out of the forest."

Dawn had only broken, the sky still dark as a glimmer of pale light seeped over the horizon, but one of the archers, a young man called Walter, waved his arm at Le Gros and David, who were sitting around the fire. "Men," he hissed. "Lots of them."

I rushed over to the palisade to see. Walter was right. One hundred Irish warriors stood on the plain ahead of us. If they came much closer, their spears would be within range.

Le Gros, William Ferrand and David walked over to the palisade too, and rather quickly Le Gros' skin turned an unnatural shade of purple. He was thinking they should have left yesterday and retreated to Carrig where it was safer. I looked away, not wanting to catch his gaze, which no doubt would be full of blame.

"There are not so many," William Ferrand said, his voice as calm as ever.

"No," Le Gros seethed. "Not as many as I thought there would be, but they don't look like they've come to negotiate. They have come to fight. Fuck."

While David looked dejectedly at the pen of two hundred cattle we had spent much of our energy herding into our camp, Le Gros looked over his men. Nine knights, including Hervey, and seventy archers. He frowned. How could he not? He was calculating the odds of charging through the Irish and Waterford warriors and making it to Carrig… and not liking the result.

"There's more," Walter hissed. "More are coming out of the forest."

"Let us ride out," William said. "Our armour will protect us from their spears, and our cavalry charge can even break their shield wall if we ride fast enough." Lowering his voice, he moved closer to Le Gros, closer than a man with leprosy should. "You will lose some of your archers, but if they try to keep up with us, most of them should be able to make it to the treeline."

Le Gros shook his head. "No, we should retreat along the coast. That way, we only need to worry about attacks on one front. I don't like the look of those forests."

"I disagree," Hervey said. "The forest provides many more hiding places than the beach. Besides, it is better to have them see we are up for a fight rather than see us retreat. That will only give them courage."

Le Gros scoffed as he looked at the forest ahead, but he was right to be afraid. The forests were not kind to those who did not understand them. But the sea was not kind either, and the Waterford Vikings were masters of that terrain. They probably half-expected us to try to escape that way and had ships of warriors ready to sail out and block our retreat.

Le Gros, sweating and biting his lips, glared at the growing army on the plain. Not one hundred anymore. More like three hundred, and still more were coming. "Damn them all to hell."

"Why are you so angry, Le Gros? I thought you wanted to win land." William Ferrand drew out his sword. "What do you think William the Conqueror did when he landed at Pevensey and heard that Harold Godwinson was coming? Retreat and hide and curse the men for wanting to protect their land? Or did he fight and conquer?" William Ferrand, usually so polite and quiet, stared at the gathering army with a ferocious intensity. He had told me once before that he wished to die in battle and that anywhere would do. Perhaps he wanted to die today? If so, it was likely that he would get his wish.

Le Gros looked set to tell him to put his sword away when a scream sounded out.

I spun around. One of the archers, who had been standing by the cattle pen, fell to the ground, a spear deep inside his neck. The archer choked on blood that gushed into his throat, then stilled. Horns from the forest blared, and the beating of shields started.

"Shields," Le Gros shouted. "We are under attack! Get ready to fight!"

The men rushed into formation. The archers moved to the palisade with their bows and arrows ready to shoot, while the knights ran to their horses.

"Run, Alys!" David grabbed me by the arm and pulled me to him. "Alys, run to the beach. Run as fast as you can. Don't wait for us."

"No." I shook my head. "I won't leave you."

David kissed me and thrust the silver ring that his mother had given to him before she died into my hand. "Run, Alys. You speak their language. Pretend you're not with us."

David gave me one more kiss, then ran to his horse alongside the other knights. All nine of them in full armour, as well as their horses, readied themselves to ride out within minutes. In the morning sun, they looked magnificent.

"They're marching toward us!" Walter shouted. "A thousand of them!"

I stared at Le Gros and Hervey, taking in the panic on their faces. The battle had started, and spears flew over the palisade. The archers pressed themselves tight against it, but it wouldn't be long before the spears would pierce and shatter the wood, or before the Irish and Waterford Vikings reached the palisade itself.

Le Gros turned his horse to face the first line of archers. "Shoot only once they are fifty feet away. Then again at ten feet. For the second rally, have the stronger archers lift you so you can shoot downward at the first line of men. Understood?"

The men nodded.

"The second line of archers, aim at the men in the middle of the shield wall, from fifty feet to the very back. Try to create a bit of space for us so that we can ride out."

"Their armour is not as good as ours," Hervey added. "Aim for their necks and legs."

"As soon as the second volley is loosed by the first line," Le Gros continued, "the knights will ride out through the gate and charge the men down, making a passage through the army. Everyone is to run after us. Have an arrow ready to loose, but don't waste time. You must make it to the forest. We will try to give you cover for as long as we can."

I looked back at the plain. There were not a thousand, as Walter had said, but certainly over six hundred. From their dress, I could tell there were Munster clansmen as well as the Waterford Vikings. They must truly be frightened of the Anglo-Normans to have united in battle like this.

The odds of our survival were not good. Six hundred of them, and likely more on the way, while there were less than one hundred of us, and out in the open these archers stood little chance against the experienced Irish and Viking warriors with their spears, swords and axes.

Tears filled my eyes. Le Gros and his army would all die, then the Waterford Vikings would tell the Wexford Vikings how easy to beat we were when they attacked first… and then it would be FitzStephen's fort at Carrig that would fall next… and that would be the end of this. The end of all my plans to win this land back. Donnchad, oh he would laugh, and say that I had acted beyond my means.

And he would be right.

"What about the cattle?" one of the archers shouted. The cows were moaning and circling their pen in agitation. They didn't like the approaching army any more than I did, the horns blaring nor the thud of beating shields – no, they wanted to break free and run away.

That was it.

They were the key to winning.

I took a deep breath and felt for my witch-magic. Drawing on it, I moved the grass underneath the cows' hooves. I wrapped it around their legs. I had the longer blades slice at their noses as they bowed down. Their moaning grew. They didn't like being held to the ground. They didn't like the pain as their soft noses were torn open. Even better, another spear flew over the palisade and struck one of the cows in the flank. The heifer screamed and bolted with the pain, but hemmed in, she crashed into another. Then it was chaos.

I ran toward the pen gate.

"Open the palisade gate!" I screamed.

Le Gros and Hervey turned.

"Open the gate. Let the cattle charge out! They will crush the Irish army."

"Do it," I heard William Ferrand shout. "Archers, get the gangplank. Alys, open the pen gate wider. Now!"

I pulled the rope that held the pen gate closed and yanked it open. The cattle, sensing their way to freedom, charged forward and ran toward the open palisade gate ahead of them. The archers on either side began to scream and whoop so that the cattle ran straight toward the gangplank over the trench.

"Loose!" Le Gros shouted.

The archers lined up along the palisade loosed their arrows. Some even re-nocked and loosed again.

The Irish on the other side, seeing the gate opening and believing that our knights were about to charge out to meet them in battle, took out their spears and swords. It was only as the first of the cattle charged through that the Irish army realised what was happening. The Irish and Waterford warriors at the very front, with hundreds of men pressing behind them, screamed as they were trampled upon, while the rest of the men scattered, their shield wall breaking as they splintered to allow the cattle to pass.

"Loose again!" Le Gros shouted.

The archers loosed, and now that the warriors were no longer protected within a shield wall, they hit their targets.

"Knights! Charge!"

Le Gros raised his sword into the air and rode out through the gate. William Ferrand and David were next, followed by the six remaining knights, who hacked their way through the scattered groups of Irish and Waterford warriors.

Soon the air was filled with screams.

I watched from behind the palisade. Le Gros was hacking with his sword. William was charging, his horse rearing up so he could stab downward at the men trying to pull him from his saddle. Le Gros and his men were winning! I couldn't believe it. Already hundreds of the Irish warriors were running back into the forest, leaving the Waterford Vikings to fight alone.

Those who were left tried to re-form into shield walls, but they were disoriented now. Arrows struck them from the sky, while knights charged at them from across the plain.

"David!" It was Le Gros who saw the danger first, and he charged toward his nephew. David, who had been chasing down a group of Viking men close to the palisade had been pulled off his horse. Only twenty feet away, I could see him fighting them from the ground. An arrow was sticking out from his shoulder, another close to his neck, and the Irish warriors were kicking and punching as they fell into the mud beside him. Suddenly, he stilled.

"Get up, David," I screamed. "Get up!"

Le Gros continued to charge, as did William, but the group of Vikings, on seeing them coming, ran to the forest.

"Get him into the camp!" Le Gros roared as he turned his horse around and rode back toward where the fighting was thickest.

"Come on," Walter shouted. "Bring him inside!"

Three of the archers ran out, lifted David and brought him inside our camp.

"Into Le Gros' tent," I shouted.

As they set him down, David's hand moved, and I ran to his side. *He was alive. Kneeling on the ground, I was about to ask the archers to fetch me some cloth to stench the cut on his head, but they had already run back to the palisade.*

"Alys," David whispered. "Help me to sit up."

"You are injured, my love," I said, pulling out the arrow that had made it through the gap in his shoulder armour.

"Yes," he answered, wincing as I pulled the second arrow away, the tip scratching the skin along his neck as I tugged it free from his chain-mail collar.

"Sorry."

"It's not that. My arm is broken, but I think, yes, I can feel my arms and legs. My injuries are not as bad as I first thought." He smiled at me, wiping away the blood that oozed from his nose and the cut along his forehead.

"Hush, my love," I said. "Take a moment. Do you hurt anywhere else?"

David shook his head and smiled. "When this battle is over, I will take you home, Alys. Damn, Le Gros, but I've had enough of this war already."

"Don't be silly. You must stay here and press your claim."

"I don't care about land. I care only about you. I'm sorry I was so angry, but I cannot bear the thought of losing you. Home, Alys. We are going home together. Together. Just what you wanted."

Crying, I kissed him on the lips. David's left arm was indeed shattered, and his ankle looked to be broken too, though he couldn't feel it yet. His fighting days might be over, but he was not so badly injured that he would die, and yet all he wanted to do was go home. A bitter anger filled my mouth. *Oh, sweet David. If only you'd had ambition flowing through your veins as well as love, what a husband you might have been.*

I ran my hands over his cheek and then moved so that my lips were at his ear. "I love you, David. Your kindness has taught me to love. It has taught me how to live. I will never forget you."

With those final words, I pressed the arrow that I had pulled from his collar into his neck. His eyes widened, and a flash of confusion ran over his face, but as the blood gushed, it faded away. Soon, he was at peace.

David was too good for this world. Too sweet. Too kind. Not the husband I needed at a time such as this. I could not be commanded to go home. I was here to be queen, not to be held back by a man, not even one as good as David.

Lying over his body, I wept. What a cruel world I lived in. It was cruel to make me do this. In a kinder world, David could have lived.

I felt myself drifting away, tired from using my magic, tired from the battle. Tired from crying.

This was how the men found me, passed out over David's body, and it was Le Gros himself who picked me up. "David has gone, Alys," he said, holding me tight.

"The arrow was too deep," I sobbed.

"I know. Come. Come out of the tent so we can prepare his body. We will pray for him. We will all pray for his soul."

Sitting by the fire, I slowly came to. David, my husband, was dead.

By my own hand.

Hundreds of dead bodies lay scattered along the grassy plain. We had won the battle, and the victorious living walked over the enemy dead, plunging swords into any man who still breathed, but it was only David that I could think of.

I stood and wept over the grave the archers had dug, while William Ferrand prayed over it. His words, spoken in Latin, sounded so grand – as if they could summon the very angels from heaven to take my sweet David into their embrace.

Crying and crying, the tears tripped down my face until the ground beneath me was wet with them. Even when William's prayers had ended, I stood by David's grave until the sun lowered toward the horizon.

Dutiful wife, sorrowful widow. Oh, I had played both these parts before, but this time, this time I felt it deep in my heart.

I had not loved David, but he had not deserved to die, and yet he was dead. Dead because to be queen I had to do unspeakable things.

The depths that these Descendants had driven me to, that my own family had driven me to, were beyond forgiveness. It was their fault David, who was mine, had to die. If they had not pursued me and betrayed me at every turn, I would already be queen, and David would still be alive.

I vowed then that they would all suffer in kind for the dreadful things they had made me do.

Wiping the tears from my face, I stared at the camp behind me. My path to power was obvious now. I knew what needed to be done and who I needed to destroy. All of those who had betrayed me deserved it, and I would feel no pity when they drew their last breath… or if I let them live, they would live to serve only me. Like Olaf.

More tears ran down my face then. This time not of sorrow, but of understanding. A true knowing of who I was and what awaited.

Later that evening, I sat by the fire as the light of the day dimmed. I did not speak. The men talked of war and where to go next, but secretly Le Gros composed his letter to Strongbow, and William Ferrand cleaned his sword.

"Will Strongbow come?" I asked him.

"I do not know, Alys," William replied. "He still awaits King Henry's permission."

"Then why does Le Gros write to him at all? If all the power resides with another man, why waste his time?"

"Because Strongbow is ambitious. Ambitious men can be persuaded if the right words are used."

Walter, the archer, who sat beside me, nodded at the dead bodies lying on the grass. "I wonder what they thought of us in battle?"

"If they had any sense, they'd be on their knees, worshipping us," Hervey said, who had now finished saying his own prayers over the dead. "One hundred against one thousand. We are like the Spartans of Thermopylae."

William Ferrand scoffed. "That was three hundred against thirty thousand."

Hervey shrugged, laughing away the correction as he stared over the battlefield.

Walter turned around and nodded at the Waterford Vikings we had captured. "What are we to do with them?"

Hervey glanced over at the group of men huddled in the pen where we had previously held the cattle. Ropes bound their ankles and tied their arms behind their backs so they could not run. Most had injuries that prevented them from escaping when the other Vikings retreated, but they were not dying men. Not like the warriors lying unconscious on the battlefield that the Anglo-Norman archers had been happy to finish off.

"How many do we have?" Le Gros asked, setting down his quill and parchment.

"I counted seventy, my lord," Walter answered.

"You could raise a great ransom for them," Hervey proposed. "That is the way of the Irish Vikings, I believe. Even better, the King of Waterford might be tempted to give you his allegiance if you allow them to return."

Le Gros snorted and spat on the grass. "I don't want their allegiance. I want the Kingdom of Waterford. What was it Donn said when he came back from Ireland? Oaths in this land mean nothing. I've come here to make Strongbow king, and so king he will be. I will not have David's sacrifice be for nothing."

Le Gros stilled, grief for David still heavy on his face. "We won a great victory. Yes, this is true. One hundred of us defeated a one-thousand-strong Irish and Viking army. Over seven hundred ran away. Two hundred lie dead. Seventy we have captured. Still, we should not underestimate them. They did not expect us to let out the cattle from behind our gates. The stampede broke their shield wall, but we cannot rely on such good fortune again." He pointed to the captured Vikings and thrust his sword into the muddy soil.

"If they mount another attack, these seventy men could escape and fight us from behind. There is only one way to solve this problem. They must die."

Hervey nodded his agreement, and brought forward a wounded Viking. Dried blood soaked this injured warrior's right leg and his ankle dragged along the grass at an unnatural angle, but his eyes were alert and sullen.

"You wish to discuss terms?" the Viking said in broken Norman French once he was dropped onto the grass at Le Gros' feet.

Le Gros didn't answer, and William strode forward, his sword unsheathed.

Le Gros gave a nod, and the sword sliced through the Viking's neck before he had a chance to turn. The wounded Vikings who had watched the exchange from the pen shouted and pulled at their ropes.

Walter smirked. "Not a chance of them escaping. I made those knots good and tight."

"Stop it." I stood and stared at Le Gros. "Please, I beg you to listen to me."

Le Gros' upper lip twitched. "Alys, I'm sorry, my decision is final. These men must die, no matter how unpleasant that may be to you."

"I don't wish to change your decision. These men and their kin have made me a widow. Believe me, I do not beg for mercy." I rushed over to him and fell to my knees, pressing my forehead against my hands which were clasped together as if in prayer.

Le Gros sighed and raised my chin, taking one of my hands in his. "What is it you want, Alys? I will grant you anything in my power."

"I wish," I said, my gaze meeting his, "to kill the next one myself."

Walter gasped. So did Hervey. One or two of the archers laughed. But not Le Gros. He stared at me until at last he nodded.

"And," I said, "I want to send a message to their friends in Waterford."

"I'll send for some parchment."

"No. I don't need parchment. You forget that I grew up here."

Waiting for no reply, I stooped to pick up David's sword and gestured for someone to bring a hostage forward. Two knights dragged one over while another forced his head down. I brought the sword up high over my head and with a force that surprised even myself, I removed the Viking warrior's head from his body in one swift motion.

"Throw his head over the cliff," I said to Le Gros. "All the heads. The current will take them to the Waterford longphort. The people there will know these men didn't have the glory of dying in battle. That is the only message they need."

Laughter erupted out of Le Gros like thunder. "What a warrior I have, and I didn't know it!" He stood and bowed to me. "I should have known that David would pick a worthy bride." He grinned as he glanced at William Ferrand. "Watch over her. I've a letter I need to finish." Without another word he marched toward his tent, grabbing the parchment and quill he'd set down on the grass on his way.

The rest of the men remained to watch what I did.

"Another," I said as I motioned for the next man to be brought over. Walter and two other archers did as I bid and grabbed the one closest to them. This man was drifting in and out of unconsciousness, with a long plait of hair matted to his neck by a mixture of mud and blood.

"Put my sword in my hand," the man muttered as his swollen eyes opened. "For Valhalla."

I tilted my head to one side and tightened my grip on the sword's hilt. "Have you not realised by now that Valhalla doesn't exist? And even if it did, no one there would want you."

Using what was left of my strength, I cut this man's head from his body and watched as it fell onto the grass. Blood spurted from his neck and oozed over the ground.

A strange silence fell then, or perhaps it was only that my world had turned silent as I watched the pool of blood spread outward and drain into the soil. How strange it was to see that the body didn't immediately realise it was dead. To see that the heart kept beating, if only for a little while.

"Alys?"

I looked up to find William Ferrand standing at the other end of the body.

"You can kill the next one, William," I said, throwing David's sword to the ground. "I think I've done enough."

It was long into the night before all the men were dead, but between William Ferrand, myself and the other knights, we removed the heads of all seventy hostages. The archers lifted their heads, drawing lots to see who would have the privilege of throwing them into the sea, and I watched in the moonlight as their heads bobbed in the water and drifted toward Waterford.

As the last of the heads were thrown in, Le Gros came out to watch, his finished letter in hand.

"Is that for Strongbow?" I asked.

"Yes."

Exhausted, I sat down by the fire and stared at him. "What words are you using to convince Strongbow to come to us?"

"I am telling him of our victory. I'm telling him of you and the heads you took from the Viking prisoners. I'm telling him that if a woman can do all that, then an earl can do more."

Isolde

The forest outside Seir Kieran

Méabh and I rode hard through the night. We were riding toward hope… but we did not find it.

Instead, we found our two friends, both already dead. Leofwynn lay on the ground just as the vision had shown me, her clothes ripped and covered with blood. I picked her up and held her tight. Why had those men killed her? *Why?* As I brushed the dirt from her face, I broke down in tears. I could feel her emotions still, for they lingered in her body. She'd been so scared.

If only I hadn't been so weak that the vision had broken. I couldn't help but feel that if I'd seen it and come to their aid earlier, I might have saved them.

"Do you know who did this?" Méabh asked me as she knelt by Gisela.

My vision had not shown me her death, only the Fomorian walking toward her, though I had no doubt it was him.

"It was a Fomorian. The one who chased me and Affraic on Rathlin and who has been in my visions. He was with a group of men, though I don't know who they are."

Méabh took Gisela's hand into hers and pressed it to her lips. Méabh had always been so cold, but I could see now from the grief on her face that this was a friendship that had endured for hundreds of years. "How did he find her, do you think?"

"I don't know."

I wish I knew the answer to this, for the Fomorians had found us at Rathlin Island too. Even Broccan hadn't understood how. The thought made me sick, that no matter where I ran to, they could follow.

I tried to calm myself by remembering that I was not alone. Colmon, Báine, Méabh and Siobhan were still at my side, but the voice of doubt niggled at me again. For how much longer? *Colmon's hair was already turning white.*

I wished Colmon was awake and with me, but seeing as he wasn't, I had to try and learn as much as I could. Using my warrior gift, I concentrated on what I remembered of the vision, then concentrated on the world around us. The smells, the sounds, the taste on my tongue. Slowing my breathing, my heartbeat, my mind, I felt for the knot in my stomach. I held it tight, not letting the heat spread through my body. Holding it tighter, a strange calmness came over me. I smelled fire. Rotting flesh. A smell so foul it almost made me heave. Fomorian. The same one who had tried to kill me on Rathlin. He was hunting me down, and poor Leofwynn had simply been in the way. He'd been so happy when he listened to her screams. There were other scents too. Thirty mortals. I could smell the sweat and blood from each of them. They had all left here together and travelled north-east.

Opening my eyes, I brushed Leofwynn's hair from her face. Once again, I had felt her fear and anguish. "I'm sorry, Leofwynn. I'm sorry I couldn't reach you in time."

Méabh, who had been watching me, gave me a moment and then spoke. "Is there anything else? Anything that might help us?"

"There were thirty men with the Fomorian. All mortal. They took great pleasure in the deaths of Gisela and Leofwynn, and I think that must be why they follow him. When it was over, they travelled north-east."

Méabh nodded. "We already knew from your vision that the Fomorians would find Seir Kieran, but we thought we had more time… and we never expected this."

I recalled then that Gisela and Leofwynn had not been in my vision of the monastery burning. I had been happy, thinking they had escaped, but it must have been because they were already dead. Hugging Leofwynn tighter, I slumped against the ground. "There is no more time, Méabh. We need to start finding homes for the mortals who live at Seir Kieran. We cannot let anyone else die on our account."

Méabh wiped the tears from her face. "I think it is time for us all to leave Seir Kieran, Isolde." Gently she pulled apart the fabric of Gisela's dress. "Look. Look at what he did to her."

I set Leofwynn gently back onto the ground and walked over to Méabh. I was horrified by the large gash in her chest, like she'd been ripped open.

"The Fomorian has the knife of immortality," Méabh said. "He used it to take Gisela's gift, and they will use it to steal more. They've stolen gifts before, you know. Before you were born."

"You mean this Fomorian has the harpist gift now too?"

Méabh nodded. "Colmon thought they were after the sword, but that's not it at all. They are after you. Can you imagine if one of them stole your gifts? They'd be the most powerful Fomorian ever to exist."

My whole body shook on hearing this.

"All of us must leave Seir Kieran," she said. "At the great Battle of Moytura, the Tuatha Dé Danann formed a protective ring around Lugh. They did not want the Fomorians to take their finest from them. We must do that for you."

"But there are not enough to do this for me, Méabh. I do not have a host of witches and druids and cupbearers to help me. Only you, Báine and Siobhan now. Colmon for not much longer. We have to fight them. We have to go looking for them."

Slowly, Méabh nodded. "Yes. I believe you are right."

Together we rode back to Seir Kieran and brought Gisela and Leofwynn with us.

What was it to feel broken? A death of feeling, perhaps. That is how I felt as I laid them to rest by the hawthorn tree. I had sobbed for Leofwynn and Gisela as I rode toward the monastery but found I could not weep by the tree. I was empty.

Siobhan readied the bodies as I watched on, not knowing what to do. But for each of the women she laid their valuables beside them. Gisela's beautiful cloak and harp. Leofwynn had her comb and a wreath that she had made.

The mortals came and laid flowers by the bodies. We told them that they had been killed by strangers – most likely from the armies that were fighting for Leinster and Connacht, and that we would be leaving soon to move somewhere safer.

Siobhan gave the mortals instructions to pack their belongings and ready the carts with food and provisions. The air was then filled with chatter and gossip and plans, but as night fell, a deathly silence came over the monastery as the mortals slept.

"It is time," Méabh said to the four of us who stood watch over the bodies. "We shall say the rites and the ancestors will come."

"I have no fear that Gisela will not be taken," Siobhan said. "Cenn worshipped her, and she was devoted to him."

"What about Leofwynn?" I asked.

"The mortals have their own graveyard," Báine said. "Tomorrow, we'll dig her a grave and say prayers over it."

"But Leofwynn didn't believe in the Christian faith."

"There are many faiths the mortals believe in, and some believe in nothing at all, but all the same, their bodies return to the earth one way or the other. It is nice too for them to be together. A place for the living to come and visit their remains."

I understood the sentiment but did not agree. "Leofwynn loved this place. Loved Gisela." I turned to Siobhan. "She loved you too. I don't understand why she wouldn't go with Gisela to the otherworld."

"We can leave her here while we wait for our ancestors to collect Gisela if you like," Báine said. "If the ancestors don't take her, though, we will have to bury her."

I nodded, and Báine moved over to help Siobhan place the flowers the mortals had brought over the bodies of Leofwynn and Gisela.

"Can you sing, Isolde?" Báine asked once they were done.

"Yes, Gisela taught me a few songs."

"Then sing now. It will let the ancestors know we are ready."

Taking a deep breath, I began to sing. A song of a great love that lived inside of the waves and splashed against the people who dove into them.

It didn't take long for a light to grow. It was so bright that I could no longer open my eyes fully, though as I tried to peer into it, I thought I could see a man with a sword at his side. His hands reached out to hold Gisela, but then the brightness became so intense I had to look away.

"Sister."

I knew that voice. Remembered it from Rathlin Island when I was waking from death.

"Aoife?"

"Yes, it's me."

I wanted to open my eyes and see my sister's face but could not. The light was too powerful.

"Have you come to collect Gisela?"

"Yes. I have come with her husband, Cenn. Her mother and brother are here too. Her aunt and two uncles. Many loved Gisela and have come to take her to the land of the dead."

"I am glad that she is now at peace and with those she loved… though I wish I had been able to save her."

"Nothing lasts more than a while, Isolde. We suffer in life, that is the truth, but in that suffering we find joy and love, and it is this that brings us onward."

"What about Leofwynn?"

Aoife paused. "You think she would want to be with us?"

"Yes. With Gisela. She was her friend and teacher. Is the love of friendship not as true as any other?"

Aoife moved away from me then, the warmth of her presence fading.

I waited, waited for an age, and soon I sensed that the light was waning. When I opened my eyes, this time I could see the outline of Aoife, the long strands of her white hair running to her waist.

"Leofwynn is with us," Aoife said. "You were right."

Glad that my friend was not alone any longer, I smiled, but quickly another emotion took me over. "Aoife, what must I do? I'm frightened."

"You must do what you think is best, Isolde. Your heart will guide you, and it will not lead you astray."

Aoife blew a kiss, then stepped away. The light was dimming and drawing back toward the hawthorn tree, which meant I didn't have long.

"Wait. Are my mother and father with you?"

"Yes."

"What do they say?" I felt tears streaming down my face. "Can they talk to me?"

"Mother says she loves you and that she is sorry."

"She doesn't need to be sorry."

"And yet she is. She is sorry for the suffering you endure without her. She tells you to trust your family."

"What about my father?"

The light drew back more, now only under the branches, and Aoife moved further and further away.

"He says for you to be strong in the face of death. He knows what it is to be broken and to be remade."

The light dimmed again. It was almost gone.

"Wait, Aoife. Don't go." Oh, how I wanted her to stay with me. For her to tell me more about my mother and father and all my family.

"What about Broccan? What does he have to say?"

"Broccan?" Aoife said, though it was only a whisper this time. "Broccan is no—"

And then she was gone. The light too.

"Come," Siobhan said, placing her hand on my arm. "Let us go inside and sleep. It's been a long day and night for you. You must make sure to rest tomorrow."

"No." I shook my head and stared at Báine. "Tomorrow we must take the mortals somewhere safe. Then we must train. We don't have long. No more resting. No more sympathy for my plight. The next time a vision comes, I need to be strong enough to see it all."

"Then we will train," Báine replied. "Whatever you wish."

The four of us walked to the monastery. My head and my heart felt heavy, but even so, I had made a decision. The time for waiting was over. As soon as I was ready, I was going to find that Fomorian, and when I did, I was going to destroy him.

Cuan

The Kingdom of North Munster

Conchobar had taken his father's command of the army with a zealous fervour and had ordered that every ráth and settlement we passed along the River Shannon be set on fire. As a result, the last few days had been a haze of smoke and ash and full of the sounds of people screaming and running away.

I did as Conchobar commanded. Set ráths alight. Burned bridges and ships. Looted, and opened cattle pens so that our men could drive the stolen cattle toward Connacht. My uncle wanted to show that oaths to him could not be broken so easily and that people would suffer if their kings made reckless decisions.

Of course, my uncle hoped these actions might turn Odhrán's people against him, or else cause another man in the Uí Brian clan to rise up to challenge him, but as I looked around and stared into the people's faces as they ran away, I did not see anger toward Odhrán. Only hatred of us.

On the seventh day of raiding, I cleaned my sword by the river as night fell and mulled over the strangeness of war. Why should the screams of people fleeing a burning dun haunt me more than the screams of men dying on the battlefield, for I'd killed many men over the years in this way when fighting for my uncle Godred? Perhaps it was merely the certainty that the men who lined up against me either wanted to fight or else took payment from their lord to do so. There was something reassuring in that – the knowing that we were all there to serve the same purpose.

The people running from our horses, they had not chosen to fight. They had chosen to live and have families.

War is a terrible thing, my uncle Godred had always told me, *and when kings play their games, the people suffer*. As a boy, I had told him this was unfair. My uncle had laughed and said I only thought that because I had been on a losing side, and if my father had won against Ruaidrí, I would not see it that way.

I had wondered then, what was worth fighting for. Using my own eyes, I answered the question by looking at the gold rings on Godred's fingers and the swathes of men who feasted in his hall. The answer I had concluded was greatness. Some might have said wealth, but Godred did not fight for that. He fought to be remembered as a great warrior. He fought for his name. And the people, even those who suffered, came to his hall to feast with him. His greatness reflected upon them somehow, though I could not understand how they did not see that it was he who often caused their misfortune.

Not all men were made for greatness. Not even all warriors were, for I was not the only one to find these raids difficult. Some of the Connacht warriors, secretly and in the darkness of night, had cried after the burning of Killaloe. Even though they were not from Munster, King Brian was a legend to every warrior in Ireland. There were rumours too, that a woman with red hair walked around the dun at Samhain, a pale ghost who shone against the moonlight and cursed those who harmed the land. The men blessed themselves every night before bed to keep her away.

"You couldn't find him? Why not?"

I glanced along the riverbank to find Conchobar shouting at two of the scouts.

"You are telling me a monk from Rome has outwitted both of you?"

"So many people have been riding along the paths, Conchobar. It's impossible to make out which tracks are his."

"Did you go to the monasteries? Didn't he say he wanted to see them?"

One of the scouts shrugged. "He's not been at any we've visited, but I'm not sure the monks would tell us. They've all heard about the burning of Inis Cealtra. Apparently, the abbot died in the attack."

Conchobar stormed off toward his tent, leaving the scouts to find something to eat and somewhere to rest before heading out in the morning to search again for the missing monk.

I found it amusing that Brother Angelo's disappearance irked Conchobar so. His reaction was selfish, of course, for he didn't crave Brother Angelo's company; rather I guessed he knew that his father would be displeased to learn he had lost the Roman monk, especially after he'd gone to so much effort to impress him. I thought, however, it was for the best. After seeing us set fire to Killaloe, Brother Angelo would probably return to Rome and tell the Pope that Ireland was as barbaric as the rumours said it was. If he knew our fuidir had killed an abbot, this assessment might be even worse.

Cuan.

A whisper of my name reached my ears.

Isolde?

I moved away from the river and rushed deeper into the forest, hoping that Isolde might be there, or at least the voice of her. Her appearance two nights ago had been the only bright light since we'd parted, but she'd not come back in the days since. I'd stayed awake most of last night, offering to take both watches, waiting for her. Hoping that she would return to me.

Once I was far enough into the forest that I thought no one in the army could hear me, I stilled. "Isolde?" I whispered into the cold night. "Isolde? Is that you?"

Nothing. No reply. Only the breeze rustling against the leaves.

"Cuan? What are you doing here? Your watch ended ages ago."

I turned to find Fearghus walking toward me.

"I couldn't sleep."

Fearghus laughed. "I couldn't sleep either. Then I realised I needed to piss."

Turning my feet, I slowly moved into fighting stance and placed my fingers on my belt, feigning fatigue, but really, I wanted my hand closer to my sword. I never had found out who told the mercenaries I would be at the bruidean. Conchobar might have wanted it and paid for it, but he was far away and could not have known where I was.

I had discounted Cathal on account of his age and naivety, which left Scolaí and Fearghus.

And now I was alone with one of them.

Fearghus wasn't the obvious suspect. He was nice. Jovial. Always had a joke and a story to tell, and a night in his company was never dull, but I could not trust him, for Fearghus' great-grandfather was King Áed Bernaig, which meant he himself could become King of Connacht one day according to the Brehon laws. It was unlikely, with men like Conchobar and Cathal of age and more closely related to the king, but that didn't mean Fearghus wasn't ambitious and wouldn't want a future rival out of his way.

"Are you looking forward to returning home, Fearghus?"

"I am. The Kingdom of Munster is not for me. The air is too warm."

"You prefer the wind and the rain?"

"Always. You know how it is. The men of Connacht complain about the wildness of the west wind but then lament its loss as soon as they ride east." Fearghus set his hand on his sword and took a breath. "You have said some interesting things, Cuan," he said after a moment. "To the king."

"Have I?" I smiled, wanting to keep the conversation going to see what was on his mind or at least what part of it he was willing to share.

"Yes. I agree with you now. We should have ridden out to face Diarmait instead of Odhrán. Now we are embarrassed by our defeat at Limerick, and the real culprit is nowhere to be seen."

"Well, we didn't know the Anglo-Normans would ride to Munster."

"No, we didn't, but you suspected that too. I remember the questions you asked Finnén. I think, perhaps, that the insult from King Odhrán was too great in my mind for me to see the sense in your plan when we spoke at Dúnmór, but now I've thought about it, after what happened, it seems so obvious that we should have attacked Diarmait."

Not wanting to criticise the king, for that would never do, I veered the conversation away to somewhere safer. "We will see Diarmait in battle soon enough. He won't get his own way next time."

Fearghus shrugged. "We'll see, but I think the king will need to be moved in the right direction. To be High King is a great thing, but King Ruaidrí's so enamoured with it, he's become scared. Scared to move, scared to act. He should have struck Diarmait and his Norman knights down last year when we went to Ferns. He says it was mercy that stayed his hand, but it wasn't. It was fear."

"Those are hard words toward your king, Fearghus. A member of his fianna should not speak so. The hour is late, and it's been a long week, so I will pretend I didn't hear them."

"They are harsh words, but they are true ones," Fearghus said as I turned and walked away. "And I know you must think them too."

I continued walking. Didn't nod or grunt. If anyone heard what Fearghus had said, he would be in trouble, but I would bear the punishment. The kingship of Connacht, as grandson of the great King Tairdelbach, was well within my reach. Ruaidrí might be scared of Diarmait, but the truth was, he was scared of me too.

As I made my way back to the riverbank, I wondered what had prompted Fearghus to say that to me. Were they even his own thoughts? I had earlier suspected that Conchobar had his ear, but perhaps my father had spoken with him, moved him in my direction, so that if I tried to take the throne from Ruaidrí, I had someone at my side. Or perhaps this *was* Conchobar's doing. He was crafty enough to think of using Fearghus to trick me into saying something against my uncle.

Once I reached the treeline, I lingered a moment, just in case I heard Isolde's voice again, but there was only silence to be found. Reluctantly, I made my way toward one of the fires and poured myself a ladle of the stew into a bowl.

"Ready yourselves," a messenger said, going from fire to fire. "Conchobar says we ride home in the morning. Back to Connacht!"

The men around the fires cheered. Everyone wanted to return home.

Everyone except me.

When I returned to Dúnmór, I was wearied by all that I had done, and so before riding into the dun, I made my way to the river. I needed to clean the dirt from my body and the dark deeds from my soul first. Only the coldest of water could do this.

As I made my way there, I found a group of men sitting on the hill. Four of them were my uncle's warriors, and over by the river was Connor. He stood by the edge with a net and a hooked line.

"Any luck?" I asked him as I reached the riverbank.

"Oh, yes. I've caught five trout already."

I took my cloak and tunic off and waded into the water. "I won't be long," I said, knowing that I had scared the fish away.

Connor shrugged.

"Can you swim?" I asked. "It's cold, but you'll feel better for it."

The boy shook his head. Not that I should call him a boy any longer. He had been at Connacht for less than a year, but he had grown taller in that time. He was not quite a man but stretching toward it. I guessed that was why he craved time alone, though I couldn't help but notice that every so often he glanced toward the part of the riverbank where Abbán had been killed.

"I was a hostage once, you know," I said. "Years ago. For my uncle Godred who had made a pact with a king in Norway."

"How did you like it?"

"It was a restful time. My uncle Godred trained me hard. As a hostage, I was fed and watered every night and not made to work. I think I came to like it more than I should."

Connor smiled. "I must confess it's not all bad. It would be nicer though if I weren't followed everywhere."

Submerging myself in the water, I shivered, then splashed the young prince. "Come now, there are worse places to be. The army has returned tonight, and there will be a great feast."

"Your uncle arrived a week ago. All anyone has been talking about is going to war with my father and rallying the other kingdoms. Nobody wants me at the feast."

"That's why you definitely should attend it." Walking out of the water, I brushed the droplets from my skin and onto the grass. "Never let anyone see that you are afraid."

"Brother Angelo said that to me once." Connor looked up then, glancing at the returning army still marching toward the dun. "Where is he?"

"I don't know. He went missing after we raided Killaloe."

Connor's smile dropped.

"Have no fear, Connor. I have a feeling we will see Brother Angelo again. He most likely wanted to tend to the injured."

"That is the like of Brother Angelo," Connor said. "So kind and generous."

Wading back out of the river, I picked up my cloak and sword and said goodbye to Connor, who had already returned to his fishing.

The feast that night was one of the best I'd ever attended. My uncle had already sent out his messages. Every king in the whole of Ireland, aside from Diarmait and Odhrán, had been invited to our dun in the summer, and my uncle had made it clear that non-attendance would be considered a sign of defiance. The warriors of Connacht had been disappointed by our defeat and had not enjoyed the burning of duns and ráths along the River Shannon. This generous feast was to show the warriors that their king had everything in hand and that he had a plan to regain our glory come the summer.

"It's nice to see you back, Cuan!" Róisín sat down beside me, out of breath from dancing with Connor, who had decided to attend. He was still dancing, or rather involved in some sort of competition with Cathal that involved tapping their feet against the leg of a chair in time with the drums. Both were laughing hysterically when the other couldn't keep up.

"Father told me that Connor will be made king when Diarmait is defeated," she whispered to me.

"That is good." I raised my glass and tilted it toward her. "To my cousin, Róisín. Princess of Connacht and soon to be Queen of Leinster."

She smirked, then clapped her hands as Connor threw his hands up in the air, having won the competition between himself and Cathal. Róisín had not been drinking, but her eyes were bright, and taking a quick sip of water, she stood up again as another tune was about to begin.

"Come on, Cuan. You can dance with us tonight."

Róisín grabbed my hand and pulled me over to where Cathal and Connor were standing.

I had never danced before, but found, given that it was already late into the night, that no one really cared what anyone else was doing. Cathal especially was enjoying himself and kept swinging me into the middle of the circle when I least expected it.

After a while, I made my escape. I needed to sleep, though I found myself glad that I was going to bed with my heart less heavy than before.

"A glass of warmed milk?" one of the servants asked. She was an old woman who stood by the outside fire, handing out cups to those making their way home.

"Thank you, yes."

As she thrust one into my hand, I felt something else along the bottom of the cup. Parchment. The old woman gave a quick smile, then moved back to the fire to fill up another cup, while I hurried over to my house at the far side of the dun. Lighting a candle, I sat on my bed. It was a letter from my father.

The time to act is soon. Make him trust you. Do everything to make that so. And then, when the time is right, be ready to turn against him. Rebellion is brewing, my son. The Anglo-Normans are readying to invade. Our time is coming, and before long, you will be king.

Donnchad

Château de Falaise

Life at Falaise was everything that FitzHubert promised and more. The food was exquisite, the entertainment sublime. Plays and poems of forbidden desires and of knights who gave their lives for their lovers were performed every evening. Men and women cheered and cried, and these sounds would sweep through the hall of the great keep like a wave.

In Ireland, poetry and stories were important, too. It was how we bonded during the long winter nights. Tales of famous warriors, ancient battles and the old gods were woven into the very land itself, and this seeped into the Irish blood. I'd seen fearsome warriors weep when they heard tales of Oisín's death and the last stand of Cú Chulainn. I'd watched grown men cower when the Morrígan's name was whispered.

When I was king, I had never understood this. I had merely paid the poets and musicians to tell their tales and keep my people happy, while I stayed at the back of the hall and plotted my next move. I had thought this kingly. To be a firm hand when those I commanded gave in to emotion and instinct.

But that was not the way of it here. Indeed, Henry and Eleanor were almost a part of the evening entertainment. They would stand and clap when a poem particularly pleased them, and the courtiers rushed to follow suit. I saw then that this display of pleasure and excitement and sadness was a strategy. A way of keeping their people attuned to their whims. A way of ensuring the people watched *them*.

There was no doubt that it worked. Every man and woman's life in Falaise revolved around the royal family. Henry and Eleanor's every whim and desire were discussed in detail. Every mind was bent on pleasing them. It was not that no treachery lay here, but rather that it had no chance to breathe.

This was the lesson my mother had wanted me to find. I saw it now. Fear was useful, but love and loyalty had their purpose. I had disliked talking to the mortal folk when I was king. I felt that those who looked after the cattle and grew crops were beneath me, for what conversation could they make that I would enjoy? But Henry spoke to all his people. Sometimes they came to petition him at court, and he listened to them as carefully as he would listen to a lord. Afterward, he spoke to them of simple things. The weather, their family, what songs they knew, and this was where his strength lay. If the people loved him, the courtiers had no choice but to love him too.

This again made me reflect on how different my rule was. In Munster, gossip and treachery were a daily occurrence. My wives sulked, my warriors followed their own strategies rather than my command, and my kinsmen could never be trusted. I realised now that by avoiding my people, I had only driven them away, and so when Toir finally declared war against me, they had let him come. None had stayed to fight for me. Not a single soul.

With this betrayal in mind, I rose from my bed, washed my face and got dressed. Rather than looking backward, I needed to focus on the task ahead, for finally I had been granted an audience with Henry. Court began early in Falaise, and I needed to be in the great hall before long to get a good seat.

"Do you want breakfast, my lord?"

A maid came into my room with a tray of hot bread and boiled eggs. It smelled delicious, but I could not eat. My stomach was already churning as I thought of how best to convince Henry to allow Strongbow's invasion. My mother believed our plans depended upon it, and in this case, I thought she was right. Change could not come to Ireland without there being chaos first, and I needed to be the man who would bring it.

"No," I said, standing as I put on my fur cloak and silver brooch. "I've a meeting with the king."

The maid curtsied, fluttering her eyelashes as she moved to the door, but I had no time for such flirtations. Not today.

As soon as I was ready, I made my way into the hall. Henry had held court here twice since I'd arrived, and I had taken the opportunity to watch him on both occasions. Holding court was another type of performance, similar to that of the evenings, but instead of delight and sadness, he oscillated between joy and fury. If anyone happened to make him angry, he would shout and scream. Once he'd even gnawed at his sleeve. I was still finding it difficult to follow the multitude of various political factions and religious disputes, but it seemed the English archbishop, Thomas Becket, was still vexing him greatly.

Sitting down, I waited for the first person to be called forward. Today, it was the count of Blois.

Henry, who had been speaking to his wife, Queen Eleanor of Aquitaine, quietened. As he did this, so did the rest of the hall.

I watched the king carefully as he studied the man walking toward him. For the moment, he was not giving anything away. Again, this was performance. He knew everyone was watching him.

The count, a middle-aged man with a balding head and narrow face, bowed. "Good morning, King Henry. I've come to discuss Archbishop Becket."

"Welcome to Falaise, Count Theobald," the king said. He gave a loud sigh and then extended his hand. "Please, tell me what he's done now."

"As you know, the ceremony to crown Henry the Younger was performed by the Bishop of York at Westminster Abbey. However,

Archbishop Becket has written to tell me that Pope Alexander issued a papal bull prior to the coronation which forbade such a ceremony taking place. I've a copy of the papal bull on my person."

"There was a sea blockade at the time, Theobald," the king answered as one of his servants took the letter from the count. "The bull did not reach us."

I smiled at this, for this was the blockade that Eleanor had put in place. A blockade that she'd insisted on precisely because she didn't want that papal bull to reach London.

"That is not the only message I have," Count Theobald said. "King Louis of France was most displeased that his daughter was not crowned on the same day."

Henry slammed his head against the back of his throne. "How could she have been crowned when she was not there? She was delayed at Caen with my wife, as everyone here can testify. What was I to do? And forgive me, but your message is a little late. I've worked out that Louis is displeased myself. He's already begun attacking the borders of Normandy. You can tell him such action will not go unchallenged."

The count tilted his head. "As a friend to both you and King Louis, perhaps I can assist you? You've always been friends. Why not discuss this in more detail and in person at Vendome? I will host the meeting myself."

King Henry glanced at Eleanor who gave him a small smile, then nodded. "Thank you, Theobald. I agree to attend."

"I welcome this, King Henry, but to return to the first part of my message, I've corresponded with Archbishop Beck—"

"And?" Henry snapped, his cheeks now tinged the same shade of red as his hair. "More threats to excommunicate me?"

"No." The count ran his hand down his long face. "He has agreed to the previous terms set out at Montmartre and has proposed the following: he will re-crown Henry the Younger, together with his wife, in exchange for permission to vindicate Canterbury's primatial authority in the Kingdom of England."

Henry sat upright, clearly delighted with the turn of events.

"I'm glad Becket has come to his senses. If he is willing to kiss me on the cheek, then I am willing to do as he asks."

The Count of Blois bowed and moved back to his seat. As this matter of business closed, another opened.

Mine.

"I now summon Donn of Ireland to speak with the king." One of Henry's servants stepped forward and beckoned me to come to the throne. I walked slowly through the hall, enjoying the stares that moved between the King and myself.

"So, you are here on behalf of Richard de Clare." Henry laughed, but as soon as his laughter faded, he got down to business. "What does he want?"

It wasn't lost on me that there was no Irish this time, no courtesies. Queen Eleanor stared at me, listening intently and not bothering to hide it. She was interested in this business then. I wished I knew whether that was a good thing or not.

"Richard de Clare wants to sail to Ireland, King Henry. He has accepted an offer of marriage to Eva, the daughter of the King of Leinster."

Henry hummed. "While I was in England, I heard that Strongbow had summoned all his fighting men to Pembroke. How many warriors does one need to witness a wedding? I doubt very much you need a whole army."

"He also wishes to hold land in Ireland, King Henry. He will inherit land via his marriage to Eva, but I have to tell you, Ireland is ripe for the taking. What if—"

"It may be, but Ireland is a Christian country. If it were not, I'd have thought to take it myself by now." He tutted then, and what was left of his smile faded. "Richard de Clare has always been ambitious. Always wanting more, but why should he have more when he stood against my mother? Against me?"

"He is your subject, King Henry. Whatever he takes will be in your name."

The king stared at me, his eyes cold, and I could sense his anger building. "Tell Strongbow my answer is no. Tell him that I forbid him to set foot in Ireland. Will that be clear enough for him, do you think?"

Faltering, I tried to find something convincing to say. "I think… I… Strongbow has promised King Diarmait to help him in the retaking of his kingdom. Didn't you promise King Diarmait that he could ask the knights of your realm for their help in taking it? If you will not allow Strongbow to hold land, will you not allow him to help King Diarmait at least?"

"This marriage he's arranged speaks of ambition, Donn. It speaks of Strongbow plotting to get his army into Ireland so he can make himself king, and that I cannot have. If I were to allow him to help this Leinster king, Strongbow would crown himself by the end of the year. That cannot happen. I am Strongbow's king. His lord. And his oaths to me still stand."

"No, King Henry. I do not think—"

"No?" the king shouted, his cheeks flashing red. "Do you dare tell me no? Well… *Donn*. I do not care what you think. Nor do I care for your presence. Go. Tell your master my judgement and tell him I shall be watching. Those who defy me do not fare well, as he already knows."

Stunned, I couldn't make myself move. Henry had not been so direct with any of the other emissaries who had come to speak with him.

King Henry rushed toward me, infuriated it seemed by the fact I hadn't yet moved, and clapped his hands in my face. "You look confused, Donn, so let me speak plainly. He can go to Ireland and be my enemy, or he can stay in Chepstow where he belongs and remain my friend. *Tertium non datur*."

There was no third option. No other way for Strongbow.

I bowed and stepped back. What else could I do? I tried to think of what Máelmórda would say. A joke, perhaps. Something witty that might make the king laugh. But the words on my lips turned to dust as the whole court stared at me and waited for me to depart.

"The next to speak with the king is Gérard of Provence. Please step forward to speak with the king."

There, already business had moved on. Still in a daze, I walked out of the hall.

"Donn! Wait!" FitzHubert came rushing toward me.

Dejected by my failure, I didn't stop. "What do you want?"

"You must return to Chepstow now and tell Strongbow what Henry said."

"I know."

FitzHubert ran to catch up, then standing in front of me, he bowed. "Good luck, my friend. Henry is allowing me to remain in Normandy, bless his soul for his generosity. I would have suggested that I accompany you, but I know you will speak the truth to Strongbow. You'll do him no favours by softening the king's words, you know."

"Agreed. I will leave directly, and I promise to repeat faithfully what the king has said." Trying to put the lessons I'd learned into practice, I gave FitzHubert a warm smile. "And thank you, my friend, for helping and guiding me during my time at Falaise. I could not have asked for a more generous host or teacher."

FitzHubert, a little flustered by my gratitude, chuckled. "It was my pleasure, Donn of Ireland. My pleasure."

He hurried back to the hall then, giving me a final wave as he passed through the doors. Off he went, allowed to remain in Normandy, while I was to travel back to Wales.

What would my mother make of what happened? Would she curse me? Tell me I was weak?

But as I mulled Henry's words over, another realisation came to me.

Perhaps she didn't need to know.

Perhaps Strongbow didn't either?

Why should I tell the truth to Strongbow or to anyone in Wales when I returned? If we needed Strongbow in Ireland, I would tell him that Henry had given permission, for it was nothing to me if Henry punished him for disobedience afterwards. In fact, it might even work to my advantage.

Smiling once more, I walked out of the castle. I'd had enough of Falaise now. It was beautiful, yes, but I had learned all I could, and home, for the first time in many years, was calling. I had been King of Ireland once, and I would be king again.

PART III

1166

Cuan

Kingdom of the Isles

(Four years ago)

I woke early as always and made my way outside.

The air on the Isles was freezing, but I didn't let that stop me from making my way to the river. I had lived on the Isles for longer than I had lived in Ireland now. I was used to the ice. *The cold is good for the soul of a warrior*, Uncle Godred always said. To feel the pain and shock of it as if it were nothing allowed the pain and shock of the battlefield to become lesser. It allowed us to become harder than those who fought against us. Warriors among men. Wolves among sheep.

This morning, I felt like a wolf. I mulled over all the battlefields I'd seen since I'd lived with my uncle. We'd fought in England, then in Norway. Then we had fought against his brother-in-law, Somerled, who declared he, not Godred, was King of the Isles. Glancing up at the walls of the fort, I stared at Somerled's head, which now rotted on a spike above the gate. That was what happened to the enemies of my uncle Godred. They died, and their body parts were displayed for all to see.

"I am nothing," I whispered as I reached the river. "If you are nothing, you can feel nothing."

Setting my clothes and sword on a rock, I jumped into the river. My breath caught. My muscles tightened. My body reacted this way every time. I let myself feel the agony of it before I rose to the top and exhaled in short, sharp bursts before breathing deeply once again.

"Cuan?"

I'd heard no one approach, and as I turned in the water, my toes clenched around the rocks along the bottom of the riverbed in case I needed to make a dash for my sword.

The adrenaline and fear pulsing inside me died upon seeing who was standing on the riverbank. It was a man I hadn't seen for many years. His hair was greying, but despite that, he looked remarkably unchanged.

I climbed out of the water, dried myself, and put on my shirt and trousers.

Out of the corner of my eye, I watched Osán in case he moved, though I took my time in dressing as if his presence did not concern me.

But of course it did. *Why was he here? After all this time?*

My sword was on the ground, underneath my clothes. Inching my toe beneath it, I flipped it up and into my hand. A trick that Bjorn had taught me.

Osán, however, didn't move, and he waited for me to put my cloak on before he came any closer. Even then, he didn't look like a man preparing to fight.

"Have you come to train me, Osán?" Grinning, I held out my sword and pointed it toward him. "What should I be today? Fast? Strong? Bold?"

Osán looked me over, that same unimpressed expression tugging at his mouth. "I'm sure you are all those things and more, Cuan. We can have a round in your uncle's square if you would like? That way we can see what you do against an actual warrior of Connacht and not a snivelling twelve-year-old prince like Conchobar."

"I've had many tests since I last saw you, Osán. There's nothing I need to prove. What about yourself? Are you still my father's nursemaid?"

"No. Just his friend."

Sharper than any knife, these words struck at my heart. Perhaps even deeper than that. I concentrated on holding in that pain… then, on letting it go. *You are nothing. Nobody.* My father had failed to keep his kingship. He had allowed his brother into his dun and not prepared for the treachery that followed. My mother had tried to save him and died as a consequence. The pain that my father had suffered was not my fault. It was not my duty to care for him. We were no longer bound in such a way.

"Your father wants to see you."

"It is hard for him to see me, is it not? He has no eyes."

"You know what I mean."

"My uncle Godred needs me. I don't have time to travel to Ireland."

"It's as well that he has come here then."

Osán tilted his head toward Godred's fort. "He's having breakfast with your uncle as we speak. Why don't you get properly dressed and meet him? Hear what he has to say?"

Osán turned, not waiting for me to give an answer, and walked toward the fort.

I let him go, making a show of tying my belt and putting on my boots, but inside, my mind was reeling. My father was here? Why?

After so many years of living in a haze of orders, I had never expected this day to come. I'd given myself over to fighting for Godred, and would do the same for whichever of his sons succeeded him. My father was a nobody. Blind. He had nothing left to offer me, and I had nothing to offer him. He'd not written, not since the last letter to my mother in Dublin saying he would divorce her if she didn't return.

I had thought to myself over the years that if he ever sent another letter, I would reply and say I was no longer his son. However, despite these well-rehearsed lines, a new emotion rose within me. *Curiosity*. Quickly, I pushed it down. I was a nobody. *A nobody who should know better than to let himself feel anything at all.*

If my father was eating with Godred, then it meant my uncle wanted us to meet, and so meet we would. My father would speak, and I would listen, and then we would part ways once again.

*

I went to my room to get ready first, the room I shared with two other warriors, Bjorn and Hálfdan. I was a simple warrior and had little in the way of ostentatious furs or jewels. I had one good tunic and one long fur cloak, though it was well worn and had belonged to another warrior before me. On Somerled's defeat, my uncle had given all his warriors gifts. Mine had been a silver ring, and I put that on. That aside, my dress was plain. No silks. No gold brooches. Nothing to say that I was the grandson of an Irish king or the nephew of the King of the Isles. I was a nobody. Just as Godred had told me when I arrived. And that was how I intended to stay.

Breathing deeply, slowly, and clearing my mind as Godred had instructed me when I was a boy, I walked into the feasting hall. Godred's two sons, Ragnall and Olaf, glanced at me, their lips curling into sly grins. They were not unkind to me, but this meeting with my father was amusing to them, and they did not care for me enough that they would bother to hide it. I grinned back, not wanting them to notice my reluctance to meet with my father. That would only amuse them further and might entice them to join our conversation.

"Cuan," Uncle Godred said, once he noticed me. He sat at the top table, while my father and Osán sat opposite him, so that their backs were toward me. "Come and sit with us. You have spoken to Osán, yes? This is your father."

"I think a son should know his own father without need of introduction," my father snapped.

Godred raised his eyebrows at this outburst but didn't say anything. This was unusual, for Godred did not allow his men or even kinsmen to raise their voices at him and certainly not in his own hall.

Deciding to speak before my father offended him again, I moved closer. "Of course I know you, Father. How are you?"

"As well as can be expected."

He turned to face me, revealing the thick knotting of skin that had formed over his eyes. My heart thudded and I was glad he could not see how my skin must have paled. The father of my memories was truly gone. Tall, muscular. Like a bull, he had once been, but he was these things no longer. Now he was like an old man. His face had sunken in since I'd last seen him, and his shoulders were narrow and frail.

"I have missed you, Cuan," my father said. "Your mother took you away from me. I divorced her for disobeying me. I want you to know that."

After glancing at Osán, who nodded along with my father, I turned to Godred. I expected him to be angry at this slight toward his sister, but he could only stare at my father, this broken man, in the same way he would at a child who had come to his table with boots covered in dog shit. Godred was holding back, I realised, and I knew then he wanted me to reply. I thought on how best to answer. I did not like how Father had spoken of my mother, but I could not let this rouse me to anger. I breathed deeply. Slowly. *I was nobody. Nothing.*

"I know about the letter, Father."

"Then why did you not come back to Ireland once she had died?"

Godred and I were the only ones who knew the truth of why I had stayed away. There was a curse in my blood, a curse of fire that would kill me if I used it... but I could not tell my father this.

"I had no wish to return to the kingdom of the man who had betrayed you and killed my mother. How could I swear an oath to a man like Ruaidrí?"

"But you are an Ó Conchúir. You must return, or else you will never be king."

This startled me. King? *How could I ever think of being king?*

"Surely my claim is as good as dead. Ruaidrí is king and Conchobar must have been made the *tánaiste* by now."

My father shifted forward in his chair, something of a smile growing on his lips. "What if I could make you king? What if I had a plan to destroy my brother and his family as they destroyed me and mine?"

"What sort of plan is this?" my uncle Godred said. "I don't want you filling Cuan's head with dreams and smoke."

My father snorted. "Ruaidrí is clever, but he is not a warrior. His son, Conchobar, isn't a warrior and he's not clever either. That's why my brother has gotten himself into a mess."

The curiosity inside of me rose up again. "What mess?"

"Ruaidrí is High King now, but he has not earned it," Father replied. "This title was built on your grandfather's work. On my work. And Ruaidrí's throne is only his because King Tigernán supports him. But it's all about to fall apart. All about to wash away now that King Diarmait of Leinster has invited the Anglo-Normans into Ireland."

"I have fought against them," Uncle Godred said. "They are wolves indeed."

My father reached forward and took my hand in his. His skin was soft, most unlike those strong calloused hands that I remembered. "You will be needed to fight in Ireland before long, Cuan. You are brave, I hear. I knew it when you were a boy, and I know it now that you have fought for your uncle and won many victories at his side. You can take Connacht back from my brother. You could even be High King."

"I don't think so, Father." I shook my head. "That's not me."

Osán sighed. Rolled his eyes. *Coming here was a waste of time*, every inch of his body seemed to say. Annoyance flared within me. Anger that he dared to judge me when he did not know me.

Stop it. You are nobody. Nothing. You cannot feel if you are nothing.

"I am not Cuan Ó Conchúir anymore," I said. "I'm Cuan the Viking. Cuan the Berserker. I am sorry you have taken such a long journey only to be disappointed, Father, but that is the truth of it."

I stood and walked away. Out of the hall, out of my uncle's fort and back toward the river.

I was not surprised to find that Osán had followed me.

"Your father wishes to say goodbye."

"Then I will come to the longphort to say farewell when he is aboard his ship."

"You are angry. I can see it within you, though you try to hide it. Why? Don't you want revenge for what Ruaidrí did to your family?"

I did want that. Hatred was a feeling I'd locked deep down

inside me, but it existed there still. Osán's words summoned it, demanded that it rise up. But to let that happen was to summon death upon myself. That was what my mother had told me. To let myself fill with anger would call the fire and then I would burn from the inside out.

"Revenge is one thing. Becoming king is another, and to that end, Father is wrong. It's beyond my reach."

"There are ways to obtain revenge without becoming king, you know." Osán's fingers brushed over the hilt of his sword. "I think you're right. The kingship of Connacht is beyond you. But killing Ruaidrí, that's not. Think about it. Your father goes to the priory at Tuam now. If you wish to speak again, go there."

I smiled at Osán as he walked away. Oh, I understood him now. He wasn't offering me a crown. He was offering me death.

It should be an insult for a man of his standing to offer this to someone like me, but instead I found only truth in his words… and better than truth – escape.

Father and Osán left quickly, and I did not speak to them again. Instead, that afternoon, I trained with Bjorn and Hálfdan, and together we went to the fort for the evening feast.

"Your father was a king?" Hálfdan asked.

"No, stupid. His grandfather was," Bjorn answered. "Don't you ever listen?"

"Rarely when Cuan is speaking."

Bjorn gave a small half-laugh but then turned serious. "What are you going to do, Cuan?"

Shrugging, I tried to order my thoughts. My answer had been no until Osán had spoken to me by the river.

"Why wouldn't you go?" Hálfdan asked me. "Your father must live the life of luxury as a brother of the High King. Living with him would be much better than being a warrior for Godred. If he was my father, I'd already be away."

Bjorn nodded. "You should think on it, Cuan, and listen, I've been meaning to tell you both for a few days now, but I'm not staying here for much longer."

Both Hálfdan and I stopped walking.

"Where are you going?" Hálfdan asked.

"Waterford. Brenna's uncle, Ragnall, is a warrior for the king there. When Ragnall visited here last week, he said I should come over with Brenna. I've paid off my debt to Godred, so I've decided to accept."

"This offer is dependent on you marrying Brenna, I presume?" I asked.

"Of course."

Hálfdan slapped Bjorn on the shoulder. "Then we shall toast you both tonight, and then come the morning, I shall weep. You will be gone and then so will Cuan and I alone will be left to fight for Godred."

"Haven't you paid off your debt yet?" Bjorn asked him.

"Not yet. Soon though. If I'm still alive when that happens, perhaps I will go to Ireland too."

"Well, I've not said I'm going yet—"

"Cuan!" Godred stood as I entered the feasting hall and beckoned me over to him.

"We'll save you a seat," Bjorn said. "Come on, Hálfdan."

Letting Bjorn and Hálfdan move past me, I made my way to Godred. As I approached his table, he pointed to the seat next to his. I rarely sat at his table. The chairs here were usually given to his sons, his brother and their kin. My uncle also rarely involved himself in my welfare outside of teaching me how to dampen my emotions so as to control the curse in my blood. Today, however, everything had changed. This was the second time I'd been offered a seat at his side. And the second time he'd meddled in my affairs.

For a while we feasted in silence and let the chatter around us grow louder. This was when my uncle leaned forward. "Osán followed you to change your mind. Have you decided what to do?"

I hadn't. Not really. And yet, as soon as this question came out of his mouth, I knew what my answer would be.

"I have. I will follow my father to Ireland."

"You will die if you do this," he said. "It is not a good plan. Ruaidrí's not stupid and will think of deception the instant you return."

"I know."

"Time has made Bardán bitter. Vengeance is all well and good, but only if you have a chance of succeeding and you—"

"Don't have a chance of succeeding," I finished for him. "I know."

"Then why go?"

Godred was a clever man, and in the ways of war, he was the cleverest of all. Somerled's head rotting on the spike along the wall of his fort was proof enough of that. I knew his opinion was the right one, that he could see the truth behind my father's ambition and the failings in his plan, but still, that was no longer my concern.

"You say it is a poor plan because I will die before I am made king. But I don't intend to be made king or to survive. If I can have vengeance first, I'll be happy."

"Ah." My uncle sliced off a chunk of salmon and ate it, chewing as he thought. "I understand now. You would have my efforts in training you wasted by dying so soon?"

For the first time, I looked at my uncle as an uncle rather than as his warrior. As blood and kin.

"You kept your promise to your sister, and for that I am grateful, but you know the curse that is in my blood and that no good can come of it. Mother told me that all with the curse die young. Is that true?"

"Yes."

"Then is this not a better way to go? To die fighting those who have hurt my family rather than die slowly, rotting from the inside out."

"I have trained you to dampen the curse. Perhaps you will live longer than the others?"

"Perhaps. But even so, what sort of life would this be? I would not have children, knowing what I might inflict upon them, which means I cannot marry. All I'm good for is fighting. So let me fight. You never know. Perhaps I might be of some use to you too."

My uncle snorted. "You are my warrior. You're already of use to me."

"Maybe. But here, I am simply a warrior, just like every other man in this room. In Ireland, I will be the nephew of the High King, and Dublin is ruled by Asculv now. Do you have no ambition to be king there once again?"

Godred ran his fingers over the bracelets on his wrist, his jaw tightening. "If you wish to go, then go. You will die, and you will die quickly, long before you can help me with Dublin. That is all I see for you. If I wanted to be King of Dublin, I would be. It is not for you to win my kingdom back."

"I didn't mean that. I simply meant my being in Ireland could be useful for you. If I'm in Dublin, I can see how much strength Asculv has."

"You'll have enough trouble with your father and your uncle and the other princes of Connacht without scheming for me."

I leaned back in the chair and stared at the fire burning in the pit.

"I still want to go."

"Then go," Godred said. "You are a man now and I cannot deny you this, but when you see my sister in the afterlife, tell her I did my best by you. I have no wish for any more ghosts to haunt me."

He sliced away at the salmon, his slaves filling his plate with smoked mackerel and buttered carrots. The conversation was over, and I found myself contented that he had not forbidden me from going. He knew it was the right thing. He knew I would die the same as I did.

And like me, he knew that this death, a death with a sword in the hand, was the best way to go.

The journey to Tuam was a strange one.

Ireland had become a place hazed by memory. Now I was here, it was hard to reconcile the homeland of my dreams and what lay before me. The trees seemed smaller, the sky a paler shade of blue, the air less damp.

I remembered the path to Connacht, though had to ask for directions to Tuam once I crossed the border, for I had never been there as a child. The shepherd I asked was incredulous that I was a man of Connacht and did not know where this great priory was. *I was a man of the Isles too,* I had replied. *Ah, you are a stranger then*, the shepherd said before walking off.

And indeed, he was right. I was no longer a man of Ireland, or at least I didn't believe myself to be. Not anymore. And yet, his words brought on an overwhelming feeling of loneliness, and though I tried to push it down, it wouldn't leave. *I was nobody. Nothing*, I whispered to myself, and after some time I was able to smother this emotion enough that I could no longer feel it.

I rode hard for several days once I landed at Dublin, stopping only to rest and sleep. Godred had let me take my own horse, Sleipnir, with me, and for that I was grateful. I was able to ride to Connacht as the nephew of the King of the Isles rather than the son of Bardán, the king that should have been but never was. However, for all my earlier determination, once I arrived at the Tuam Priory, I pulled Sleipnir to a stop and paused.

I could turn back.

Godred would accept me. He always needed good warriors, and life, if not easy, would at least be known to me. The path ahead of me here was a hard one. A shorter one, yes, and that was what I desired in a way, but something held me back. I thought then of my mother, of her black lips and cold hands, and the way she screamed when she saw my father's eyes being taken.

"Come on, boy," I said, stroking Sleipnir's neck. "We're here. You can rest now."

Dismounting, I led him into the priory stables and asked one of the novice monks for my father.

Osán came out of one of the small outhouses a while later, smirking as he saw me. "I knew you'd come," he said. "Your father had his doubts, but I knew."

His self-assurance annoyed me, but I said nothing as I followed him to the outhouse. "My father lives here?"

"Yes. It's a small house he's been given, to be sure. The monks here don't believe in luxury, not even for the son of a king."

"Then why stay?"

"Because Ruaidrí rarely visits, and that's good enough for your father. In any case, the monks are kind, and that counts for something."

"You stay here too?"

Osán nodded.

"What about your family? What about Dáire?"

"They are well, and I visit them when I can." His voice turning short, Osán opened the door, and we walked inside. There was a fire burning in the middle of the room, and my father sat on a wooden chair beside his bed. The furnishings were plain but well made, and I noted the blankets were made of fur rather than wool. *The monks allowed him some luxury then.*

"You've come to me, Cuan," my father said, reaching out with his hand.

I took it and kissed it. "I have, Father. How are you?"

"Better for you being here."

Smiling up at me, the scarred skin over his eyes was all I could see. Trying not to let my unease filter into my movements, I sat in the chair opposite. Osán sat on the bed. There was no turning back now. No leaving to return to the Isles. Taking a deep breath, I stared at my father, forcing myself to see his scars with acceptance rather than pity.

"You spoke of a plan when you came to the Isles, Father."

"I did, but are you ready to hear it?"

"Yes, of cour—"

"Truly ready, Cuan? What I ask of you will be difficult, and you didn't seem so keen when we last spoke."

"I had put the memories of what happened far away from me, that's all. I didn't know if I was ready to face them, but once I thought about it, I knew I had to. And now the memories have resurfaced, there is no pushing them back down."

My father nodded, seeming to understand.

"Then we will face our revenge together, my son. Now," he shifted forward in his chair, "the first thing you must do is to go to your uncle. He's currently residing in his newly restored castle in Galway. He built it with stone, if you can believe it." He gave a small laugh and shook his head. "Once you find Ruaidrí, you will ask to join his army and stay with him at his dun."

"And he'll let me?"

"You are his nephew, the grandson of a High King. Custom dictates that he must say yes, although he will keep you at arm's length."

"Why do you want me to do this? Why not simply kill him?"

"Oh, that would be too easy, Cuan. I want him to know he is losing everything. I want him to suffer and to understand why he was never supposed to be king… and of course, *you* must be king after him. If you were to walk into his dun, somehow reach him and strike him down, you would not last much longer. No, this is a more delicate plan. A plan where not only do we destroy him, but we turn everyone else against him and raise you up."

I glanced at Osán as he said this. He said nothing, only lowered his eyes, which meant he didn't think the second part was possible.

"Perhaps I should try to grow my own power in Dublin. Meet Ruaidrí with an army at my side?"

"Dublin?" My father snorted. "What has Dublin got to do with anything? I cannot contemplate why your mother suggested such a thing when she fled Connacht. You are an Ó Conchúir. If you were to make a move for power there, it would only make people see you as a Viking. To take Connacht that must not be. By stealing you away, she has done terrible damage that I now seek to rectify."

"Mother did what she thought was best."

My father waved his hand, his expression moving to annoyance. Quickly, however, he recovered and gestured for Osán to come closer.

"Give Cuan his present," he said. "Seeing as he remembers his mother so fondly."

Osán opened the small chest at the bottom of my father's bed and took out a bundle of blankets, which were wrapped in a thick leather binding. Pulling the leather and fabric away, my mother's sword was revealed. The one that had belonged to her father and had an engraving of Odin's eye on the hilt.

Rushing forward, I reached out to take it. It was just as I remembered it. So beautiful. So sharp.

"I've also purchased a new cloak for you and two new tunics and trousers. Godred may think it appropriate for you to be dressed in rags, but not I. And this is my last gift." Taking a silver ring from his finger, he held it out for me to take. "My father gave it to me. Now it's yours. You are an Ó Conchúir again, my son, and everyone will know it."

"Thank you, Father."

"There is one last thing," he said. "Before you go, you must make a vow to me."

"A vow?"

"Yes. Your word that you will do as I say. That you will follow my orders and my orders only."

Osán pulled out a gold cross from inside the chest and handed it to me. "You must hold it as you make your vows."

"I don't believe in that."

"Then what do you believe in?" my father asked.

I brushed my hand over my sword, letting my fingers rub over the engraving of Odin's eye. "This."

"A blood vow will suffice if it holds you true."

Kneeling at my father's feet, I cut the palm of my hand and smeared my blood over the silver eye. "I swear to go to Connacht and bring down my uncle. And I swear to follow your orders, Father, so that it's done as you wish."

My father smiled and patted my cheek. "You are a good boy, Cuan. Now go. Your first task is to gain your uncle's trust. Only once his other enemies move against him will I give you further instruction, but be prepared. I have a feeling it will not be long."

Summer 1170

Cuan

Dúnmór

On the morning of the gathering, I awoke with the first flush of dawn. I could hear the slow footsteps of the serving women around the dun as they lit the fires, the sound of voices drifting with the wind. It would not stay this quiet for long though. The gathering was to start after breakfast, which meant Dúnmór would soon be full to bursting.

I got dressed and went to the feasting hall with the rest of my kin and those chosen to be in my uncle's fianna at the Tailteann Games. It was only meant to be a ceremonial title, but my uncle wanted to showcase the might of Connacht and our link to old Ireland and Fionn Mac Cumhaill. Ruaidrí had spared no expense. He'd brought in the best of food, the best wine and ale, as well as imported fruit from Iberia. Added to that, the best musicians had been summoned to entertain us this evening.

As the morning passed, other kings entered the hall and approached the top tables. King Tigernán of Bréifne was the first king to arrive, then King Maghnus of Ulaid. The kings of the Northern Ó'Neills and Meath followed. It put me in mind of the Tailteann Games, except the men looked around the room with no laughter upon their lips. War was a serious business, and war was all we had to speak of today. No games, no lawmaking, no weddings.

Soon, the hall was filled. Not just with the kings of all the kingdoms in Ireland, aside from King Diarmait and King Odhrán, but with brehons and advisers, too. As more and more came inside, the sound became almost deafening. Everyone was talking, or else whispering and glancing at my uncle. There was a lot to talk about. Not just of our defeat in Limerick, but also the arrival of a new set of Anglo-Normans, who seemingly, with fewer than one hundred men, had defeated a force of six hundred warriors from Waterford and the Irish Uí Dróna clan.

As I closed my eyes, I tried to listen through the din to hear what was being said.

How can it be that the warriors of Waterford were defeated so easily?

And they cut off their heads, you know. Threw them into the sea so that they washed up at the longphort.

The Normans are a savage lot. We've let them stay here too long as it is.

What was King Ruaidrí thinking when he let Diarmait remain at Ferns last year?

The whispers were interesting, but nothing I could not have guessed myself. Ruaidrí now had to get us all out of this mess. For the moment, everyone seemed content to let him try.

"Welcome, everyone!" Eoghan shouted. "Please take your seats."

My uncle, unable to hide his delight that all the kings he'd invited had come, raised his hand to indicate the meeting was about to begin, and once everyone had settled, the guards at the back of the hall began to close the doors.

They stopped just as they were about to pull them to and allowed a final couple of men through.

To my surprise, Osán came into the hall first. Behind him, even more unexpectedly, was my father.

My heart pounded and I clutched the arms of my chair. I could feel myself losing control of my emotions, and I bit the inside of my cheek to push them back down or at least dampen them into something physical. A physical pain that I could focus on.

What was my father doing here? *Why had he come now?*

I don't know why his appearance at Dúnmór had such an effect on me. I knew my uncle had blinded him, I'd lived with that every day since, but somehow seeing my father here, in the place of his blinding, made my head ache. I might have expected Osán to come, but not him.

My father walked to the front of the hall, refusing to sit at the back with the lesser Connacht kings. I watched him as he moved, as did everyone else in the hall. Frail and blind as he was, the men here remembered him. Some greeted him by name, and he gave them a greeting in return.

"I am glad you came, Bardán," Uncle Ruaidrí said as a space was made for him and Osán at one of the front tables.

"I am a man of Connacht," my father replied. "I will always come in its hour of need."

A silence opened up with this unexpected interaction, but Ruaidrí seemed determined to continue as if this had not flustered him. It had though. Now that I knew him better, I noticed how the skin under his eyes turned white.

"You have all heard about the battle between the Anglo-Normans and Osraige last year," he began, softly clearing his throat. "And no doubt you have also heard rumours of what happened at Limerick and Waterford."

The men in the hall mumbled. *Yes, they had heard.*

"I can confirm that we lost the day at Limerick. King Cormac had not kept his scouts on the forest paths and as such we were surprised by the Anglo-Normans who King Diarmait has in his thrall. We retreated to save our men, but to show I cannot tolerate defiance, we burned every dun and ráth along the Shannon, including Killaloe."

The hall was silent now, the men listening intently to Ruaidrí and watching his every move.

"As to what happened at Waterford, I have only heard the same rumours as yourselves. That is why I asked the King of Waterford to send a messenger to describe what happened."

My uncle held out his hand and the Waterford messenger came into the hall. I sat forward in my chair as I realised it was my friend Bjorn.

Bjorn came to a stop once he reached the top table, but not before nodding his head at me. "Before I begin, I must greet a fellow warrior, a man I fought with in Norway and again when King Godred retook his Kingdom of the Isles. Cuan Ó Conchúir, it is an honour to be in your company once more."

Smiling, I placed my hand over my chest. "It is an honour to be in your company too, Bjorn. I wish it were for a happier reason."

"Indeed," Bjorn said, "for I have come here to tell you of the loss of hundreds of our men. Only a few weeks ago, a ship of warriors arrived from Pembroke, under the flag of Richard de Clare, or Strongbow as his men call him, and they set up camp at Dun Domhnall. The Waterford Vikings and the Uí Dróna clan met them in battle there. Despite the low numbers of the Anglo-Norman party, we could not drive them back. By the end of the day, we had lost hundreds of men, and seventy were taken hostage. We were about to send a messenger to negotiate their release when we saw their severed heads floating on the sea."

"The Anglo-Normans are as vicious as the rumours then?" King Tigernán asked.

"More vicious, I believe," Bjorn answered. "These men were all injured, but not dying, and slain as if they were animals."

King Ruaidrí stood and once more held out his hands. "Men of Ireland, we find ourselves at war. It has come to us quickly and we have delayed too long. Now is the time to act."

The men in the hall nodded. Not one disagreed.

"We must plan for war today, Father," Conchobar said. "We must decide where to face Diarmait and then ride out."

King Ruaidrí nodded. "I regret not destroying him at Ferns last year during the negotiations. I was too kind in allowing him an opportunity to become King of Leinster again."

"He was an old man, you mean, and you saw the potential of marrying your daughter to his son?"

Everyone turned to the person who had uttered these words. *My father.*

"I am blind, but any fool can see what your plan was. And it was a good plan, but by now you must know that Diarmait cannot be controlled. Even worse, the Anglo-Normans who have come to his aid have found us wanting. They won a great victory against the men of Osraige last autumn. Then they defeated you at Limerick. Now, fewer than one hundred of them have won a great victory outside Waterford. You should expect an invasion from Strongbow himself imminently."

My uncle shook his head. "There is no way the King of England would allow one of his earls to come here. An invasion of a Christian country by another is not permitted by the Church. If Strongbow comes, it is for land in Leinster through his marriage to Eva. He is a fool, for once Diarmait dies, the men of Leinster will rally around Connor and not his daughter and her Norman husband. But it seems he doesn't understand our ways and has thus been duped by Diarmait."

"What of Domhnall?" someone shouted. "They might follow him."

"Domhnall is a bastard. The Brehon law says they cannot," Conchobar replied.

Ruaidrí nodded as did several of the brehons in the room. "Connor is the only suitable heir, and with him married to Róisín, once again Ireland can be united. I did the right thing negotiating with Diarmait. My only mistake was in thinking that he was a rational man. I will not make the same mistake again."

"So… what should we do? Where will we fight?" King Tigernán asked.

"We should gather an army from each of our clans, and we should all ride to Ferns. This time we will fight King Diarmait until he surrenders and hands over the kingship to Connor. Once he is defeated, the Anglo-Normans will go home. Without a king to support them, they will see staying here is a lost cause."

Another silence opened up, and I leaned forward. "I disagree, uncle."

Ruaidrí raised an eyebrow at this. "You do?" He smiled as if inviting conversation, but I knew my interruption had displeased him. Osán seemed surprised by my interruption too. Telling my uncle he was wrong in a room full of people was not the best way to endear myself to him, but it could not be helped. I had to speak the truth.

"I have fought for my uncle Godred as you know. I fought for him in Norway, and I fought for him to regain his kingdom in the Isles. The world has changed. Men are hungrier for land than they ever were, and the style of war has changed in these lands too. I fear that if the Anglo-Normans come in greater numbers, they will not leave when Diarmait dies. I think they will see all the land we have to offer and will want to take it. Just as the kingship in England passed through Queen Maud, they will say it has passed to them through Eva and will not care that our laws say different."

I paused for a moment, but the hall was still silent. The men here were listening to me.

"As my father said," I continued, "they have won three battles against us now, each time with fewer men and less knowledge about the land. Why? Because they have learned their lessons fighting in Jerusalem and Frankia and Hastings. We must drive them out now. This is more important than dealing with Diarmait. Rather than go to Ferns, we must destroy their camps at Carrig and defeat them in battle. Only once we have done that, should we go to Leinster and fight Diarmait."

Once I finished, the hall filled once again with chatter. I half-expected for the kings to dismiss my idea, but I found instead that many of them agreed with me.

"This is an interesting thought, Cuan," King Ruaidrí said. "But if we attack the Anglo-Normans first, we will need more information about their fighting style. Don't you agree?"

"Yes."

"Then I would like you to accompany your friend Bjorn back to Waterford and learn all you can about the battle and the strategies used. I will have Fearghus do the same and travel to Osraige. We cannot fight an enemy until we know him."

I agreed, for there was nothing else I could do, but I knew this was him wanting to get me out of the way. My father's attendance had spooked him. Bjorn's arrival and greeting hadn't helped. But I found I didn't care. Leaving Dúnmór for a few weeks to once again be with my friend Bjorn was music to my ears.

The meeting continued for a while, mostly the kings discussing how many warriors they could raise and if it was worth waiting until the harvest was in to assemble. After a while, Ruaidrí called a stop to the conversation. "This is what I have decided. Firstly, Cuan and Fearghus shall visit Waterford and Osraige. Meanwhile, I'll have scouts verify the position of the Anglo-Norman army and the routes we can take to reach them. I'll also have scouts keep an eye on King Diarmait so that if he moves from Ferns, we will know. But know this. We strike within weeks. Ensure your army and suitable provisions are ready and then come to Dúnmór. If we fight as one army, we will march as one army, and God help anyone who stands in our way."

With the meeting over and the hall emptying, my father came over and embraced me. "You spoke well today, my son."

"Thank you, Father."

"Is there somewhere we can go to talk in private? Your house perhaps?"

I agreed and led him and Osán out of the feasting hall. Given that I was not allowed to be with my father without Ruaidrí's permission, I also glanced his way, but he was occupied with the kings who had flocked to ask him more questions. I then thought I should invite Bjorn to my house, but he was being interrogated by King Tigernán and King Maghnus, both of whom wanted to know more about the dead hostages. Making a silent promise to rescue him later, I walked toward my house at the back of the dun with Osán and my father.

Once I had closed the door behind us and helped my father into a chair, I poured us each a glass of ale.

"You said the right thing at the meeting," Father said.

"I don't think Ruaidrí will go for my plan."

"He is full of pride, so probably not, but the other kings will remember the sense you spoke when it goes wrong for him. There is much I know that my brother doesn't seem to."

Curious as to what he meant, I handed him the cup of ale. "Such as?"

"Such as Strongbow's army is already encamped at Pembroke and the ships are being readied as we speak. Diarmait is preparing his army to move. Whatever Ruaidrí decides to do, it will be slow because he always seeks for the kings to favour him. Diarmait will act faster. He and his Normans will probably attack Waterford first. If not Waterford, then Dublin, and it will happen within days, not weeks."

"Are you sure? It seems late in the year for Strongbow to come over, and he'll have a hard time invading either of those cities."

"I've told you before, Asculv is weak. He has no fight in him, and already Strongbow sends messages to other men inside the city offering them land and wealth. They'll turn against Asculv when Strongbow arrives at the city gates."

"Unless Ruaidrí and his army are there in time."

"I can't see Ruaidrí having the army ready in time. Did you listen to the kings complaining about needing men for the harvest?" My father rubbed his hands together and a gleeful smile spread over his face.

"This is not good news, Father."

"Not for Ruaidrí, but it is good news for you."

I took a sip of my ale. Yes, this was the plan. This was what my father wanted. For Ruaidrí to fail so badly that I would find it easy to oust him. That had always been the plan, and yet for it to happen, Connacht would have to suffer. Men from all over Ireland would have to suffer. I didn't want that. Not anymore.

No. I wanted to go to Isolde, and with her I wanted to leave this land. Leave behind all this scheming and talk of revenge. But I couldn't, could I? Isolde had not returned to me, not in person or in her dreams. And I had made a vow to my father.

"When you go to Waterford, find out what you can," my father said. "Strategies, battle tactics, who the leaders are. This knowledge will become your power. Remember that."

Osán touched my father's shoulder then. "It's time for you to go, Bardán."

My father stood slowly.

"A great war is coming, Cuan. You must be ready when it arrives. Not just to take the kingship of Connacht but to destroy all of those who took it from us. You remember your vow, don't you?"

"Yes, Father. I remember."

I said goodbye to my father, watching him until the door closed. I wished now I had never agreed to kill Ruaidrí, for when I closed my eyes, I no longer saw my uncle dead at my feet.

I only saw myself with Isolde.

But that was impossible. Isolde was far away from me. She lived now only in dreams or else as a ghost who visited me in hers. And the truth was, the curse was still inside of me. There was nowhere I could run, nowhere I could escape with Isolde where that would not be so.

Donnchad

Bristol

The ship sailed north. This time, I'd been able to find one that would sail me directly to Bristol, rather than having to travel via London. I had dreaded the long voyage but was grateful that it was summer rather than winter. Weather on the sea was always unpredictable and the mild sunshine of Normandy faded rather quickly. By the time we reached Bristol, a storm had blown in, and the wind was so sharp that the sailors' teeth chattered as they worked to anchor the ship.

I had huddled in my seat for most of the voyage, my cloak wrapped tight about me. My Fomorian blood kept me warm, but the wind was still sharp enough to cause discomfort. I had never been good on the sea, either, much to Sitric's amusement when I was a boy. The rolling swells reminded me of the time that I vomited over the side of the ship with my father when we sailed from Munster to the Kingdom of the Northern Ó'Neills. My father had comforted me. Sitric had laughed. Mother had barely been able to conceal her disgust.

Now I was close, I dreaded the conversation I was about to have with her, fearing that she would see through my lies. Somehow, Mother would know I had failed. *Sitric would have argued harder*, she would say. *Máelmórda would have charmed the king*.

But there was no point in worrying about that now. It was Strongbow whom I needed to convince. He was the one who needed to believe that Henry had given him permission to leave. I therefore had to settle on how this conversation would have gone. What words would Henry have said if his reply had been favourable? He was often vague, perhaps leaning into this was best. Not to lie outright and say he had given permission but to allow Strongbow to think he had.

I was still mulling these thoughts over, when the ship docked at Bristol. It took me the rest of the day to reach Chepstow Castle, easy enough once I found someone willing to sail me over to the other side of the river, and once there, I was greeted as one of Strongbow's men and given a horse. Taking some time to buy food and provisions, I then rode on to Pembroke, where Strongbow had gone for the summer.

Six days later, as I approached the castle at Pembroke, I found a group of knights waiting for me outside the entrance. Dressed in full armour, they were impressive, and Strongbow was with them. *Were they going hunting?* No, if they were going hunting, they'd be on horseback. I slowed my horse to a walk.

"Greetings, Donn," Strongbow said as I approached. "We had word from Falaise that you were on your way back to us. My man at Chepstow rode on ahead when you arrived, so I thought we should come out to greet you."

My mouth dried. *He'd already had a message from Falaise?*

"Pigeon," Strongbow said, seeing the confusion on my face. "They are useful birds. I have one or two kept at most castles in England and Normandy. You never know when one will be needed."

"Ah," my voice faltered, the lies I had rehearsed falling away. He already knew Henry's response. He just wanted to know the details.

"So, tell me what happened," Strongbow said. "Henry must have had a good reason for denying me."

"It is true, my lord. He forbids you from going to Ireland."

Strongbow leaned forward as if a heavy weight that I could not see pressed down upon him. "Did you not convey my messages? Did you not explain to him the opportunity?"

"I did, my lord, but he did not agree."

"So, what did he say? I'm sure it wasn't just the word *no*."

"He said you were too ambitious and thinks you want to make yourself the King of Ireland. He told me to remind you of your vows, and that he is your king and lord."

"Did he forbid my marriage to Eva?"

"No, not the marriage. Just your setting foot on Irish soil."

Strongbow smiled at this and rolled back his shoulders. "I see. Well, I've tried to please him and cannot. The truth is, Henry does not trust me even though I've done everything he has ever asked."

I stared at the river and at the ships harboured there. The ships were ready. I could see that from here. Did that mean he still meant to go to Ireland? Did it mean that Strongbow had it in him to defy his king?

Strongbow followed my gaze. "As you can see, Donn, his refusal comes too late. I have committed to go. I've made an oath to marry Eva, the daughter of Diarmait Mac Murchadha, and to fight for him, and so I've decided that my only option is to beg for forgiveness once the deed is done." He nodded to the knights beside him. "Go on ahead and tell the men we leave as soon as I board."

"I think this is the right decision, my lord," I said as Strongbow and his men turned. "The king was much preoccupied by his falling out with King Louis and Archbishop Becket. I'm sure once you take Ireland, he will forgive you."

"You are sure, are you, Donn? Has a few months in the company of the king allowed you to know him?"

"No, I just—"

"Never worry, I am teasing." Strongbow smirked; the weight now lifted from his shoulders. "I sent you to do a job, and you could not do it for me, but have no fear. I forgive you."

Forgive me? What need did I have of his forgiveness?

I lowered my head. "Thank you, my lord."

"And I thank you for doing your best. You're now free to go."

"Free to go?"

"Yes. I have no further need of you."

"But I can help you, my lord. The language, I—"

"I've others who can help on that front. You are welcome to stay here as my guest, and the horse you are riding is yours. A token of my gratitude."

My mind couldn't quite keep up with what he was saying. He didn't need me? What arrogance had persuaded him of such a thing? He'd be dead within a week without me there to guide him.

But perhaps that was for the best.

If I found another ship to bear me to Ireland, I would be there to form a plan for those who survived the Irish rebuttal, which would surely come if such a large army landed there. But first, I needed to find Cecile. She was key to my plans, and it was time to have her at my side.

"What about my cousin?" I asked.

"Oh, yes, you still want to marry Cecile? Well, she is a free woman, so I suppose you'd better find her and ask. The women of the castle are in the tower."

Strongbow and his knights hurried away then and made straight for the harbour.

Still reeling from our interaction, I made my way into the feasting hall where the servants were clearing away the breakfast. It was strange to be in a hall of this size and find it empty of all except a few servants.

"Do you know where Cecile is?" I asked one of them.

The servant stared at me blankly.

"She worked here before. Serving the food and wine. Strongbow said she would be in the tower."

"There is no one in the tower yet, my lord," the servant answered. "But I think I remember who you speak of now. The women in the kitchens will know where she is."

I made my way outside. Even though I had not been to

Pembroke before, the kitchens were easy to find, for I could hear the kitchen maids screeching from the courtyard, and if that hadn't led me there, the smell of curdled milk and raw fish surely would have. As I turned the corner, I found the women laughing with each other as they took turns sipping at a bottle of wine.

"Cecile!" I shouted.

A maid walked out of the kitchen. This one was young and carried a bucket of fish guts in her hand. Swerving to avoid me, some of them spilled onto her apron.

"What's wrong with you?" she snapped, her voice as sharp as any knife. "You shouldn't be here."

"I'm looking for Cecile."

"Who?"

From behind the kitchen maid, a plump, older lady peered at me. The cook. She had just taken a swig of wine and wiped her lips as she passed the bottle to her friend, a woman with grey curls that peeped out from under her headscarf.

"What business do you have in my kitchen?" she asked, eyebrow raised.

"I merely wish to speak with my cousin, Cecile."

The cook sniggered, revealing a gap where her two front teeth used to be. "She's away."

"Away where?"

"With the earl. To Ireland. She was made a lady's maid for his daughter, Alina. Too good for the likes of us then, so she was."

Cecile had gone with Strongbow to Ireland? *Surely not*. If she was on the ship, she must have heard of my arrival. Why had she not disembarked?

"Left you in the lurch, has she?" the cook said, her grin widening.

This statement led to a peal of laughter from the other kitchen maids, and the old cook wiped the dampness of her eyes with the backs of her hands. "You're too late, son. She's been making eyes at the earl for months, and he's been making eyes back. You'd best be off and finding some other lady to woo. Cecile is the lord's whore now, so she won't be wanting you." She pointed at the young girl who was wiping away the fish guts from her apron. "If you want a wife, why don't you marry young Mildritha? She's a pretty girl when not covered in fish."

I kept my emotions tight, trying my best to ignore their ridicule. "What about my sister, Alys?"

The old woman's smile slipped then. The laughter faded. "Oh, I forgot that Cecile and Alys were kin. I'm sorry to tell you that Alys' husband, David, has died. Your sister took it very hard, from what I've heard."

"Where is she?"

"Ireland."

"Alys is in Ireland?"

"Yes. They left months ago. What was it Alys did?" The cook nudged the woman with the grey curls in the ribs.

This woman hiccupped. "She killed the man who killed David. Cut his head off and threw it into the sea."

"Seventy heads she cut off," Mildritha said.

"Don't be stupid," the cook said. "Alys could never cut off seventy heads. It was just the man who killed David and one more."

I edged away from them and their argument about how many men my mother had killed. I knew enough to understand the truth. My mother had always intended to go to Ireland and had tempted me with Henry's court to get me out of the way. That was why Strongbow didn't need me. He had Alys and Cecile.

Even though I had always suspected Mother was lying to me at the time, the betrayal hurt, for it wasn't just my mother who had turned against me, but Cecile too.

And there – that was another reason Strongbow had not wanted me to sail to Ireland with him. I had told him of my plans to marry Cecile, and he wanted her for himself. Oh yes, and no doubt my mother fanned those flames in the right direction – and now she was in Ireland, famed for having killed either one man or seventy, while I had been left in Pembroke like an unwanted dog.

I made my way back into the feasting hall, and one of the serving maids there fetched me milk, watered ale and a selection of the roasted meats and breads from the table. Stabbing the table with a bread knife, I tried to think. So, my mother had Cecile on side. But what about Angelo? Where did he fit into all this?

Was he even alive?

Had any Descendants found him? I wished more than ever that I had not left him behind. If he were with me, I'd be in a much stronger position.

Another issue was that Mother and Cecile had no idea I suspected any Descendants could be alive. Making plans in my head, I decided that when I went to Ireland, I would concentrate on finding them. I was a Fomorian, a warrior and a cupbearer, but if I found another Descendant, I could take another gift. I could make myself so powerful that even my mother could not stand against me again.

I ripped the thread I had used to seal my cloak pocket shut and took out the Descendant's knife…

Except it wasn't the Descendant's knife.

It was Angelo's.

Another betrayal.

My son had stolen my knife from me before I left Ireland. This time, I could not keep my emotions in. I stood and screamed and threw the plates onto the ground, where the clay shattered into hundreds of pieces. Then I stormed out and took my new horse.

"He's not ready yet," the stable boy said.

Pushing the boy out of the way, I jumped up onto the horse's back and rode him out of the castle. My plan had changed. I was not going to Ireland now. No, I was going back to Falaise. Back to Henry.

It was time to find out what this king did when he was betrayed by his men. I had a feeling his justice would come sharp and swift, and it was this thought that kept me riding through the night.

Gormflaith

The Hill of Carrig

Le Gros and his army had moved to Carrig not long after the battle outside Waterford, and here we had stayed ever since. I itched to be away from this heap of rocks, but where else would a loyal widow wish to be other than with the kinsmen of her late husband?

Robert FitzStephen, fresh from his victory in Limerick, had welcomed his Norman allies with open arms, though he asked more than once why we had landed outside Waterford rather than come straight to Carrig. Le Gros, to his credit, did not lie and said it was to stake his claim on Waterford. Given he had not actually won the city, this now depended on if Strongbow gave it to him. I suspected that at present he had not done enough to earn a prize of that size, and of course, for Strongbow to give it away, he had to win it himself.

Robert and his brother Gerald must have known this too, and so didn't complain or argue. They simply got on with reinforcing the fort and readying themselves for war, and this was why each day felt like the same day over and over. Ad infinitum. Oh yes, we were ready for war, but it was late in the summer now and still Strongbow had not come.

Le Gros, Robert FitzStephen and Hervey sent letters upon letters to Strongbow, all begging for him to come, and every morning and evening, they sent their men to the coast to see if a fleet of ships were headed our way. None had yet appeared.

"He said he would come," Le Gros said as he cleaned his sword for the hundredth time. "And Strongbow never goes back on his word. Not to me."

I didn't know how Le Gros stayed so wilfully hopeful, for he must have known that if Strongbow didn't come soon, the weather would turn and then the Irish kings would put their bickering aside and unite. Word had it that King Ruaidrí had already summoned every king in the land to attend his dun. If he could convince them to go to war against us, it was over. The Anglo-Normans were good in battle, but not good enough for FitzStephen's remaining three hundred and Le Gros' remaining sixty-three to face an army of over ten thousand.

And so we waited. Waited and waited. *Would Strongbow come or not?* That was the question that burned in all our minds.

Never before had I prayed to my ancestors, but on this occasion, I did. *Make Strongbow come*, I whispered into the smoke of the evening fire. *Don't let David's death be for nothing*.

Rage flooded through me when I thought of David. Memories of how unfairly I had been treated by my family was all I could think of. Perhaps this was why, when I slept, I could no longer search for them in my dreams. Now all I could see was David lying on the grass, and the way he looked at me when I sliced his neck open.

It was my family who had made me do such a thing. My family, the Descendants and Olaf.

"Alys, will you collect some more firewood?"

I looked up to find two of the Anglo-Norman archers staring at me. It was Walter and his friend Baldwinn. Walter was cooking a hare stew while Baldwinn gutted the fish.

"We need to get the second fire going," Walter added. "Get the fish brewing, otherwise we'll be short for dinner."

I set down my comb and silently agreed. Food. That was the problem with keeping an army this size at a camp like Carrig. The whole day was spent in the catching and cooking of it. The men had discovered by now that I was no cook, and so instead sent me to collect wood or mend their clothing.

I preferred collecting the wood. At least when doing that, I was able to get out of this camp for a while. Wrapping my scarf over my head, I walked into the forest below the hill and collected the larger branches that had fallen. I was only there for a short while when a golden eagle landed on the oak tree beside me.

Olaf.

I'd dreamed of him several times while at Carrig. He had still not found Angelo, and I had not ordered him to return to me. His return now might be because he could no longer bear to be away from me, or it could mean he had finally found my grandson.

Walking further into the forest, just in case any of the Anglo-Normans came in to pass water, I stopped in a clearing, then waited until all around me was silent. Olaf, who had followed me, landed on the ground. Moving over to touch him, I transformed him back into himself.

The newly formed man stared at me. Naked and old and haggard and absolutely disgusting. I hated him more than ever as he writhed on the forest floor. It was his fault I was here collecting wood like a peasant. If he had been more like David, he never would have betrayed me, and I would already be queen of this land. By killing Svein, he had destroyed Sitric's chance of winning Dublin and ruined all my plans for the battle at Clontarf. All for a stupid vow he'd made to avenge his dead mother. He'd chosen her memory over me – the woman he said he loved – and that was a betrayal I could never forgive.

He loved me now, though. I could see that from the way his eyes shone when they took me in. This was the love potion in all its glory. A potion that could only be broken by seeing someone else he truly loved. Olaf had no one left alive that he loved, and so his devotion to me was complete and unbreakable.

A few months ago, I'd found this comforting. *Now it reviled me.*

I felt for the vials that I had sewn into my cloak. One of them was the potion of truth, the other the potion of forgetfulness, though there were only a few drops of that left. Perhaps I should give him these last drops, and send him toward Wexford? He'd be like a madman to the mortals there. An old man with no memory, but at least he'd be gone from me, and I'd never have to look at his wretched face again.

"Gormflaith," he said, crawling forward on hands and knees. "I have news for you."

"You found Angelo?"

Olaf knelt up, hands clasped together. "No. I did not. Could not. I searched everywhere. Every dun and every ráth I came across."

Angelo was dead then. The realisation hit me, stung me as if a sword had just pierced my heart. Damn it. Why had Donnchad left him behind? *Because Donnchad was a fool, that was why*. How I'd ever trusted him was now beyond comprehension.

Who had killed Angelo, was the next question. Mortal or Descendant? I found that I no longer cared. Isolde was dead. I would destroy any other Descendant who might try to hurt me. Back in Ireland, I could feel my power was stronger. The fire burning within me, oh, one day I would let it out.

One day soon.

Olaf tugged at my dress. "I even flew back to Bristol and Chepstow in case he had returned there looking for you, but he hadn't. And that's how I know..."

He trailed away, his hands tightening around each other.

"Know what?"

"That Strongbow is coming. The ships are readied."

Ah, some good news at last. "What about Cecile?"

"She has boarded the ship. They are coming, I tell you. I flew over Strongbow and listened to him. He has sent letters to Hervey and to Diarmait only, not Le Gros or FitzStephen. They are all to meet at Waterford. The messenger has already set sail. He'll be here this evening. Tomorrow morning at the latest."

"Strongbow plans to invade Waterford first and not Dublin? Are you sure?"

Olaf nodded, his blue eyes wide and sincere.

"That is why I have come to you, Gormflaith. You are heading to war now. It is not safe for you. I had to come here. To you. To be with you."

Giving him the smile he so desperately craved, I tilted my head to the side. "You would protect me?"

"Yes. Give me my young body and a sword, and any man who tries to harm you will die a painful death." He crawled a little closer. "Please."

Deciding I could no longer stand the begging, when I spoke next, I put some emotion into my voice. "You've done well, Olaf."

"So have you," he replied, beaming at my kind words. "You are rid of that man now. You told me you would get rid of him, but I had no idea you planned to do it so quickly."

David. He spoke of David. My smile faded. *How dare he speak of him.*

"Yes," I replied, my voice suddenly dry. "He's gone."

"Then what is next, my love?" Olaf reached forward, tentatively touching my foot with his hand. He stank of bird. Reeked of fish too. He wanted to kiss me. I could see it in his eyes. He wanted to bed me and for me to tell him once again how much I needed him and that when I was queen, he would be at my side. Well, I would rather vomit all over myself than ever lie with him again.

Crouching down, I met his gaze. "I need you to work hard for me, Olaf. Now, before the messenger comes. I will need you to fly over and around Waterford and search for signs of weakness along the walls or longphort. Can you do that for me?"

A pained expression flooded Olaf's face. "It is a well-defended city, Gormflaith, and the walls are made of stone. Its weaknesses will be few, if any."

"Surely that is not the great Olaf Tryggvasson giving up before he has even tried? Have no fear, Olaf, I have faith in you, even when you don't have it in yourself. I am sure you will find something. If you do, I can tell Strongbow. Now that David is not here,

I need to find another way into his social circle so that my plans to betray him can begin."

Appeased that I had shared my plan, he nodded. "Yes, yes, I can do that for you."

"And then when you return, I will turn you back into human form and you can be at my side."

Olaf's eyes brightened, his every expression full of joy. "I don't know what to say, Gormflaith. Thank you. Thank you for once again letting me be by your side."

"Now go and do as I ask, oh, and find something to wear too. A monk's or priest's attire should work best. That way you'll be allowed in my company without a chaperone."

Olaf, delighted with this outcome, smiled at me even as I transformed him back into an eagle. Only once he had flown away did I shudder. The smell of bird lingered in the air alongside the hatred in my heart. By all my ancestors, I couldn't wait to be rid of him.

Quickly, I returned to camp with my bundle of wood. As with every other evening before this one, I ate dinner, mended the men's shirts, trousers and boots, and then fell asleep. For the first time in many months, however, I felt excited. My patience had been rewarded, and war was about to begin.

David was gone. So was Angelo. But I, Gormflaith, was alive.

The next morning, I walked into the woods to pass water, hopeful that Olaf might have returned with information about Waterford, but with no such luck, I collected the firewood before returning to Carrig.

"You took your time," Baldwinn said as I trudged through the gate.

"Sorry," I answered. "We've picked the forest dry. I had to go further in this time."

I set down the firewood. However, I quickly noticed there was a flurry of excitement around Le Gros' tent.

"What's going on?"

"A letter has arrived," Walter said, rubbing his hands together. "Strongbow has left Pembroke. Twelve hundred men he's bringing, as well as provisions for a siege. We've got to meet him outside Waterford, by the River Suir, I think. We're going to ride out this afternoon after we've eaten."

Grinning, I set down the firewood and stoked the fire. The march to Waterford would take two days if the men kept to a good pace. Even better, Strongbow had brought provisions with him, which meant there would be no stops to forage.

"Will you watch over the stew, Alys?" Walter asked. "I've got to get my clothes ready."

Seeing as I had nothing of my own to pack, for everything I owned I was wearing, I did as Walter asked and even ladled it out once it was ready. The men handed me their bowls, smiles on their faces, all eager to be away.

The final stages of preparation were now finally underway, with the men either eating or packing up their tents, and the knights readying their horses. Just as the archers and foot soldiers moved into marching formation, a golden eagle flew overhead.

Olaf.

It was poor timing, but I wanted to know if any danger lay on the road ahead. Quickly, I ran to the gate.

"Where are you going, Alys?" William Ferrand called after me. "We are leaving shortly."

"I have to pass water. I won't be long."

William grunted. "I'll have one of the men ready David's horse for you, but don't be long. The army won't wait. Not even for you."

I hurried into the forest and glanced at the old brown woollen robe, lying on the ground, that Olaf had foraged. Perfect. I checked that he hadn't torn it with his talons, which he hadn't, then brushed the dead leaves and debris from the fabric. As I did this, he flew down from the oak tree he was perched upon, and I transformed him back into human form.

With more enthusiasm than I'd ever seen, he put on the robe, and as soon as this was done, he held out his arm for me to touch.

"I'm sorry, Olaf. You must stay like this for now."

His mouth parted. "No, Gormflaith. You cannot desire me like this. Give me my younger body. The one that gives you pleasure."

"You think they will allow you to be with me if you look like that?" I shook my head. "They would part us, and I can't have that. You must appear as you are now. Just for a time. I promise once I have more control, I will change you."

Olaf, desolate, eventually nodded. He wanted to seduce me, for me to desire him as he desired me, but he didn't want to anger me either, not when I dangled such a promise under his nose.

"Tell me, Olaf. What did you find when you flew over Waterford?"

"It is fortified, just as I thought. It is located between two rivers. Both of these things will make it difficult to breach. It is filling with warriors from Munster too. The King of Waterford has a spy in Pembroke, and they know an invasion is imminent."

I sighed. This was not good.

"Was there anything at all that might help?"

"One thing. In some places along the outside of the wall there are watchtowers. One watchtower on the northern side hangs from the wall. This one is supported by a beam that goes through the wall, and it is also propped up by a post. I believe the weight of the watchtower makes the wall weak here. If Strongbow was able to break the post, the watchtower's weight would all be on the beam, which in turn would weigh on the wall. It's possible this might bring part of it down… but equally, it might not do anything. The wall is thick and well made."

"Very well. That is something at least. What about the road ahead? Is it safe?"

Olaf nodded.

"Good." I gestured then for him to approach. "Come then, Olaf. Come to Carrig and I will introduce you to my friends."

Olaf, stinking of bird and fish, followed me up the hill. How differently the men would have reacted to him if he looked as he used to. They'd have brought out their swords and bows and would have barred him entry. But this old man, he was almost ignored as he followed in my wake. This time, I moved past the fire and went straight to Le Gros.

"Ah, Alys!" he said, already seated upon his horse. "Are you ready?"

"Yes. Where is David's horse?"

"Here it is, Alys," William Ferrand, who always kept his promises, brought it over for me, and I used one of the tree stumps to elevate me so that I could haul myself up.

"Who is your friend?" William asked.

"He is a priest. He asked to bless us, and I felt I should let him come in."

"Tell him to leave," Le Gros said. "We're almost ready to go."

"I think we should bring him with us," I replied. "My grief weighs heavy on me, and I should like a priest to talk to. Besides, he says he is from Waterford. Wouldn't that be useful, for I'm afraid I am of no help when it comes to the city."

"Can he keep up?"

I shrugged. "I suppose if he can't, then he won't be a bother to you."

"Very well," Le Gros said. "But tell him we cannot spare a horse, and no one can carry him either."

Le Gros looked around, checked one more time that everything we needed had been packed away and that the men were ready. "Men, let's ride out."

I followed Le Gros, leaving the old and haggard Olaf to walk with the archers.

It took us less than two days to reach Waterford, for Le Gros and FitzStephen had their men march through the night so that we could reach Strongbow's camp before any of the Irish kings might hear of us travelling to reach him.

We found him easily enough, just outside Waterford on the

estuary of the River Suir. The camp was huge and already was in some sort of order. What impressed me the most was the number of horses they had brought over from Pembroke, which in turn meant the number of knights. At least two hundred. Yes, this was more like it. This was a force that might be able to take whatever the Irish kings threw at them.

Strongbow's tent was in the middle of the camp, and Le Gros and FitzStephen lost no time in making their way there. I should not have followed, but I did anyway. I could say I was looking for Cecile, if nothing else. Or I could say I was frightened of being in a camp with so many men I didn't know. Le Gros hadn't quite fallen for the act of innocence that had so ensnared David, but he liked me enough not to want to cause me discomfort.

Walking close to the tent, I was glad to see that Cecile was there. She was brushing the hair of Strongbow's daughter, smiling as the curls fell nicely over her shoulder.

"Is that how you like it, Alina?" Cecile asked.

The young woman gave a shy nod, then turned her attention back to her embroidery.

I crept a little closer, close enough that I could hear what the men were saying.

"It's time," Strongbow said, his map rolled out on a makeshift table. "We begin as soon as the men have rested."

"You don't wish to wait for King Diarmait?" Robert FitzStephen asked. "He can't be far away."

"I have no intention of waiting for Diarmait. In fact, I'd much rather take the city without his aid. That way it's mine rather than his."

Oh, this was interesting. Already Strongbow had thrown off the pretence of fighting for Diarmait. Already he was here to serve himself.

"How long before he arrives?" Le Gros asked.

"I guess we have two days, which is why I want to begin as soon as possible."

Robert and Le Gros both bowed and smiled. I couldn't help but smile myself. Strongbow understood that to win, you had to take rather than be given. With ambition like that, our fortunes rapidly improved, which meant it was time for me to make a move of my own.

"Cecile! Is that you?" Running into the tent, I focused only on Cecile, and opening my arms, I wrapped her in my embrace.

"Alys," Cecile said as I buried my head in her shoulder. "How are you?"

"All the better for seeing you."

Strongbow waited for me to pull out of our hug and then gave me a kind smile. "I've heard much of your bravery, Alys. And I can only join you in your grief. David is a loss to all of us."

Curtseying low, I wiped my eyes. "Thank you, my lord."

Strongbow pulled me up and kissed my hand. "Why don't you stay here with Cecile for now? I know you'll want her with you. Alina will enjoy your company too."

With my agreement given, he marched out of the tent and gave directions to the knights who had camped around it. His patience for women was gone. Now it was time for war.

Talking in Irish, I whispered to Cecile. "How are you?"

"Well."

"Where is Donnchad?"

"He returned from Normandy to give Strongbow Henry's verdict, which was no. Strongbow sent him away then. I have no idea where he is. He'll be furious, wherever it is."

I nodded and sat on a chair, exhausted from the two days of riding. I needed peace, but not yet. If the battle was to begin, I had to stay alert to what was happening. Peering out the door, I watched Strongbow beckoning for Le Gros, Hervey, William Ferrand and Robert to come closer. "Bring the ladders to the front," he said. "Tell the foot soldiers to get in line."

"Now? Before we set up camp?" William asked.

Strongbow nodded. "It is warm. We have no need of tents just yet, and I've had enough of waiting."

From the comfort of my chair, I watched as the men readied the ladders they had brought over with them. Next, I glanced at

Waterford. The walls were high and from here I could see hundreds of men on top of them, ready to defend.

"Would you like some lemon cakes, Alys?" Alina asked. "I brought them with me from home."

Smiling brightly, I accepted one and began to ask the young woman about what she made of Ireland. There was no point telling anyone about the watchtower just yet. Best to let the men attack and fail first. Only then might Strongbow be desperate enough to listen to the advice of a woman.

"March!" Strongbow shouted.

All three of us walked toward the door of the tent and watched as the Anglo-Norman army marched toward Waterford. Alina and Cecile were wide-eyed, curious but also horrified by the thought of what was to come.

I was so excited, I couldn't even hide my smile.

Isolde

Seir Kieran

"Can you hear the water? Sometimes it has a voice. Sometimes it has music." Méabh splashed the water at me, her expression hopeful, but I was sure by now she was beyond exasperated.

I swirled my fingers in the river. "Nothing. I hear nothing."

"Why don't you try getting into the water? Let it surround you?"

I didn't particularly want to. It was cold, and there was little heat in the air today. Still, I did not want to say no. Time was moving onward and still I had not been able to master anything about the cupbearer gift. Not so much as a droplet of water had moved on my command.

Taking off my cloak and dress, I waded into the river until it reached my waist.

"Now, take a deep breath and go under," Méabh said. "See if the water interacts with you. When it responds, the water forms a ball and comes into your hands. Or sometimes it will swirl around your arms like a fish."

I swam out into the deeper part of the river. The current was stronger here than by the bank, but years of swimming in the sea around Rathlin had more than prepared me to handle it. Taking a deep breath, I used my hands to propel me downward and then I stilled.

The water tugged at me, pulled me downstream, and I let it take me. Closing my eyes, I tried to empty my mind of thought.

Come to me, I said in my head. *Let me feel you.*

The water continued its journey downstream, the current still carrying me. *And then I felt something*. The river was pushing me downward too, deeper, and a loud sound filled my ears. Like a wolf howling, only lower, so low it made my bones vibrate.

Spreading out my hands, I waited for the water to come into them like Méabh had said, but the water didn't do that. Instead, the sound grew louder and louder, so loud it hurt my ears. I waited and waited, still hoping that the water would swirl around my arms or form a ball. Running out of air, I pushed myself upward.

"Anything?" Méabh stood on the riverbank, a little further back than where I had come to, and she jogged to catch up.

"Did you hear it? The noise?"

"There was no noise."

"There was. It was so loud. It was like… an animal growling."

Méabh pressed her lips together. "I've never heard of the water sounding like that before. When I hear it, it is light. That is what the other cupbearers said too. Are you sure it just wasn't the sound of the blood rushing to your head?"

I pushed my hair from my face. "Maybe?"

Méabh twisted her lips. "Try again."

I tried again. And again, and again. Each time I submerged myself, I waited for the water to come. Sometimes in my head I asked it to come into my hands. Other times I moved my arms, trying to swirl the water about myself. But there was nothing. The water did not come to me, nor did the strange noise return.

"I think that's enough for now, Isolde," Méabh said as I swam up from the water for the fiftieth time. "We can try again tomorrow."

I nodded, rubbed myself dry with a blanket and got dressed, then together we walked back to the monastery. The shadow of it loomed toward me and I found myself walking slower than usual. If I had not enjoyed living at Seir Kieran before, I hated it now. With all the mortals gone, it was devoid of joy. There was no laughter. There was no Leofwynn to come and talk to me. No Gisela to lighten my mood. My grief for them came to me often. Usually at night when I was alone. And in my dreams, I had not again travelled to Cuan even though I had wanted to many times. I was alone. Completely alone.

"Isolde!" Siobhan called my name on seeing us returning. "Colmon has woken up. He wants you."

Running toward the monastery, I made straight for his room. He had trained me seven days ago, and it had tired him so much that he had gone straight to sleep and had remained sleeping ever since. The amount of sleep he needed between bouts of wakefulness was getting longer and longer. Even worse, over half of his hair was white. The time of my vision was approaching.

"Hello," he said as I entered his room. "What have I missed?"

"Nothing."

"No visions? The wind hasn't spoken to you again?"

I shook my head.

"How is everyone? How are you?"

Closing the door behind me, I sat on the chair beside his bed. "We all miss the mortals. The monastery is very quiet without them."

"Yes, of course you do." He edged back in his bed, trying to get comfortable against the pillows. "What about your training?"

After the training session I'd just had, I didn't really want to answer, but denial would not get me anywhere. "I've made progress with Báine. I've been trying to transform into a crow. Yesterday, I grew feathers on my arm, so she thinks I'm close. Siobhan is happy with my healing too."

"What about Méabh?"

"That's still a problem. I trained with her this morning, and I thought something was happening, but no, I'm as hopeless as ever."

I smiled at him, trying not to let him see the worry that dwelled inside me. And my worry was deepening. Not just because of my lack of progress in training with Méabh, but also because of Colmon himself. He looked so much frailer today. The muscles on his arms and shoulders were disappearing. I knew he would suggest going out into the forest to train, but I didn't want to. Despite what he said about me not hurting him when he used his warrior gift, I knew this couldn't be true. His gift was fading, which meant his warrior strength and ability to heal quickly were fading too.

"Will you talk to me, Colmon?" I asked.

"I am talking to you."

"I mean, will you tell me more about the Descendants and what life was like before I was born? There is so much I don't know about our ways and history. I feel today, me knowing that is more important than moving faster or hitting you harder."

Colmon nodded. "How about we still go to the forest, just for a walk, and I will talk."

"Are you sure?"

"Oh yes. I don't know about you, but these grey walls seem to press down on me if I stay under them for too long."

Knowing exactly how he felt, I helped him stand, and the two of us made our way outside.

"You should have seen our fortress at Fennit Island," Colmon said, his arm linked into mine and a walking stick in his other hand. "The halls inside were beautiful and covered in golden tapestries. No grey walls there. No. It was full of colour. The courtyard had flowers, and of course, the hawthorn tree, and all around us there was the sea. Sometimes flat and calm and other times tempestuous and chaotic. You never knew when you woke up what it would be."

I loved listening to him talk like this. He was ageing and frail, but his voice was so animated. So full of life.

"Tell me about your friends."

"Your grandfather was my greatest friend when I was a young man. My mentor. But all the warriors were close. Cerball, who was

Méabh's father, had such a way with the sword. Then there was Fiachre, the weapon-maker."

He paused then, and some of the joy left his voice.

"I remember Gisela telling me about him. She told me he became sad as he got older."

"That's right, he did. At the end, he helped me though. He gave me the sword, a treasure of the Tuatha Dé Danann, and I thank him for this trust every day. Otherwise, the sword would have been lost to Tomas and the Fomorians he was helping."

"So the sword and spear are on Rathlin, and the cauldron is at Fennit Island?"

"Yes, under the hawthorn tree there, although the hawthorn tree here is from its cutting. That is why the ancestors can come to collect the dead here."

"And the Lia Fáil? The fourth treasure. Where is that?"

"Tomas had that in his keeping. It is supposed to be under the Hill of Tara, but I do not know for sure. Tomas never told any of the other druids where it was, and so that is lost to time."

We walked a little further, picking at the berries growing on the bushes and eating them. He had done all of the talking so far, of which I was glad, but I had a few questions of my own. Questions I hadn't the courage to ask anyone else.

"Colmon, can I ask you about Rónnat?"

"Of course."

"She was a prophetess?"

"That's right, though she didn't tell anyone."

"Why?"

Colmon sighed as he leaned on his stick. "She saw into the future and knew that she would be used. Tomas banished her for lying with a mortal, and I can only suppose that was what she wanted. To be banished. To be away from Tomas, and to spend her final years helping us, though we didn't understand it at the time."

"But she went mad listening to the wind. At least that's what Báine told me. Why would anyone want that?"

"She didn't want to go mad, but she wanted to help us, and I suppose she also didn't want anyone to see what was going to happen to her." Colmon walked toward me, his grey eyes shining. "All prophets go mad in the end, Isolde. The wind speeds it up, is how Rónnat explained it. Is that what worries you?"

"Yes, though that is selfish of me."

"No, of course it isn't, and you don't have to listen to the wind, Isolde. All this talk of prophecy, it is a weight and a burden. It is wrong that it is left to you – as young and innocent as you are. Perhaps that is something I should have said a long time ago. Whatever you decide to do, if this all goes wrong, it is not your fault."

"But in the vision… you tell me *I tried but not hard enough*."

A tear fell down Colmon's cheek as he reached forward to take my hand. "In the vision, my sweet Isolde, I was afraid. My words of anger were meant for me. Not you. It is I who has not tried hard enough."

I wrapped my arms around him and held him tight, feeling how tired he was as he sagged against me.

"Let's go back to the monastery, Colmon," I said. "We can talk more around the dinner table."

Colmon nodded and together we walked toward the grey and the stone that had become our home.

That night we ate and spoke a little more with Siobhan, Méabh and Báine. Not sad stories, but happier ones, and by the time evening fell, Colmon was ready to sleep once more.

"Goodnight, Colmon," I said as he walked away with Méabh. "I look forward to training with you when you wake up."

"Me too, Isolde. I hope I won't sleep for so long this time."

"I did not tire you out so much today, so I hope so too."

"Oh, don't be deceived, Isolde. Using the mind is more tiring than using the body sometimes. Especially when you must remember things you've tried to forget."

Giving Colmon a final wave, I ate the last bite of my supper, glad that he seemed to be happier now than when we were talking in the forest.

"I might go to bed myself," Siobhan said, once Colmon and Méabh had left the room. "I've got to harvest the crops in the morning."

"I'll help," Báine said. "Or else Méabh can if I'm training with Isolde."

"I can help too. Before training."

"Very good," Báine said. "And then we must set our minds to the last of the packing. We go at the next full moon. Agreed?"

"Agreed," we all replied. It was time. We all knew it.

Both Báine and Siobhan said goodnight, and as soon as they left, I made my way toward my room. Colmon was right. Talking was exhausting, for I felt I had not been so tired as this in an age. Eyes closing as soon as my head touched the pillow, I was asleep within seconds.

A tower, whitened with lime paste, stood tall. Two men watched outward from the tower, though more men lined the walls. An army moved against them. The men on the walls sounded the alarm, rang the bells, and the air filled with roars and screams.

An army marched. Ladders went up against the wall. Arrows flew. All was chaos. Screams. So much screaming.

"Come with me, Sichfrith," a man said. I recognised this man. It was Bjorn. Cuan's friend who had spoken to him in the tent at the Tailteann Games. "They are coming. Waterford will hold, but we must fight."

"How many are there?"

"Nearly two thousand, I think. They must have brought the ladders with them from Pembroke. Come and see for yourself."

The man Sichfrith nodded and ran up the steps, two at a time, so that he could see over the wall. When he reached the top, Cuan was there. Cuan said something that I couldn't hear. Sichfrith nodded again.

Blood. It covered the ground. There were no roars now, no loud screams, just silence.

The air swirled, as if I were flying away from the walls. The vision changed. This time, there was a man covered in flames, and another man stood beside him and spoke. The man who was speaking was a Fomorian. It was not the Fomorian from my visions, though. It was another. Dark curls and a long face. I couldn't hear his words. The second man… the man covered in fire. It was Cuan. The flames grew and grew until they touched every part of his body. He was screaming.

"Cuan!" I shouted his name. "Cuan! Run!"

I woke up sweating. This time, I didn't vomit or have black phlegm rushing into my mouth, but I felt sick all the same.

The Fomorian had Cuan. He was burning him.

Jumping out of my bed, I got dressed and ran outside. I had to save Cuan. I had to warn him about the Fomorians that were coming for him. Taking a horse, I rode out of the monastery gate. He was in Waterford; that was what the vision had shown me. I knew where that was. South and along the coast.

I rode hard and fast… until I reached the river that I'd been swimming in earlier that morning.

No. Wait. I was supposed to be training tomorrow. Learning how to use my gifts so that I didn't lose control.

Pulling the horse to a stop, I dismounted and walked over to the river. I held out my hands, trying to feel for the water, to make it move at my command. But the river did not listen. It simply continued to flow downstream. *Why couldn't I summon it?* I had been here for months now. Months and still nothing.

Putting my hands down, I examined my reflection in the water – blurry, murky and dark. What was I doing? *What was I doing?*

I had to save Cuan, but I had to learn to use my gift. The Fomorians were coming here, and I had to learn how to fight them without destroying everything. I felt as if my body was torn in two.

As if tragedy lay in every direction. I didn't want Báine, Siobhan, Méabh and Colmon to die. I didn't want Cuan to die either.

Perhaps… perhaps it was better if I went now? Perhaps it was best that I searched for the Fomorians alone instead of dooming my friends to certain death.

I stilled, mulling it over and over, and then I remembered what Aoife had said.

You must do what you think is best, Isolde. Your heart will guide you, and it will not lead you astray.

Running back to the horse, I hauled myself up onto the saddle and rode south.

Angelo

The Kingdom of Connacht

The forest of Connacht was a peaceful place for the most part. Not luxurious by any means, for my bed was one of leaves, and the food was whatever the men could catch. On good days that could be deer, wild boar and hare. On bad days, it was mice and other rodents that scurried across the forest floor.

This didn't matter to me. Food was food, and I took what I was given.

The reason I was here was so that I could have a period of calm to work on my new gift. *Time is the most valuable thing a man can spend*, Theophrastus had once said, and I was spending it the best way possible. In improving myself. In becoming a harpist.

Unlike Cecile, who could never be bothered to practise – her biggest vice aside from the blandness of her personality – I dedicated myself to learning. As soon as I awoke from my fever, practising my new gift was all I could think of. All I dreamed of. And after only one cycle of the moon, I had all the fuidir under my control. Well… nearly all.

Thirty was now twenty-nine. It couldn't be helped. Early on, one of the men, cleverer than the others, had resisted my words. He had realised somehow that I was manipulating him. It made him angry. It made him want to kill me, for my harpist gift was already strong enough to show me his emotions. Initially, I had been annoyed that I was unable to bend him to my will, but it had provided me with an opportunity to see how far the other men would go on my behalf. *Would they kill one of their own for me and the salvation I offered?*

It turned out that persuading murderers to kill a friend was very easy.

As the weeks progressed, and my skills improved, I decided another challenge was required. A harder one. It was time to go, but I needed to prove that I had my new gift under control, for once I left these forests, my time of calm would be over. I would be heading toward war and chaos. Toward Gormflaith and my father. Toward Cuan and Isolde, whose gift I still wanted so desperately. To die and yet live. That was the best gift of all.

"We have them!" Luchóg said, his voice shaking with excitement. Rushing into our forest camp like a child, he clapped his hands.

"Bring them to the clearing then."

I could hear the fuidir returning from where I sat. We were deep in the forest, far away from any dun or ráth, and so they whooped and cheered at the tops of their voices.

Sitting down on the log chair one of the men had crafted for me, I took out the necklace Luchóg had stolen and waited for them to arrive. I turned the necklace over in my hand, staring at the lines within the shiny green stone. The harpist had held onto this stone when she had convinced me to leave her alone. I wondered if some power resided within it or whether she had merely held onto it to stop herself from screaming. Luchóg, the thief, had taken this trinket for himself, but as soon as I realised, I had made him hand it over to me. Closing my fist around it, I took a deep breath and prepared myself for what was to come.

As soon as the fuidir arrived at the clearing, they dropped the two men they'd been carrying onto the ground. These two men were tied up with ropes, their mouths gagged. Two monks from Leinster they were, captured from a small monastery just over the border with Connacht. I doubted the fuidir had bothered to hide their tracks, but it didn't matter. I didn't plan on remaining at this camp once I was done.

"Are they related?"

"Yes," Luchóg replied. "They are brothers."

All the fuidir gathered around the clearing now. Ready for my performance. *Ready to be amazed by the power God had given me.*

For a few moments, I stared at the monks. They were old men, or at least they seemed old to me. It was hard to tell sometimes with holy people who never saw the sun and never did a day's work. Their skin sagged around their arms from lack of muscle, and their hair and skin were pale and grey, and yet their faces were not lined in the way that people who worked the fields or shepherded often were.

"Do you want us to kill them?" one of the fuidir asked.

"Don't be foolish," I replied, gesturing for them all to sit.

A couple of the men seemed confused that I had asked for monks, and that I had specified a close kinship. The killing of women was an easy thing for them... but holy men, that was different. As I read their emotions, I felt doubt from one or two. *Why did a man sent here by the Pope want to hurt two fellow monks?*

Despite their doubts, I had to do this. I had to pass this next test because since stealing the harpist gift, I'd noticed two things. Firstly, and more obviously, it was easier to get somebody to do something they were already predisposed to enjoy. Secondly, when given the chance to do good, inexplicably, the worst men would sometimes take it. They couldn't explain their decision afterward, but something not yet dead inside them wanted a chance to atone. Often this glimmer of goodness revolved around children. Sometimes animals. Sometimes it was only that the required deed reminded them of a childhood memory.

The real test was this... getting someone who was good to do something bad.

And with a group of fuidir, this was the one thing I had not yet had the chance to practise. Until now.

"Remove their gags, blindfolds and hand-bindings," I said. "We must give our guests a chance to speak."

"Who are you?" the first one asked as his blindfold and gag were removed. This was the older of the brothers. I could tell by the way the skin along his throat sagged when he spoke. "Where have you taken us?"

"My name is Brother Angelo, and the Holy Father has sent me to Ireland. You are currently in Connacht."

Both monks stared at each other now the second monk was free of his blindfold and gag. "The Holy Father sent you? Pope Alexander?" the younger one questioned.

"Yes. There is only one Holy Father."

The first monk, the oldest, laughed. "And he asked you to forcibly remove us from our monastery, tie us up, and take us deep into the forest?"

"The Holy Father has given me a mission. There are devils in this land. Devils I have been sent to destroy. He says that the monks and bishops of this land have not done a good job in keeping this evil at bay."

The elder monk snorted. "And what does a young man such as yourself know about devils?"

"Oh, I've met many devils during my life, and just as Jesus and his apostles exorcised them, so can I." I switched to Latin and began the prayer of exorcism that I had once heard spoken in Rome when a little girl was taken over by a fit. "Most glorious Prince of the Heavenly Armies, Saint Michael the Archangel, defend us in our battle against principalities and powers, against the rulers of this world of darkness, against the spirits of wickedness in the high places."

The younger monk, recognising the words of Paul to the Ephesians, frowned. "You think *we* are devils?"

"No," I smiled and took a step toward them. "No, but I need your help. I am sorry, I must pause here. I feel very rude speaking and not knowing your names."

"I am Brother Pádraig," the eldest said. "This is Brother Mark, who also happens to be my youngest brother."

"Yes, yes, I can see the resemblance. Tell me this, are you close?"

"Very," Brother Mark replied. "Brother Pádraig has taught me everything."

"That is good. This relationship is exactly why I picked you."

"For what?" Brother Pádraig asked, more sceptical than his brother.

"God and the Holy Father have sent me here. They have given me gifts with which to fight the devils that haunt this land, but before I fight them, I must put these powers to the test, otherwise I may fail in my sacred duty."

I walked forward and with a sharp knife that had once belonged to the dead fuidir, I cut the ropes away from Brother Mark's legs.

"What must I do?" he asked, standing.

"You must kill your brother." I handed him the knife.

The younger monk looked at me as if I might be joking. "I cannot," he said. "I could never commit the sin of murder, and if ever such a dark sin did lurk inside of me, I could never hurt Pádraig."

Using my harpist gift, I breathed in deeply and turned the green stone in my hand. "I think you should."

"Mark, put down the blade," Brother Pádraig said. "If they kill us, they kill us, and our souls will be clean. Nothing is worth being barred entry into the Kingdom of Heaven."

Brother Mark nodded. "My brother is right. I cannot break God's holy commandment."

I turned the stone again. "Oh, but you can. If God commands it, you must do anything he says. Was Abraham not willing to kill his own son for God? That is faith. That is true faith. And now God is talking to you, Brother Mark. He is asking you to kill Brother Pádraig. Why won't you do it? You must do it. You must."

Brother Mark turned toward his brother, the knife held out. After a moment, he took a step toward him.

"That's it, Brother Mark. Keep going."

"Stop! Stop! You are right," Brother Pádraig said, his eyes focused on me. "We have not done enough to keep evil at bay in this land. Is that what you want to hear? Well, it's true. That is why the Anglo-Normans are coming. They are coming, and the Bishop of Armagh has said he will welcome them when they do."

Now this piqued my interest. The Irish Church would not only allow an invasion… but they wanted it. "Tell me more, Brother Pádraig."

"Our abbot told us. The bishops of Ireland have spoken about the invasion, and they hope for more Anglo-Normans to come. The faith in this land is weak, and the kings do not adopt the doctrine of the Church as they should."

"I see."

Brother Pádraig, relief sweeping across his brow, knelt back onto his heels. "Even better, I've heard that they are on their way. Within weeks, days maybe, they will be here, and they can help us win the fight against the devils. Mark and I can help you too."

"I'm afraid you cannot, Brother Pádraig. God has sent me to cleanse this land, and you are the sacrifice that must be made." I turned then to Brother Mark, who was shaking, beads of sweat trailing down his forehead and nose. Concentrating, sensing my gift and holding it as I did with my fire-magic, I rubbed the stone.

"Go ahead, Brother Mark. Kill him."

Brother Mark ran toward his brother and thrust the knife deep into his stomach and then into his neck.

It didn't take long for Brother Pádraig to bleed out, leaving Brother Mark to watch. As I withdrew and stepped away, Brother Mark began to cry. "What have I done?" he sobbed as he took his brother in his arms.

"You killed him, Brother Mark. Your own brother too. How could you?"

"But… but you told me to?"

"And in doing so you have only proven yourself unworthy and full of the devil. Just as I suspected."

Brother Mark sobbed even harder. "I'm sorry. I didn't want to do it. I don't know why I did."

Standing forward, I removed the knife from Brother Pádraig's neck and handed it to Brother Mark.

Not speaking this time, I said in my head what I wanted him to do. I felt his mood shift. Away from anger and sorrow and toward self-loathing and despair. Staring at the blade, hands shaking, he turned the knife around and thrust it into his own stomach.

It took him much longer to die than Pádraig – but die he did.

"Did you pass the test?" Luchóg asked, once Brother Mark had stopped breathing.

"I did." I stood and gathered the fuidir closer. "It is time for us to go west now."

"Not Seir Kieran?" another of the fuidir asked. "I thought that was where the devil woman lived."

"Oh, she is there to be sure, but I believe the Holy Father has sent another like me to come to our aid. We will need them."

"Where? Where are they?"

"We go to Wexford. There is a hill known as Carrig. We shall begin our search there."

"What about the monks?" Luchóg asked, glancing at the two bodies.

"Do whatever you wish with them, just so long as tomorrow you are all ready to leave this place."

Walking away from them, for I needed to take in what had just happened, I smiled as I stared up at the trees. What joy there was in life. *What absolute joy.*

Cuan

The River Barrow

Bjorn's men, who were sailing their ship down the River Barrow, had moved us at great speed over the last few days. We would be at Waterford soon they said, though I was in no rush. The first part of the journey had been on horseback, and we'd ridden over the mountain paths in Munster to avoid Leinster territory. This had meant long days and sore legs. Now, I could lean back against the mast and watch the land as it passed us by. Summer in Ireland was a beautiful season, and the bushes we passed were filled with berries and flowers. Purples and yellows and blues. I found myself thinking of Isolde and how much she would enjoy this.

It was nice spending time with Bjorn too. He was in good form, delighted that Brenna was pregnant, and seemed happy with his life in Waterford.

"What is King Ragnall like?" I asked him. "Is he a good lord?"

"He is. Generous too. More generous than Godred, that's for certain… and until now, I've not had to actually fight for him, aside from breaking up a few arguments here and there. Waterford is a peaceful city."

"And now these Anglo-Normans are coming to ruin it."

"I don't think they'll ruin it. The walls are strong, and our warriors are well-trained, even if I say so myself. Our defeat on the plain, that was a shock to be sure, but they had luck on their side. The cattle won the battle for them, and that's the truth."

"But didn't the Anglo-Normans cause the stampede by hemming the cattle in and then releasing them once your warriors arrived at their gate? That doesn't seem like luck to me. It sounds like strategy."

Bjorn shrugged. "There are lessons to be learned, but still, if the Anglo-Normans try to attack us again, this time we will fight along our own walls. I think rather than Waterford being in danger, it is your uncle's army. You were right at the meeting, Ruaidrí should attack Carrig before Ferns, but whatever he does, it needs to be done quickly, otherwise he'll find himself in trouble."

I nodded, knowing that this was the main problem. Ruaidrí was already moving too slow in my opinion… Still, he had united the kings at the meeting. That was something. If he could just get them ready for battle and marching, this could all be put to rights before the weather turned.

"Enough about Waterford and battles, anyway," Bjorn said. "How are you, Cuan? The truth this time."

I gave Bjorn the smile he wanted. "I'm good. I told you at Kells that I was fine."

"Well, I didn't believe you then and I don't believe you now."

Opening my arms, I ran my hands down my thick fur cloak.

Bjorn snorted. "Your uncle might give you fine clothes, but he doesn't like you. His son, Conchobar, doesn't either."

"I know."

"They're frightened of you. That's why they sent you away. All you're going to get from this trip is a view of the plain, and I could have described that to you at Dúnmór."

"Again, I know."

"Then why do you stay with them? Come to Waterford. Find a woman. Live your life."

I shrugged my shoulders, and when I next spoke, I put some enthusiasm into my voice. "Perhaps I will one day. When this is all over."

As ever, I didn't fool Bjorn, and he rolled his eyes at my attempt at nonchalance. "If life with Godred taught you anything, it should be that war is never over. All that changes is who you're fighting. I've been lucky these last two years, that's all. But if life is to be short and full of fighting, it is better to spend the time you *do* have with someone you love."

"When does Brenna expect the baby?"

"In the next few weeks, but don't change the subject." He eyed me then, his expression turning harder. "I heard about Hálfdan. Something about him giving you up to King Diarmait."

"Yes, that's true."

"He's living at Ferns now, or so I heard," Bjorn added, anger leeching into his voice. "What I wouldn't do to him if I found him."

"Don't trouble yourself with Hálfdan. Asculv gave him up as a hostage to Diarmait, and that put him into a difficult position."

"We fought together, Cuan. Lived together, the three of us. I would rather die than give you up, and I know you would do the same for me."

"Still, I'd rather you did nothing. In fact, I'm glad Hálfdan didn't give his life for me. If you ever happen to see him, let him be."

"Why, Cuan?" Bjorn shook his head. "Why don't you care? It is as if your life is meaningless to you. You were always a little like this, but it is even more so now."

I stared at Bjorn. He'd been a friend to me. A good friend. A brother of the shield wall who had never let me down. He did not deserve me the way I was now – vague and dishonest.

"I am sorry, Bjorn. You're right. I am in danger, and this is just how I must be to survive. Ruaidrí fears me because he knows my father plots to make me King of Connacht. It is custom that allows me to live in Dúnmór, but if they had their way, I'd still be in the Isles with Godred. Or dead."

"Do you want to be king?"

Away from Dúnmór, I tried to order my thoughts. If I could be honest with anyone, it was Bjorn, but more than that… perhaps it was time to be honest with myself.

"I never did, but now I have lived in Connacht and have come to know my family and the people… and I see how poorly

Ruaidrí has managed this… I do not know. Ruaidrí is not brave. He is clever to a point, but the truth is he doesn't really care about anything except for himself. I don't think… I know he isn't a good king."

Bjorn nodded, seemingly satisfied that I had finally revealed what was on my mind. "Well, I don't understand the path you are on, Cuan, though I know it must be a hard one to walk. While you are in Waterford, Brenna and I will look after you. It would be nice to see you smile for once."

"I should like that, Bjorn, and know this: I'm glad you are happy."

The river ship sailed onward, and after a while Bjorn stood up, eager to catch a glimpse of Waterford. The old man, Ingvar, who sailed the ship with his two sons, smiled as he turned a bend in the river. It was always the same. No matter how old or how jaded, the sight of home always brought a smile to a man's lips. It made me wonder then… *where was my home?* I had lived in so many places. Dúnmór, the Isles, Norway, Dublin, then the Isles again… I wasn't sure… except I remembered the feeling in my chest when I saw Dúnmór after escaping from Diarmait at Ferns. Despite everything that had happened there, I had felt relief when I rode through its gate.

"Stop the ship, Ingvar. Quickly!"

The old man did as Bjorn said and let out the sails, while his two sons dropped the anchor stone.

"What is it?" I asked.

"There are hundreds of people outside the city. An army."

I walked to the front of the ship and stared at the land between the walls of Waterford and the two rivers flowing on either side. Bjorn was right. There was an army encamped on the western plain.

"It's the Anglo-Normans," Bjorn said through gritted teeth. "More have come over."

"It must be Strongbow himself for there to be such a number."

Calming my breathing, I tried to think of what to do, for this was exactly what I had feared. This was not a battle to win King Diarmait's kingdom back, as was the excuse for Wexford, nor was it for revenge, which had explained the Anglo-Norman battle in Osraige. This was conquest, and now it had started. Ruaidrí had been too slow to act, and the Anglo-Normans had taken it as a sign that they could win.

Bjorn paled as he realised the truth of what I'd just said. He knew as well as I that if Strongbow had come over with an army of this size, there wouldn't simply be a negotiation for loyalty and vows. They had come prepared for a siege.

"Ingvar, sail us closer," Bjorn said. "But stop before the next bend. You and your ship need to stay out of sight. Once Cuan and I disembark, I want you and your sons to hide in the forest. If I need to get a message out, I'll need someone I can trust to carry it."

Ingvar's boys raised the anchor stone, and Ingvar steered us slowly to the next bend. The bank on the left side was low and grassy, and it was here that Ingvar beached the ship.

"We will cover it with bracken," Ingvar said. "Make it hard to see."

"Thank you, Ingvar," Bjorn said. "Thank you."

Bjorn and I hastened toward the city, keeping close to the river and low to the ground.

As we reached the final hill, we lay flat against the grass and looked over the camp. According to Ruaidrí's spies, the men at Carrig had numbered around three hundred. The numbers here were significantly higher. Maybe close to two thousand. I could see the foot soldiers carrying their ladders to the front of the army, and the knights organising the archers. An attack along the western wall was imminent.

"It's too late to get in through the gates," Bjorn said. "We'll have to get to St Bran's River and then climb over the wall."

Quickly, I cast my eyes over the city. The walls were high with watchtowers at every corner and every midpoint, and there was a trench along the western wall too. The walls were constructed in the same way as Dublin's. However, Waterford had only three walls, for it was triangular in shape rather than rectangular. The northern wall was built running alongside the River Suir, while the south-east-facing wall ran alongside St Bran's River. A shorter wall on the western side was heavily fortified with two towers and a trench. At first glance it would seem this would be the hardest wall to breach, but there was no other option for the Anglo-Normans, not with the rivers running so close to the other two walls. This was good for Waterford. It meant their enemies' options were limited and that they could focus their defence on one wall rather than all three.

"Follow me," Bjorn said. "We'd better hurry, otherwise they'll see us."

Together we made our way into the forest and ran along the treeline until we came to St Bran's River. Creeping low against the riverbank, we moved past the plain and then over to the watchtower at the northernmost point of the city.

Bjorn waved up at the man sitting in the watchtower. "Sichfrith. It's Bjorn."

The man leaned over the edge and waved. He disappeared for a few moments, only to return with another warrior and two ropes, which they threw over the wall.

"I hope you can still climb," Bjorn said. "More to the point, I hope you can climb with the weight of that lovely fur cloak on your back."

Sprinting forward, the two of us reached the wall and climbed. Bjorn threw himself over the top just ahead of me, though he looked like he was about to vomit as he collapsed onto the wall scaffolding.

"Thank you, Sichfrith," Bjorn panted, saluting the man who had waved at us from the watchtower.

"No problem, Bjorn, but you are a little late," Sichfrith said. "Indeed, if you'd arrived any later, you'd have only been able to watch the battle from the hill."

Bjorn grunted.

"Who's your friend?"

"Sichfrith, this is Cuan… nephew of both Godred of the Isles… and the High King Ruaidrí Ó Conchúir."

"Greetings, Cuan," Sichfrith said, smiling and holding out his hand to help me up. "And welcome to my father's city. It is a shame you've come at such a time, or perhaps it is lucky. I do not know yet."

Taking his hand and standing, I brushed away the white lime paste that had rubbed off the wall and onto my cloak. "Well, you have an army at your walls, which wasn't what I was expecting. Strongbow, I assume?"

Sichfrith nodded. "They've sent no message, but a trader here says Strongbow's colours are on one of the tents. I think it's safe to assume it's him."

"When did they arrive?" Bjorn asked, standing.

"This morning. The Normans from Carrig joined them not long after. We received word a few days ago that a fleet was crossing from Pembroke and so we were able to call the Uí Dróna and Déisi clans to our aid. They are here and ready to fight. Don't worry. We can hold the city."

Despite the confidence in his voice, I did not feel so sure as I leaned over the wall scaffolding to look at the city below. There were thousands of people living in Waterford, but how many of them were women and children? It was true you did not need as large a number to defend a city as was needed to win an open battle, but still I worried that there were not enough warriors.

"Have you sent out calls for aid to anyone else?" Bjorn asked.

"We sent a messenger to Wexford and to King Ruaidrí. Only yesterday though, and I'm hoping they won't be needed. As I said, the men here are ready to fight."

"Good." Relief swept across Bjorn's face. "These Anglo-Normans are going to find out what it's like fighting against a city that's ready for them."

Sichfrith smiled and once the other warrior had pulled up the two ropes from the wall, he clasped Bjorn on the shoulder. "Come, we'd better see what my father wants. He's allocating posts and weapons to the men now."

Bjorn followed Sichfrith to the end of the walkway, then climbed down the ladder. "Where are we going?" I asked as I followed.

"To the square. I need to hear what King Ragnall has to say, and then I need to find Brenna."

"Ragnall first? Before me?" Brenna spun around at the bottom of the steps, her arms folded and eyes wide. She'd always been beautiful, with long brown hair and freckles over her nose, but now she was radiant.

"I misspoke," Bjorn replied. "I meant to say I need to find Brenna first and then the king." He pulled her toward him, kissed her, and set his hand on her swollen stomach. "How's the baby?"

"Kicking all the time and not letting me sleep."

Bjorn kissed her again and pulled her closer. "I want you to stay in the house, do you hear? The Anglo-Normans have lots of archers, and they will shoot into the city once they are ready. Make sure you have plenty of food and water in the house so there is no need to leave."

"I have already done that. I'm not stupid." Peering around Bjorn, Brenna gave me a quick smile. "Hello, Cuan. How are you?"

"Better for seeing you."

Laughing at this, she pushed Bjorn on the shoulder. "Now off you go. I'll stay inside and keep safe, like you've asked. In return, you'd better not do anything stupid." She glanced at me again. "Look after him, Cuan. I want him to come home to me when this is all done."

"I'll do my best."

"See that you do."

She kissed Bjorn one more time, then marched off, hands resting on her stomach as she made her way home.

Bjorn watched Brenna for as long as he could still see her.

"Brenna will be fine," I said. "She knows how to stay safe."

"I know. I just don't like that she has to." He took a deep breath, then turned. "Come on, let's find Ragnall."

We, along with Sichfrith, hurried through the market and made our way to the square just outside the fort. Here, King Ragnall,

Sichfrith's father, a burly man with a greying beard, was calling his warriors forward. He then pointed out which part of the walls he wanted them to defend and told them what provisions to bring. He was sending most of the men to the western wall, but every so often another position was allocated along the other two walls.

"Hvitserk, you're next," King Ragnall shouted.

A tall, bearded warrior walked forward, an axe and sword in either hand.

"Hvitserk, you and your sons must look after the watchtower at the midpoint of the northern wall," King Ragnall said. "It is unlikely they will attack from this side, but there is the gate leading to the longphort and a post under the watchtower itself. They might think of climbing up it somehow. Take spears, oil and stones with you. Sound the horn if you need more men."

I listened to Ragnall as he gave out more of these orders, happy with what he was saying. It was wise to organise most of the defence along the western wall while also ensuring that the other walls and watchtowers were manned too.

As we reached the front of the crowd, Bjorn and Sichfrith greeted Ragnall.

"Father, this is Cuan," Sichfrith said. "Nephew of High King Ruaidrí and also nephew of King Godred."

King Ragnall, who'd been glancing at the store of weapons, pulled his gaze away and stared at me. "Yes, I've heard of you. Are you here to fight, or do you come on behalf of one of your uncles?"

"Both. King Ruaidrí sent me here so I could understand the Anglo-Norman attack that happened at Dun Domhnall, but now I'm here, I think another warrior will be of help."

"That's kind, Cuan, honourable, but I'd rather you went to the High King and told him of our plight."

"I can do that if you wish."

The king nodded. "I do wish. Once it gets dark, I'll have the men cover you so you can get out."

"Ingvar has hidden his ship up the River Barrow," Bjorn said. "I told him to wait there in case we needed to get a message out."

"Good." The king gave Bjorn a quick smile. "Tonight then, Cuan. Be ready. Until then, we must fight. Sichfrith, I want you to be in charge of the western wall. I will command from the fort and direct men where they are needed. These Normans are sneaky, and so we need to be ready to react. Bjorn, you go with him."

I nodded and turned to leave with Bjorn, but then Ragnall grabbed my arm.

"Will Ruaidrí come to our aid? Is he ready to fight?"

How to answer this? Ruaidrí would not necessarily do what I advised him. In fact, it was more likely he would do the opposite, and if he felt Waterford was lost, or else a sacrifice that was required so he could launch an attack elsewhere, Ruaidrí might not come here at all. But I couldn't say that to Ragnall. Not now.

"Do you think you can hold out for three weeks? That's how long it will take his army to reach here."

"I don't see why not," Ragnall replied. "We've plenty of warriors and provisions."

"Have you thought of sending messages to more of the Munster kings?"

"Yes, I sent messages to them yesterday. I believe they will come, but it is the High King who must help drive these men out. When I swore my oaths to him, he swore to protect this land. If I keep my vows to him, he must keep his to me."

I nodded. "I will do my best to see that he comes, Ragnall. That is all I can promise."

"Then that will have to do."

Suddenly, the horns along the western wall sounded, and the Waterford warriors standing there began to beat their shields with their fists

"They're coming," Sichfrith shouted. "Warriors, positions!"

The warriors who were not already standing along the walls or guarding the gates as they were told, ran. The other people, the elderly, women and children, ran into the fort or else their houses until the streets themselves were almost empty.

"Come on," Sichfrith said as he hurried to the western wall.

"Bjorn, I want you to oversee the right watchtower. Cuan, I'll let you go there too if you promise to stay low. I know you want to see them fight, but my father will kill me if you're too injured to get out to speak with your uncle."

Nodding, I followed him and Bjorn and climbed up into the watchtower. The Anglo-Norman army on the plain was organised now, and the foot soldiers at the front were marching forward. Two lines of men behind the foot soldiers, however, didn't move.

"Be careful of those archers," I said to Sichfrith, pointing them out. "They will loose when you least expect it."

Sichfrith nodded and glanced at his warriors along the wall. "Hara! Thorfinn! Shields at the ready!"

The Anglo-Normans came then at speed. Using shields to cover themselves from our spears and stones, they ran in rows of ten. Boards of wood to breach the trench came first, then the ladders.

"Throw!" Ragnall shouted. "Use the long sticks to push the ladders back."

The Waterford warriors did as he commanded, repelling the ladders and hooks trying to get a hold on the wall, while the Irish spearmen from the Déisi clans threw their spears into the throngs below. The best of them timed it for when the Anglo-Norman shields lifted to allow the ladders through. However, much of the Anglo-Normans' armour was too good to allow penetration of the flesh from this distance.

"Arrows! Shields up!" Sichfrith shouted. The men on the walls lifted their shields. With that terrible hissing sound I remembered from Limerick, they soared over the walls, some of them hitting our shields, but many landing in the city itself.

As the wave of arrows came to a stop, the warriors on the wall lowered their shields, but the Anglo-Normans had used the arrows to their advantage. Not one but two ladders had landed against the wall, and already they had too many men climbing up them for the Waterford warriors to push them back.

"Oil!" Bjorn shouted. "Stones too."

Lifting a few of the stones in the baskets that lined the wall scaffolding, I threw them down the ladder. I hit one of the Anglo-Normans in the arm, and downward he fell, causing the two men underneath him to fall too.

"Oil coming up!"

Two warriors climbed up the ladder with two pots of boiling oil. Using thick cloth to protect their hands, they threw the oil down the other ladder, covering and scalding the men who were climbing. One of the Irish warriors soaked a cloth in the oil, then wrapped it around his spear, and lit it with one of the torches that burned on the side of the watchtower.

The men on that ladder were already trying to climb back down, but they were not quick enough, and the flames of the newly lit spear hit the oil that had soaked into their trousers and shirts. The men screamed as they burned. One could only writhe on the ground, while another tried to reach the river. He didn't make it.

"More spears!" Sichfrith shouted. "Oil! Fire! Stones! Don't let a single one of them over the wall!"

The whole day was full of this. Arrows flew over, ladders hit the walls, men tried to climb, but as night approached, none had made their way over. Even better, almost one hundred corpses littered the trenches below us while only eight of our men had fallen to the Anglo-Norman arrows.

Ragnall was delighted with the outcome, and as darkness fell, the Waterford Vikings cheered and shouted insults as the Anglo-Normans retreated to their camp.

"Don't get complacent," Bjorn shouted. "They will rain arrows down on us during the night so that we cannot rest. If you are on the walls, keep your shields up. Protect yourselves. Take turns to keep watch."

While Bjorn and Sichfrith ordered the men, I helped carry more baskets of stone up onto the wall scaffolding. That was until King Ragnall approached.

"Are you ready to leave, Cuan?" he asked.

"I am."

Bjorn and Sichfrith came over then.

"How do you want to get him out, Father?" Sichfrith asked.

"We will hang a rope down over the northern wall – the middle tower will be easiest. I'll have the men watch your escape, but I think the Anglo-Normans are done for the day."

Plan agreed, the four of us made our way to the northern wall. While Ragnall and Sichfrith searched for rope and a few spearmen to cover me, Bjorn and I climbed up the scaffolding. I gave the city one final look over, feeling hopeful that Ragnall and his men might last until my uncle arrived. Then I looked out over the river, trying to see if any Anglo-Normans were out there. A few archers perhaps, looking to catch a warrior walking along the walls.

That's when I noticed something glimmering on the ground underneath the watchtower.

The sky was cloudy and moonless and so I leaned over to try to make out what it was. Grabbing Bjorn, I pressed my finger to my lip. "What's that?" I whispered.

"Armour," he said after a few moments. "The fire on the watchtower is reflecting off it."

The two of us listened. It was hard with the jeering on the western wall, but… yes, I could make out voices.

"Get more torches up here so we can see," I said. "They're up to something."

Bjorn climbed back down the ladder and reappeared alongside Sichfrith and Ragnall, who each carried lit torches. Sichfrith, who could see the light reflecting beneath us too, dropped his torch to the ground. It only lit the air beneath us for a few moments, but it was enough.

"There are at least fifty men along this wall," I said to Ragnall.

"What are they doing?" he asked.

"They are doing something underneath the middle watchtower."

"Are they climbing the post?"

"No. They're all on the ground. In a circle."

Hvitserk, who had not noticed the men underneath the

watchtower, came out and looked over the edge. As he did this, the paste of the watchtower ceiling crumbled onto his hair. I pressed my hand onto the wall and ever so slightly, it shook.

They weren't climbing the post. They were taking it down. Sawing through it or hacking at it with their swords. I turned to Bjorn. "Why is the post there?"

"The soil is soft along the riverbank," he replied. "We put it there to help hold the weight of the watchtower. Why? What's wrong?"

I grabbed Bjorn and rushed over to where Ragnall and Sichfrith stood. "They are sawing through the post. If they get through it, and the post is holding the weight of the tower, the tower will collapse, and it will bring down the wall with it. Hurry, we need to get rid of them before they get through."

Ragnall and Sichfrith ran to get more warriors, while Bjorn and I ran over to the bucket of rocks inside the watchtower and threw them down at the men below. Hvitserk and his son did the same. We heard shouts as we hit the Anglo-Normans, but there were too many, and now I was closer to the watchtower, I could feel the stone shaking underneath my feet. We had to get rid of them. *Now.*

"Hvitserk, the horn. We need more men."

Hvitserk blew it and as the horn sounded out, more warriors from within the city ran to help us. As more men came up the scaffolding, bringing torches and weapons with them, I could make out the men beneath us more clearly. Not just foot soldiers and a couple of knights, but at least fifty knights on horseback were riding along the riverbank and toward the northern wall. Damn it. They must be close to sawing through the post.

"Spears!" I shouted.

"More stones!" Sichfrith shouted as he clambered up the wall. "Bring the oil too!"

Panic soared inside of me. It wasn't just our voices I heard now. The Anglo-Normans underneath us were shouting too. "Faster, Le Gros. Hurry!"

The wall swayed and stones crumbled down the side of it. Bjorn felt the shudder too and took hold of my arm. "Down the ladder. We'll get you out on the other side."

"I cannot leave you."

"You must. If the wall collapses, the city will fall. You need to tell your uncle. He needs to ride here, even if we are defeated, to drive these men out before they can rebuild. Otherwise, you'll never get them out."

Leaving Ragnall and Sichfrith and the growing number of warriors to defend the northern wall, we climbed down and ran to the south-eastern wall.

Before we reached it, a mighty crash shook the whole city.

"It's falling," Bjorn said, horrified.

It happened slowly at first, but then there was another boom as more of the wall gave way. Not just a few stones, but a whole twenty-foot section. The Waterford warriors screamed as those on the scaffolding fell too. Then more screams as the wall collapsed onto the church and the surrounding houses. There was a terrible silence which only lasted a few moments – broken by horns sounding out as the Anglo-Norman cavalry charged into the city.

The warriors still on top of the western wall rushed down the ladders to meet with this charge, then suddenly many of them fell to the ground. A volley of arrows had flown into the city. I hadn't even heard them this time, not with the horns blowing and men roaring.

Bjorn grabbed my arm and forced me to run beside him. We were almost at the wall, but then he turned and ran into a house, practically breaking the door as he ran through it. "Brenna. Hurry. Now."

Bjorn came back out of the house, holding Brenna's hand. "You're leaving with Cuan."

"What? No," Brenna said.

"They've made it into the city. You're leaving. Don't argue."

"But I can't. I can't climb…"

"You don't need to climb. I'm going to open the gate. There will be no one here. Not now they've got through the northern wall. As soon as I open it, move to the other side of the wall and wait for ten seconds, then run. I'll climb onto the wall and make sure you get to the river."

Bjorn didn't wait for me to say anything. He didn't even wait for Brenna to argue. He just pulled her toward the gate, lifted the wooden beam that sealed it shut, and kissed her.

"Look after her, Cuan. And the baby."

With that he pushed us out and sealed the gate shut behind us.

Brenna shook, lost for words at what had just happened. Bjorn had done that quickly to stop us from arguing – to stop himself from caving in and letting her stay. Well, I had to repay him by getting her to safety. Taking her hand in mine, I counted to ten. As soon as the count was up, I pulled her toward the river, and holding onto her, I towed her to the other side. "That's it, Brenna," I whispered as we climbed up onto the riverbank. "We have to run into the forest now."

"I can't. Something hit me."

Picking her up, I saw an arrow had struck her leg as we had swum across. As I glanced up into the sky, I could see that the archers were shooting at the western and southern walls of the city. Hoping to strike down the warriors rushing to defend the northern side of the city.

Setting one of her arms over my shoulder, I ran and pulled her alongside me until we reached the forest. As soon as we were far enough inside, I paused to take the arrow out of Brenna's leg and ripped up her hair-scarf. "Tie this over the wound. Then we need to make it to Ingvar's ship before anyone can follow us."

Brenna nodded, tears streaming down her cheeks. Even as she tied the cloth over her wound, she couldn't take her eyes off the city, as if somehow hoping that Bjorn would follow us.

"Listen, Brenna, Bjorn knows how to fight. You will see him again."

Brenna nodded and stood. Her left leg was weak now, but I could see from the fierce look in her eyes that she was determined to make it to Ingvar's ship.

I put her arm back over my shoulder and we ran until we reached the bend in the river.

"To Connacht," I said to Ingvar and his son as they ran out of the forest.

"What happened?" one of his sons asked.

But I could not answer. Nor did I need to. As the wind blew us north, voices could be heard upon it. It was the sound of war. The sound of screaming. The sound of dying.

Gormflaith

Waterford

The fighting lasted for hours. From our tent, we could hear the screams and shouts of the warriors as they battled. The cries of horses. The sound of arrows as they flew overhead. War, it was something to behold, but it was the sound of it that surprised. The din. In my two-hundred-year life I had only heard such a noise once before, and that had been at Clontarf.

Now that the men had breached the city, I could not see what was going on. It was hard not knowing. I remembered this feeling from Glenmama. How wretched I had felt as I waited, and then the disappointment when the men came back to tell us they had lost. Sitric had to flee. Flee before Brian and his son Murchad – and their army – came into Dublin to claim it as their own.

Pulling myself away from my memories, I watched the walls of Waterford, my eyes fixed on the part of the wall that had collapsed. The Anglo-Normans had breached the city as they wanted, yes, and I had told Le Gros how to do it, but I had no idea how many men were inside waiting for them. Were the screams and shouts from the men of Waterford… or were they ours?

It was Walter who came to speak with us first. Bloodied and weary, he ran out from the crevice in the wall and across the plain, then practically fell into our tent. Cecile and Alina reached for their cloaks in case he uttered the word *retreat*, but not I, for his expression was not filled with fatigue or worry, but with joy.

"We have won!" Walter said, his voice completely hoarse. "We have won!"

My hands rose to my mouth. What relief to hear those words.

Walter grinned, then turned to Alina and gave her a clumsy bow. "Strongbow... Sorry, I mean, my lord, Richard de Clare, wishes his daughter to enter the city. He has sent Robert FitzStephen and I to escort you in."

Glancing outside, I could see FitzStephen riding toward us now. He was bloodied too, though much more than Walter. His armour and the armour over his horse's neck and front legs had so much blood dripping from it that the horse's tawny lower legs were stained red.

It surprised me that Strongbow would want us in the city so soon, but who was I to refuse? Who were any of us to refuse? Quickly, the three of us women stood and readied ourselves to leave the tent.

"Just his daughter," Walter said. "It might be safer if you two stay here."

"You think I'm going to let an innocent maid such as Alina enter the city with two men?" I snapped. "Absolutely not. She requires a chaperone. Cecile and I will accompany her. Hurry now, we don't want to keep Strongbow waiting."

I spoke forcefully, a different Alys to the one that gathered sticks for the fire. This Alys was the one who had chopped off the Waterford Vikings' heads. Walter gave a quick nod, then held open the tent door so we could leave.

Outside, the sky was clear, and the morning sun was warm. A beautiful day for Ireland which was usually damp and grey. Olaf, who'd been sitting by a nearby tent, stood, eyes glancing at me hopefully. Gods, what was I going to do with him? I'd never had to bear his presence in human form for this long before. Tonight, or as soon as I was able, I was going to change him back. Even looking at his face made me feel sick.

"Priest," FitzStephen said, clicking his fingers at Olaf. "You should come too. There are men in need of last rites and confessions."

When Olaf gave him a strange look, I spoke to him in Irish.

"Are you coming, Olaf? You are being invited into the city."

"They want me to come?"

"You are a priest, and they want you to tend to the men. Come. This is part of my plan, and I need you to see what has happened."

I wasn't sure if he knew how to complete any of these rites that FitzStephen wanted, but I supposed those dying or already dead would not care. Olaf didn't seem to care either. My words and my apparent need of him cheered him, and he came to stand behind me as we made our way into the fallen city.

Our walk into the city was shocking, more shocking than the earlier noise would have led me to believe, and I thought I was too old to be shocked. There were bodies everywhere. Warriors, of course, I expected those. But there were hundreds of women and children too. From their remains, I could tell horses had charged into some of them, crushing skulls and bones. Others had slashes across their necks and faces from the knights' sharpened swords.

Cecile and Alina shivered behind me. Alina even let out a sob as we turned one corner. Here, the ground had turned red from the blood flowing over it.

This is war, I wanted to say to them. But it was unlike any war I had ever seen. For the Irish, war always happened out on the plains, away from the women and children. Men died in their droves, yes, but not their children or their wives. That was not our way.

But as with so much else, Strongbow was bringing the Norman ways of war to Ireland. They said they were more Christian than us, and yet I could no longer give that any credence. There was nothing godly about the sight before me.

I snatched another glance at Cecile, who was holding Alina's hand, to see what she made of it. She was trying to comfort Alina but could hardly look at the slaughter and instead stared at her feet. But this was the work of the man she loved. Why then look away?

Why not see it and know who it was that you had given your heart to? Youth. This was the answer – the only reason for her inability to look, for she still believed in the fantasy that men wrapped around themselves in the light of day. And here, in Waterford, was what men could do when shrouded by thick walls and the dark shadows they cast.

"Careful," Olaf whispered. "There are Waterford warriors hiding inside the houses."

Nodding, I moved closer to FitzStephen and Olaf while ensuring that both Alina and Cecile were behind me. I had been stabbed once before and had no intention of allowing that to happen to me again. Not here. And not by some peasant fisherman who'd been too afraid to come out and fight the men.

"Nearly there," Robert FitzStephen said as he turned into another street. From here, one of the towers loomed in the distance, and I could see people congregating around it. However, it was only as we reached the end of the street, that I could make out how many. Over a thousand Anglo-Normans had survived. This was good considering how long the battle had lasted. But also gathered here were the leaders of Waterford, the kings and the chief warriors, though their hands were bound behind their backs. Le Gros and his men marched them up onto a stone step that led into the tower, setting them above the rest of us so that we could see their faces. The man who stood in the middle was their king. Though he wore no crown, I could tell by the fierce look in his eyes and the sorrow upon his brow.

Strongbow, still on horseback, urged his horse forward a little so all could see him too. "On their knees," he commanded.

The Waterford king and his men didn't speak as Le Gros and his men pushed them down. They didn't beg. What was the point? They had already surrendered, and so there was nothing left to say. These men, this king, they all knew what was about to happen to them. A king could not hope for life when the bodies of women and children lay lifeless upon the ground.

"My name is Richard de Clare, Earl of Pembroke, Lord of

Striguil," Strongbow said loud and clear for all to hear. "The Kingdom of Waterford is now mine by conquest." He pointed his sword at the man with the long beard. "Who are you?"

"Ragnall, King of Waterford, and this is my city."

"*Was* your city," Strongbow replied. "It is mine now."

Ragnall shook his head. "And look at what you have done to it. So much destruction and death. There was no need to kill the people here. You are a king of ghosts now. A king of the dead."

"Death is the result of conquest," Strongbow answered. "You must destroy what came before. Always." He stared at Ragnall, examining his features, the long face and greying hair. "You and I are from the same people. And what our ancestors did was admirable. We fought and fought and then befriended and married into our enemies and slowly we took the land from them. Rollo did this in Normandy. Amlav the Red did this in Dublin. But times have changed. We no longer have the patience to take what we want slowly. At least, I do not."

Ragnall spat on the ground.

"Are these men beside you your kin?" Strongbow asked.

Ragnall didn't speak. Didn't move.

Strongbow dismounted and walked onto the step. In one swift motion, he lifted his sword and swung it down and through the neck of the former King of Waterford. As Ragnall's head fell, blood spurted from his neck, spraying over Strongbow's armour and face. The body twitched a few times before thudding forward, and then all was still.

The man beside Ragnall, younger but alike in every way, lowered his neck so that Strongbow could strike him next.

"Make way for the King of Leinster!"

The silence was shattered as the sound of horses and men running into the city grew.

Intrigued, I turned to catch a glimpse of King Diarmait and his army. Donnchad had not told me anything about Diarmait or his family on his return to Chepstow, though I knew he had withheld many of his thoughts from me. I wondered now what he made of him, for he was our kin through Máelmórda. A last little link between who we once were and what we had become.

Surprised by my own reaction, I gasped as they approached. Yes, I could see our features in him, and in the dark-haired man who rode at his side, I could see Máelmórda. Cecile noticed it too. I could tell by the way her eyes followed him as he passed by.

All was quiet as Diarmait rode into the courtyard. He did not smile, did not wave, indeed he showed no emotion on his face at all. No acknowledgement of the blood and dead he had passed, though he must have been shocked to find that Strongbow had taken the city without him and in such a manner.

"Let him go," he said, pointing to the man who had just lowered his neck. "That man is Sichfrith, and he is known to me." He paused and stared at Ragnall, or rather, at his body. "In this country, when your enemy concedes defeat, we leave them be. And from the looks of it, there has been enough bloodshed for one day."

Strongbow stared at the king, jaw clenched. His blood was up, and I knew he wanted to say this was his city and he would act as he saw fit. But perhaps in seeing that Diarmait's men were behind him, clean and fresh and spoiling for a battle they had missed, he thought better of it and sheathed his sword.

Diarmait clicked his tongue. "I believe you want to marry my daughter?"

"Yes," Strongbow replied.

"Then let us make that happen."

"Now?"

"Yes. Now. You will marry my daughter today or not at all, but know this, once you are wed, we will plan where to go next."

Strongbow smiled at this. "Where do you want to go?"

"Ah," Diarmait said. "I wish to be High King of Ireland, and if that is to happen, there is only one place to go."

"Connacht?" Cecile whispered in my ear.

"No. Dublin," I answered.

Connacht indeed. Cecile had clearly never listened to a word I said. There was nothing in Connacht of any value. The only reason

King Ruaidrí held the high kingship was because he had the biggest army and had forced the other kings to submit to him. But if Strongbow had his own army, an army that could capture a city of this size in a day, then Ruaidrí had lost his advantage. That meant wealth was the biggest asset now, and by taking Dublin and cutting off Ruaidrí's access to gold and silver, Diarmait understood what it took to win.

Strongbow moved back toward his horse, but before he had a chance to mount it, a bishop and a young woman with a veil covering her face moved into the square.

"This is my daughter, Eva," King Diarmait said, pointing at the young woman. "This bishop is my cousin, and he can perform the ceremony here."

Strongbow shook his head. "We're not in a church."

King Diarmait nodded over at the church beside the fort which part of the wall had fallen into, and then at the dead bodies upon the steps. "We cannot have the ceremony in the church now. We will have the formal wedding once it is rebuilt, blessed and washed, but if you want us to join forces, you must say your vows on the Holy Bible today."

"Then today it will be." Strongbow moved away from his horse and stood in the middle of the square. Taking a breath, he held out his hand for the young woman to take.

Diarmait smiled and gestured for her to approach. Oh, the Leinster princess was so young and sweet, I could see that even through the veil. Too sweet to be walking upon a street still awash with blood. Too innocent to be wed when the street was still filled with corpses.

She shivered as she passed me, her eyes darting around from under her veil as she took in all the strange faces staring at her. The hem of her dress was red now, drenched in the blood that she walked upon, but still she kept moving. An Irish wolfhound walked at her side, and a blind boy, holding its lead, followed in the dog's wake.

Cecile stared at all of this, sometimes looking at Strongbow, sometimes at his bride. She was not crying – she was hardier than that by now – but such jealousy swam in her eyes that anyone who looked upon her face would see it. It was hard, I supposed, to be spurned in love, though it had never happened to me. Poor Cecile. She'd chosen the wrong man, or else did not have the wiles to capture him completely.

And this man was now about to wed a bride full of the qualities he espoused to adore. Virgin. Innocent. Chaste. Rich. These attributes could only have made Cecile burn. However, from the way Eva glanced at Strongbow, I suspected this new groom was *not* who she wanted. With every step, slower than the one before, I could feel her unwillingness. I could sense that she saw him as a monster.

And a monster Strongbow was. If Cecile did not see that, I certainly did. Had always known. What man spoke of invading another land and was not? Worse still, to agree to a wedding like this was beyond barbaric. No feast first? No gifts and dowry? Even my wedding to Brian after Glenmama had been better than this.

What was Strongbow thinking?

Yes, he wanted to tie himself to Diarmait, but it was unfortunate that they'd chosen speed over tradition. It would come back to haunt him when he moved to take the kingship of Ireland. This day would be remembered as a day he married a princess with blood on his armour and no gold to give. A king who kept a poor hall could not stay a king in Ireland for long, that was the truth.

I supposed it was just as well that I was here to save him.

Isolde

The River Barrow

Once I reached Munster, I followed the path along the River Barrow. Three days I'd been travelling now, and my horse had covered many miles. Using my gift, I healed him when he was tired, and so we hadn't needed to stop unless it was to take on some water or to sleep. We had to be close to Waterford, I thought, as the sun began to fall. The river was widening, the land was getting flatter, and I'd spotted a couple of seagulls flying overhead.

"I'd be careful going that way," a voice said.

I turned my head and found a woman sitting on a large boulder on the other side of the river. She was old, this woman, so old her cheeks were hollowed from lack of teeth. A young girl sat beside her. She had long dark hair and skinny legs, and she gave me a small smile before snuggling into the old woman.

"Why? What's happened?"

"Waterford is at war."

Oh no. I was too late. *Did that mean the Fomorians already had Cuan?* My horse stepped backward, sensing my panic, and quickly I tried to calm myself.

"We were walking along the River Suir when the ships came. My grandson told us to get upriver, and we are waiting for him to come to us. He will come. I know it."

"Who came on the ships? Do you know?"

The old woman tutted. "The worst kind. Men with swords and armour."

"My father wanted to find my sister," the little girl added. "He told us to wait for him here, and so we will wait. Won't we, Grandmother?"

The old woman nodded and wrapped her arm around the young girl. "Yes, my love. We will wait, and he'll be here soon. Best for us not to get too close to the city. That was your father's thinking." She stared at me then. "You should listen to my grandson too. No point in going that way. You'll only find trouble."

I thanked the old woman for her advice, but I had no choice other than to keep going. Cuan was in Waterford. I had seen him there in my vision. Burning. I had to save him. *Had to.*

So rather than turning, I did the opposite and urged my horse to go faster, and we rode until the sun met the horizon. Determined to keep going, even as the night approached, I stopped only to allow my horse to take on food and water.

Finding a part of the river with a low embankment, I dismounted and led my horse over to the river. As he drank, I opened my waterskin. The river water here wasn't clean enough for me to drink, but it was inviting, and I splashed my hand in it and rubbed the cool water over my face and neck. The sensation of the cold against my warm skin was delicious, and I reached back for another handful.

But the water… this time it swirled under my fingers. Moved against the current. *The water was listening to me.*

Smiling, I felt for the knot inside my stomach, reached for my gift and summoned more. Watching in disbelief, the water spun in a circle and formed a ball which moved into the palm of my hand. Music came to me too. Within the gushing and gurgling, there was a song. The most beautiful song I'd ever heard. Oh, I wished Méabh were here to see this. She would be so relieved, as relieved as I was, that finally the water was moving at my command.

This thought made my breath catch. Méabh right now would be wondering where I was. She'd probably be worried sick. The others would be too, thinking perhaps I'd been taken like Gisela and Leofwynn. But how could I say that I needed to leave? They would ask why, and I couldn't tell them. Not about Cuan. Not about what my vision had shown.

The ball of water pulled away from me then, jumping out of the water like a fish, and moved downstream. Curious, I followed, but the ball of water seemed to have disappeared now, or else had moved deeper where I could not see it.

I followed the river a little more, listening for the music and watching for the ball of water, and then I heard something else. Sobbing. Crying.

Holding the reins of my horse tight, I used my warrior gift and reached out with my senses. The sound was coming from a woman. She was in pain, and I could smell blood. She was sad too, full of sorrow.

"I am sorry. I'm just so tired," she said.

Using my harpist gift, I knew her words were true. I could feel her fatigue, her physical pain, but it was still her grief that I felt the most. What had happened to this poor woman? War, I thought. Like the old woman had said, *men with swords and armour.*

"Don't be sorry, Brenna. Stay here and rest. I'll be back with some food and water soon."

The woman gave her thanks, and I would have thought to hide from them… but there was something about the man's voice that made me run toward them instead. I came to the forest just in time to see the man running out of the treeline.

"Cuan?"

The man stilled, and my heart pounded against my chest as I took him in. He was the last person I had expected to see here, but my joy could not be contained. It meant he was alive. It meant he was safe.

Cuan rushed toward me, as shocked to see me as I was to see him. On reaching me, his hand moved to my cheek, the part of the cheek where I had touched him in my dream. But this was no dream… not this time, and when I touched him, he could feel it too.

Opening his arms, he pulled me closer and held me tight. He kissed me, his hands rushing to my hair, fingers locking around it, as if to prove that I was not a ghost.

"I am so glad to see you, Isolde. So very glad."

"What are you doing here? I had a vision of you in Waterford… I thought it was under attack."

"I was in Waterford. The Anglo-Normans laid siege to it. King Ragnall told me to leave just before the city was taken so I could tell Ruaidrí what had happened. When we left, the screams were unimaginable. I think there must have been a massacre."

"A massacre?" I whispered. Yes, I had seen the start of this battle in my vision, had heard the screams and sobs. "The vision showed me some of this. A man called Sichfrith was with you, and I knew you were in danger."

"You came to find me because of this vision?" Cuan whispered.

"Yes."

Cuan wrapped his arms around me again, and this time I let myself be held – let the weight of my body fall into his. I could have stayed there forever, but that could not be. The woman in the forest was suffering, and it was only growing. I could feel more about her now, could sense there was a child growing within her.

"Who is your friend, Cuan?"

"Brenna. She's Bjorn's wife. He wanted me to take her with me when I escaped, but she isn't well. An arrow hit her leg while we were escaping, and she is heavily pregnant too. We travelled part of the way by ship with a man called Ingvar, but he couldn't take us any further, and now she's struggling to walk."

"Let me help." I took out my waterskin. "You were looking for water, weren't you, and I have plenty."

The two of us walked into the forest and made our way to Brenna. Yes, I could feel her pain now. All of it. "Brenna, my name is Isolde. I'm here to help you."

Holding out the waterskin, I removed the lid and brought it over to her lips.

Brenna drank, but as soon as I took the skin away from her, she burst into tears. "I wish I had stayed in the city now. I don't think I can live without Bjorn."

"Don't say that," Cuan said. "Bjorn wanted you to survive. You and the baby, and we do not know that he is dead. If he is alive, he will come to Dúnmór. You must stay strong."

I held Brenna's hand tight and while she and Cuan spoke, I felt for the arrow wound. The skin here was inflamed and hot, and I sensed that dirt had got into the flesh. If left untreated, it would get into her blood and then her fever would grow. But more than this, she was shaken by what had happened. Her breathing was shallow and sharp, and sweat covered the back of her neck. The baby was agitated too, kicking and moving as he felt his mother's anguish rush through their blood.

Using my healing gift, I mended the tear in her leg, leaving just a graze that would heal over in the next few days. The sorrow, I could help with that too. Not forever, but just for tonight, and so using my harpist gift, I eased it and gave her a feeling of calm that allowed her to fall asleep.

"Using your gift doesn't make you sick anymore?" Cuan asked.

"No, not now I know how to use it properly. That's what the Descendants have been able to teach me."

"That is good." He looked sad for a moment but then took my hand and kissed it.

Now that Brenna was sleeping, I led Cuan to the river. It was beautiful here, even in the moonlight, and together we sat on the grass.

"Tell me what happened in Waterford."

Cuan sighed. "Ruaidrí sent me there to speak with King Ragnall, but when I arrived, a group of Anglo-Normans had landed. Nearly two thousand of them once they were joined by the

Anglo-Normans already in Ireland. They were able to make part of the wall collapse and in they came like a wave. I need to warn my uncle as soon as possible."

"You should take my horse in the morning."

"I cannot do that."

"Of course you can. Brenna is exhausted, and you said yourself that you need to reach your uncle quickly."

He nodded, then reached out with his hand to touch my cheek. His thumb rubbed against my lip. "I just had to check again that you were really here. Every time I blink, I fear you will be gone."

Leaning into him, I kissed him... part of me wanting to make sure he was real too. "You told me you loved me once. Do you remember?"

"How could I forget?"

"I couldn't understand it at first. You had never indicated that you felt such a thing. No sweet words. No soft touches. But once you said it, I knew it was true. Just as I knew then that I loved you too. I hadn't realised it, but during my travels, I always sought you out. When you spoke, I listened. And when I was alone, I thought of you and the things you had told me. I was so naïve I didn't even understand my own feelings."

Cuan smiled. "I tried very hard to keep those feelings in. You saw what happens to me when I feel too much. I lose control. It's how my mother died. She loved my father and when he was attacked, the fire came out of her, and a week later she was dead. Keeping my heart to myself is how I have survived all these years, and so when I told you that I hadn't wanted to love you, you have no idea how much I meant that."

"You were scared of loving me?"

"Yes. If I had been a free man, a man without the curse, I would have told you I loved you long before I did."

"When?" I laughed as I asked this, trying to trace back our time together.

"There were a few times. After the attack at the bruidean when you were lying asleep under the tree. You had been so brave, I had not expected it. Next, when I saw you under the tree at Kells, staring at the ladybirds crawling along the grass. I thought to myself that I would like to watch you like that always. Not running, not fighting, not arguing. Just happy."

A sadness swept over me, a sadness that this could not be. The wind spoke to me now, and one day soon I would lose my mind like Rónnat. He wouldn't want me then.

"When you visited me in your dream," he said, "if that's what it was, I meant it when I said that I wanted to be with you."

"You cannot, Cuan. It's not possible."

"What if you explained to the others that I was your friend? Would they listen?"

I didn't know. Perhaps. I had come to know them so well over the last few months, but this was still unknown. They hated Fomorians, that was all I knew… but if I explained to them about Cuan. Told them he was good…

"You would leave your family to come and live at the monastery with me?"

"Not right away. Not while Connacht is in such danger… but after… yes."

His words were tempting. I wanted them to be true, even if I only had a short time left where my mind was not broken. "Are you sure, Cuan? The love you have for me, are you sure of it? We had so little time with each other. Do you think that if more time passed—"

"That I would forget about you?" He shook his head. "No. Never. Don't you understand, I was never meant to love anyone, and I still fell in love with you."

I kissed him again. Not soft and gentle like the time in the cave when I didn't understand my own feelings. I kissed him as if this was the last time I would see him. I kissed him as if this was the last time I would kiss anyone.

⋆

We lay there until the dawn broke, fingers interlocked and my head resting on his shoulder as we drifted between kissing and talking and sleeping. Cuan was asleep now and he looked so peaceful. The concentration in his brow was gone, as was the worry he held in his shoulders. I traced my finger down a thin line that crossed his face. A shallower version of the scar line I had healed after his escape from Ferns. He must have cut it back in so that his kin didn't notice that it had gone so suddenly. I wished that I had more time to talk to him. To ask him about his family and his father and what had happened. No, I did not want to leave him, but the others would be worried about me, and now I knew Cuan was safe, I had to return to Seir Kieran.

Standing, I wiped the grass from my cloak.

Cuan stirred as I moved and opened his eyes.

"I will see you soon, Cuan Ó Conchúir."

Cuan sat, his hand reaching up to hold mine. "We will be together soon, one way or another. I swear it."

I didn't know if this was true. I hoped it was. Wanted it to be. But our lives, they were both so filled with danger. Not only mine, but also his.

"Before I go, Cuan, there is something else I must tell you."

"Yes?"

"In my vision, I saw another Fomorian. He was burning you. Killing you. I thought it was happening in Waterford, but it must be some other place. Some other time."

"Was it one of the Fomorians who tried to kill you on Rathlin?"

"Maybe? He had long, curly dark hair. Pale skin. He seemed older than you, but I could not see his face clearly nor hear what he was saying. Not all visions come true, but I need to tell you just so you are prepared. It might mean that if you come to live with me, I will put you in danger."

Cuan pressed his lips together. "I will remember this warning, Isolde, but if anything, this only shows that we should be together. I would rather my life was forfeit than yours."

Standing, he embraced me again. "As soon as I am sure

Connacht is safe, I will find you. Until then, you should stay with Colmon and the other Descendants."

"Yes, and when you find me, we will talk to them. Together."

"I agree with this plan." Cuan kissed my lips. "It is a good plan."

I wanted to kiss him again, to feel his lips upon mine, but instead I pulled back. We would be together soon. The kiss we had just shared, it was not our final kiss. Just one of many.

"Goodbye, Cuan. I love you."

"I love you too, Isolde."

Ripping myself away, I walked to the river and made my way north. Toward the monastery and the grey stone, and the questions that would surely come. This time, however, I did not feel so scared of what they might say. Nor did I feel so alone.

Angelo

Waterford

After weeks of travelling, we had finally reached the City of Waterford. Seeing the lime paste walls in the distance was as joyous a feeling as I'd had since the death of Brother Pádraig and Brother Mark. *Finally*, our long trek through the forest was over. Luchóg walked beside me. He was grinning like a fool, but the other fuidir were further behind. They were probably complaining about their feet or hunger, and not yet aware that we had reached our destination.

I was hungry myself and eager to be in the city, but as soon as I breached the final hill, I knew something strange had happened here and I came to a stop. Usually, a city of this size had ships sailing along the longphort and people walking in and out of the gates with carts of goods. But there was nothing. No movement, no people, even though the gates were open.

Where was everyone? Had Waterford's warriors heard that the Anglo-Norman army was coming this way and left the city to ambush them somewhere else?

"Your friend is definitely here?" Luchóg asked.

"Maybe. I'll need to go inside to know for sure."

Luchóg cast an eye over the city. His eyes were sharp, and he knew as well as I did that something strange was afoot.

"You go on ahead," I said. "I'll wait for the others to catch up. See if you can find out what has happened."

I waited on the hill for the rest of the fuidir, a smile on my face and a kind word for each of them as they reached me. They were exhausted after walking for so long, and one of them even dropped to the ground, declaring he was unable to go on. I didn't say anything this time, for I'd heard all these complaints before. Instead, I quietened his foul mood and tried to give them all a sense of excitement that they had finally arrived.

Using my gift like this was tiresome, and during our trek I'd had to use it often. You'd think men living in the forests would be used to walking, but it turned out a life of scavenging and stealing required less effort than I thought. This fatigue had made controlling them difficult. Their usual anger, sharpened by physical discomfort, was more potent, and it took every ounce of skill with my new gift to soothe them and stop them from deciding to go back to Connacht.

Thankfully, Luchóg did not take long to return.

"The man at Carrig said the Anglo-Norman army had come here, but I didn't expect them to take the city so quickly," Luchóg said. "A day. That was all it took."

Oh, so that was it. Not that the Anglo-Norman and Waterford armies had clashed elsewhere. The Anglo-Normans had actually taken the city.

"I don't believe it," one of the fuidir said. "How?"

"The knights cut down a watchtower is what I heard," Luchóg said. "It brought down the northern wall. It's hard to see from this angle, but a large section of it has fallen in. There are dead bodies everywhere."

"And the gates are open?" I asked.

"The guard I spoke to said that the city is trading today, and the market is already open. Come and see for yourselves."

The mood of the fuidir lifted, and I gestured for them to walk down the path that led into the city.

What to do? What to do?

There was no doubt my grandmother was here if the Anglo-Norman army had won. From talking to the men at Carrig, I knew she was with that part of the army. And it was more than likely that my father and Cecile had sailed over with Strongbow. What did I want to say to them? Who did I want to be? The old Angelo or the new?

"Listen," I said to the men as we approached the gate. "Do not cause trouble here. The knights will cut you down if you commit any crime."

"Then what will we do?"

"We will tell them the truth."

The fuidir scratched his head.

"We are pilgrims of the Holy Father," I said. "And we have come to help bury the dead."

"We have?"

"Whatever gold and silver you find is yours. Better that it's in your hands than buried in the earth."

This cheered the fuidir even more, and once we arrived at the gate, it didn't take much to convince the guards that we were indeed pilgrims seeking to pray over the dead.

"Why don't you and your men look after the bodies over by the western wall?" one of the guards said to me. "We haven't cleared that side yet."

Yes, I could tell. There was a stench already permeating the air.

"Once you wrap the bodies," he added, "bring them to the gate on the western wall. A grave is being dug there."

The men, hardly able to hide their grins, hurried over to where the bodies lay, like a plague of rats. I walked with them for a while, taking in the city and making sure that the fuidir knew how to behave, but I had no intention of staying with them. The city was a feast for the eyes, and now inside the walls, I could see exactly what had happened. Oh, but it was a mess. Blood covered the streets, the market stalls, even the walls.

"Luchóg." I walked over to the fuidir leader, rested my hand on him and gave him the feeling of caution. "Keep them in check, yes? The Anglo-Normans deal out harsher punishments than the Irish kings."

"Yes, Brother Angelo."

"Good. I will go now and look for my friend. Once I'm ready, I'll find you."

With that order given, I made my way toward the Anglo-Norman camp, which had been set up around the fort.

Pretending to administer prayers to the injured Anglo-Normans who lay down on makeshift beds, I walked along the streets. Glancing around, I could see, even with so many dead and injured, that the work of life was continuing. Some of the Anglo-Norman warriors were already rebuilding the wall and church, while others were reorganising the stores of food that the Waterford leaders had hoarded for the siege. I also noted that some of the Waterford survivors were trading goods with the Anglo-Norman knights and archers. It was nice to see that greed always won in the end.

In this manner, I walked all the way to what was left of the church, and it was here that I heard my grandmother laughing. Hiding behind a stall, I watched her walking arm in arm with another woman to the fort. Oh yes, she was with Eva, daughter of Diarmait Mac Murchadha. I remembered her from my time in Ferns. My distant cousin. Her blind brother sat on a chair outside the fort... Enna, yes, that was his name, while the older, bastard one, Domhnall, was standing by the fort door and eating an apple.

And then I saw another woman I recognised. She walked behind Gormflaith and Eva. Eyes down. A frown upon her face.

Cecile.

If Gormflaith walked about the city as if it was already hers, Cecile was quite the opposite. Younger than me, she had only ever known peace and luxury, for Máelmórda spoiled her as if she were a princess. To him, I supposed she was, and I had never minded. But now, the effects of such treatment were apparent. She did not see the dead bodies lying on the street as signs of victory. No. It pained her, the brutality of it, and a silent tear fell down her cheek.

Gormflaith didn't seem to notice Cecile's misery. She was too overjoyed by the unfolding of her plan, whatever that was. She wanted to be queen, I knew that, and I was sure that in some way this victory at Waterford was to her advantage.

I could only admire her for such ambition. How she planned on turning Strongbow's army against him was the question. My father didn't seem to be here, which confused me. He would find it easier to take command of an army, but perhaps there was a reason. All of it intrigued me enough for me to be willing to reveal who I was.

I waited by the church for a time, saying prayers and talking with the wounded, and while I did that, I used my gift to seek Cecile out and strengthened the emotions she already felt.

It didn't take long for her to reappear. Come to torture herself some more – to look at the dead bodies and wallow in her own misery – both things I had wanted her to do. In the midafternoon light, she looked as if she had lost the will to live. She was scared though, too scared to leave the place she hated. As she walked toward the church, she sat on the steps and placed her hand on the stone.

Gormflaith ran out after her, and once again, I hid from them. Lowering my hood, I held the hand of a dying man and pretended to pray.

"Come inside, Cecile," Gormflaith said. "You are making a show of yourself."

"But I love him. It's too hard talking with Eva knowing that she is married to him and I am not."

"Oh, Cecile. You don't love him. How could you? He gives you nothing, and now that he is married, he hardly even speaks to you."

"Only because he finds it hard to be in my company and yet apart."

Gormflaith hissed. Even without looking at her, I knew she'd be rolling her eyes. "Oh, Cecile, please. I don't have time to argue with you. Just think about how idiotic that sounds. *He doesn't want to break his vows?* Well, he broke his vow to the king by coming here, and he brought Alina here, who he fathered out of wedlock. How is it he can break every other vow but this one? He's using you. Fanning his ego with your forlorn looks and teary eyes."

Gormflaith paused. "Grow up, Cecile. Be who you are capable of being. I've brought you here. Taken you away from Donnchad who would be married to you by now if he had his way. When I am queen, you can have whomever you want. Any mortal. Several if you wish."

Gormflaith sighed and stepped away. "A feast has just been prepared, and you are invited to attend. Why don't you cheer up and come and eat with us?"

When Cecile didn't answer, Gormflaith huffed and turned, making her own way back to the fort. Enna and Domhnall had gone inside too now, and yes, the smell of cooked venison was drifting in the air.

Cecile, however, was unmoved by this. She was still forlorn, grieving. *Lonely*.

I paused for a moment. Was this the right move? Grandmother would be of more use. She was a powerful Fomorian and a witch… but she also had more ambition. If I told her about Isolde, she might want her gift for herself.

To that end, Cecile was a better fit.

Her gift was the only problem – the strength of it.

I remembered us teaching her how to use her fire-magic when she was younger. She was a natural to start with, but as she grew older, it was as if her gift had weakened, and her desire to use her fire-magic receded too. Perhaps that was the problem. Desire. Well, then, all I had to do was awaken it. She was Fomorian, after all. It had to be in there somewhere.

Taking down the hood of my robe, I walked toward her.

"Angelo?" She wiped her cheeks and rushed over to me, her eyes widening as she took me in. "I've been so worried about you. Where have you been?"

She bent down and picked up a stick so that I could draw in the mud a picture that might explain my absence, but I did not take it from her.

"I've been in Connacht."

She started. "You can speak?"

"I've always been able to speak. I just didn't want to. I needed to protect myself."

A frown swept over her lips. "Who from?"

"From Gormflaith. From Donnchad. They use people, haven't you noticed?" I wiped her cheeks. "I think you have. That's why I can finally reveal myself to you."

She pushed my hand away. "What a little snake you are. How is it even possible for you to have kept up such an act for so long?"

Using the harpist gift, I stared at her and took in her anguish, her despair, and made it even deeper

"Because they hurt me, Cecile, just as they are hurting you now. I didn't speak to keep some part of myself safe. Can you not understand that?"

"I… Yes…" She nodded as she wiped away another tear, freshly fallen. "I suppose I can."

Her loneliness seeped out of her like blood from an opened vein. I let her feel this but also gave her some hope. I was here after all. A cousin. *Someone who might understand her*.

"Why don't you come with me? Away from this place?"

She shook her head. "I don't think so."

"Why stay? Gormflaith has used you. What is left for you here?"

"There is someone I love, Angelo."

"Who?"

"Strongbow. At least I thought I did, but he did all this, Angelo. All this death and destruction was at his command. And then he married Diarmait's daughter, Eva. I knew he had agreed to it, but he told me he loved me. How could he set me aside so easily?"

"Men will do anything for power, Cecile. That is a hard lesson we all must learn."

I pulled her into a hug and rested my chin upon her shoulder. She felt safe with me. I had played with her as a child. Given her presents and never asked for anything in return.

"How are you so wise, Angelo? How are you so wise when I am not?"

"You are like a princess, Cecile, and here you are working like a slave. What if I told you I could take you somewhere better? Somewhere beautiful."

I took out my necklace and rubbed my thumb over it. "What if I told you, you could have a purpose?"

"A purpose?"

"Yes, you can help me. I would be grateful. In fact, I need you, Cecile. I need your help."

She glanced up at me, a small smile growing on her lips. "I want to be helpful, yes."

"Even better, Cecile, I have found another Fomorian. He wants to meet you. But we must protect him from the others. Will you come and speak with him?"

She nodded.

"But first, there is someone else I'd like you to meet. Her name is Isolde."

I held out my hand and she took it, and together we walked toward the gate. As we left the city, Luchóg saw me in the distance and smiled once he saw I had someone with me. *A woman.*

Cecile, sweet Cecile, no longer wanting to be lonely, kept going, and together we walked along the path and into the forest. Glancing back just the once, I saw the fuidir were following.

Cuan

Road to Dúnmór

Brenna and I rode toward Dúnmór as fast as we could.

Brenna was much better now that Isolde had healed her wound, but I still could not ride as hard as I wished, not with her so heavily pregnant. She sensed this, and wanting my uncle's army to avenge what had happened in Waterford, she didn't complain and kept riding long into the night, long past I felt she should. The journey was arduous over the mountain paths, though the good summer weather had helped. Once we reached Connacht, it became easier. Here, my name alone provided me with another horse, as well as shelter and fresh food.

At one bruidean we had stayed in, Brenna tried to insist that I ride on ahead and leave her, but I could not do that when Bjorn had entrusted her to my care, and so I slowed my pace and kept her at my side, and once I felt she needed to rest, I insisted we stop.

These times of rest were not always easy. My mind often moved to thoughts of Isolde. Of our promise to be together. I wanted this more than anything. Seeing her, feeling her, it had been intoxicating, and yet I couldn't think when this would be. *When Connacht is safe*, I had told her. Right now, that seemed like a far-off dream. The Anglo-Normans were here now, a whole army of them, and my uncle was not prepared.

⋆

Finally, we reached Dúnmór, and as the dun came into view, I slowed my horse to a walk. Brenna pulled hers into line beside mine and stared up – gazing over the thick stone walls and circular trenches dug around the bottom of the hill.

"Is that it?" she asked.

I supposed after living in a city like Waterford, with its large stone walls, longphort and huge fort, Dúnmór seemed small, and I couldn't help but smile at the way her nose wrinkled.

"The High King lives *there*?"

"Yes. Dúnmór is an old dun, though King Ruaidrí has another one, much finer than this."

"Then why doesn't he live in that one?"

"Sometimes he does, but this one is safer, for you are in the heartland of Ó Conchúir territory. You might think it would be easy for an army to invade such a dun, but I tell you, no army would ever make it this far."

Brenna looked at the dun again, still bemused. "Where are all the warriors then?"

As I glanced up at the fort, I could see her point. There didn't seem to be many by the gate or at the posts around the wall.

"I thought you said the High King had called up all the armies. Shouldn't there be thousands here by now?"

"Oh, you mean the warriors from the other kingdoms? They are marching this way as we speak. They'll be here soon."

Brenna's chin quivered, her disappointment turning to anguish. "How soon?"

"Any day now."

"*Any day now* is not good enough. If Bjorn is still alive, every minute counts."

"Don't worry, Brenna. My uncle will be ready to march once they arrive."

I hoped rather than believed this to be true, but I didn't want to trouble Brenna. Once we reached the dun, I wanted her to rest and eat and make sure that the baby was well. Bjorn, if he were alive, would find a way to reach us. I tried not to think of the alternative, and what my head told me was the more likely outcome.

"You are nobody," I whispered to myself. "A nobody cannot feel anything."

"What did you say?" Brenna asked.

"Nothing of interest." I tilted my head at the dun. "Come on, let's go a little faster. Once we are at Dúnmór, we can get off these horses and rest."

Brenna didn't need to be told twice, and we took off along the path.

When we rode through the gate, there were no guards there to greet us, and to my surprise it was Fearghus who came to help us with the horses.

"Morning, Cuan." Fearghus took hold of Brenna's horse, while one of the other guards, an older one with a bad leg, hobbled away to fetch the stablemaster.

"Greetings, Fearghus," I replied. "Where is everyone?"

"Eoghan is training the warriors in the forest. Not just ours but the ones from Bréifne too. Seeing as I'm part of the fianna, I offered to stand watch. They'll be back soon, and then you'll hardly be able to move."

"King Tigernán's here?"

"Yes, he's in the feasting hall. He and his army arrived yesterday and have set their camp upriver. The other kings are expected to be here by the end of next week, though a scout said he spotted King Maghnus' army not too far away. I'd say they'll be here by this evening." He patted my horse's nose and gave Brenna a quick glance. "How was Waterford?"

"Waterford is taken," Brenna snapped. "Already gone. This army of yours is much too late."

Fearghus tilted his head, his eyes seeking out mine to see if this was true or not.

I answered his unspoken question with a nod. "Where's my uncle? I need to tell him what happened."

Fearghus hurried into the feasting hall, while I dismounted. Helping Brenna down next, I walked over to one of the serving women. An older woman whom I recognised as having lived here when I was a boy. "Brigid, would you fetch the healer for Brenna?"

Brigid nodded and walked out of the dun. In the meantime, another of the serving women brought over a cup of milk.

"What's all this, Cuan?" my uncle asked as he came out of the feasting hall. Fearghus, Conchobar, Cathal and King Tigernán followed in his wake, and I couldn't help but notice all the rings on my uncle and cousin's hands – more than usual – and how they sparkled in the sunshine. "Surely this is some kind of jest?"

"I'm afraid not. Waterford has been taken by Strongbow and his army."

My uncle's mouth dropped open. King Tigernán's did too.

"How many came over with Strongbow?" Conchobar asked.

"I'd say around fifteen hundred. Closer to two thousand once they were joined by the Anglo-Normans already in Ireland. They have three hundred knights. A significant number of archers too."

My uncle's head was shaking. "For you to be back so soon, they must have taken it quickly. Did Ragnall surrender?"

"No. They put up a good defence, but the Anglo-Normans spotted a weakness in the wall. Once they brought part of it down, the cavalry came in."

"Please," Brenna said. "Please do something. The screams we heard from the city – the cries of the women and children, it was unlike anything I've ever heard."

King Ruaidrí pressed his hand against his head, the skin around his eyes and lips blanching, but he somehow composed himself enough to smile at Brenna and gestured for two more of the serving women to come over.

"Who is your friend, Cuan?" he asked.

"This is Brenna, wife of Bjorn."

"Eisten, take Brenna into Róisín's house. Get her warm and fed and then somewhere comfortable to rest."

Brenna looked at me. I could tell she wanted to stay and tell the king what had happened, but that was not a good idea. Rage was hidden underneath his politeness, and I didn't think it would be good for her to see that. "Brenna, you must rest now. I'll come and speak with you later."

Brenna reluctantly walked to Róisín's house with the serving women, while my uncle beckoned for the rest of us to follow him into the feasting hall. Moving close to the fire, we sat in a circle around one of the tables.

King Ruaidrí leaned forward in his chair, twisting his rings about his fingers, one at a time. "My spies told me that Diarmait was riding out to Waterford, but I thought it was merely to meet with King Odhrán. Not this."

"The invasion is starting then, and Diarmait has made his play. He means to bring you down, Father." Conchobar leaned forward in his chair too, a fierce look in his eye.

"We must go to war, Ruaidrí," Tigernán said. "And quickly."

My uncle nodded. "Seeing as Diarmait is no longer at Ferns, we need to head to Dublin instead. That's where he and the Anglo-Normans will go next. It has all our wealth, and all the trade links. We must reach it before they do, for I wouldn't put it past Asculv to switch his allegiance."

He turned to Conchobar and Cathal. "The other armies are all marching this way. They need to know there can be no rest once they arrive. We march to Dublin as soon as we can. Send messengers out to tell the kings what has happened and this change of plan."

"While we wait, I'll have scouts look over the roads to Dublin," Fearghus added.

"Yes. We need to think about what path Diarmait will take from Waterford so we can block it off. Have the scouts check the condition of all the paths – forest, river and mountain." Ruaidrí banged his fist on the table. "There, we have a plan. Let's see it done."

"And what about the boys?" Tigernán asked King Ruaidrí, his voice soft and low.

"What boys?"

"Diarmait's hostages."

Ruaidrí tapped his finger against the arm of his chair. "What about them?"

Tigernán sneered as he leaned forward. "They cannot live while their king has broken all his oaths. They must be killed as forfeit."

Silence. Then King Ruaidrí laughed. "They are boys, Tigernán. Besides, Connor is to wed Róisín. He will be King of Leinster once Diarmait is dead."

"You are going to give Diarmait's son *a kingship*?" Tigernán practically spat out this sentence. "I'd rather die than let his son be king of any part of this land. The whole line needs to die. They are poison, all of them."

"Hush now, Tigernán."

"Hush? You forget who made you High King. Damn it, you've forgotten who made you king. Without me, you'd have nothing."

My uncle took a breath and stared at him. But if he hoped this would make Tigernán stop talking, he was wrong. Tigernán was in a fury now.

"Kill them or I'm leaving."

"You cannot leave. We're going to war."

"And why should I fight for you? A man who cannot do what needs to be done. I'd rather go home."

My uncle's temper flared now too, and as he stood, the chair flew out from underneath him. "You will fight, Tigernán, or we will be at war next. How dare you say that to me."

"I do dare. Diarmait has broken his oaths. His hostages' lives are forfeit. If you cannot kill them, how can I trust my army to your care? Has being surrounded by so much silk and gold fooled you into thinking you are a holy man rather than a king?" Tigernán licked his lips and took a step back. "But if you don't think I'm right, we can wait for the other kings to arrive and see what they say."

Another silence, but I could tell from the way that Tigernán glared at my uncle that he wasn't going to back down. The old man had always been filled with pride, and when he said something like this, he meant it. Ruaidrí knew this too, *and knew that he needed*

Tigernán's army. Not to mention that if Tigernán left, so might some of the other kings. If my uncle hadn't wanted to fight three hundred Anglo-Normans at Limerick alone, he certainly didn't want to take on two thousand.

"Fearghus," my uncle said, "fetch our men from the forest. Tell them to come back to the dun."

Fearghus walked outside while King Ruaidrí sat in his chair, eyes closed. Conchobar paced by the fire, and King Tigernán stood. It was only Cathal who glanced at me, his eyes showing a sense of panic that I was feeling too.

Killing the hostages was the wrong move. If Ruaidrí killed those boys, any chance at negotiations with Diarmait would die. But more than that, they were boys. My heart pounded in my chest as I realised what was about to happen. *But what could I do? I was not supposed to be arguing with my uncle, and to argue on behalf of King Diarmait's sons would only cause Conchobar to call me a spy once again.*

A few minutes later, Fearghus came back into the feasting hall. "Our men were already on their way back. They are in the dun now. What do you want them to do?"

"Tell Eoghan to have our warriors take the Leinster boys out of their house. Take them down to the river."

Before I could think of something to say, my uncle rushed past me and stood at the doors of the feasting hall, watching as the men gathered outside the hostages' house.

A few moments later, the warriors smashed through the door and dragged the boys out. They were shouting and screaming, turning the tables and beds to try to keep the men away from them. But with so many warriors there, they couldn't hold them off nor break free. As Caomhán and Olcán were brought out, tears streamed down their cheeks, and they struggled against the men and ropes holding them. Connor was brought out last. Tears streamed down his cheeks too, but he did not cry or struggle now that he was out in the open. He stared straight ahead, chin held high.

"What are you doing?" Róisín came out of her house and frowned as Connor was led to the dun gate by the guards, but her confusion didn't last for long. How could it? Even the daughter of a king knew that the world could be harsh.

"Father. Connor and I are to be married. What are you doing to him?"

"Yes, daughter, you were to be married," Ruaidrí said. "But his father has broken his oaths. Strongbow has invaded Waterford at Diarmait's invitation and massacred the people there, and now his hostages' lives are forfeit."

Róisín sobbed. "No, Father. Don't kill him. Please don't kill him."

My uncle stared at his feet, unable to look at his daughter's face.

"Mother, tell him, he cannot," Róisín pleaded as Queen Gráinne came outside. "Connor will be king after Diarmait. That is what Father promised. He will be a good king. I know him."

Queen Gráinne held her daughter's hands, her words of comfort fading from her lips. She too stared at Ruaidrí, her eyes pleading with him to change his mind.

"Well?" Tigernán snapped. "Are you going to get on with it or are women's tears going to undo you?"

Ruaidrí shook his head. "Eoghan, take them to the river."

"Father. Don't do this!" Róisín screamed this time and ran in front of her father. "Don't! Please!"

Gráinne, weeping now too, ran after her daughter, trying to take Róisín's hand to pull her back, but Róisín pushed her away and screamed all the louder. "Why is he doing this? No! I won't let him."

A few of the warriors herded Róisín back into her house, her screams and pleas for help only growing louder, while the rest of us walked down to the river, where the boys were forced onto their knees.

My uncle watched this white-faced, while Tigernán couldn't hide his smile. He hated Diarmait, hated him for stealing his wife all those years ago, and this hatred had become all-consuming.

It made me hate *him* all the more.

I had to do something. I had to speak. Stepping forward,

I opened my mouth, then quickly shut it. I felt it. *The fire inside me.* The tingling in my fingers.

Breathing deeply, I tried to control my emotions. *I was nothing. Nobody.* I needed to stay quiet. That was what I was supposed to be doing. Agreeing with my uncle and keeping him onside as per my father's instructions. Not arguing. Not getting angry. But as I opened my eyes and looked at Connor, Olcán and Caomhán, I realised I couldn't do that.

Clenching my fists and taking another deep breath, I walked over to my uncle and Tigernán. "Róisín is right," I said, doing my best to keep my voice calm. "Connor will be a better king than his father and is the last heir that the brehon laws will allow. If you kill him, Strongbow will have no one to stand against him who can rally an army in Leinster."

Tigernán spat at my feet. "Diarmait broke his oaths. There are consequences to this."

"You are always wanting death and destruction, Tigernán. And always so happy to let others do your work for you."

Tigernán laughed at this, his lips curling into a sneer. "Watch yourself, boy."

"Perhaps it is you we should be watching. Lurking over us with your one eye, like Balor, destroying everything he sees."

This shut Tigernán up, and I turned to my uncle. "Don't kill the hostages. Diarmait will soon see the mistake he has made in inviting the Anglo-Normans here. Don't make it so that he cannot turn on them."

This gave my uncle pause, and he stared at the three boys, biting his lip.

As he pondered my words, another army approached, and I could make out King Maghnus at the front.

Tigernán grinned and beckoned for the King of Ulaid to come over. "What say you, Maghnus? Strongbow and Diarmait have taken Waterford. I say Diarmait's hostages must die, but King Ruaidrí is hesitating."

"Why do you hesitate, Ruaidrí?" King Maghnus asked.

“The hostages are of value,” my uncle replied. “If Strongbow declares himself King of Leinster, as we’ve heard he means to, then Connor is the only legitimate heir Leinster has left.”

“We may also need them when negotiating,” I added. “If we kill them now, we’ve lost that advantage.”

“Why are you standing up for them?” Conchobar snapped. “Perhaps you are a spy for Diarmait, after all?”

The fire rose within me again. The anger. The wrath. Breathing deeply, I tried once again to control it, to bring it under. I am nothing. Nobody. *Nothing.*

“No answer this time?” Conchobar sneered. “Or is it that you have no Brother Angelo to lie on your behalf?”

My anger bubbled inside me. Lies. Greed. Oh, it was all here. Not a thought for what was best for Connacht.

Lifting my sword, I pointed it at him, then turned around in a circle so that all the men saw me. “My name is Cuan Ó Conchúir. My father’s name is Bardán. My grandfather was King of Connacht before King Ruaidrí. But many of you will not know me because I was raised on the Isles with King Godred. With him, I fought in England and in Norway and in the Isles. I tell you now that the wolves are at our gate. These Anglo-Normans are not here to fight for Diarmait; they are here to win land for themselves.” I turned again, this time until my sword pointed at Tigernán. “If you leave the battle now, as you say you want to, all you will do is buy yourself a few years. And then the wolves will be at your door, and there will be no one left to fight with you.”

Tigernán stared at me, and his men gathered around him, fingers brushing their swords. But I could not stop now. *I am nobody. Nothing.*

“I am also of my uncle’s fianna and will not have him be insulted by you. So, either fight with us or leave, but if you do that, you will know in your heart that you are a coward, as will every man here.”

My hands ached, and I could feel the sword turning warm beneath my fingers. The fire was coming.

"Your uncle is a High King," King Tigernán answered. "He must fulfil his oaths too."

I closed my eyes, trying to control myself, but the fire was close now. To speak again would cause me to unravel.

"A compromise, perhaps?" King Maghnus said. "King Diarmait has broken his oaths and so his hostages' lives are forfeit, but what Cuan says is true. If we kill them now, we will weaken our position if we negotiate."

"So, what do you think we should do?" Ruaidrí asked.

"Keep his son alive," Maghnus suggested. "Kill the other two. That way, we will punish Diarmait for his behaviour, but have something left to barter with."

Ruaidrí nodded. So did Tigernán.

"Eoghan, see it done," my uncle said.

I still couldn't speak. So close was the fire that I lowered my sword and breathed in and out. *You are nobody. Nothing. A nobody cannot feel.*

When I looked up, Olcán and Caomhán were dead. Eoghan had slit their throats, and their bodies lay still on the grass. Connor knelt beside them, shaking. Cathal rushed over to him and quickly led him back up the hill, not even waiting to be given the order.

I was glad Cathal did this. It meant the opportunity for Tigernán to complain or persuade the others to change their minds had gone.

The men dispersed quickly. I did too. I had to get away and be alone until I calmed down.

As I reached the dun, I walked straight into my house, and leaning over the wooden bedpost, I heaved.

A thick black liquid came to my lips, and I spat it onto the ground. *The curse*, as my mother called it, had finally caught up with me.

Gormflaith

Waterford

Living among the Anglo-Normans, victorious in the City of Waterford, was a glorious thing. The city was not so big, nor so grand as Dublin, but the fort had the same style of table, the same smell of carved wood and spiced wine. The Viking Irish way of living had changed little in the last hundred and fifty years, and I found I liked it. Had missed it.

Life would have been perfect, me sitting by the fire with a glass of wine in hand, talking to Eva and Alina, all the while watching and listening to what the men were plotting, if Cecile hadn't ruined it all by running away.

Her disappearance had caused a commotion for the first few days – for the feasts were set aside in favour of sending out search parties. Thankfully, they had now been called off, and Strongbow had sent a few of Diarmait's men to track her, though so far, she had eluded them. I was confident she was somewhere in the city. Perhaps hiding in the church and crying herself to sleep every night because Strongbow had abandoned her. She'd come out soon – when she became either hungry or bored. I had no doubt of that, for she would have been found by now if she'd ventured out into the wilderness. She had no aptitude for travel and certainly wouldn't know how to hide her tracks. As an added precaution, I'd turned Olaf back into an eagle and sent him to search for her. He'd been more than a little unhappy about this, but I'd promised him on his return, I would change him back, not just to mortal form, but to his younger self.

Cecile's absence wouldn't have bothered me so much, except as her *kinswoman*, I was expected to worry. I couldn't laugh by the fire – no, I had to be asking where she was or pretending that I couldn't sleep.

Strongbow himself had seemed a little preoccupied by her disappearance, but certainly not heartbroken. He was being kept busy in any case. King Diarmait wanted to march to Dublin with all haste, while he wanted to fix the wall at Waterford so he could keep hold of his hard-won territory.

This wasn't the only disagreement between the two factions. Strongbow had declared himself Lord of Waterford, but Diarmait had declared himself King of Waterford. Who ruled then? For the moment, it wasn't being discussed. However, Strongbow had made the fort his home, declaring he needed somewhere suitable for his new bride, in which case, it seemed to me that he was the one who had gained control.

Today, I sat by the fire. Eva and Alina were either side of me. They embroidered while I spoke to them. Eva's French was good; she'd obviously been tutored over the last year or so, but Alina's Irish was terrible. Switching between the two languages, I helped both to learn more of the other.

Eva was not as attentive today as usual. She sat in her chair, face pale and staring absentmindedly at the fire.

"What's wrong, Eva?" I asked after a while, moving to Irish.

She glanced over at Alina to see if she was paying attention – she wasn't – then at the men who were talking at the table, her new husband being one of them. Edging her chair closer, she whispered, "My monthly blood hasn't come."

I placed my hand on hers. "You think you are with child?"

"Can it happen so quickly?"

"Well… you married three weeks ago. It is possible that his seed took on the wedding night. There are other signs. Your breasts might feel tender. You might feel nauseous or tired. Do you feel either of those?"

Eva nodded and wiped away the tears gathering in her eyes. "I don't want to have his child."

This showing of emotion was unexpected, and quickly she tried to pull it in lest Alina should look up. She'd been the dutiful daughter until now. Doing what her father and older brother told her. Now reality had sunk in. She was a wife, married to a man she didn't like. And now she was to be a mother.

Her story was so similar to mine. Oh, how I had hated Amlav when my father had married me to him. Old and foul-breathed. Every time he touched me, I shuddered. At least Eva had been spared that. Strongbow was in his prime, not young, but not wrinkled and sagging either.

I held her hand tighter. "It is hard to bear the children of men you do not love, but I promise you, you will love this child you have together. Your husband is a powerful man, and your child will be safe with him as their father."

Eva nodded, dried her eyes, and sat back in her chair. There was nothing else she could do but accept the small glimmers of hope amidst the gloom.

I, however, began to think. I'd had a plan swirling in my head for weeks now. Was it too soon to act? It felt too soon. Babies were lost at this stage as often as a pregnancy continued, and yet with the talk of marching to Dublin within the next couple of weeks, I had little time to play with. I reached for the lining of my cloak, feeling for the vials I had sewn into it. The potion of forgetfulness and the potion of truth.

"Eva… I have a favour to ask of you." I lowered my eyes.

"Yes?"

"My husband died in the fighting, and I grieve for him."

Eva reached out to take my hand in hers. "I am sorry for your loss. I know you have been sad. Alina told me about it."

At the mention of her name, Alina looked up, and noticing that I appeared upset, pulled her chair forward. "What is it, Alys?"

"Alina, Eva," I said, switching to French so that Alina could follow the conversation. "My grief for David has become so strong that I have decided to take holy vows. Eva, do you know if there is a nunnery close by that would take me in?"

"Yes. There is one not far away at Kilculliheen, just over the river. I know it well. My father founded it, and my mother's cousin is the abbess there."

Eva was so sweet, so enthusiastic because of her ability to help. Alina, too, rubbed her hand on my shoulder.

"Do you think if you went there with me, Eva, that they would take me in? I am too scared to go alone. They might think poorly of me for having an Anglo-Norman husband, but if you came and spoke for me, I know they would treat me well."

"It would be an honour for me to go with you, Alys," Eva said.

"Are you sure?" Alina asked. "It is a big decision."

"Yes, Alina. I'm sure. Do you think you could tell your father that I request an audience with him?"

Pliable as ever, Alina ran off to do my bidding.

Eva edged a little closer. "I'll be sad to see you go, Alys, for you've been my only friend these last few weeks, but I am glad you have found your peace. When should you be ready?"

"We could ride out today?" I squeezed her hand. "Wouldn't you like to get out of Waterford?"

"Today?" Eva frowned. "My father might not let me."

"Ah," I said, giving her a slow smile. "Then you are going to learn the benefit of being married. You don't have to ask your father anymore. You can ask your husband, and a husband only just married is usually quite willing to say yes." I gave her a soft wink. "Come, it is very easy. All you need to do is compliment him and give him a small smile. Do that, and he'll agree to anything you want."

"Alys!" Alina came running over to me. "Father will speak with you now."

Walking toward Strongbow, with Alina and Eva holding my hands, I smiled. Even better, Le Gros and William Ferrand were with him.

I curtseyed low and Strongbow turned toward me, more than a little surprised.

"What is wrong, Alys?" he asked. "Alina says you wish to speak with me."

Rising, I took a step forward. "My lord, I have been full of sorrow since the death of David. I've tried to bear it as best I can, but it will not do. I've decided to take holy vows. Eva knows of a nunnery close by where I can say them. I should like to go there. Today."

Le Gros placed his hand over his heart, a look of surprise passing over his ruddy face. "Alys, it breaks my heart that life has parted you and David in such a cruel way."

"I know. I know you miss David as much as I do. You will understand then why I wish to dedicate the rest of my life to the saying of prayers for his soul and the souls of all his family."

This lit up Le Gros' eyes. A nun saying prayers day and night was sure to wash away many of the sins he had committed in his lifetime. Men like him paid fortunes for nuns and monks to pray for them, and here he was getting it for free.

"Then as your guardian, for you are my nephew's widow, I say you can go."

I smiled and glanced at Eva, who smiled back. "Eva has agreed to come with me. The abbess there is her mother's cousin."

Strongbow frowned at this. "Is it not dangerous?"

Eva shook her head. "It is not far. Just over the river. And you will come with us, yes? To say farewell and keep us safe." Slowly, she smiled.

Oh, I couldn't have picked her words better myself. For Strongbow to say no now would be akin to him admitting that he couldn't keep his wife safe in the lands he was declaring as his.

William Ferrand stepped forward. "A large group of us could go. If God has called Alys to his convent, we should do all we can to help her."

Strongbow gave his new bride a warm smile. "Of course we will go. Yes, Le Gros. Call up the knights. We ride within the hour."

★

The journey to the nunnery didn't take long, for it was only on the other side of the river and the bridge was not too far away from the city itself. Far from it being dangerous, the path was clear. Not a single warrior, spear or sword stood in our way, only a few shepherds who quickly hurried into the hills with their sheep once they spotted us.

The nunnery itself at Kilculliheen was smaller than I expected. The church was the focal point, and then around it were a few scattered houses where the nuns lived, a storeroom and a shed for the cows and goats. Poor fare for a nunnery that had been founded by a king. My, Diarmait was miserly – a trait he'd probably inherited from Máelmórda.

On seeing such a large group riding toward them, two of the nuns screamed and ran inside. This brought the abbess out. If she had been afraid on hearing the screams, she did not show it, for her weathered face was the picture of calm serenity by the time we reached the gate. Recognising Diarmait and Domhnall, who had decided to come with us, she raised a hand in greeting.

"Welcome," she said. "How may I be of service this fine day?"

Eva urged her horse forward. "Good day, Abbess Darlughdach. This is my friend Alys, who wishes to take holy vows."

Abbess Darlughdach took us all in, then gestured for me to come to her. I dismounted my horse, and at my request, Eva did the same.

"All friends of Leinster are welcome here," the abbess said, "and we do have space for a new novice, change these em-dashes to spaced en-dashes "trade has suffered here these last months with there being so much talk of war. An extra mouth to feed will be a great burden upon us."

Diarmait grunted something about already having given her money but still handed her a purse of silver. Strongbow did the same. "This is for my men who have fallen. I would like some prayers said on their behalf."

The abbess stared at Strongbow's purse, twice as big as

Diarmait's, and raised an eyebrow. "Of course, my lord. Of course. If you give me the names, I shall have my nuns dedicate a special mass on their behalf."

Another of the nuns came forward with a piece of parchment and took down the names that Strongbow called. While this was being done, the abbess led me and Eva toward one of the houses behind the church. "I will show you your room, Alys. On the bed, there are the clothes we expect you to wear while you are training."

As we reached the stone house, the abbess opened the door. The room was dark and plain with only two small beds inside. "Sister Ruth will be your companion."

"Where is she?"

"At prayer right now. Why don't you get dressed and then I will introduce you to everyone?"

Nodding, I reached out to hold Eva's hand. "Will you help me with the clothing? And then I can give you my clothes which I will no longer need. I would like you to give them to those in Waterford who are without."

Eva nodded, and the abbess gave her a warm smile. "I'll be by the church."

Once the abbess closed the door, I took off my cloak. Removing my water skin from my belt, I opened the lid. "Here, Eva, take a drink of water. It's not good to be thirsty when you are with child."

"Thank you, Alys." Eva took the waterskin and drank.

I sat down, and hiding my face in my hands, I used my witch-magic to transform. Then, I took hold of Eva's hand for a moment. Awkwardly, she snatched it away, for I'd held her too tight and too long. But it was too late. I had changed myself into Eva and then Eva into me. As I raised my head, I took Eva in. The new Eva who looked like Alys. It was strange to look at myself like this. At my black curls and pale face. At my beauty.

"What have you done?" Eva said. "What have you done to your face? Why do you look like me?"

Eva rushed toward me, instinctively knowing she was in danger.

Her fingers gripped my neck, her fingernails scratched my cheeks. Oh, she was feisty, this one. I cowered underneath her, not answering, just letting her hit me, until she suddenly stopped.

As she did this, she stepped away from me and stared around the room. "Where am I?"

"You don't remember?" I asked, gazing up at her, using my witch-magic to hide the scratches she'd just given me.

"No." She shook her head, her eyes widening with fright. The potion of forgetfulness had taken hold now. She was devoid of all memory. Of everything that had ever happened to her.

"Your name is Alys," I said. "You lost your husband in battle, and you told me that you wished to take your vows at this nunnery so you could pray for his soul." I pressed my hand gently onto her stomach. "You are with child also."

"And you are?"

"I'm Eva." I smiled sweetly. "My husband is Richard de Clare, Earl of Pembroke, and once my father dies, he will be King of Leinster. Your husband fought for mine, and so he has paid your way into the nunnery. You will be treated well here. You have my word."

She frowned as she looked around the room.

"You must take your clothes off now. Here are the novice robes you must wear instead."

"I… I don't understand what is happening to me."

"Can you really not remember anything?"

"No. Not really. I mean, I know how to speak, and I understand what it is to take holy vows, though I can't remember wanting to take them. But… I can't remember the names of my father and mother. Where I lived. I can't even remember the name of my husband."

"His name was David. You loved him very much. His death has caused you to lose your memory. With time and prayer, I'm sure you will make a full recovery." Holding out the novice robes, I placed them in her hands. "Now, you need to get dressed. Give me your clothes. And your rings and necklace too."

In a daze, Eva put on the new robes and handed over the ones she had removed. Her fancy cloak and silk dress as well as five rings and a gold necklace.

Just as she had finished getting ready, another nun came running into the room. She was young with plump cheeks and rosebud lips. "Hello, Alys," she said cheerfully. "I'm Sister Ruth. I'll take you into the church and introduce you to everyone."

The real Eva gave me a worried glance, but I gestured for her to move along. "I'll come and visit you soon, Alys."

Sister Ruth closed the door as they left, chattering about the church and the other nuns. Quickly, I undressed, put on Eva's dress, cloak and jewels, and then made my way back to the church.

The abbess was there, talking to the other knights and taking coins of silver and gold to say prayers for them too. Another Sister followed the abbess, taking down the names on her scroll, ink now splattered all over her hands.

"Abbess Darlughdach," I said, "can I speak with you for a moment?"

The abbess nodded, though I could tell she would much rather be taking more of the knights' silver.

"About Alys. She is a dear friend of mine," I said. "And she is with child."

"Oh." The abbess raised an eyebrow.

"It is, however, not her husband's. That is why she has come here. Do everything you can for her in this trying time and, when the baby is born, send for me. I will take care of it."

I passed over one of the silver rings Eva had given me, which the abbess squirrelled away in her pocket.

"That's for keeping this secret. She doesn't want the men to know that she slept with another. She doesn't want it to taint the memory of her husband."

The abbess gave a sigh and shook her head. "The way of sin is strong within our sex. I'll work her hard so she atones, but have no worry, I will look after her and send for you when the baby arrives."

"Only me, mind you," I added. "No one else. If I cannot come myself, my messenger will be wearing my ring." I showed her the gold one with the purple stone. "If you have kept the baby a secret, the ring will be yours."

The abbess nodded again.

"Thank you, Abbess Darlughdach. You are very good."

"No, child, it is you who is the most deserving. Thank you for bringing her here."

Giving her a kiss on the cheek, I walked outside the monastery as Eva.

"You took too long, daughter," Diarmait chastised me as I reached him.

I bowed my head as a sign of contrition, but inwardly I seethed. What an old goat to speak to me in this manner. That was the first thing that was going to change going forward.

"All is well?" William Ferrand asked as I mounted my horse. "Alys is settled?"

"Oh yes," I replied, making sure to speak in Eva's accent. "Alys was quite delighted with the nunnery, and she will be very well looked after. I promise."

Isolde

Seir Kieran

When I arrived back at the monastery, Siobhan, Méabh and Báine said nothing about my disappearance.

At first, I thought it was because they didn't want to push me, or perhaps that they worried asking questions would only make me run away again.

In many ways, these thoughts made their kindness harder to bear, and with no Leofwynn or Gisela here, and no Cuan, I felt more alone than ever. I knew I should apologise for leaving without telling them. I should be trying to bring us back together, but every time I was tempted, I could never bring myself to do it.

This led to a realisation. They weren't asking me questions because they were waiting for Colmon to wake up, and the truth was, I only felt strong enough to have this conversation once… and so I let the awkward silences linger. I let the distance grow.

In the meantime, I rehearsed over and over what I would say.

Cuan and I had said we would talk to the Descendants together, but that couldn't be. It was not his responsibility to explain who he was. It was mine. And so I decided once Colmon woke up, I would tell them the truth. All of it. I would tell them about Cuan and what he meant to me, that he was a good person, that he wasn't like the other Fomorians. He didn't even know that he was one until I told him.

And so, instead of talking, the four of us kept busy with

preparations to leave the monastery. The mortals were all gone. Most of the animals had been given away, though some chickens and goats were coming with us, and the cart was loaded with possessions. Finally, it seemed they had got themselves organised. All that was left to do was harvest the last of the crops in the garden, plot our path west, and then once Colmon woke up, we'd be on our way. Away somewhere safe where the vision I'd had wouldn't come true. *A future where I didn't kill everyone around me.*

On the fifth day of this strange life of half-silences and packing, Méabh came to me in the garden.

"Come to the hall, Isolde. Colmon is about to wake."

Glad but also nervous that things were finally about to change, I made my way into the hall. My stomach churned as I went over my well-rehearsed story. The story of how Cuan and I had met, and how he had helped me, and how I discovered his fire-magic. Fear came to me too. *What if they didn't believe me.*

"Is he up yet?" Siobhan asked as she came into the hall behind me.

Báine shook her head. "Soon."

I sat at the table and took an apple from the bowl. "Are we ready to go once he is?"

"Yes," Méabh answered.

My breath caught as she said this. I wasn't supposed to use my gifts on Descendants, but my harpist gift came to me without me calling it. *She was lying.*

Lifting my eyes to meet her gaze, I set down the apple. "Why did you just lie?"

"I didn't."

"You did. And you lied again. I can tell."

"You aren't supposed to use your gifts on us," Méabh answered.

"I didn't mean to, but that's not the point. Why aren't you ready to leave?"

I stared around at the three of them and at the furtive looks they gave each other. What were they hiding?

Báine took a deep breath. "Perhaps you should tell us why you left first? We were worried sick about you."

"Stop, Báine." Siobhan held out her hands. "We are supposed to be waiting for Colmon."

"No, she can tell us now." Báine tilted her head and folded her arms. "Come on, Isolde, tell us why you left."

How quickly her kindness had gone. There was so much anger in Báine's voice now that it took me by surprise. "I… I had a vision."

"A vision? A vision of where that man would be?"

This revelation startled me. *She had followed me?*

Of course she had. That's why they hadn't been worried when I returned. They *knew* I was safe, but this meant Báine had watched me with Cuan. How much had she seen? Had she listened to our conversations? *Watched us kiss?*

I shouldn't have left without telling them, but I was angry now too. "You tell me off for using my gift on you, but really, you've been using yours to spy on me."

"After what happened to Leofwynn and Gisela, you thought you could just leave and we wouldn't try to find you?" This time it was Méabh who answered, only she didn't speak, she shouted. "Isolde, everything we do is for you. We do everything to help you. And you just left. We thought you'd been taken."

"I'm sorry about that. I am. I saw—"

"I tracked you as soon as we realised you were missing," Báine interrupted. "And when I found you, I found you with him. The same man who left you here last year. Do you love him? If so, why have you been keeping him a secret?"

"I didn't know he'd be there. I was going to Waterford. The vision showed me a battle there… and a Fomorian. I wanted to see if my vision was true."

"But if that's the case, why didn't you tell us? We would have gone with you?"

Oh, how could I answer this? There were too many reasons. Because I didn't want to tell them about Cuan. Because I didn't want them to die trying to save me. Because I had lied to them for so long, I couldn't bring myself to admit all I'd withheld.

"What's his name?" Báine asked.

"Seeing as you clearly were watching us the whole night, why don't you tell me?"

"Stop it, the two of you," Siobhan said, cutting in on whatever response Báine was about to give. "Let us calm down. We must wait for Colmon to wake."

My anger only grew at this. Why wait for Colmon? So he could tell me off? I was about to storm out of the room, run away from the lot of them, when something caught my ear.

"Shh," I pressed my finger to my lip. Something was moving outside. I'd heard footsteps. And now there was a strange smell. "Someone is coming toward the monastery. More than one."

"It could be someone wanting to trade for the animals?" Siobhan said.

"No." I shook my head. "It's not… it's a Fomorian. I…" Trailing away, I knew what it was. It was a Fomorian. *The Fomorian*. He was close by. He'd found us.

Using my warrior speed, I ran toward Colmon's room. "Let's put him in the cart," I shouted as I ran along the corridor. "We need to get out of here now."

As I slammed the door open and stormed into the room, I rushed over to Colmon, who was lying on the bed, still sleeping, but it was his hair that stopped me moving. It was completely white.

"When did this happen?" I asked Méabh as she ran into the room behind me. "Why didn't you tell me about his hair? We could have left days ago."

"He didn't want us to tell you," Méabh said. "He'll be awake soon. Then he'll explain."

"No." I shook my head, suddenly understanding. "You lied to me because you never intended to leave, isn't that it? You're all fools. You need to leave, Méabh. You too, Báine and Siobhan. In my vision, you are all dead, and it was my fault. I lose control."

Báine's eyes filled with tears, but she did not move.

"Go, Báine." I shoved her back. "Your mother gave her life to save mine. Don't let me be the one who is responsible for taking your life too. Please go."

Báine bit her lip but slowly she pushed my hand away. "We've trained you now, Isolde. You won't hurt us. The vision was a warning, that's all. Look around you. There are no mortals for a start. Already we have changed what's going to happen."

"Are you so sure that you're willing to gamble your life? What if I lose control? What if I—"

"We're staying," Méabh said. "This Fomorian is here now. It's time for us to destroy him. No more running. No more hiding."

No. No. They had to leave. They didn't understand. They hadn't seen the vision, the destruction… the death.

"Don't worry, Isolde. We all die in the end. Everyone here has decided to see this through."

I turned around.

Colmon was awake. Old and frail as he was, he sat up in his bed and stared at me.

"If you are scared, you can go, Isolde. I told you before that the burden on you is too great. But we are staying."

"Colmon… but you are too weak."

He laughed at this. "I am weaker than I would like, yes, but I am a warrior, Isolde. You think I can lie in a cart and run from my enemy? You think I could let myself die peacefully of old age, while you live on to fight alone? No. Never."

He moved forward, shoulders sagging, but as he drew on his gift, his shoulders straightened, and he stood up. Colmon the warrior was here once more. "How many can you sense, Isolde?"

Using my warrior gift, I felt for the danger outside. It was worse than I imagined. "I sense… not one but two Fomorians. And there are mortals. At least twenty, but I'm not sure."

"Twenty-nine," Colmon answered. "And all with evil in their hearts." He held out his hand and smiled. "Now, Isolde. Pass me my sword."

Angelo

Seir Kieran

"They've all gone inside," Luchóg said. "All four of them."

Smiling, I rubbed the stone in my pocket. This was the news I'd been hoping for. "Thank you, Luchóg. Now, go and ready the men. It's time."

Patience. It was the virtue most often required to win.

Armies charged in. Kings made decrees, and their warriors rushed to follow their commands. But assassins – they hid, they waited. They watched. They held their breath until the right moment.

That's what I had been waiting for. The right moment.

And it was now upon me.

But before I acted, I had to go over what I'd already learned.

One, there were no warriors here.

I'd sent Cecile to the outskirts of the monastery yesterday. Placing her along the walls as a few shepherds haggled over the goats the Descendants were selling, all but begging a warrior to reveal themselves. None had appeared.

Gormflaith had told us once that the warriors could smell our fire, and that was why we never used it when we were trying to escape Broccan. Cecile had not used hers in over a decade, nevertheless, I was sure a warrior would smell her from so close a range.

Two, there were only four Descendants.

Yesterday, I had also sent Luchóg into the monastery to buy one of their chickens. He offered to help them pack up their cart.

During this time, he watched as the four women who lived at the monastery walked between the gardens and stables and the monastery itself. One with a rounded face and light brown hair, another with short, dark brown hair, and another with long black hair that reached her waist. And then, of course, a young woman with red hair tied back in a plait. *Isolde.*

During this time, a local woman had come by, seeking a remedy for her child's cough. Only one Descendant, the one with light brown hair, had tended to them.

Three, this Descendant was a healer.

That left two Descendants whose gifts were a mystery. Luchóg said that the short-haired one walked around the monastery with a gloomy face, while the one with the long, dark hair seemed angry. Druids, perhaps? Weapon-makers? Harpists? They were the final unknowns.

And of course, there was Isolde. I did not fully understand her gift. I knew only that she had been dead and was now alive. Luchóg said she had spent her time digging up vegetables and barely spoke to the others.

Four, the Descendants were leaving Seir Kieran.

This meant I had to act quickly. I'd rather there not be any unknowns, but timing was everything, and the right time was now.

Closing my eyes, I drew upon my harpist gift and approached Cecile.

"It's time."

My cousin sat up, eyes uncertain. She'd been difficult to control since we'd left Waterford. She was intelligent, and she questioned often where we were going and why. It might have been easier if it were only me, but the fuidir made her uneasy. They looked at her, leered in her direction, and this led to fear and hesitation. Today, I'd kept the fuidir away from her, and slowly, slowly I'd built upon the emotions I wanted her to feel.

"Are you sure Cuan is there?" she asked.

"Yes, I'm certain. The men saw him last night. These Descendants have taken him prisoner. We must set him free before they kill him."

Cecile nodded, but she was frightened. Underneath her fear, however, there was anger at the Descendants for taking one of our kind against his will. I pulled at this righteous anger and made it burn stronger than her fear.

"What must I do to help free him?" she asked.

"You must use your fire-magic, Cecile." I took her hand in mine. "We will draw them out, and once they're out in the open, we will trap them."

"What if the Descendants come for us before we can do that? What do I do? What... what if my fire-magic doesn't come?"

"You kill them, Cecile. Any way that you can."

I held out one of the knives the fuidir had stolen from a dead warrior in Waterford, keeping back two for myself. "Take it."

"No. I can't. I can't use a knife."

"Don't you remember the years we had to run from Broccan?"

She nodded, but she didn't really understand. She'd been so young back then, and Máelmórda had never wanted to worry her. He'd made everything a game. Every time we left our home, it was an adventure and a chance to see somewhere new.

"Don't you realise what he would have done if he had found us? He'd have ripped us apart limb by limb. Even you. And that's what they're going to do to Cuan if we don't rescue him."

Pulling at her anger again, she took the knife.

"Now, we will go to the monastery. Once there, I will send the fuidir into the buildings to drive the Descendants out. That is when we will use our fire-magic to destroy our enemies once and for all."

Cecile stood and walked toward me. She was ready. *Finally.*

Holding hands, we made our way into the clearing where the fuidir were waiting.

"Men, I am glad to see that you are ready," I said. "I told you there were devils here, and here they are. Tonight, we fight them. Tonight, you will see God act through me and Cecile, and salvation will be won for all."

The men smiled. I had given them anger too. Rage. The desire to see death and destruction.

"All you must do is kill three of the devil-women. The red-haired woman is the only one you must leave alone. She is too dangerous and only I can destroy her. Do you all understand?"

Again, they nodded.

"Luchóg has told me the women have all gone inside, so now is our chance. We will walk to the monastery together. Once we reach it, I want half of you to enter the buildings. Kill any you come across. If you can't kill them, chase them out to where we are. The other half are to stay close to me and Cecile, except for you four." I pointed at three of the most murderous fuidir as well as Luchóg. "You hide behind the wall. If you see an opportunity to attack, you can take it, otherwise you will wait until I call you."

The fuidir, delighted, nodded in agreement.

Plan made, we walked through the forest, the fuidir keeping a few paces ahead of me and Cecile.

With my harpist gift, I sought out the people inside the monastery. Feeling for their emotions. I felt anger. Pain. Worry.

Good. Heightened emotions were easier to sense.

As we climbed over the boundary wall, the men split into two groups as I had told them. The first half ran into the courtyard, some then moving to the front door, while others slipped in through the church.

"I don't like it," Cecile said. "It's too quiet."

She looked set to cry with fear, but I savoured this sensation. This feeling of anticipation that came before the carnage. They would come out soon. They had to.

It didn't take long.

Just as I suspected, the four women soon hurried out. Isolde gazed around the gardens, her hands holding the healer Descendant's hand, while the other two moved ahead of them. The one with the short hair had water spinning in her hands. Ah, *cupbearer*.

The other held out her hands, and a mist began to swirl around the group of women, thin tendrils wrapping themselves around their bodies. *Witch.*

"Now, Cecile. Use your fire-magic."

Using my harpist gift, I heightened her fear. That's all I wanted her to feel now. Like an animal trapped, I wanted her to panic.

She held up her hands, and fire burst from them. She set the stables alight and then formed balls of flame in her hands, which she threw at the Descendants. Beyond the flames, the four fuidir sneaked along the other side of the wall to get into a better position. This was good. Very good.

I ran forward, using my flames to strike at the cupbearer. The mist was thickening, but I could still make them out.

"Now!" I shouted at the fuidir behind the wall. "Kill them!"

Three of the four fuidir jumped over the wall and sprinted toward the Descendants, knives and swords out.

"Cecile, strike at the cupbearer!"

Cecile did as I asked, while I made my fire slither along the ground, and through the noise of the fuidir's roars, I could hear the Descendants screaming. The fuidir were close now. So close to the women.

Then, there was a blur. Something moving. The fuidir, who had been running, dropped to the ground, and through the white of the mist, blood spurted in the air as one by one they fell.

A warrior was here after all.

Isolde

Seir Kieran

We did as Colmon asked and let the mortal men chase us to the front of the monastery, while he killed them off, one by one, as they gleefully hunted us down.

Colmon had told us this needed to be done first. *It was often true that killing the leader of an army was the smartest move*, he had said. *But when facing such a foe, one cannot afford to have enemies fighting us from behind.*

I should have offered to help him, but the words wouldn't leave my mouth. Last year, I had killed the man in the bruidean when he had tried to kill me, but to seek out my enemies, to creep up behind them and drive my sword in their back… I did not know if I could do that.

With no more mortals in sight, we moved to the front door, and here we waited for Colmon to join us. All was going to plan, but I was still afraid. Outside there were more mortals wishing to kill us… as well as two Fomorians. I could smell them standing by the stables, even though one of their scents was faint.

Footsteps in the hallway. Coming our way.

Taking out my sword, I pointed it toward the noise.

I could fight for my friends. I could do this.

To my relief, it was Colmon who turned the corner, and I returned my sword to its sheath. *Fool.* If I had used my warrior gift instead of panicking, I would have known it was him.

"That's all of them who came inside," he said, "but there are more outside, plus the two Fomorians."

"What should we do?" I asked.

"We need to kill them. That is why we stayed and what we promised we would do." Colmon looked at Méabh and Báine. "Are you ready?"

"Yes," they answered.

"Then I will run to the back of the monastery and then into the forest. From there, I will circle around so I can attack the Fomorians from behind while they are fighting you. Keep Isolde safe."

Méabh and Báine nodded, but I didn't like that they were being asked to protect me. Pushing aside my fear, I shook my head. "I can fight too."

"And you may have to, Isolde, but not to start with." Colmon reached out and touched my cheek with his hand. "We are hundreds of years old, and we have fought them before. Never in the past would we have allowed someone as young as you to fight, and never when someone was so new to learning their gift. So let us do what we're trained to do before you put yourself in harm's way."

Colmon removed his hand, gave us all a nod, then ran back along the hallway.

"They're by the stables," Méabh said to Báine as she peered through the door. "Are you ready?"

"Yes. I will summon the mist once we step outside."

"And I will call the water." Méabh stared at Siobhan and then at me. "You two stay behind us. We must fight for as long as we can to give Colmon time to get behind them. Understood?"

I still didn't like this, but Siobhan took hold of my hand and held it tight. "You stay with me, Isolde," she whispered. "Méabh and Báine know what they're doing."

Tightening my grip on Siobhan's hand, we walked outside. The two Fomorians were to our left, with ten men gathered around them, knives and spears in their hands. I recognised them. I'd seen some of these faces before – in my vision where they had tracked Gisela and Leofwynn through the forest. I felt sick upon seeing them, but it was the sight of the male Fomorian who made me shake. This was the Fomorian who had trapped me and Affraic. *The one from my visions.* I feared him, yes, but I hated him too.

As soon as Méabh set foot on the grass, she drew water from the ground and the well to herself, while Báine called the mist. It thickened quickly, swirling around our bodies as if it were a shield between ourselves and the Fomorians. But it was no true shield, just a cloak, and I knew the fire could still find us. Burn us. Kill us.

As I turned to face the Fomorians, flames smashed against the stables, and the wood and the thatch over the roof caught alight. Seconds later, a bolt of fire hit Méabh. She used the water spinning in her hands to stop it from burning her, then quickly she summoned more water, until a great ball of it swirled between her hands.

"Now!" one of the Fomorians screamed. "Kill them!"

Through the haze of mist, three men jumped over the wall and ran toward us, the gleam of steel in their hands.

Another blast of fire soared through the air. Screaming, Méabh drew up more water as the fire moved closer, and finally she pushed it back.

Méabh smiled at this victory, but no sooner had she put those flames out than a trail of fire sped along the grass toward us, wanting to catch and encircle us. Just like on Rathlin. I remembered how the fire had formed a wall around us, trapping Affraic and me inside.

"Get back!" I shouted, dragging Siobhan and Báine with me.

Méabh used her gift to draw more water and threw it at the fire snaking along the grass. Still it inched closer, the two Fomorians stronger than her alone, and the men who were running toward us were getting closer.

I had to do something. Had to.

You. It is you who did this, Isolde. I told you that you must learn to control your gift. You tried, but not hard enough.

Colmon's words from my vision gave me pause. I didn't want their deaths to be my fault, but I had to fight now. I had to fight, or else we'd all die anyway.

Quickly, I sped toward the men running our way and drew my

sword. I felt for the knot in my stomach and pulled on my warrior gift. These men were not innocent. They had killed Gisela and Leofwynn, and they had come here to kill us. My sword danced in my hands as I reached them, and blood filled the air. One. Two. Three. Throat. Stomach. Chest. Down they fell onto the grass.

"Méabh, look out!"

It was Báine who screamed. The male Fomorian had taken a knife out of his cloak. Spinning it in his hand, he threw it, using his fire-magic to propel it toward Méabh.

"Méabh! Get out of the way!" I screamed.

I ran toward her, using my warrior speed, but before I could reach her, the knife plunged into her chest, and the force of it flung her backward. A blast of fire followed, and with no water in her hands, her body burned.

No. No. Not Méabh.

Grief and shame burned through me. I should never have let her fight for me. *I* was the girl to destroy fire. *This was my duty.* It was time for me to stop being afraid. Closing my eyes for a moment, I summoned a storm. Above me, clouds formed, thickened. The wind blew away the mist and drove the fire back toward the Fomorians. There was no more hiding now. It was time for me to fight.

"Run, Siobhan," I said. "You too, Báine. Leave us."

"No, Isolde," Báine said. "I'm staying. I can help."

"No. Please. Go."

The Fomorian laughed, and another ball of flame shot forward, this one aimed at me and Siobhan. Pushing Siobhan out of the way, I focused on my gift and pulled the knot in my stomach tighter. *Closer*, I whispered to the storm. *Hurry*.

The clouds swirled above me, and hailstones began to fall. Light at first. Then heavier. The laughter faded, and the two Fomorians ran into the forest, knowing the damage the storm was about to bring.

"Scared?" I called after them, my anger growing. "The last time you saw a storm like this, it nearly killed you. I know. I saw it."

The ten men who had been standing guard around the Fomorians screamed as the hailstones fell upon them. They tried to follow their masters but didn't make it to the protection of the wall or the forest in time. The hailstones smashed into them, crushing legs and arms and skulls. I ran past them as they fell, swerving through the hailstones, and then jumped over the wall.

The two Fomorians were just ahead of me, setting the trees on fire as they went, but still I followed. Colmon had to be close by now. Together, we could trap the two Fomorians.

"Why are you running?" I shouted. "You came to find me. Here I am."

The male Fomorian came to a stop in a clearing just ahead of me. Twisting his body, he threw a ball of fire at me, then another. I swerved, moving so fast I could hardly breathe. Skidding to a stop by an oak tree, I noticed him watching me, a small smile growing on his lips. Opening his hand, he blew, and like a rope, a bolt of flame soared through the air and circled me.

I held out my hands, trying to summon the water. It had responded to me at the river outside Waterford. It had to come to me now. But I couldn't hear it. Couldn't feel it.

I told you that you must learn to control your gift. You tried, but not hard enough.

Quickly, I reached for my witch gift instead and searched for the surrounding trees, the roots, the branches, asking them to move and shield me. A large branch slammed down on the ground between me and the Fomorian, but he slid out of the way in time and threw another ball of fire my way. I jumped to the side, but I was losing control now. I could feel the knot in my stomach loosening despite my efforts to hold it tight.

Then I heard something. Someone running and running fast.

"Colmon!" I shouted. *It had to be him.* "Colmon!"

"Hurry, Luchóg!"

As I turned toward the noise, a spear flew toward me. A mortal man with sharp eyes and long, thin hair grinned as the shaft left his hands.

I turned my body to get out of the way, but then more fire hurtled toward me. I froze for a moment, my instincts at odds over which way to move.

Spinning away from the fire, I waited for the spear to hit.

But it thudded against someone else.

Falling, I turned to find that the mortal man was dead, Colmon's long knife in his throat, but the spear… the spear had pierced Colmon's chest. His chest instead of mine, and he collapsed to the ground. "My gift," he said. "It's faded, Isolde. I'm so sorry… I couldn't get… to you… in time."

I crawled toward him. I could pull the spear out of his body and heal him. *If I could just touch him.* Black phlegm was gathering in my mouth, and my arms were beginning to shake, but I had enough strength left to save him. *I had to have enough.*

Before I could reach him, the female Fomorian moved out from behind a tree, held out her hands, and used her fire to build a wall of flame around him.

"That's it, Cecile," the male Fomorian shouted. "Kill him!"

The female Fomorian stared at the fire, but for some reason she didn't make the flames grow.

"Do it, Cecile. Now!" the other Fomorian screamed.

Cecile shook, tears streaming down her cheeks. "I can't, Angelo… I can't…"

Taking hold of my sword, I stood and tried to gather my strength before charging at Cecile, when Báine dashed out from the haze of smoke. The roots of the tree beside Cecile wrapped around her feet and dragged her down. Báine kept running, knife in hand and ready to plunge into Cecile's chest, and then suddenly she stopped. "Neasa, is that you?"

Cecile's eyes widened and with this she threw a bolt of flames toward Báine, who flung herself to the ground. Báine seemed to disappear, her dress crumpling flat to the ground, but then a crow moved out from under the fabric and flew into the smoke-filled air. Cecile, sobbing, ran away.

I was glad Báine had escaped, for the trees burned all around me now. Sweat dripping down my arms and face, I could barely breathe, but I had to get to Colmon. I had to get him away from the fire that circled him.

To do that, I needed my cupbearer gift to work. Summoning the water again, I felt it this time. Water from the ground moved into my hands, but before I could manipulate it, more fire found me. It circled me, the walls around me high and burning the lower branches of the oak tree that stood over me.

The male Fomorian, Angelo, walked inside the circle of fire. His golden eyes took me in, and reaching forward, he thrust a knife into my stomach and dragged the blade down. Gasping, I fell to my knees, unable to move as he took out another knife from his cloak and aimed for my chest. *My heart.*

Using the last vestige of strength within me, I pushed my hand upward. The blade pierced it instead of my chest. Angelo stared at me, his eyes glistening with anger, when something grabbed at his leg. At first, I thought it was a root or branch, though I had not called it. *It had to be Báine.* She'd come back to help me.

As Angelo was dragged along the ground, the wall of fire disappeared, and I pulled the knife out of my stomach and healed the wound there. I had to get out of here.

"Báine, run."

But it wasn't Báine who was fighting the Fomorian. It was a wolf. A large wolf with blue eyes was biting at Angelo's leg.

The Fomorian kicked it, causing the wolf to yelp, and a ball of fire grew between his hands.

"Get away from him!" I screamed.

A great wind blew up, hurling Angelo against one of the trees. He smacked his left shoulder against the trunk and gasped as he fell to the ground. I stood then, and using the knife I had just taken out of my stomach, I threw it at him. It sliced Angelo on the side of his neck, and he screamed as he tried to stop the blood from spilling out. The roots along the forest floor slithered toward him too, wrapping around his legs and trying to drag him under, but using his fire-magic, he burned through the roots and ran into the smoke.

Collapsing onto the ground, I felt myself fading, and more black liquid poured into my mouth. I was close to exhaustion, close to blacking out, but I couldn't give up. Not yet.

Rolling onto my side, I pulled the knife from my hand, put it into my belt, and crawled toward Colmon. As soon as I reached him, I knew he was dead. Already gone. Tears streamed down my cheeks, and I lay there, drifting in and out of consciousness, when I heard a noise.

The wolf that lay on the grass… it was whimpering.

What had caused it to help me?

I forced myself back onto my hands and knees and crawled over to see if it was alive. It was. Barely.

"Be careful," said a voice.

I turned to find a woman with long dark hair and green eyes staring at me. "You must heal him in his true form or else you will hurt him more."

I was too tired to run, certainly too tired to fight, but for some reason I was not afraid of this woman. "What do you mean, *true form*?"

The woman ignored my questions and crouched down beside him. "He has travelled hundreds of miles to be with you, and we found you. Just in time. But now we must hurry and get out of this fire."

She moved over to Colmon and transformed him into a crow. "You carry him. I'll carry the wolf."

The two of us hurried out of the burning forest, moving downhill and toward the boundary wall of the monastery. As I climbed over the wall, I was glad to find that the monastery still stood, and that aside from the stables, nothing was on fire. The grass was not filled with dead bodies, and Siobhan and Báine were alive.

Setting down the crow on the grass, the witch transformed Colmon back to himself.

"Senna, is that you?" Báine came over to us, limping at first, and then trying to run.

The witch, Senna, if that was her name, knelt on the grass, and as she touched the wolf with her hands, it began to transform. Fur became skin. Paws became hands and feet.

"Broccan?" I stared at the man in front of me. He was unconscious, but breathing. "Broccan." I said his name again. I couldn't believe it. Collapsing at his side, I wept and I wept. *Broccan was alive.*

Cuan

Dúnmór

Sleep did not come to me easily after the death of the two Leinster hostages. Two nights had passed, and I hardly slept as I waited for more of the dark liquid to come to my mouth. For blood to seep from my gums and nails. For my lips to turn black.

So far, I was well, and nothing had happened to make me suspect I was dying like my mother, and yet I feared it. Not the dying, but in dying the way she had.

On this second day, as a faint light began to build on the horizon, I walked outside and checked myself over. There was no more black liquid. No blood. No aches or pains.

It had been a warning, that was all, and it was a warning I had to heed. With so much turmoil over the last few days, I had nearly lost control. The fall of Waterford, worrying about Bjorn and also Brenna. Missing Isolde, and then Ruaidrí bringing out the three Leinster hostages to kill. It had been too much, and as a result, I had nearly lost everything, for not only could I have killed myself, but I could have killed everyone standing around me. The fire, I had felt it in my hand. Had felt the blade warm against my skin.

Knowing I could not fall back to sleep, I dressed and walked to the river. Keeping on only my shirt, I plunged myself into it as if the coldness could somehow kill the fire inside of me. As I sank under the water, I remembered the lessons Godred had taught me.

How to detach myself from reality. How not to feel. To breathe and be apart from the world.

It was harder now than it used to be.

As a child and then as a young man, I'd had very few friends, but all of us were warriors and had accepted we might die. We had no sympathy for each other because we had none for ourselves, and that had made death easier to understand. I had wanted for nothing, because I was given nothing.

Here, in Connacht, I wanted.

I wanted Isolde. I wanted there to be peace. I wanted to be free.

Until this war was over, I had to push these feelings deep down. Finding a way to restore peace to Connacht came first. Then I had to tell my father that I could no longer do what he wished of me. I was no king. No ruler, and the truth was I could not kill my uncle in cold blood anymore.

Doing this would mean breaking my vow to my father, something I was loath to do, but I couldn't live this life anymore. It was tearing me apart – killing me – and for the first time I found myself wanting to live.

Feeling calmer, I waded out of the water and dressed. It was dawn now. The men would be rising and getting ready to train, and I would need to be ready to speak with my uncle about our strategy once we reached Dublin. The scouts were due back within the next couple of days, and with them, news of the various paths open to Diarmait and Strongbow.

As I made my way onto the path, I saw Osán standing there, waiting. His presence startled me. Like a bad omen, he had reappeared the very moment I had decided to break my vow. It was as if Odin himself had spotted my weakness and was forcing me back into line.

"What are you doing here?" I asked more sharply than I should have.

"Your father sent me to fight for your uncle. Don't worry. Ruaidrí knows I'm coming."

"You're going to fight for Ruaidrí?"

"I'm a man of Connacht, and I have answered the call of the High King. Why shouldn't I be here?"

"Because you hate him."

"I do, but I'm still of Connacht and know we must win this battle against the Anglo-Normans. Hatred can wait."

I shook my head, already too irritated for lies. "Why don't you be honest, Osán, and just say you've come to watch over me?"

"That is true too."

I licked my lips and continued along the path. Osán didn't move. He simply stared at me, a strange smile on his lips.

"Your father has a message for you," he said once I passed him.

"Oh?"

"This is your time now. The army of Connacht is about to march to Dublin. You must use this link to your mother's kin to your advantage, which I hear is growing."

Coming to a stop, I turned my head.

"I heard about your speech before the Leinster hostages were executed," he explained. "You spoke well. Your father was most pleased. You stood up against Tigernán when your uncle could not. The warriors of Connacht will have noticed that. They will have noticed that your word carries more weight than a High King's. Once the pressure on Ruaidrí increases, which it will, you must tighten your hold further. You must push him to breaking point."

I didn't want to ask how I was supposed to do this. I didn't want that on my mind. All I knew was that I had to speak the truth.

"I don't want to follow my father's plan anymore, Osán. I don't want to overthrow Ruaidrí, and I don't want to be king."

Rather than Osán chastising me and calling me an oath-breaker, which I thought he would, he laughed. "We shall see, young prince. We shall see what you do when the crown is at your fingertips."

He was the one who walked past me then. I watched him as he reached the dun and greeted the men there. The older ones remembered him. Revered him. He was an experienced warrior who had won many victories for my grandfather. Even Ruaidrí, knowing that Osán despised him, would be glad to see him when riding out to war.

That evening, there was another feast. Five more armies we were waiting for, even though they'd been told to hurry, but for those kings who had arrived, my uncle had to put on a show.

Brenna at least was here tonight, and I waved her over to sit beside me at the top table.

Sitting in the chair beside mine, she groaned. "I can't wait for this baby to come. I can't even see my feet anymore."

Laughing, I put some food onto her plate, making sure to give her the best cuts and a variety of buttered vegetables. "How long do you think you have left?"

"Another cycle of the moon. Hopefully less."

"Then I shall not be here when you give birth."

"No, you shall be fighting." She picked at the meat. "If Bjorn did not survive… I think he must not have or else he would be here by now, then I will be alone."

"Don't say that. He might have made it to one of the ships, or he could—"

"Cuan, stop. I must be serious now. If Bjorn didn't survive, then I am alone and must make my own way in this world."

"I will look after you, Brenna."

She nodded but did not smile.

I knew what this meant right away. "You worry I might die too."

"I don't worry for myself. Just the baby. Like I've already said. All my family were in Waterford, and if Bjorn is dead, so are they. You're the only person left whom I can rely upon. I wish I didn't have to place that burden upon you, but there it is."

"Then if I die and Bjorn is dead, go to Godred."

Brenna snorted. "And be his thrall again?"

"If I am dead, say that the child is mine. Godred will take you in." I stared at her. "I am serious, Brenna. If I die, this is what I want you to do." I took the small silver ring from my finger that

Godred had given me after the death of Somerled. "Give him this, and he will think it is true."

Brenna took the ring. A flush of red coloured her cheeks, but even so, she put it in her pocket. "Everyone is talking about you, you know."

"Are they?"

"You did a good thing saving that boy."

"I didn't save them all, though. Is that what the people say? Do they blame me?"

"No. They say that King Tigernán conceded to you where he would not concede to the High King."

This was what Osán had told me the warriors would think, but I didn't want that. I shook my head. "That's just small talk. It doesn't mean anything."

"You need to be careful, don't you?" she whispered. Her eyes filled with worry, but this time I could not lie to her. She said that I was the only friend she had left. Well, apart from Isolde, she might be my only friend too.

"Yes."

"Then be careful."

"I will."

She took a piece of meat in her fingers, using it to cover her mouth. "And what about Dublin?"

"What about it?"

"Bjorn told me that Asculv was going to let Diarmait have you last summer. That he and Hálfdan betrayed you."

"That's true."

"Then not only are you in danger here, but you are in danger where you are going. Be careful, Cuan. Be careful."

She put the piece of meat in her mouth while I took a drink of ale. She was right. My father saw an opportunity, but Brenna saw the truth of it. There was danger in Dublin. Asculv would be a fool to think I didn't know what he'd done and might try to kill me before I even set foot in the city.

Breathing deeply, I took another drink.

Everything Brenna said was true. That was why I had to be careful and leave Ireland with Isolde once this war with the Anglo-Normans was over. I had tried to tell Osán earlier, but I would tell him again. Tomorrow.

This life I'd been living, it was finished.

"What is it?" Brenna asked.

"What?"

"You're smiling. Tell me why?"

Raising my glass, I smiled again. "I've made a decision, that's all. And I feel better for it."

Gormflaith

Waterford

The argument between the two factions only grew as the days passed. Anglo-Norman against the Irish who had invited them here.

As Eva, daughter of Diarmait, wife of Strongbow, I'd witnessed all of these rows and bitter words.

The crux of the matter was this: Diarmait and his son Domhnall wanted to march to Dublin immediately, but Strongbow wouldn't leave until the walls were repaired and the city was strong enough for a garrison of his men to hold Waterford against a counter-invasion.

"When will we march?" Diarmait snapped every morning.

"Soon," Strongbow replied, his voice remaining calm every time. "Soon, we will go, but only when we're ready."

For all Strongbow spoke about the walls, repairs and counter-invasions, this delay was a power play. Strongbow was making the man who had begged him to come over, beg again. In Chepstow, I'd not overly admired Strongbow. His courtship of Cecile and his endless piety had bored me, but here, as a warrior, he impressed. He was certainly not going to be pushed around by Diarmait, who was so used to getting his own way.

As I sat down for the evening, the same conversation started up again. I quickly removed myself to my bedroom, tired of the same argument and scathing looks – but if I had thought I'd escaped, I was wrong. In a fury, Diarmait stormed into my room while

Strongbow left the fort to examine the walls. Diarmait slapped me across the face as he passed. Hard enough to leave a welt on my cheek. "Can you not control your husband?" he seethed.

"Leave her, Father." Domhnall pressed his hand against my shoulder, which I supposed was meant to reassure me that Diarmait would not strike me again. Domhnall did this sometimes when Diarmait was in a foul mood – to reassure me. Not just me either, but Enna also, his blind half-sibling, who seemed to live in a state of perpetual anxiety, even more so when his father approached.

Somehow, Domhnall was immune to Diarmait's temper. I didn't know why, or what he'd done to be elevated so. Perhaps it really was as simple as Diarmait had loved his mother, but I guessed there was more to it than that. One day, I would find out, but now there were more pressing matters at hand.

"You want him to march to Dublin, Father?" I spoke demurely. Softly. Just how Eva spoke.

"Yes. We need to get there before Ruaidrí. If he gets to Dublin first, everything becomes more difficult."

"And why do you suppose Strongbow would listen to me?"

"I shouldn't have to spell that out for you," Diarmait snarled, but at this he sat on my chair and closed his eyes. He truly was the very worst of men… but he did know war… which meant it was time to move the Anglo-Norman army to where he needed it to go.

"I should like to help you, Father, but I cannot do so unless I know what you want. When do you want to march? What path? How many men do you need?"

"I'm hardly going to tell you such things," Diarmait answered.

"Well then, don't chastise me for not persuading my husband to do things I know nothing about. You are putting me in an impossible position." I eyed Diarmait and walked over to him, chin held high. "If you won't tell me anything, then next time you are angry, don't hit me on the face."

Diarmait laughed at this. I knew he would. Old men didn't like insolent children unless they needed something from them, and right now, he needed Eva. "Fine. Here is something for your pillow talk with your new husband. Tell him that the wealth of Dublin is not ten times that of Waterford. It is a thousand times. Maybe more. Tell him, whoever can get Asculv on side will win Ireland. As for the path to Dublin, this is the most difficult question. It cannot be by sea. Asculv will have his fleets at the ready, and his men are better at fighting on water than we are. That leaves the rivers, the main road, and the mountain passages which are narrow but hidden. That is why the mountain path is best, but to make it to Dublin before Ruaidrí we need to leave soon. Within the next two days. All this delaying and fixing walls, it is nonsense. It's like trying to repair a clay bowl when you're being offered one made of gold."

I nodded. "That will do."

Enna came into my room then, Eva's wolfhound at his side. The wolfhound took one look at me and growled.

"Delaney, don't do that!" Enna said, rubbing his nose. "I don't know what's gotten into him." Enna stumbled forward, reaching out for the wooden railing he knew was to the right of the door.

"He's jealous," I said. "Jealous that he's no longer my favourite and is punishing me. Keep him away from me until he learns to behave. I don't want him to bite me."

Enna tutted. "He wouldn't hurt you."

But as I looked at the dog's raised lip and sharp teeth, I thought he probably would. He was clever, this dog. He knew I was not Eva. How funny that animals so often saw what people did not.

Raised voices from the feasting hall caught my attention and I moved to the door. Strongbow was back.

"I suggest you all leave me now," I said. "I've got to speak with my husband."

Diarmait snorted and stood, marching out of my room without saying a word. Domhnall followed. "Come on, Enna. Come on, Delaney. I'll get you both some supper before bed." Domhnall held out his arm for Enna to take, and they walked out of my room together.

Enjoying the silence, I prepared the bedroom. It was time for me to speak to my husband... but first I had to pray.

★

That night when Strongbow visited my room to say goodnight, he found me on my knees.

I let him find me in this position on purpose. To tease. To provoke. He'd bedded Eva on their wedding night of course, but since then he'd kept his distance. Certainly, there had been nothing between us since I'd transformed into her, not even so much as a kiss or a tender touch of my hand. He was courteous instead. He asked about my health and comfort.

That had to change.

"Husband," I said. "Can you come here?" I patted the chair beside the bed.

He nodded and sat, looking down at me. Staring at my pale skin and innocence in the nightdress that was just a little too low.

"My father is angry."

"Has he asked you to talk to me on his behalf?"

I shook my head, concealing my face behind my long, thick hair. "But I know things, and I think it is best that my husband knows them too."

"Then tell me." His voice was soft, but beneath the veil of politeness, I could hear his suspicion.

"I cannot. You are not truly my husband yet, are you?"

"We said our vows."

"Not in a church, which means you can say our wedding was invalid. And the truth is, under Irish law, I can divorce you at any time if I wish."

"Do you want to divorce me?"

I reached out and took his hand and placed it on my stomach. "No."

He reacted to this. Finally. His pulse quickened, and he even smiled as I pressed his hand tight against my nightdress. There was no bump there, not yet, but soon there would be. I'd use my witch magic to make it so.

"Are you sure?" he asked.

"I have missed my monthly blood twice now, and that is why I must be honest. If my father breaks with you, he'll take me with him and give my baby away so he can marry me to another."

"I wouldn't let him." Anger tinged Strongbow's words this time. Pride.

"He will take me when you do not expect it. That's why I have not told him about the baby. We…" I let a tear fall onto my cheek, and I wiped it away. "We would not be safe with my father." I lifted my head and tilted it, showing the red mark that bloomed upon my cheek.

"Your father did this to you?"

"Yes, but that is not what I want to talk about." I turned toward his chair as if I were praying no longer to God, but to him. "I want to help you."

"How? How can you help me?"

"Say that you will go to Dublin, but that first you must be married to me properly. In the church. Demand the dowry that my father promised and demand that it be handed over on the day of the wedding."

"Why?"

"That is all my father's wealth. Once he hands that over, he will be dependent on you. This is also why he wants Dublin, for the wealth… but you must be the one to take it. If my father takes it, he will kill you. Do you understand? He doesn't mean for you to keep this land or to have any part of it. That is why he hasn't married us properly. That is why he doesn't care about the walls." I put my hand in his. "But I care about you."

Strongbow stood and pulled me up with him. Touching my cheek, he kissed me. I kissed him back. "I do not want you to go, Richard," I whispered in his ear. "I want you to win."

Pulling me onto the bed, he removed my nightdress. After weeks of abstinence, he had finally given in to temptation. Not just of the flesh, but for the promise of gold and silver and a city called Dublin.

*

Two days later, Diarmait knocked on my door.

"Come, daughter," he said. "It is time."

He didn't stay to offer me words of wisdom, for Eva had already married and bedded Strongbow. According to Diarmait, this wedding was only being held so we could be blessed in a church with a bishop in attendance. However, I was pleased to see that Strongbow had insisted that the dowry was exchanged. This meant he was listening to me.

Diarmait, terse and as unaffectionate as my own father, gave me a kiss on my cheek and a golden brooch to put on my dress, while a chest of jewels and gold was given to Strongbow. It was everything the King of Leinster had, but Strongbow had promised to march to Dublin as soon as the ceremony was over, and so despite the poor position Diarmait had bargained his way into, he was happy.

Eva's half-brother, Domhnall, stayed behind and offered his arm, while the blind brother, Enna, leaned against the stone wall. Delaney, the wolfhound, growled.

"Can you take the dog away, Enna? I don't want him to jump up and dirty my dress."

Enna frowned. "Delaney wouldn't do that."

I rolled my eyes as I fixed my brooch. "Take him away. Just in case. There are quite a lot of people outside waiting to watch the ceremony, and I don't want to look foolish."

"Go on, Enna," Domhnall said. "Don't upset Eva right now."

Enna frowned, his fingers scrambling along the walls to find a marker that he recognised. "It's your voice," he said.

"My voice?"

"It's lower than usual, and you smell funny too. Delaney doesn't like it."

"Tis the perfume Alina made for me, is all. And my voice is hoarse from talking so much. Why do you have to insult me when you know I am nervous?"

Enna finally found the door and led Delaney outside. Those two were a problem I needed to take care of. A blind brother and a clever dog, I could do without.

Domhnall rolled his eyes and gave me a broad smile as they left. "Come, you know how sad he gets. It's making him bitter. Once the wedding is over, we can feast, and then he'll be in a better mood."

Holding out his arm for me to take, he smiled.

Once again, I wondered what he thought of all this. Domhnall was kind, unlike Diarmait, but he never said anything of his own. He barked Diarmait's orders or else tried to ease his temper. Who was he underneath, in the dark of night? How much of Máelmórda resided inside him?

"Ready?" he asked.

"Yes, I'm ready."

Holding onto Domhnall, I walked toward the church and remembered my first wedding to Amlav. Everything was so similar, how could I not? Oh, I had wanted to run away that day. I had wanted to run and run and never come back. Amlav was old and sagging, with dirty teeth and foul breath. But I had stayed. My mother had seen to that, and I had endured what many young women must suffer at the hands of old, wretched men when given a virgin as their new bride.

My second wedding was only a little better. That time it was Máelmórda and Sitric who had forced me down the aisle. Brian had been gentler, kinder, but still, I hadn't wanted his hands on my body nor his words in my ears. He was cold. Ruthless. My enemy.

There had been countless husbands since then, beginning with a Spanish lord who took pity on me and Máelmórda after our loss at Clontarf, and ending with sweet David, who had been my way back to Ireland. I had married some of those men willingly enough. David perhaps the most. But still, they were a means to an end, a path to somewhere new, even David, who I'd come to enjoy.

Today, I felt this path keenly. That I had reached the end of it, or at least, that I had only one more step to go. This was exactly where I was meant to be, and finally, I was married to a man who was of real use. I was with a man who wanted to be king and had the desire and the means to make it happen. And now, I was his wife.

Not a wife who could be set aside and divorced, no, these Normans didn't believe in that. I was here at his side *to stay*. Eva was already with child, which meant soon I would have a son or daughter at my side. An heir.

But perhaps, after a while, I would not need even them. Fire tingled at the tips of my fingers. Perhaps soon I could reveal my true self and watch as the mortals of Ireland worshipped me as they had once worshipped my ancestors. *Perhaps*.

The whole church was silent as I entered. Everyone watched me as I walked toward my husband. Le Gros. Hervey. William Ferrand and Robert FitzStephen. Today I was officially to be made the wife of an earl.

But soon… very soon… I would be a queen.

Angelo

The forest outside Seir Kieran

I fled for as long as I could, but eventually I collapsed onto the grass. Rolling onto my back, I stared up at the sky and the stars sparkling within it.

The fire was not far enough behind me, but there was no point in running anymore. I was dying. A knife had sliced my neck, while the wind Isolde had conjured had flung me against a tree and crushed my arm and shoulder. I could not go on, which meant sooner or later the Descendants would find me… if my wounds didn't take me first.

Death smiles at us all, Marcus Aurelius had once said. *But all a man can do is smile back.*

I closed my eyes, waiting for death to come. I was not afraid of it. There was nothing within the nothingness beyond. Even Marcus Aurelius was wrong sometimes. Death did not smile – and so I did not waste my strength in giving death one of mine.

I simply lay, feeling the blood seep out of me and into the ground.

Something rustled in the grass beside me, and I licked my lips. They had come for me. The witch, perhaps. Or Isolde.

She had been the flaw in my plan. The unknown rather than the other two Descendants. How magnificent I might have been if I'd only been able to kill Isolde. But alas, I had been foolish. Not patient enough. She wasn't only master of death and life, but she was a witch too. And a warrior. Could it be that she had all the gifts? Was that possible? It had to be. I had not understood before – Gormflaith's fear of them. I did now. Too late though. Too late.

"Angelo, is that you?"

It was Cecile who crept out of the forest and walked toward me. I had to confess I was a little disappointed. I wouldn't have minded seeing Isolde again before I died. To see her grief and her fury – both things I had inflicted upon her.

Instead, it was my cousin who stood over me. Not with a look of concern or sadness, but of acceptance. A low emotion, but I did not blame her. She knew I was going to die as well as I did. Lamentations and tears were for fools who had hope.

"I hate you," she said. "You used me, just like the others. You got inside my mind."

Ah, this was better than I had first expected, and I roused myself enough to open my eyes. "I did, Cecile… but there is nothing… can be done now. I'm dying."

She crouched down beside me and rolled up her sleeve. "Look at this."

I couldn't turn my head, for it would only make more blood pour out of the slice in my neck, so I glanced out of the corner of my eye. "What… am I supposed… to see?"

"You're supposed to see the blood on my clothes and the lack of cuts on my skin."

My mind was not working as it used to, the blood loss was making it slow, but even so… this seemed important. *Cecile had healed herself.*

I thought back to my memories of the battle on Rathlin. The woman who had been with Isolde, the woman whose gift Cecile had stolen, was not a witch, like she had claimed. She'd lied to Donnchad. But of course she had. She had said she'd summoned the storm, but that must have been Isolde. My mind ran then to my cracked skull. My father had told me he thought I would die, and yet I had woken up completely healed after Cecile and I had slept in the same cart, as my father took us to Chepstow.

"Heal me," I muttered, almost unable to get my tongue to move.

Cecile touched the open wound on my neck and ever so slightly pushed her finger inside. I nearly blacked out with the pain, but Cecile grabbed my face, her nails digging into my cheeks.

"I'll only heal you if you tell me something. And don't even think of getting inside my mind again."

"Fine." Coughing up some blood, I dribbled over my chin and neck. Weak as I was, I had no choice but to agree. Besides, life seemed like a fair exchange for secrets. "What do you want to know?"

"Why did the Descendant know my mother's name? She even thought I was her for a moment."

Now this was a secret. I could lie. It would be better that she didn't know, but she'd already worked it out. All she wanted was confirmation.

"Your mother was—" I couldn't get the words out. Quickly, Cecile pressed her hand against my neck. Within moments, I felt better. A little more like myself. "Your mother was a Descendant."

Cecile took her hand away, healing me just enough so that I could continue talking. "How is that possible?"

"You see how Olaf is around Gormflaith. Your mother was like that for your father."

"My father used a love potion on a Descendant? He wouldn't do that."

"Oh, sweet Cecile. Your father did many terrible things in his life. The least of them was using your mother."

"You're all as bad as each other."

"And you are one of us," I returned. "There is darkness… inside of… you too. I felt it."

She inched away, was about to stand.

"No. Don't leave. Heal me. Please."

"You'll only use me again."

"I won't. I promise." Lifting my good hand, I reached up toward her. "Please, Cecile. Don't leave me… for them… to find."

Cecile bit her lip, then pressed one hand against my neck and the other against my shoulder and arm.

"My leg too."

"No, not your leg." Cecile stood up and walked away. "I don't want you to catch up with me."

"Why, where are you going?"

"Away. Away from all of you and away from the Descendants who will come looking for me now." She stared at me as I tried to sit up. Now the pain in my neck, arm and shoulder was gone, all I could feel was where the wolf had bitten my leg.

"But before I go. I saw something. For what our friendship used to mean to me, I'll tell you."

"What?"

"When you ran away, I hid behind a tree. Another Descendant came. A witch. And when she touched the wolf, it turned into a man. It was the warrior who always followed us around. The one my father fought on Rathlin. Broccan." She stared at me, her eyes filling with tears this time. "You know what that means, don't you."

"It means that Donnchad's warrior gift didn't come from Broccan after all. It came from your father."

"Don't you see?" she said. "This is why I have to get away from you all. You'd all kill me without a second thought to get power. But I don't want power. I want to be free." She sprinted into the forest then. Ran and ran until I could no longer see or hear her.

Dragging myself up, I limped forward.

Now that I was in somewhat decent shape, aside from the bites and tears to my leg, I had to get out of here. I could steal a horse and ride to Connacht. Lie low for a while.

For yes, Angelo had failed, but *Brother* Angelo, he had not, and while I was hiding, there was another Fomorian at Dúnmór who I could use.

I needed him, for I had lost the knife that stole the Descendants' gifts in the fight. To make up for this failure, I needed a gift before I could return to Gormflaith. A long-lost great-great-great-grandson might do the trick.

Isolde

Seir Kieran

While Broccan slept, I held his hand tight. I didn't want to let him go. Not ever. Never again.

He was alive. I couldn't believe it. I couldn't believe that he'd broken his back, and Senna had transformed him into a wolf, any more than I could believe he had dragged himself here with a broken leg and burns covering half of his body. But here he was.

Lying in a bed in the monastery, he slept long and deeply. He was no longer wounded or injured, for Siobhan had healed him. It was exhaustion that held him. I could see it in his face, in the weight he had lost, in the burns that covered his body.

I understood this exhaustion, for I'd slept for two days myself, drained from overusing my gift and bereft with grief for Méabh and Colmon. I was angry too that the Fomorians had escaped. If I'd only had some energy left after I'd conjured the storm, I could have chased after them. Found them. *Killed them.* Those two words would have sat uneasily with me before, but I had to face the truth now and accept what was to come – that I was a warrior, and I would have to destroy those who sought to destroy me.

I didn't want to think of Fomorians now though. They were long gone and tracking them could wait. For now, I needed to see my cousin. I needed to speak to him.

What had he gone through since we'd parted?

Which of the Fomorians had hurt him on Rathlin? I'd heard him talk of Senna before, but how had she found him?

I ran through these questions and possible answers countless times. I went over our recent battle too. It was the younger Fomorians who had found us at Seir Kieran. Did that mean the others were dead? And why had Báine known one of them? Neasa, she had called her, though the other Fomorian, Angelo, had called her Cecile.

Broccan stirred beside me, pushing all thoughts out of my mind. *Finally, he was waking.*

"Broccan, can you hear me?"

Broccan's eyes opened. "Isolde," he whispered, smiling. "You're alive."

"You're alive too." I took hold of his hand and pressed it against my lips. "Siobhan has healed your back and leg. You can stand if you want to."

Broccan's eyes opened a little wider and, using his arms, he sat up in bed, relief spreading over his face as he moved his legs and feet. "Oh," he said, resting his head against the pillow. "I thought I'd never get here."

"But you did, and you saved me, like always."

"If I could just have reached Seir Kieran a little earlier." His eyes filled with sorrow then, and I understood his meaning. If he'd reached us sooner, Colmon and Méabh might still be here. But there was no point in thinking such things. Only the future could be changed, not the past.

"Don't say that. You are alive. Senna too. Báine and Siobhan. Me." Gently, I touched the new red scars over his shoulder. "I wish I could heal them for you."

"It was Fomorian fire that gave them to me. You cannot heal it, but it doesn't matter. They don't bother me."

Once, I might have thought he was lying, but I could tell this was the truth. I could tell that he was as happy to be with me as I was to be with him.

"I've missed you, Broccan. I've felt so lost without you at my side."

"And I without you."

His smile made me smile, despite the pain of loss, and I wanted it to stay on his face forever. He had spent my whole life protecting me. Now, it was I who wanted to protect him. My harpist gift came to me for a moment, and I could feel how broken he was on the inside and how the scars over his heart were deeper than those over his body. I had seen this sadness break through on Rathlin occasionally, but he'd never let it affect me. It must have been so very hard for him to do that.

"What was it like being a wolf?" I asked, forcing my harpist gift away, and instead trying to find something lighter to talk of.

"Strange. As if I were not really myself any longer, but it was better than being a crow, which Senna tried first."

"Why is that?"

"Hares are tastier to eat than worms."

I laughed at this, and Broccan laughed too, but as my laughter faded, he stared at me with his blue eyes. "I think you have had a hard time too. You must tell me everything."

Could I? Could I tell Broccan about Cuan? Yes, I could. I had to. *No more secrets.*

Just as I was about to speak, Báine knocked on the door and entered the room. "How are you, Broccan?"

"I'm well, Báine."

"Good, because it's time to say goodbye to Colmon and Méabh."

Broccan swung his legs over the bed and nodded. "Come, Isolde. We should not make Méabh and Colmon wait any longer. We can talk more tonight."

When Broccan and I walked outside, we made our way toward the hawthorn tree. Colmon and Méabh were lying on the grass with their possessions placed over their bodies. Colmon had been dressed in his thick fur cloak, while Méabh was wearing her green silk dress. Flowers had been placed over her neck and hands to cover the burns underneath.

Siobhan was kneeling beside them, putting a final chain of daisies in the hair of each. Tears fell down her rounded cheeks as she whispered words of farewell. She'd known them both for hundreds of years, and I could see the pain of this parting on her every expression. Báine stood slightly aback, her grief as present, but held more tightly. She stared at me for a moment, then turned away to stare at the hawthorn tree and her friends who lay underneath the branches.

Senna was here too. Although she didn't know Colmon or Méabh, or at least I didn't think so, she seemed sad. Staying further back, she found somewhere to sit on the grass, and there she closed her eyes, breathing slowly in and out.

Yes, it was time for Méabh and Colmon to leave us now. The otherworld awaited them, and everyone here had to let go of their grief. I just had time for a final goodbye.

Kneeling at Colmon's side, I thanked him for all he had done for me. For being there when Broccan could not. For teaching me. For giving me hope. I also thanked Méabh. For looking after Colmon and for her patience with me.

"Will you sing, Isolde?" Siobhan asked as I stepped away. "Like you did for Gisela and Leofwynn? It will call our ancestors and tell them we are ready."

Drawing on my harpist gift, I sang the song Gisela had taught me and almost instantly the light around the tree grew.

As before, I had to shut my eyes, but I could hear footsteps this time. The ancestors. Gisela had told me that Colmon loved my mother, loved her at a time when he'd pushed Méabh away. This was how I knew that my mother would come for him, and that if I could just keep looking into the light, I might catch a glimpse of her.

Staring as long as I could, a woman's figure sparkled within the light. I could see her long hair and a flash of red within the white before the brightness became so much that I had to close my eyes.

"Isolde."

Once again, I felt Aoife's presence.

"Hello, Aoife. Tell me, did I see my mother just now? Is she bringing Colmon to the otherworld?"

"Yes. She was the first to come for him, although there are many who wish to bring him over. Méabh too. Her father, Cerball, was the first to come for her."

"Then they will be happy."

"Yes."

Already I could feel the brightness fading. I held out my hand as if to stop it. "Thank you, Aoife. Thank you for guiding me."

I opened my eyes just a little, and saw the outline of my sister. Not as clearly as on Rathlin when I had taken the potion of death, but I could see the shape of her face and the long strands of white hair over her shoulders.

Aoife reached out and pressed her hand against my cheek. For the first time, I felt her. I felt the pressure of her hand against my skin.

Quickly, she pulled her hand back, her eyes widening.

"What just happened?" I asked.

She shook her head. "I do not know, Isolde, but it is best I do not touch you again, at least not now. I have power over the otherworld, and I do not want you to come here just yet. There is much you have to do in this life first."

She stared at me as the light dimmed. "Do not lose yourself, Isolde. Promise me. Hold on to who you are."

Not quite understanding, I watched her until the light faded. The bodies of Méabh and Colmon were gone now, and with them all the joy that I had left within me. Broccan came to me then and pulled me close.

"Do not despair, Isolde. Do not despair."

With Colmon and Méabh gone, Báine called us to gather. Wiping my eyes, I walked over with Broccan to where the others were standing. Senna came over too, though once again she stood slightly back from the rest of us.

"Where do we go now?" Báine asked. "Where can we rebuild?"

"We need to go to Rathlin," I said. "To find the sword and spear of the Tuatha Dé Danann. Colmon has hidden them there."

"What do you think, Broccan?" Siobhan asked.

"I think we should listen to Isolde."

Báine nodded. "Then I will go and fetch my belongings so we can set out."

Siobhan gave a small nod and followed Báine, though there had to be little for them to fetch. All the food we had collected into the cart was burned, all the animals slain too.

Broccan squeezed my hand. "It will be just like old times, Isolde."

"Yes. We're going home." I smiled then. Rathlin had felt like a dream these last few months. I couldn't wait to return, and more than this, my anguish was further eased knowing that Broccan was travelling with me, but no sooner had this thought given me comfort than my mind went to Cuan. I had to tell Broccan about him, but when? When was the right time to do that? Now? When we rested tonight? Tomorrow? Also, what if Cuan came here looking for me and I was gone. What if he gave up on me?

Concern tugged at Broccan's lips. "I'll keep you safe, Isolde."

"Don't say that."

"Why not?"

"I'm sick of others putting themselves in danger. There's to be no begging me to save myself or to run this time. I'm not doing that ever again."

Broccan gripped my hand and held it tight, but didn't answer, which I took as a sign that he didn't agree with my request. Well, he would understand soon that I was serious. So many had died to save me. My father. My mother. Affraic. Colmon. No more. No more.

Are you listening, child?

The faintest of whispers reached my ears.

"Broccan, could you fetch me another cloak?" Senna asked. "I'm cold." She shivered as she spoke even though the evening air was warm, but Broccan did not question it and walked into the monastery to see if Báine or Siobhan had any spare clothing.

This left Senna and me alone.

"I sent him away on purpose," she said once he was gone. "The wind wants to speak with you. Did you hear it?"

"I heard it, yes. Did you?"

"No, the wind does not speak to me, though your aunt does sometimes. She's the one who told me that the wind would call you once Colmon and Méabh had been taken to the otherworld."

"Does that mean you are a prophetess too?"

Senna shook her head. "Rónnat is able to find those she knew from before, and she can speak to them. It hurts her to do this. But the wind, it can only speak to you. This is not Rónnat, or at least not Rónnat alone. There are hundreds of voices on the wind. Each who has seen into the past and into the future."

The leaves by the hawthorn tree shivered. The wind blew up around it and suddenly the branches swayed. Yes, I could hear the wind now. It was calling me.

Walking toward it, I held out my hands and listened.

Hello, child. Are you listening?

Yes.

The vision I am about to show you will break you. It will break you in two. A crack in your mind and heart, but you must see it. Do you understand?

I understand.

A vision of colour and light and dark came into my mind, the wind swirling around me. When I opened my eyes, I stood upon a mountain and could see all around, hundreds of miles in every direction.

The colours changed. Away from the greens and yellows and blues, and instead moved to orange and red. The land was burning. Everything was alight. From the ground to the sky to the heavens. Thousands of screams rang through the air.

Everyone in this land will die, Isolde. Everyone. And the land will never heal, never return to the land that is. Even the otherworld will wither away. That's what will happen when the magic of this land is gone.

Shaking, I stared at the destruction. At the burning.

Can you bear to see more, Isolde? The truth is yours if you want it.

Before I had been afraid of the truth, but I could be afraid no longer. Everyone who had sacrificed themselves for me deserved my courage in return.

Yes. Show me.

The vision changed. A vision of death and what the otherworld would become. My mother was there at first, but then she was on fire. Burning. Then dust. Everything around her burned too, until the otherworld was empty, and the air was smoke. The images inside my mind shattered and splintered until there was nothing of the otherworld left but fire.

And then, not even that.

Cuan

Dúnmór

As I walked outside the dun gate, I stopped and looked over the hill. Finally, everyone who had said they were coming was encamped outside Dúnmór and ready to march to Dublin.

I strolled around the perimeter of the dun, staring over the tents and men who were laughing and talking. I heard the Irish of Ulaid being spoken alongside the dialects of Bréifne, Meath and Munster, and I was glad of it. United, we would be able to defeat any foe who came our way.

"Two days," Fearghus said as he walked over to me.

"What's happening in two days?"

"That's when your uncle says we are to march."

I smiled, even though this news frustrated me. We should be moving now. Already I felt we had left it too late, and there was no reason for the delay this time. Still, I did not want to say this to Fearghus.

"I'll be glad to get moving," I said instead.

"Well, the delay makes *some* sense. Not everything's been decided, so I guess at the meeting tomorrow night we will finalise our plans."

"Yes," I agreed. "Now that the scouts have returned, we can plan which way to travel and which passages to block."

Fearghus paused a moment as if he were about to say something else, but instead he gave a nod of farewell and continued along the path.

I was glad, for I did not want to talk of battle right now. Indeed, I didn't really want to talk at all, but alas, my solitude was not to last. In the distance, I could make out Meallán running toward me.

"Cuan!" he shouted. "He's returned."

"Who?" I asked.

"Brother Angelo, of course. Come on. He's in the dun and in a bad way. A wolf attacked him."

Meallán grabbed my hand and then ran back the way he had come. Smiling at his exuberance, I let him drag me up the hill until we reached the dun gate.

"There he is!" Meallán said. "I told you."

It seemed Meallán wasn't the only one excited by Brother Angelo's return, for both Róisín and Connor were helping him to a chair by the cooking fire.

"Don't take me into the feasting hall," Brother Angelo said when Róisín suggested this. "Not when the king has so many guests. The fire here is good enough for me."

"But you need a healer," Róisín said. "And you need to eat. You look half-starved."

"I'll not say no to a healer and food, but I'd rather not disturb so many kings with my tale of foolishness. I got lost, you see. Lost deep in the forest. I had to escape more than just wolves, I tell you, but I shall save those stories for another day."

"Oh, you must rest, Brother Angelo." Róisín looked quite distressed at the suggestion he continue to sit by the cooking fires. "Tell him, Cuan. Tell him he must."

A group of men had gathered around us by now. I heard them whispering already the story of how the monk had got lost and attacked by wolves, and I was sure he'd rather not be such a curiosity.

"Why don't you come into my house, Brother Angelo? You can lie on the bed, and then the healer can get a look at your leg. Wolf bites are nasty things, and it would be best that you got it treated sooner rather than later."

Brother Angelo closed his eyes and sighed. "I will accept your kind offer, Cuan. God, as always, works through you."

Trying my best to ignore this compliment, for I didn't deserve it, I set Brother Angelo's arm around my shoulder. The men surrounding us moved back, allowing us to walk to my house.

"Why don't you find the healer, Meallán," I suggested as I set Brother Angelo on the bed. "Connor and Róisín, why don't you fetch some clean garments and food?"

The three of them hurried away, eager to help.

"You have more friends than you used to, Cuan," Brother Angelo said. "When I first arrived here, everyone avoided you. Now I see that everyone is watching you."

"You must take some of the blame for that. All your talk of miracles has put strange ideas into people's heads." I found myself suddenly curious about this, and seeing as we were alone, I sat on the chair beside the bed. "I never asked, but why did you lie for me?"

Brother Angelo lay back. "Shut the door, Cuan. I've something to tell you."

Doing as he asked, I closed it. "Yes?"

"I know your secret. The one that keeps you up at night and that eats away at you during the day."

"What secret is this?" I asked, guessing what he was about to say. That he knew I wanted to betray my uncle. That he had been working for my father all along. Or perhaps that he was working for my uncle Godred.

But he didn't speak. He only held out his hand. "This secret."

A flame suddenly appeared on his palm and then ran along his arm. "You are like me, Cuan. I know you are."

I watched the flame. Watched how it danced on his skin and yet didn't burn him. "How... how can you do that?"

"Because I am a Fomorian, and I've been taught how to use my fire-magic. You could do this too if you let me train you. There are more of us. One of them is your direct ancestor, the mother of Sitric Silkbeard. Her name is Gormflaith. She's very powerful."

I shook my head, confused by much of what he was saying. "No. I don't think so."

"Why not? Wouldn't you like to control your fire? To use it? With everything that is going on, I'm sure it could help you."

Staring at Brother Angelo, I re-examined my knowledge of him. He was no monk, that was for sure. If that was the case, then why was he here? To watch me was the only answer, but that in itself led to more questions. "Why are you only showing me this now?"

"Because I didn't know if I could trust you. I know you are friends with one of our enemies. Isolde."

"If Isolde is your enemy, then so am I." I took out my sword and pointed it at his throat.

Brother Angelo stared at the blade and smiled. "Come, Cuan. She was only ever friends with you because the Descendants hadn't worked their influence on her yet. Next time you see her, she will not trust you. I swear it. They will turn her against you. I could help you, of course, but we would need to act quickly, while there is a chance she will believe you over them."

A great panic built up inside that Isolde would turn from me. Was that why she was so frightened of the other Descendants? Had she already told them about me? Had they forbidden our relationship? She loved me, I knew that, but I also knew how hard it was to survive in this world and how hard it was to turn against those who claimed to care for you.

Brother Angelo took out a smooth stone from his pocket and rubbed his fingers over it, lying back on the bed as if deep in thought.

"What do you think she's been doing there all this time, Cuan? Praying?"

"No. She's been learning how to use her magic."

"The truth is that the Descendants have been training her to kill us. They hate Fomorians, you see, and Isolde has all the gifts. Did she tell you that? She's not just a healer. Not just a witch. She's a warrior too. Once she's strong, the other Descendants will make her crush us. Even you."

I didn't like the things Brother Angelo was saying… and yet… there was truth within them. She had been so much stronger when we met outside Waterford… and she herself had told me the other Descendants hated Fomorians. *They would never let us be together, would they?*

"Isolde wouldn't use her gifts against me. She saved me." I said the words, but already they felt strangely hollow.

"Then, let me promise you this. I will train you, and when the Descendants come for us, which they will, you can see what she does. If she tells the others to leave you alone, then you will know I'm wrong. But if she uses her gifts against you, then at least you have a choice. You can stand there and die, or you can fight back."

Uncertainty swam inside me. I loved Isolde. I didn't want to fight her.

"Even better, if Isolde joins us, you and Isolde and I can fight the Descendants. They are using her, after all. If we can just convince her of this, then she can be with you. Love you. Be with you always."

The uncertainty that had swum inside me for weeks seeped away. He was right. This was the best way. Isolde should be here with me.

"What else do you want, Cuan? Deep in your soul? Do you want to be king? I've heard some of the men say you should be."

"I don't know anymore."

"Then why are you here?"

"I'm here because Ruaidrí blinded my father and because of that action my mother died, and so I promised my father that I would kill Ruaidrí. When I made that promise, I believed I would be killed in the attempt, so wanted nothing beyond that… but I don't know anymore. To kill Ruaidrí would weaken Connacht, but he is not a good king. He doesn't care about the people."

"What if I told you, Cuan, that you could be king and more? What if I told you that all those who have hurt you will bow at your feet? Should you like that?"

I nodded. I had never wanted power before, but after seeing

the damage Ruaidrí had wrought, it was better that I had it rather than he. Power, it was not a bad thing when held by the right people. *Why had this thought not come to me before? It felt so obvious now.*

Angelo held out his hand, and the flame grew there. He held it there so easily, smiling even.

"You are a god among men, Cuan. We both are. Soon, everyone will know it. Understand?"

"Yes."

"Then tonight, when everyone is asleep, I will train you in the forest. All I ask in return is that you help me kill my enemies. Is that an agreement, Cuan? Do you swear?"

"Yes, I swear."

EPILOGUE

Olaf

Dúnmór

Love. Love was everything. The only thing. Love.

Gormflaith was love. *Is* love. Everything. The only thing. Love.

My wings soared. I wished she were here so she could see them. See the power within me and that I would do anything for her. Now that David was dead, she must see me again. Once I did this for her, found Cecile, she would want me. Want me forever. Want me. The only thing.

Eyes. *They see.*

But not Cecile. I had followed the wrong trail. It was Angelo.

Finally, I could return to my mistress and tell her this. To my love. To my everything. To the only thing that mattered. Cecile was still missing, but she'd want to know about Angelo. Angelo.

As I flew overhead, I watched him sitting on the ground. Injured leg. Good. For he had evil behind his eyes, this one. I'd seen it. Known it from the first moment I had laid eyes on him. He moved around his family, thought I could not see who he truly was because I was a bird. But I could see everything. *See every thought.* Smell it when he thought of evil things to do. Have flown over him while he's done them. Skinned dogs. Skinned cats. Children. Killed. Killed. Killed.

The man beside him was readying his sword. I landed on a branch above them. To watch. Watch. Watch the evil one so I could save my love. Gormflaith. To warn her. To warn my love.

"You swear you can teach me?" the strange man said to Angelo.

Angelo, weak, nodded. "You are one of us. Imagine being able to use your fire at your will. No one will be able to take anything from you ever again."

"And the others will help?"

"Of course. Gormflaith especially. I told you – she speaks of her son Godfrey all the time. You are of his line. She'll weep when she sees you. Weep with joy."

I leaned forward on the branch. This one was Fomorian too? Fire. Fire. But how? How could it be? I watched the man. Stared at him. Eagle sight could see so much. Every freckle. Every wrinkle.

Blue. The palest shade of blue in his eyes. *Like me. Like my mother.*

Godfrey. That was my son. My son that I never saw. I remembered the name now. Remembered.

This man was descended from Godfrey.

From Gormflaith.

From me.

I watched. Listened.

"How will you teach me?" the stranger asked.

"I will teach you as my father and my grandmother taught me, Cuan. I can teach you while we travel to Dublin. In the forest at night when you stand watch or else when the others are sleeping."

Cuan. That was his name. His name. My seed. The son of my line. Of Godfrey. My mother's eyes.

Her face came to me. I saw her smiling. Saw her die at the hands of Svein Forkbeard. I had loved her, and this act had torn me apart. How had I forgotten all this? My mother, I had loved her. Loved her.

A strange feeling moved inside me. I shivered. Shivered. I remembered now. Remembered that I was Olaf, King of Norway. I remembered my ship, the *Long Serpent,* and how it crashed on the waves.

Gormflaith had poisoned me.

Given me a potion from the wretched druid. I remembered.

Remembered. Given me this fate that was worse than death. Made me love her. Forced me.

Love was nothing to me. Nothing at all. Death was all that I wanted now. Only death. But before I let it take me, I would take the lives of those who had used me. Enslaved me. Humiliated me. Gormflaith… yes, I hated her. Hated what she had done to me. Humiliated.

But this seed of my son. I would save him. Save him.

Save him.

Historical Note

When we left *Daughter of the Otherworld*, King Ruaidrí believed he had successfully subdued the King of Leinster at Ferns. Richard de Clare (Strongbow) was procrastinating in Chepstow. Things, however, were about to change.

In *Son of the Serpent*, the chess pieces are being moved into position, and we examine a small but pivotal period in Irish history between the autumn of 1169 and the summer of 1170.

When I looked at the real history of this time, I couldn't help but note how interesting Strongbow is. He is bound by oaths to King Henry II, but he is ambitious. He sees himself as a military leader, but has been ignored by his king. In fact, he is a rival to Henry II in many ways, and Henry doesn't want him to rise against him after fighting for Stephen in The Anarchy. Out of favour, Strongbow is looking for opportunities.

Diarmait, King of Leinster, has now provided him with one. In *Daughter of the Otherworld*, Strongbow assisted Diarmait by sending Robert FitzStephen over to Ireland with around six hundred men, but this was just an opening move, a way to assess what Ireland was like. In *Son of the Serpent*, Strongbow needs to make a decision. To invade and face the wrath of his king, or to stay put in his own lands and plead for the return of his title as Earl of Pembroke.

In August 1170, he sets sail for Waterford.

If you were to read Wikipedia or a general overview of the Anglo-Norman invasion, it will tell you that Strongbow's invasion of Ireland was sanctioned by Henry, but this is not true. Those who left with Strongbow were in fact fined by the king.

We will get to see more of the simmering rivalry between Strongbow and Henry II in *Queen of the Ashes*, the next Gael Song novel, but in *Son of the Serpent*, you can perhaps understand why Strongbow has left. Firstly, he has a young bride to marry. Henry so far has not permitted him to wed. I should mention here that Eva was actually called Aoife in real life, though anglicised to Ava or Eva in historical documents. I used the name Eva purely to avoid mix-ups with Fódla's daughter. Secondly, Strongbow must believe that in Ireland there is land for the taking, not to mention a promise from King Diarmait that he will inherit the Kingdom of Leinster. The victories of FitzStephen (at Osraige and Limerick) and Le Gros (at Dun Domhnall) are probably what entices him the most. The Irish kings and warriors so far have not shown themselves to be cohesive. And of course, the actions of a woman known as Alice of Abergavenny become known too.

Legend has it that Alice cut off the heads of all seventy Viking hostages after the battle at Dun Domhnall, and had them all thrown into the sea; revenge for the killing of her husband/lover at the battle. We know little of her, except that she was thought to be in her twenties and a servant.

I've commandeered this historical Alice (using the spelling Alys) and set Gormflaith over her. It was too delicious a detail to pass up, and it felt like a very Gormflaith thing to do, although I didn't have her killing all seventy of the Waterford Vikings, which I think would be impossibly tiring… but legends do grow, and so I gave her two.

Of course, what happened at Dun Domhnall is nothing compared to the battle at Waterford. Here, for the first time in Ireland, we see a strong defence. The Waterford Vikings understand their Norman cousins and see that an invasion is on the horizon. They also have the benefit of walls and a proper defensive strategy. However, a watchtower, propped up by a post, was their undoing. Once the post was cut through by the Anglo-Normans, the watchtower fell and brought down a portion of the wall with it.

This just goes to show how an army with many members who had fought in the Crusades would have learned a thing or two about siege strategy. The city is then invaded and many of the people are massacred.

Strongbow and Eva marry after this battle, and there is a very famous painting – *The Marriage of Strongbow and Aoife* by Daniel Maclise – if you wish to see how it is represented in art.

Now, let's move away from Strongbow and back to the Irish kings. Here, motivations are less clear.

What is Diarmait thinking when he makes this deal with Strongbow? He has a legitimate son who could be the next King of Leinster, as well as an older illegitimate son who is a renowned warrior. Why promise his kingdom away when the laws of Ireland don't allow it? Did he really think Strongbow would be able to take the land from his legitimate son once he died? Or did he believe that by marrying his daughter to Strongbow, he could simply avail himself of his new son-in-law's warriors and then watch as they sailed away?

The other main player is King Ruaidrí. He comes from a brutal family where power is everything. His father blinded two of his own sons when they revolted against him. His father also wanted to blind Ruaidrí, though Ruaidrí was able to escape this fate. Ruaidrí, in turn, was brutal to his own family and is recorded as having blinded one of his own brothers to ensure the kingship stayed with him after his father had died. This brother was called Brian, though I have changed it to Bardán, so as not to confuse readers with Brian Boru, who I think still looms large after *The Land of the Living and the Dead.*

However, now Ruaidrí is High King, retaining that title is a difficult thing. Even Brian Boru struggled to hold on to his power. Not only did Dublin and Leinster turn on him, but when called, the Northern Ó'Neills wouldn't fight for him either. King Ruaidrí faces similar issues. At the end of *Daughter of the Otherworld,*

Leinster had broken their oaths to Ruaidrí and demanded their own oaths from Asculv, King of Dublin. While Asculv's oaths are meaningless, it does reveal intent. Ruaidrí understands this. He knows that Diarmait is not truly subdued.

Having taken three hostages from King Diarmait, including his last legitimate heir, Ruaidrí is slow to act, and when he does, he is loath to commit. The King of Northern Munster turns on him too, and with this, Ruaidrí's grasp on power begins to crumble. However, at the end of *Son of the Serpent*, Ruaidrí still has enough power to amass a great army for a showdown with King Diarmait and his Anglo-Norman knights.

However, here I must stop. The events of *Queen of the Ashes* are about to begin…

If you wish to read more about this time in Irish history to see what you think, I suggest the following books:

The Conquest of Ireland by Giraldus Cambrensis (translated and edited by Thomas Forester, revisions by Thomas Wright)

A New History of Ireland II: Medieval Ireland 1169–1534, edited by Art Cosgrave

The War of the Irish Kings by David Willis McCullough

Strongbow: The Norman Invasion of Ireland by Conor Kostick

Dermot, King of Leinster, and the Foreigners by Nicholas Furlong

Acknowledgements

Son of the Serpent, the second book of Era II, moves us closer to the end of the Gael Song series. It was a thrilling book to write, and I am going through a whole mixture of emotions as I move onto drafting the final book in the series.

As I veer between excitement and sadness over finishing a series that has been part of my life for so long, I must be thankful for those who keep me calm and grounded. Firstly, I wish to thank my husband, Gerard, and my three children, Darragh, Shay and Finan. Their love and joy are everything to me and are what makes my life as wonderful as it is.

A huge thanks to my mum and dad and the rest of my family. I am lucky to have you all by my side, to have your feedback and support. I'd be lost without you.

Five books in, I am so delighted to say that my publication journey has been a wonderful one. There is no doubt in my mind that this is due to my fabulous agent, Ed Wilson, and my fantastic editor, Greg Rees. As the Gael Song grows, the support I've needed has grown too, and your advice and enthusiasm has never been in short supply.

And finally, a big thanks to my critique group, my beta readers and my fans for sticking with me and spreading the word about my books. A special shout out to Michael Sugarman, Keytelynne Radde, Michelle Hossack, Kalindi Shah and Shelley Stefanik.

About the Author

Shauna Lawless is an avid reader of Irish mythology, folklore and history, which inspired Gael Song, her historical fantasy series set in turbulent mediaeval Ireland. Her critically acclaimed novel, *The Children of Gods and Fighting Men*, was nominated for Best Debut at the British Fantasy Awards. She lives in Northern Ireland with her family, where you can often find her writing or curled up with a good book.

Follow Shauna via her newsletter or at shaunalawless.com
Instagram: shauna_lawless_author